## Frankfurt, 1932

"From the data presented thus far, I would have to assume that the patient was a plague victim." The tall, good-looking young man looked across the long table to the examining board of medical school professors. They were the best four that Goethe University could muster, and he had just begun to deal with their barrage of questions in diagnostics. It was an open-ended practicum, and they had been at it all day with a number of senior medical students. But Eric had spent the better part of a month living like a monk, poring over his notes and texts. He was prepared.

"What kind of plague and in what stage, Herr von Kleist? Be precise. Diagnostics is a combination of memory and precision." Doktor von Schleicher folded his arms over the vest of his brown suit and sat back, peering at Eric over the tops of small, round spectacles. He was the finest epidemiologist on the teaching staff and the toughest on students. Eric's standing as first in his senior class would have no effect on Dr. von Schleicher's part of the practicum. Nor would the name von Kleist be a factor. It might make the others pause before becoming abusive with a particularly tricky part of the exam, though. For Bismarck himself had said that the von Kleists, along with the Krupps, were the aristocracy of the rolling mill; perhaps the richest and most influential industrial triumvirate in all of Germany—and in much of the western

1

world. But none of that would help in the practicum, nor would Eric have wanted it to.

Eric glanced quickly at his hurriedly scribbled notes, made as von Schleicher had read off the symptoms that had to be assembled into a diagnosis. He looked up, and the two men's eyes met for a second. He *had* written that particular question; there was no doubt about it. It was the bulwark of his field.

Eric brushed back a comma of dark brown hair from his forehead and cleared his throat before he spoke. "Specifically, Herr Doktor Professur, the severity and color of the lesions indicate pneumonic strain. Lymphatic distension, apparent dehydration, and elevated temperature would clearly point to a tertiary involvement."

Von Schleicher grunted and nodded. He leaned forward. Eric could see that the man was moving in for the kill. "And what, Herr von Kleist, would you prescribe?"

"At this stage the patient is already morbid, Herr Doktor Professur. However, ice packs should be used to lower the body temperature. But treatment of the patient is of less importance at this stage than other measures."

There was a rustle of papers among the other three physicians. Eric's choice of words had rattled them, and he knew it. Conversely, von Schleicher nodded, and the hint of a smile creased his stony face. "Enumerate, Herr von Kleist."

Eric had won, and they both knew it. All that remained was to spell out the steps. "Immediate isolation. Incineration of clothing and personal effects. Interrogation of all whom he has come in contact with, and their subsequent quarantine. A public health alert for plague symptoms for a period of twenty-one days...." Eric paused. There was something missing, something fighting its way back up from his memory. Dr. von Schleicher leaped into the pause.

"Yes, von Kleist? Is there something else?"

His tone reminded Eric of his father. A Prussian mentality always jumped onto weakness or the barest hint of it. Dominate or be dominated. Utterly humiliate or utterly submit. The attitude was ruthless and unforgiving, but it was the one

"BE SILENT, YOU...INGRATE.
YOU ARE GIVEN THE WORLD AND YOU SPIT
IT BACK INTO MY FACE...
YOU THANKLESS CUR."

Lotte came quickly to her feet. "I will not hear this. Eric *will* go to medical school and Gelsen funds... my funds will pay for it. And, Nazi swine will not be entertained in my home!"

She turned and started toward the tall double doors that led to the entry hall.

"HOW DARE YOU!!" Johann shrieked as Lotte strode with determination toward the hall.

Still shaking and terrified, not knowing where he mustered the courage to move, Eric pushed himself to his feet and followed his mother, with Reinhildt and the sobbing Horst in his wake.

"Eric. Come back here."

Eric stopped but did not turn. "I'm sorry, Father."

"You will be sorrier. I... I disown you. You will never get another pfennig... Kurt will... Kurt will get it all. HE is my oldest son, now." The door closed.

## CRIMSON COMES THE DAWN

*A family divided by the passions
of politics and love*

# CRIMSON COMES THE DAWN

## Gene Snyder

GOLDEN APPLE PUBLISHERS

CRIMSON COMES THE DAWN

*A Golden Apple Publication / June 1985*

*Golden Apple is a trademark of Golden Apple Publishers*

ISBN 0-553-19845-9

PRINTED IN THE UNITED STATES OF AMERICA

0  9  8  7  6  5  4  3  2  1

**Dedication**

*As ever, to Nancy and Laura*
*and most specially to Michael Philip*
*with joy, hope and love.*

**Acknowledgments**
*To Phil Leonhardt and Tim Keating
for research; and to Dr. Jules Delcau for
his wisdom and guidance about
the years of the Holocaust.*

# Prologue

## Frankfurt, 1967

He watched the massive conference room door close and heard the quiet, satisfying sound. Turning, he walked slowly to the end of the long, glistening conference table, gazed down its length, and exhaled with a sigh. The table was neatly surrounded by a dozen plush leather chairs. The rich amber carpet provided a subtle contrast to the furnishings and warmed the dark, paneled walls. The atmosphere spoke quietly of wealth, of power, of decisions made in tranquillity.

As he looked at it, he nodded slowly to himself. It was fitting, he thought. The board room of one of the largest corporations in the western world should have the comfort of a living room and the gentle silence of an empty cathedral. For, what he was about to do would indeed be . . . an act of faith.

He was a study in contrast. Though he was not yet sixty, his face was creased and weathered like that of a man a decade older. Oddly, set in the craggy face were striking blue eyes that hinted at a mental quickness and dexterity of a man half his age. His blue suit outlined a physique that was still athletically lean. He allowed himself the luxury of another deep satisfying breath.

*It was gone!*

The weight in his chest, the heaviness he had carried for so many years that it had become part of him, almost unnoticed, was suddenly gone. He marveled over it for a minute while his eyes moved to the large window that overlooked the rolling lawns of the Frankfurt suburbs. The warmth of early May in the Main Valley had brought a sudden spring. In the distance he could see lawns and trees exploding into color. New life . . . a new beginning.

His eyes moved down to the neatly arranged folder that sat on the end of the table just in front of him. Ironic, he thought. A new beginning also meant an ending. But there would be time for pondering ironies later. Now, the task—the act of faith had to be completed.

He opened the folder and leafed through page after yellowed page, each mounted on thick bond paper. Every page had been meticulously initialed by witnesses, all carefully selected, handsomely paid and, above all, sworn to absolute secrecy. It took only a moment to insure that everything was completed, in order—in readiness.

He picked up the folder and strode across the thick carpet. He removed the plastic dust cover from the machine and stared intensely at the controls for a second before he pushed the button that started the machine humming. Inside, a dozen scalpel-sharp circular blades spun hungrily . . . waiting.

He opened the folder and carefully removed the first sheet. He fitted it into the stainless steel feeder tray and paused for only a fraction of a second before nudging it forward until it was snatched up by the blades. In a second the shreds fell out of the back of the machine into a tray. He shredded the next sheet and the next. The rhythm was almost hypnotic.

In minutes it was over.

He carried the tray back to the table, set it down, and slowly fingered the shreddings. There was a certain sense of comfort in the gesture and perhaps a small, lingering ghost of disbelief. How long had it been? Thirty years? No! Thirty-five.

He removed a gold Ronson butane lighter from the jacket pocket of his blue suit.

*Dear God! Thirty-five years . . .*

He moved the lighter to the edge of the paper shreds.

*and all the lives . . .*

He pressed the button. A jet of flame flashed to life.

that had created the von Kleist empire. While Eric knew that in a perverse way it was a necessary part of business, he could not condone what it was doing to his family. Power had become a disease to his father, a contagion, not unlike the pneumonic plague. His father had thoroughly infected Eric's brother Kurt with it. Eric had seen the symptoms years earlier, at about the same time that he had caught fire with the curiosity and excitement for medicine. He remembered that he had been fourteen, then....

Eric sat in the shade of the great Lombardy poplar and looked at the small bird in the box. The heat of the afternoon sun would have been too much for his "patient" to take. It had long since stopped trying to drag itself toward an escape. Instead, it sat huddled in the corner of the box, quivering, terrified. Occasionally Eric would cautiously extend a not-too-sterile, fourteen-year-old hand into the box and stroke the bird's back feathers. He flattered himself that this was an anesthetic of sorts.

His eyes moved to the ornithology book that lay propped open against the poplar. The bird was an English sparrow, and after peering for a minute at the text, Eric determined that there was only one bone in the small wing that could be broken. A hollow, delicate primary. With the tiny pieces of splint his friend Karl Mittenberg had gotten for him, and the slender strips of white tape that his mother, Lotte, had cut for him, he started the delicate and nerve-racking procedure of splinting.

It took him the better part of an hour to finish, and when he did, he couldn't contain his excitement. He looked down toward the beach at his eight-year-old sister Reinhildt. She was quiet and slender with long dark hair, like her mother.

Eric gingerly picked up the box and headed toward the spot where she was sitting and watching Horst, their seven-year-old brother transform a pile of wet sand into a fortress. It was something Horst did every time their mother took them to spend a quiet weekend afternoon at the estate's lake.

"Reinhildt, look at this. You must see!"

"What?" She got to her feet and started toward him

As Reinhildt looked down in wonder at the bird in the box, Eric glanced toward his mother, Lotte, who was sitting quietly on a beach chair some yards away. She had been jotting things in her diary-journal, as she sometimes did when they were at the lake. Perhaps it was the animation of Eric's comment that made her look up. It was she who had encouraged and helped him when he had first become fascinated with healing things, at six. His first patient had been a rabbit with a broken hind paw. Lotte had gotten him splints and bandages, then shown him how to set the bone. She had learned such things from *her* mother, she said. He remembered telling her that he would become a doctor, if it was what she wanted. Her face had grown stern.

"If you are to be a doctor, it should be because you want it for yourself, *not* for me," she had said.

And so, she had advised and supported and loved. But there was a sadness in her eyes now. A loss. Was it father? he wondered. She hardly ever saw him now. None of them did. Did father still really love her? Did he really love any of them?

"Did you do it, Eric? Did you really make it better?" Reinhildt peered into the box at the small sparrow.

Eric nodded vigorously. "I think I did. We'll have to give it time."

Reinhildt turned to Horst. "Come see this, Horst. Look at what your brother, Herr Doktor Eric, has done."

Horst looked up from his project only for a second. "In a minute. I'm almost finished."

After sculpting the last battlement, he got to his feet, making a few perfunctory attempts to sweep the grit from his knees as he walked. "What did he cure this time? A field mouse? A turtle? I don't know how he finds all of these sick animals."

Reinhildt frowned. "He looks for them, silly. And besides,

how would you ever see anything with your nose in the wet sand all afternoon?"

Horst stuck his tongue out at her and looked furtively in the box, then up to the beaming Eric. "How did you—"

"*Sigfriiieeeeeddd!*" The shriek startled them. Kurt, three years younger than Eric, had spent the afternoon charging up and down the beach, a young warrior in quest of dwarfs and Rhine gold. He carried a tree-limb lance. The other three had almost forgotten him.

He had lowered the lance and was starting to charge toward them with a whoop. But they were not the target, and suddenly Eric realized what was. He gently set down the box and ran to head Kurt off. Horst saw what was happening a second later and also started to dash. Both of them were too late.

"No!" Horst cried. Kurt was assaulting the just completed sand castle that Horst had spent all afternoon lovingly constructing.

In seconds it was gone, just an unrecognizable pile of sand again. Horst slipped to his knees, tears cutting jagged lines down his grimy cheeks.

Eric lunged for Kurt as he passed, but missed and fell in the wet sand.

Kurt turned to the two of them and yelled as he ran. "The fortunes of war, Horst. You must guard your castle."

Reinhildt ran to comfort the crying Horst, and in the distance, Lotte got up from her beach chair and put her diary aside. She started to approach.

Eric got to his feet and, with sudden, growing horror, watched Kurt. "Kurt, stop! Look out. You're—"

In a second it was over. Unknowingly, Kurt had crashed into the cardboard box. By the time he realized what he had done, it was too late. The bird was dead, crushed underfoot.

He got to his feet and turned to face Eric, who was running toward him, enraged. It was only the arrival of Lotte that prevented Eric from throttling his younger brother. As Kurt's square chin jutted out and his eyes flashed with dark defiance, he resembled his father. "It would have died, anyway,

Eric. Something would have eaten it, if it couldn't fly. Besides, how do I know it wasn't dead already? . . ."

"I said, Herr von Kleist, was there something else?"

Von Schleicher was again leaning forward over the table, looking for an opening, a weakness. Eric blinked. His thoughts about the past evaporated.

"I would extend the quarantine to twenty-five days, order cultures on all of the medical staff who have come in contact with the victim, and include them in the quarantine."

"Why, twenty-five, Herr von Kleist?"

"Assuming that the victim had symptoms within four days of exposure and that the transfer vector was virulent up to the time of diagnosis, a safety factor of four days is reasonable."

The old epidemiologist nodded tersely and made a note on the sheet in front of him. He then looked to his right. "Gentlemen, is there anything to add to the diagnosis on this case?"

The other three shook their heads, and Eric exhaled in relief.

"Eric?" It was Doctor Waldman, Eric's mentor. The man was a superb doctor. His questions would be fair, though by no means easy. But Eric was pleased to hear his first name used. He knew that Waldman would be the only one on the examining board to use it. Still, he was looking at a man who wanted the practicum to teach the student rather than baffle him. It was something of a relief to know that he would be the next interrogator.

"Yes, Herr Doktor Waldman?"

The bald, florid-faced man cocked his head to the side and folded his arms over a starched lab coat. "A patient arrives in emergency. A male of thirty. He is suffering from a crushing pain in his lower left quadrant, just off the center line. No apparent trauma or wound. His wife brought him in, saying he simply doubled up in bed with it. What is your immediate diagnostic reaction?"

Eric didn't pause a second. "Check for invertrable disc herniation, subluxation or neurological constraint."

Waldman was shaking his head. "Nothing. What next? Quickly. An immediate reaction. The man is screaming, and you have to restrain him. He's writhing in agony. You have to diagnose fast. What is wrong? What do you do? Do you sedate?"

"No. Just restrain. We don't have enough information to sedate. It could kill him, depending on what's wrong. Palpate the kidney area to look for a pain reaction. If the pain is that exquisite, the chances are that it might be a kidney stone."

Waldman's face split into a wide grin. "Well done, Eric. You even got the illness I had in mind. And you didn't sedate. Well done—"

There was a knock at the examining room door. Eric and the four examiners sat in silence for a second. Interruptions in a practicum simply did not happen, certainly not at Goethe University. It was something just short of sacrilegious.

The expression on Dr. von Schleicher's face was grim. Eric pitied the person on the other side of the door. "Come."

The door opened, and Margaret Braun looked nervously into the room. She was the secretary in the administration office, a woman addicted to frumpy brown dresses and rich helpings of Black Forest cake, bursting with chocolate and cherries. It was perhaps why the dresses looked frumpy. She was just over two hundred pounds.

"I am so sorry, Herr Doktor Professur. But, you see, there is this call—and the young woman said it was urgent—and—oh, dear."

Von Schleicher nodded. "Calm yourself, Margaret. For whom is the call?"

Margaret looked to Eric. "For Herr von Kleist. They said it was urgent."

Eric's eyes darted to her and then to the four men across the table. Suddenly he felt as though he were in a dream in which he had arrived at a formal reception without his trousers. There was no acceptable way to interrupt a practicum for a call. It simply didn't happen.

Von Schleicher cleared his throat and started to speak, but Waldman interrupted.

"Excuse me, Doktor. Eric. I'm sure it's important or the

party wouldn't have called. Perhaps you could take it at the extension just outside." He looked to Margaret, who appeared terrified. Waldman smiled. "Margaret?"

"*Ja*, Herr Doktor Professur?" It seemed to all come out as one word.

"Can Eric take the call on the extension in the hall?"

"Of course, Herr Doktor Professur. I had it switched there when I came in."

Waldman nodded. He was senior to the other three, and Eric was, after all, Waldman's candidate. "Take the call, Eric. It won't be much of an interruption, I'm sure."

Eric nodded and managed a half smile. He got to his feet, feeling bewildered and more than a bit disturbed. He followed the scurrying Margaret Braun out into the hallway. As he picked up the receiver that lay on the table, he glanced back through the open door to the four men at the table before he spoke. "Eric von Kleist."

It was Reinhildt. There was a mixture of fear and anguish in her voice. "Oh, Eric. I—I couldn't get an answer in your apartment, and then that woman said that there was no way you could be disturbed. I—"

Eric could sense her voice was a hairbreadth from panic. He could feel the cool detachment of a medical professional slip over him like a coat of mail.

"*Liebling*, calm down. What is it?"

She told him.

At the table in the room only a few yards away, Waldman could catch snatches of the conversation. He liked Eric and had championed him for admission when the board had balked three years earlier. Being a von Kleist had its drawbacks, and one of them was the envy and bitterness of medical professors, who could barely keep body and soul together in a massive depression, considering one of the richest men in the world for admission to medical school. Waldman had shamed them, criticized their professional ethics, and eventually gotten Eric a slot in the school. Eric had repaid Waldman by quickly rising to number one in his class and remaining there for an unprecedented three years. Eric spoke quietly. "When did? . . . And how? And when is? . . . Tomorrow? So soon?"

There was a long pause, during which Waldman could hear nothing. Then, from the back he could see the tall, lean, handsome doctor-to-be nod slowly. Waldman could see that the call was having an impact, though he wasn't sure what it meant. Moments later, the conversation ended. "Very well. I'll leave late this evening or early in the morning. No. I'll drive. Expect me just past noon."

There was a noticeable difference in Eric when he came back into the room. All four of the men on the panel could see it, though Waldman was perhaps the only one who could see the turmoil through Eric's emotional armor.

"Is everything all right, Eric?"

Eric nodded. "Yes. Well, it's nothing to further take your time for. I—I can take care of it tomorrow. I'm sorry for the interruption. Truly."

Von Schleicher cleared his throat. "Very well, Herr von Kleist. Let's move then to the next case."

It was nine in the evening when it was all over and the panel had assembled its results. Yes, he had passed the practicum. Yes, Eric had retained his status as head of the senior class. Waldman moved down the hall with him as Eric pulled on his trench coat and hat against the inevitable rain that he knew would be falling outside. The two shook hands, and Eric walked out into the courtyard.

He crossed the campus and headed for his apartment. He was glad he had chosen to walk earlier, rather than take his car. He stopped for a second under a streetlight and looked down at his hands. He could see them quivering, even through the warm kid gloves. He would not have been in condition to drive, especially not all the way to Tübingen, not tonight. He resolved to leave early in the morning.

Reaching his building, he walked up the stairs and unlocked the door of his apartment. He shucked his trench coat and put it on the hall coat rack, then turned on the gas heaters. Then he followed his normal procedure for getting over the tension of a hard day. He went to the bar and poured two therapeutic ounces of Dornkaat, which he bolted down. He stripped off his clothes and took a shower, until the hot water heater had emptied, then slipped on a robe and poured another glass of Dornkaat. This one he sipped, while he felt the effects of the first shot of hundred-fifty-proof schnapps hit his bloodstream. He moved to the window and peered out into the wind-driven rain that was battering the park across the street. In a strange way he was pleased with himself. They had not seen it—except perhaps for Waldman. He had been ever so solicitous in his farewell, though far too tactful to pry. Nothing had gotten out through Eric's walls. He had not asked for a postponement, nor even a delay. It was an accomplishment to take pride in; the kind of thing he would need to perfect as a doctor.

Looking out the window, he could see that the kiosks that lined Grunebergweg had been repostered. They stood on line like silent sentinels, each carrying an identical message. Red oblongs, white circles, black swastikas. *Deutschland Erwachet!* Germany Awake! They were professionally done these days. When Eric had first taken the apartment, the posters been crudely drawn and hastily put up, the product of maniacs and gangsters. Now a movement had been created. The swine, the vermin had created a movement to be respected. He shuddered and turned away from the window. He set the small alarm clock for five and downed the last of the schnapps. The world was teetering on the brink of madness, but there was nothing he could do about it, not tonight. Perhaps at Tübingen tomorrow. He sat on the side of the bed and thought about what he would have to deal with in the next twenty-four hours. A sob erupted from deep inside, and tears welled over the rims of his blue eyes. For the first time since he was ten, Eric von Kleist cried. He let himself think it was the schnapps. Perhaps he was becoming a crying drunk, he told himself. But in his heart he knew it was a lie.

The gray Frankfurt dawn arrived almost unnoticed. The oppressive, omnipresent cloud bank that hugged the damp Main Valley through the fall of the year barely shrugged at the arrival of the sun. The evening rain that had spread outward from the Taunus Mountains had chilled into a cold, wind-driven drizzle. The gun metal sky promised that the gloomy weather would last the day and perhaps far into the night.

Eric's small red Laconda sports car roared along the graveyard-quiet streets. He had slept an hour past the alarm, and the chances were that, unless the weather turned better as he drove southward, he'd be an hour later than he'd told Reinhildt. For a fleeting second he wondered what his father would say, if indeed, old Johann chose to say anything at all. It would perhaps be better for everyone if the old man said nothing at all.

Passing the Messegelande, Eric remembered browsing unobserved through the huge von Kleist trade exhibit a few months earlier. It was pure public relations, and Eric knew it. Von Kleist had little need to attract customers. Still, the show had been impressive. Large, lighted charts had graphed the burgeoning production of the massive Von Kleist *Fabrik* in Frankfurt-Höchst. Photos and models depicted the Von Kleist shipworks on the Weser River, near Bremerhaven; nitrates and munitions works near Köln; steel and heavy industry plants in Elmshorn and Leinzig; farm machinery factories in Stuttgart. It went on and on. Public relations men drank steins of beer while they bragged to potential European and American clients that at least one in twenty Germans was somehow connnected to or in the employ of the Von Kleist AG.

Eric had slipped through the exhibit unnoticed, perhaps because his presence was not really expected. Had it been, the public relations crew would have had a field day. He was, after all, the heir apparent, the oldest male child of the legendary Johann "König" Von Kleist, the fast growing "king" of German industry. They would say in their press releases that he was a crown prince in the royalty of industry, destined to stamp the family name indelibly on history. Moreover, he looked the part. At twenty-three he was tall and athletically lean with finely chiseled features, striking blue eyes, a warm smile, and an engaging wit. It would have all been too much.

And so Eric had gone anonymously, quietly through the displays. He and only he knew that if they had thrust him into the public eye, almost every word the press would have said would have been wrong. He was not the heir apparent. Not the inheritor. His father had angrily assured him of that just after his seventeenth birthday. Seven years ago, he thought. And yet, he could feel the anger, the pain. What had he called him? Disloyal? Ingrate?

The explosion that had taken place at the exquisitely appointed dinner table of Schloss von Kleist that warm summer night in 1925 was much like a volcanic eruption. The pressures had built up in all of the parties for years before they flared up in a rage that had left the family structure hanging by a thread.

In his youth the elder von Kleist had sped through the military academy at Spandau, gaining a reputation as a brash young genius in military engineering and logistics. His development of a more powerful, lighter, and more portable artillery piece brought his name to the attention of Bismarck and thence to Kaiser Wilhelm. But Johann had cultivated a taste for money and power. And he realized that a military career would never really get him the former, while taking precious years to gain him the latter. He courted and married Lotte Gelsen, a small, slender, radiantly dark-eyed girl, who at seventeen was fifteen years his junior. Astute beyond her years, Lotte had no illusions about the marriage. She knew that Johann hungrily eyed the nearly bankrupt steel mill her father owned. Still, she found the dynamic, brash Prussian exciting.

Gelsen Fabrik soon became Gelsen von Kleist Fabrik, and a year later, after her father's death, it was simply von Kleist. Johann swept through the plant like a man possessed. Rolling mills were redesigned. An improvement on the Bessemer process was patented, and wartime colleagues were persuaded to buy better, cheaper steel from the boy genius of Spandau. In five years Johann tripled production and sales. He ruthlessly drove failing competitors out of business. Then he expanded. Steel meant guns, he reasoned. And guns and ammunition went together. He bought a chemical plant and turned it to the production of nitrates. The rest was history.

His career rose like that of Andrew Carnegie, his American counterpart, until the Great War, which would later become known as World War I, shattered everything.

Johann was embittered and thoroughly radicalized by the humiliation of defeat and the forced dismantling of all his munitions-related production. Pressured from without, he became a man obsessed with a hatred of the Allies. He staved off bankruptcy and swore he would find a way to defeat them, to "avenge Germany." He endured, but at the cost of his wife and young family.

As the years passed, he saw them less and less. Even his traditional dinner appearances became infrequent. And oddly, though he saw Lotte and the children rarely, he assumed that *his* plans for the children's futures would be instantly carried out. Lotte, in effect a widow raising orphan children, would have none of it. Small spats developed at the dinner table over a period of time. They increased until it was clear that an axis had formed, pitting Lotte, Eric, Reinhildt, and Horst against Johann and Kurt. The pressures mounted until the volcano erupted on that night in 1925. . . .

Eric had spent weeks planning how he might approach his father about his decision to become a doctor. He had asked his mother about the best timing, approach, method. She counseled him but added a reminder: she did not know Johann as well as she might once have.

The dinner that evening had been exquisite. Afterward, Johann sat at the head of the table like a monolith. Amid the gleaming silver and glistening crystal, he slowly lit a cigar. His black suit made the gray stand out in his black close-cropped hair. His cold, intelligent blue eyes darted to Kurt, then moved across the rest of the family. Eric, uneasy about the announcement he was about to make, glanced to his mother, who nodded reassuringly. Eric took a deep breath and turned to his father.

"Father, I—"

"A moment, please, Eric." Johann gestured with the cigar.

"I have a rather important announcement to make before we get to the idle chatter for the evening."

Eric sat stung and then quietly crushed by his father's words. He folded his hands in his lap and looked at them. He had been prepared to capsulate his life's ambition in one phrase, and his father had unknowingly snuffed it out. It was merely "idle chatter."

"I want to share a—shall I say—decision with all of you." Johann was smiling. "We have all fought hard, very hard to rebuild—to make von Kleist the strongest corporation in Germany. You also know that my goals have not been for us alone. They are for Germany. Today I took a step, a giant one I am convinced, toward supporting Germany in her growth. As of today, I have committed myself and the—" He paused to search for the right word. Eric looked toward his mother. Her dark eyes flashed, though her expression was icy. Somehow she seemed to know what was coming.

"—modest holdings of Von Kleist Fabrik to the full political support of the National Socialist party."

Kurt beamed. The others were stunned and silent.

"I might add I have personally contacted their leader, Herr Hitler, this very day. He was immensely pleased to receive our supp—"

"No!"

Eric's head snapped toward his mother as he heard her voice. He had never heard such anger in it. It frightened him.

She shook her head. "A gangster? A man who has spent time in Landsburg Prison for making a rebellion in Munich? A common criminal?"

Johann's eyes flashed with anger that matched Lotte's. "A *visionary*! A man who will see Germany on the road to greatness. A decorated war hero, wounded in action, gassed by the French and the British. And it is clear, Lotte, that you have been swayed by the slander that the Jewish and Communist press have printed about him, about the whole movement." His tone softened slightly, though there was still an edge to it. "You will have to meet him—speak with him as

I have. You will see that what is printed in those scandal sheets is trash. You will see."

Lotte shook her head slowly and drew herself up straight at the table. "No, Johann. I will not see, and how dare you patronize me and the children in this way. I will not accept those barbarians—not on any terms. Nor will I accept that maniac that sits at their head. He is not even a German."

Johann brought a fist down on the table. The glassware rattled. Eric, Reinhildt, and Horst were startled, but Kurt never flinched; his eyes remained focused on his father.

"He is more of a German than most who were born here. We are committed, and that is the end of it."

"They will not come into my house."

"I remind you, madam, it is not *your* house. It is mine."

"There would not have been a von Kleist company, Johann, if there had not been a Klaus Gelsen. Or had you forgotten?"

*"Enough!"* Johann's face was red, and the veins stood out on his neck. "We will speak no more of this. The subject is closed."

Eric looked from his father to his mother and back again. He was numb, confused. The announcement so vital to him had been totally eclipsed in the fury that was building between his parents.

Suddenly Eric thought the time might be right. The silence was oppressive; the tension was unbearable. Perhaps to mention it at that moment would be to calm things.

"Father—I . . ."

"What is it?" Johann's eyes moved to his oldest son.

"I've come to a decision about something. I—"

Johann folded his arms. "You, too? It seems everyone is making pronouncements tonight."

Eric swallowed hard, feeling a hard knot of fear in his stomach. "I have decided to go to Heidelberg University. I am going to study pre-med." He managed a small smile.

"You what?" Johann looked incredulously at Eric.

"I've been accepted. I took the examination three months ago. I—"

Johann closed his eyes and shook his head, as if to shoo

away a bothersome fly. "Don't be silly, Eric. You are going to be an engineer. You have responsibilities to the family. You are the oldest."

"But, I—"

"You will study engineering. The issue is closed. Is that clear?"

"The issue is not closed, Johann." Lotte's voice was cold and icily calm.

Kurt looked at his father, who sat only a few feet away. He nodded quietly. "You see, Father. It's as I said."

Johann looked at Kurt for a second and then down the table that had so suddenly become a battlefield. He paused, puffed on his cigar, and blew a cloud of bluish smoke out across the table. "You will please explain your comment, madam."

"That is the second subject you have closed in a row, Johann. I refuse to allow it. Eric has dreamed of being a doctor for years. He will be allowed to pursue that dream. I will not permit you to stop him."

"What you will not do, madam, is say another word on the matter. Nor will you again outrage us with your slanderous comments about the National Socialists."

He looked to Kurt and then to Lotte. A realization seemed to dawn. "I see, I see. You recruit our oldest son in your cause, do you? You subvert him? You turn him against his father—and his country? Well, there are ways of dealing with that, madam. There are ways."

Eric was shaking uncontrollably. It had all gone so wrong—dear God—so wrong. "Father?"

"Be silent, you—ingrate. You are given the world, and you spit it back into my face, you thankless cur."

Lotte came quickly to her feet. "I will not hear this. Eric *will* go to medical school, and Gelsen funds, *my* funds, will pay for it. And, Nazi swine will not be entertained in my home!" She turned and started toward the tall double doors that led to the entry hall.

"*How dare you!!*" Johann shrieked as Lotte strode with determination toward the hall.

Still shaking and terrified, not knowing where he mustered

the courage to move, Eric pushed himself to his feet and
followed his mother. Reinhildt and Horst followed. "Eric.
Come back here."

Eric stopped but did not turn. "I'm sorry, Father."

"You will be sorrier. I—I disown you. You will never get
another pfennig—Kurt will—Kurt will get it all. *He* is my
oldest son, now."

Eric closed the door.


In that agonizing quarter of an hour it was over. The family
was ripped in two. Eric remembered that after that evening,
his mother changed; grew more intense, more committed to
her children getting exactly what *they* wanted from life. She
was still a Gelsen and had a legacy from her family that gave
her independent wealth. Though it was only a fraction of her
husband's holdings, it was enough to pay for Eric's under-
graduate and medical school expenses. It was also enough to
nurture a study of music for Reinhildt and to encourage
Horst's deepening love of art and architecture. Eric had often
wondered how much of his obsessive drive to be first in his
class had been a psychological pattern of support for Lotte
and revenge on Johann. But it didn't really matter. Being a
good doctor was all that mattered. At least it had . . . until
Reinhildt's call.

He drove past the great rail terminus of the Hauptbahnhof
and the fleshpots of the Kaiserstrasse, which were deserted in
the early morning. He'd sampled the wares of the brothels
more than once in the years that he'd studied in Frankfurt.
Early in medical school, he had frequented them, even
haunted them. He had become something of a regular. He
had long since attributed his youthful licentiousness to a
prescription for getting over Anya. Odd, he thought, as he
turned her name over in his mind for a second, he had not
thought of her in months. His friends would have said that
meant he was "over" her. He wondered for a second if he
really was, before he shook the thought away. There was no
time to ponder broken love affairs. He had to get home.

He arrived at Heidelberg, stopped the car, and hurriedly purchased some buttered rolls from a sidewalk stand. The rolls were fresh and crisp, and they quieted his grumbling stomach. In fifteen minutes he was again on the road, climbing the winding, steep Bergstrasse, which overlooked the ancient fortress that was now Heidelberg University. Eric had spent four years there, before moving on to Frankfurt. He crossed the peak of Königsstuhl, the mountain aptly named the Seat of Kings, drove to Stuttgart, then on to Tübingen.

As he sped up the gravel road that rose with the incline of the hill toward the gates of Schloss von Kleist, he glanced at his watch. He had managed to regain the time lost in his late start. As he drove through the open gate, one of his father's security men waved him through. Eric knew news of his arrival would be reported to the main house before he got there. He pulled to the side of the road under a grove of fruit trees and looked at the house for a moment.

It was massive, looming, marble faced. Its four stories dominated the hill and were visible from every spot in the valley. It was a tribute to Johann von Kleist. It would be his monument, Eric was sure.

On the great oval path that led to the columned front entrance, Eric could see them standing, rigid, brown shirted; an honor guard of Kurt's maniac colleagues...*Hitlerjugend*— the Hitler Youth. Ironic, he thought, and infuriating. They would manage to turn it into a propaganda coup. The Nazis had come to support their long-time patron, Johann von Kleist, in his bereavement and loss.

Eric remembered Reinhildt's words on the phone. "Eric, it's mother.... She's dead—in the night. Heart failure they've said."

The house was festooned with swastika flags, hurriedly trimmed in black crepe.

*Dear God.* The men she'd called barbarians—madmen— would pretend to mourn her passing so they could parade Johann as their patron. He gripped the steering wheel until his knuckles stood out in ghostly white. After a few minutes, the anger passed. Control returned. Mother was dead, suddenly, unexpectedly... and there was nothing he could do about it. Grief was a luxury he had no time for.

With mother gone, Reinhildt and Horst would need his strength, his protection.

For now, they would be sheep—in a house of ravenous wolves.

## 2

Reinhildt von Kleist watched as Eric's red sports car roared up the long driveway of Schloss von Kleist. For a fleeting second she could feel the icy knot in her stomach start to loosen its grip. Eric was home; he would make it all better. It was the way that she had thought when she was a little girl, running to him with a scratch or a cut finger. Eric could always make things better. A bandage, a kind word, some tenderness—and everything was well again.

But those were the things of childhood. *Mother is dead.* She could remember the words as Horst had said them yesterday. They had echoed through the halls of the schloss like a litany. Now, the anguished words of her younger brother returned, and with it came the mental picture of his terrified face, tear streaked and unbelieving.

The icy knot formed again in her stomach. No. There was nothing that Eric could do. It was time to abandon the things of childhood. There was no bringing her mother back from the grave. The thought of her mother brought tears to her eyes, and that was something that she could not afford with the funeral beginning in less than an hour. She had cried for the better part of the day her mother had died, and now she had no tears left. Besides, the Nazis were turning the whole funeral into a propaganda issue, and loathing the Nazis as Reinhildt did, she had to be sure to keep a lock on her emotions.

As she watched from a tall French window upstairs, she could see Eric's car skid to a stop, spraying a shower of pebbles across the waiting *Sturmabteilung*—or SA—honor guard. Standing at a stony attention, the men did not flinch as the pebbles pelted them. Stone, she thought. They are stone lions obeying the whim of a madman. And her brother Kurt was one of them, rushing mother's funeral so he could return to his precious unit. How could she hate a brother? she wondered. But how much of a viper he was now.

Kurt had stood stonily near the door to Lotte's bedroom as Doctor Karl Mittenberg had ordered the morticians to remove Lotte's body. Karl had asked them to pause so that Reinhildt and Kurt could take a last look at their mother. Reinhildt had seen the ivory skin mottled with patches of purple. They were blood vessels, Karl had said; places where the blood pooled in the hours after death. Lotte's body was stiff with rigor mortis as Reinhildt embraced her. Her lips were cold to the touch.

Reinhildt stood straight, and then she staggered a step backward from the bed, into Karl's strong arms. His voice was speaking to her, but she couldn't make out the words, which seemed to come through the distant, roaring sound in her ears.

"Your mother will always live," he had said. "The part of her that you love will live forever in your memory. Everyone's immortality is in the children's memories."

She had leaned against his chest, stunned by the tenderness of his words. It was something that she'd never heard from Karl before. She had cried, in great racking sobs and he had taken her to her room and given her something to sleep. By the time she awakened, the word had gone out on the wire services that criss-crossed Europe: the matriarch of the most prestigious industrial family in Europe had died suddenly and unexpectedly. Huge bags of condolence telegrams had been deposited on the marble foyer of Schloss von Kleist. Flowers jammed the front hall, and still they came. Lotte von Kleist was a woman of incredible international prominence. And yet, for Reinhildt, all of it had the taste of ashes. Her mother was gone.

She walked to the huge dresser and stared into the mirror. She was tall, dark and lean, with broad shoulders, a tapering back, and a slender waist. Her black hair framed a face with sharp features, deep set brown eyes, a strong straight nose— the legacy of her father—and a broad, sensuous mouth. She was her mother all over again, except for her nose, and she knew it. The very thought of the resemblance again filled her eyes with tears.

There was a knock at the door. *"Ja?"* She forced her voice to have no quiver in it.

"It is Kurt."

She stiffened, feeling the muscles in her back tighten. Why him? He was the last person she'd want to see now.

"Come in," she said, knowing that his entrance was one way or the other inevitable.

Kurt was wearing the uniform of the SA, the storm troopers.

Reinhildt looked at him in the mirror. The swastika on his left sleeve was reversed. Somehow it seemed to her less offensive that way. What had it been? Greek? American Indian? But that did not matter now. Now, it was fast becoming a national religion, and if one did not accept it, one was subject to the inquisition.

She spoke without turning from the mirror. "What is it, Kurt?"

He cleared his throat. That always meant that he was troubled by something. "There is a problem with Horst."

She turned from the mirror, surprised by his cryptic tone. "What do you mean?"

"I mean—" He paused and took a few paces into the room. "Well, he got upset when he saw the honor guard and more upset when he saw me in uniform. I couldn't help it. I *have* to be in uniform, I am heading the honor guard. You have to speak to him. All of this is too important. Do you understand?"

Reinhildt shook her head. "No. What are you talking about?"

"I mean that he has refused to come to the funeral. It is out of the question. He has to be there. The family must present a strong front in this time of crisis."

Horst had retreated from the death of his mother. He had spent the previous day, following his discovery of the body, in his room. When Reinhildt had gone to talk to him, his cool reserve had told her that he was a bomb whose fuse had been lit. It would only be a matter of time before someone or something triggered him into an explosion. As usual, it was Kurt.

She looked up at Kurt and took a deep breath before she answered. "If he doesn't want to go, he doesn't have to. We should all be allowed to say goodbye to *Mutte* in the way that suits us best."

Kurt clasped his hands behind his back. "You don't seem to understand. . . ." He paused and thought for a second of the impact if Horst really did boycott the funeral. It would be a clear slap in the face to the Nazis and tell the world that the von Kleists were split on the issue of support for the party. The thought gave him more than a chill when he thought of the kind of reaction that would elicit from his party superiors.

"What I mean is, it is not fair to the other members of the family for him not to be there. Mother would have wanted him there, she would have wanted the family together."

Reinhildt took a step in his direction, and she could feel the anger start to well up from her stomach. "You are a cold-blooded hypocrite, Kurt. The reason that you want Horst there is the propaganda victory that it would mean for your precious Nazis. Your appeal to Mother's memory disgusts me. But, as it happens, I, too, believe that Mother would have wanted Horst there with the rest of us, and for that reason *only*, I'll talk to Horst."

Kurt took a step back and nodded tersely. "Thank you, Reinhildt," he said, turning to leave the room.

Eric stood in the doorway.

"Eric." Reinhildt called out, seeing him for the first time.

Kurt stopped in his tracks, and his eyes locked with his brother's. "Good morning, Eric."

"Good morning, Kurt," Eric intoned, surprised to see his brother in uniform. "One of your—colleagues informs me that you are wanted downstairs in the main hall. It was something about where the hierarchy will be in the procession and at the graveside."

"That has already been established," Kurt said. His tone blended a querulous quality with a twinge of annoyance that something had escaped his meticulous planning. "But thank you. I'll look into it." He walked quickly down the hall.

Eric and Reinhildt looked at one another for a minute, sharing the silence of disbelief. Then Eric embraced his sister, and it seemed that as he held her, he could feel the courage that had been holding her together evaporate. Sobs started to shudder through her, and it took a good ten minutes for her to be able to stop.

As he helped to calm her, she started to tell him how things had transpired. "H-Horst went to her bedroom when she didn't come down for breakfast. He knocked and found that the door was locked. That made him nervous because she never locked her door. When he couldn't rouse her, he forced the door. She was in bed. . . . Karl Mittenberg says he thinks that the time of death was the night before—sometime around ten."

"Did Karl say how—?"

"He said heart failure, and that it seemed to happen very suddenly."

Eric gestured in the direction of the window. "Why are *they* here?"

"Father and Kurt." Their eyes met. "I hate it as much as you do, Eric. I'm even starting to feel that I hate Kurt, and I don't want to do that."

For a moment she thought she might cry again. With an

effort, she held back the tears. "When Horst saw Kurt in uniform and that army of brutes outside, he refused to attend the funeral. Kurt was here insisting that I persuade him to come."

Eric folded his arms.

"And what are you going to do?" he asked.

She shook her head. "I'm sure that Kurt will think it a major victory, but I'm going to go and talk to Horst. Would you come with me?"

Eric nodded, then looked at his watch. "We should be quick. We'll have to be leaving in less than an hour."

They left the room and moved through the wide hall of the third floor of the schloss. The third floor had fifteen rooms, all reaching from a central hall, which led to a grand staircase. The stairs swung in a graceful arc to the second landing. The steps and rails were a rich but quiet teak. The huge balustrude staircase that moved on from the second floor to the main hall was marble. It bespoke permanence and quiet power, two things dear to the heart of old Johann von Kleist. They were the things that the four children had grown up with.

Eric and Reinhildt moved down the ornate hall until they came to Horst's room. Reinhildt tapped gently, and then, after a few seconds, she tapped again, harder.

"Yes?" The voice was distant.

"Horst? It's Reinhildt. Eric is here. Might we speak to you?"

There was a pause. After a moment the door opened.

Horst, tall for sixteen, had the dark good looks of Eric and Reinhildt. They formed an unusual contrast to Kurt, who was as fair as any Nazi might have wished. Horst, in shirt-sleeves, seemed numb, distant, glassy-eyed. Eric could see that the boy still manifested the traces of shock. After all, Eric thought, it was he who had found his mother's body. Eric thought that actually his youngest brother was not doing badly, considering.

"Little brother." Eric stepped forward past Reinhildt and took the boy into his arms. Together they went into the room with Reinhildt trailing along, making sure to close the door.

"I know he's my brother, but he's a swine," Horst said

through clenched teeth. "Telling me that I owe an appearance at my own mother's funeral to the fatherland. Dear God."

Eric looked at him. "We all owe an app    nce to Mother—no one else."

Horst nodded and moved to the window. He could see the large cortege of black Mercedes limousines forming in line for the trip to the church, only a few miles away in Bebenhausen. There seemed to be hundreds of cars. To the left of the cortege, the Hitlerjugend detachment stood as they had all morning, in the drizzle and in stony silence. Next to them, Horst could see his brother Kurt, quietly speaking to a stranger, who Horst thought, had to be one of his Nazi friends.

Sighing, he turned from the window, His eyes met Eric's, then Reinhildt's. "Very well. You're right. Both of you. We owe it to Mother. I will go."

Eric slipped a gold watch from his vest pocket and snapped it open. "All of us will have to be ready quickly, then." He paused for a second, as if he had forgotten something. Indeed, he had.

"I'd better see Father before we go. I came straight upstairs, and it wouldn't do to see him for the first time at the funeral. I know him. He'd take it as an affront."

The other two knew what he meant. Almost anything was an affront to old Johann, these days, especially since almost all communications with him had to go through Kurt. "Where is father?" Eric asked Reinhildt.

She paused for a second, as both of them stood at the open door. "He's in the study downstairs. He's been up since dawn and dressed for the funeral. He's seen no one at all."

Eric was not surprised. Johann would be sitting at the desk from which he managed the largest industrial machine in Germany, and he would be armoring himself in a mental equivalent of von Kleist steel. He would appear for the funeral as the perfect image of the ultimate Prussian.

Eric considered skipping the formal visit, but he dismissed the thought. Form dictated that he at least make the effort.

He reached over and quickly hugged his sister, then started in the direction of his own room, while she moved off to hers, and Horst, resigned now, started to don a black suit.

Eric's room was two doors down from Horst's, and as he opened the door, he could smell the antiseptic blend of cleaning compound and wood polish. For a split second, the smell made him think that he was making rounds in a hospital again. It was so clean that it was almost stinging. The staff, under the intense and meticulous direction of Klaus Schmidt, the estate manager, would have had the room clean and ready less than an hour after the announcement that Eric was coming home. Eric had always thought that Schmidt was a man with something missing in his personality, but he could never quite determine what it was. Schmidt was short and stout and pushing fifty. He had been with the family for more than a quarter of a century and had worked his way to the highest position on the staff. He had been directly responsible to Lotte and old Johann for all functions of Schloss von Kleist, and he made the place, Eric remembered from his childhood, run like a Swiss watch. Still, there was something about the man's personality—something missing. Eric had never been able to figure out what it was.

He pushed the thought aside and looked at his watch. He would have to hurry. He showered, then shaved and dressed in a three-piece black suit, deciding to use the new soft-collar American shirt, rather than the stiff-winged collar, still popular on the Continent. It chafed his neck far less than the harder one, and the last thing that he needed was more discomfort.

He looked in the mirror, examining himself, as he knew that the news cameramen would be doing at the funeral and burial. No matter what the political ramifications, he knew that he had to be a von Kleist. Not for Kurt and his Nazi gangsters, but for his mother. It was the least that he could do for her. He noted that there were dark circles under his clear blue eyes, the legacy of preparing for the practicum. Well, there was nothing he could do about them. He took a last look and quickly headed out of the large bedroom and down the stairs in the direction of his father's study. At the bottom of the stairs, he was headed off by two Hitler Youth boys who straddled the door to the study. He stopped for a second and stared at them.

"Excuse me," he said, moving toward the door.

The taller of the two, standing at the right side of the door slipped sideways, directly in Eric's path. The boy was a teenager though as tall as Eric and clearly outweighing him by thirty pounds. He had the look of a farm lad or perhaps of a star soccer player. The young man, never taking his eyes from Eric, clicked his heels and bowed formally, though stiffly.

"I beg your pardon, sir. It is forbidden to enter."

Eric was outraged. "I am Eric von Kleist, and I wish to see my father. Do you understand? Get out of my way, please."

The two stood eye to eye. The boy did not move a muscle. He repeated his earlier words. "I beg your pardon, Herr von Kleist. You are forbidden to enter."

Eric contemplated hitting him. It would have been a fine release for the tension.

"Eric?"

The voice startled him. It was Kurt's, and it came from a few feet behind him.

Eric wheeled, still ready to hit something—anything. He couldn't understand the anger inside him. "Yes?" he barked.

Kurt stood only a few feet away from him, and in the distance there stood another man. He was short and slender with blue eyes and sandy hair. Eric judged that the man was in his late thirties. He stood in a morning suit and simply watched Kurt as he spoke to Eric. He was Baldur von Schirach, *Gauleiter* of the Hitler Youth. Von Schirach watched carefully as Kurt took a few steps in Eric's direction.

"I am sorry, Eric. Father is seeing no one until the funeral. No one. That is his order. The two guards who stand before you are my comrades. They simply obey my orders and those of father."

Eric turned back to the youth and again, their eyes met. "Then, tell *him*"—he poked a finger in the direction of the young man—"that he might learn some manners and that he is a rather unwelcome guest in this house." His eyes never moved from the young farmer as he spoke.

"You may go, Heinrich." It was von Schirach who spoke, and both of the boys before the door snapped to attention as he did. Heels clicked in unison as they raised their right arms in the Hitler salute. They moved off quickly, stopping before the large exterior doors in the main hall.

Von Schirach turned to Eric, and the tall, thin-faced man managed a polite smile. "My apologies, Herr von Kleist. Excuse the lads. I believe they all suffer from an excess of zeal. They—"

Suddenly the door to the study swung open. Johann von Kleist stood in the doorway, staring at them.

Eric eyed his father carefully and with a strange sense of dismay. He was a mere shadow of the man Eric remembered. The once tall, robust titan of industry seemed to have shriveled. There were lines in the old man's face that Eric did not recall. There was more gray in the close-cropped hair, and he had lost perhaps twenty pounds. But it was Johann's eyes that told Eric the most. It was not just the lines and the slight circles under them, it was the look of fatigue. Eric made a note to speak to Karl Mittenberg about it. If there was anything wrong with Johann, Karl would reveal it—as one professional to another.

Baldur von Schirach snapped to the best caricature of attention that Eric had ever seen. He was rigid as a corpse, and as he steadied his gaze on Johann, he snapped his right hand up in the Nazi salute.

"Heil Hitler."

Johann nodded and raised a hand partway up in a faint imitation of the salute.

"Allow me to speak for the Hitlerjugend in conveying the condolences of the youth of Germany for the loss of one of the most important and beloved women in the Reich."

The speech was blatantly rehearsed, and if Eric hadn't been studying his father so carefully, he might have been driven to anger or perhaps to laughter. Still, von Schirach's tone made it clear what sort of charade the funeral would be.

"Thank you very much," the old man said, perfunctorily. Johann's eyes met Eric's, but there was no real communication in them. It might have been the natural anesthesia that Eric had many times seen in the faces of those whose loved ones had died. But he doubted it.

The old man scrutinized the people in the hall before he spoke. "I asked that I not be disturbed. What is all this noise?"

Eric nodded inwardly. It was the same father he remembered from childhood: an order was to be obeyed no matter the circumstances.

"A small discussion, Herr von Kleist. Nothing more. I am sorry that it disturbed you at this time of mourning."

Eric noticed that the rigid position of attention that Schirach affected as he spoke made the man look like he had a broom driven into his rectum. If it hadn't been so frustrating, it would have been laughable. "Father, I wanted to see you before we go to the funeral. I got in and changed so quickly that I did not have a chance to say hello. That was all I wanted to do. I had words with one of Kurt's"—Eric looked down the hall at the two Hitler Youth near the door—"colleagues. I don't think it's suitable that he give orders in our home. I'm sure you understand."

Johann turned to glance down the hall, and the glint from the gold swastika pin in his father's buttonhole caught Eric's eye. It had been a gift from Hitler himself. Eric remembered the incident clearly.

Hitler had dispatched Goebbels, the small, limping gnome of a man with the strangely manic smile, to the schloss in the last week of September. The von Kleist endorsement had been a major factor in gaining the National Socialist German Workers Party an enormous number of seats in the Reichstag. Following the election, their numbers burgeoned from a mere twelve deputies to an incredible one hundred seven. This had been due in large measure, Eric knew, to the huge number of von Kleist employees who felt it necessary to vote for the Nazis if they wanted to keep their jobs in the mills and the factories. There had been no threats, of course—no real coercion. It had simply been made clear that the "Senior," as Johann was called by the workers, was throwing his support to Hitler and that a success for the Nazis would mean many contracts for the factories.

Goebbels had been the one who had orchestrated the propaganda that had made the election a success. He had arranged for the radio broadcasts and written the speeches that Johann had made to the German people. So it was only right that Goebbels be appointed to deliver the small pin and personal note from the Führer. He had pinned the swastika on Johann amid the popping of flashbulbs, and the presentation was plastered on the front pages of all the German pro-Nazi newspapers in a matter of days. Eric had watched from a distance.

Now, Eric could suddenly guess what his father's reaction to the interruption would be.

"The order included everyone, Eric."

Right. The look of strain was not because of Lotte, but because of the old man's effort to hide the antipathy of years—so as to present a united family at her funeral. There was nothing else there. Certainly no affection. Nothing.

Eric nodded tersely, his eyes never leaving his father's. "I understand, Father."

"However, I would like to speak to you. Not today, but perhaps in a few days, when things get settled down."

"Of course," Eric said, inclining his head slightly, curious about why his father, who for years had spoken to him only when necessary, should want to talk with him now.

The door opened at the far end of the hall, and another Hitlerjugend entered and conferred briefly with Kurt. The two saluted, and Kurt strode up to his father. Eric could not help but see that Kurt was focusing on the old man exclusively. He wanted again to laugh but stifled the urge. Kurt was torn by trying to impress his father and Schirach at the same time. It was indeed laughable.

Kurt snapped to attention, and his heels clicked. "Father,

everything is ready. May I get the others—if you are ready to leave?"

"I'm ready. Are you and the others—Eric?"

It was the way Johann worded the statement that made Eric wince. It was as if Horst and Reinhildt were little more than distant relatives in the house rather than the children of his body. He had adopted the attitude over the years, but Eric had not seen his father in some time and had forgotten his attitude. Now, it returned with all of the bitterness that Eric remembered from the past. They were indeed all poor relations—save only Kurt, darling of the Hitlerjugend.

"Yes, Father. I'll get Reinhildt and Horst. We'll be down in a moment."

Eric turned in the direction of the stairs. As he started up the long staircase, he could hear Kurt below. "Father, with your permission, I will go to the head of the honor guard. I regret that I cannot go with you in the car."

"Not at all, son," the old man said.

The funeral cortege moved with agonizing slowness through the narrow, gray, rain-swept streets of Tübingen. Sitting next to his father in the huge Mercedes limousine, Eric had positioned Reinhildt on his right and Horst opposite them facing their father. He had made sure that Horst did not face the honor guard with Kurt at the head marching to the rear of the five flower cars and the hearse. Behind the car that carried the family, the cortege stretched for nearly half a mile. There were representatives of such families as the Farbens and the Krupps, as well as dozens of party functionaries.

As the cortege wound through the curving streets of the medieval town, Eric was surprised by the crowds held back on both sides by Hitler Youth and police. Apparently these people had experienced Lotte's generosity and warmth. The thought warmed him, but he pushed it aside. It was not the time for such musings. There would be time later for all of that.

He looked to his right, past Reinhildt, in time to see the open-topped press car pass, driven by a storm trooper. Propped in the back was a camera tripod and a man shooting motion

picture film. It passed slowly, the camera panning across the
family, and then it accelerated, pausing to get shots of the
honor guard, the hearse, and the flower cars.

Eric's eyes moved along the crowds again. Many of them
waved handkerchiefs, while some stood in rain gear and
simply bowed their heads. Among them were still photographers, snapping away. He began to wonder if they all were
just extras in the drama that the Nazis would plaster across
the German papers. He wondered if it mattered at all. Still,
though, he could share a great deal of Horst's anger. Lotte
von Kleist's funeral was going to be a massive political coup
for the "Brownshirts." It was something that, in life, would
have made her cringe. Eric was glad that she was not there to
see it.

A few drops of cold rain spattered on the windshield of the
car as the procession moved toward the family chapel and
burial plot at Bebenhausen. It was the chapel and plot that
Johann had chosen earlier, and the choice was significant.
The chapel was ancient, having been built by Dominicans in
the early 1400s. The monks had cultivated vineyards on the
steep hills that slid down to the winding Neckar. These
vineyards produced a fine, light white wine that was shipped
by barge through the Swäbian states and all the way to the
burgeoning Homberg area in the north. The wine made the
monastery wealthy and, the Dominicans, having taken vows
of poverty, could do little with the income, save put it back
into the abbey and the construction of even larger facilities. It
had been rumored that the income was what prompted the
construction of the fine chapel.

It was in the midst of the Reformation that things had fallen
apart for the monks and their thriving business. The more
zealous, local liege men of Luther, always envious of the
wealth of the monastery, especially as many of them were
vintners in competition with the Dominicans, hired merce-
naries to liberate the monastery from the Papists.

The church, the abbey, and many of the outbuildings had
been put to the torch, and a number of Dominicans who
refused to leave were put to the sword. In a few years, the

Lutherans had rebuilt the abbey and resurrected the lucrative wine trade with the Hansa.

Old Johann had first seen the abbey in the years after World War I, as he was building his industrial empire and its symbol, the Schloss von Kleist. He had seen in the abbey the same Phoenixlike quality that he had envisioned in the rebuilding of postwar Germany. He purchased the eastern portion of the graveyard and contributed heavily to the refurbishing of the abbey and the environs. The Bebenhausen Kirche got to be known among the townsfolk of Tübingen as Kirche von Kleist—the private family chapel of the family. Old Johann had said on more than one occasion that when Reinhildt found the *right* man to marry, the ceremony would be in the chapel. But Johann's idea of the *right* suitor was far from Reinhildt's. His fumbling attempts to foster "accidental" meetings with "appropriate" young men were awkward and transparent. All of them were connected to industrial interests that somehow related to the von Kleists. Reinhildt often complained to Eric that she felt like a medieval princess who was being bartered for political treaty or trade considerations. She was grateful that, recently, the attempts had been fewer.

The flower cars moved in the direction of the cemetery as the hearse stopped in front of the church, followed closely by the family car.

The small, chubby form of Klaus Schmidt approached the car door. As manager of the estate, Schmidt had been charged with all of the preparations for the funeral, in cooperation with the members of the Nazi party. Though Eric did not think that Schmidt was a Nazi, it mattered little. Efficiency was the little man's lifeblood, and he would almost compulsively organize anything that he was ordered to. He had been with the family for more years than Eric could remember. It was Klaus who made things run. The schloss was his domain, as was a large portion of the decision-making of the family. There had been more than one time that Eric had overheard his father ask Schmidt's opinion about a business endeavor. It seemed that the man always managed to come up with a well-informed opinion. With him setting things up, the funeral would tick like a Swiss watch.

"Herr Eric? Herr Horst?" he said, his voice just above a whisper.

Both of them turned to him.

"We hoped that you might be the left and right front pallbearers. Herr Kurt will be on the middle right and Herr von Kleist"—he nodded his head deferentially in Johann's direction—"you will precede the casket along with Fräulein Reinhildt—if that is satisfactory?"

Eric and Horst nodded and slipped out of the car. They took their places at the door of the hearse, where Kurt joined them along with two men from the SA and one from the Hitler Youth. The last pallbearer was just coming up through the rain from one of the cars. Eric recognized him immediately. Karl Mittenberg.

Karl extended his hand, and Eric took it. They said nothing but simply allowed their eyes to meet. Eric sensed Karl's sadness. He too, had been close to Lotte von Kleist. As a girl, she had wanted to be a nurse, and she had done volunteer work in his clinic on the mountain that overlooked Tübingen.

But there was more in Karl's eyes than sadness and loss, and Eric could see it. It was a look that he had not seen there before. It was one that he could not identify.

"We must speak—later," Karl said, his voice just above a whisper.

Eric nodded.

The cortege moved through a crowd, to the doors of the church, where the light casket was slipped onto a rolling bier that slid slowly down the main aisle of the church. The first two pews were roped off and reserved for the family. As he took his place, Eric heard a noise and glanced to his right. It was the high-pitched whirr of a camera accompanied by the glare of camera lights. The swine were going to spare nothing in publicity, Eric thought.

The ceremony was brief and simple as Lotte von Kleist would have wanted it to be. From the opening prayer to the closing hymm, it took little more than half an hour, after which the procession reversed itself and moved out of the church in the perfect order that Klaus Schmidt had devised. The clouds had thickened as the winds from the north blew cold over the mountains. It would be winter soon, and snow would blanket the area. But now, it only looked like rain. Eric noted the clouds with a sense of victory. At least it would foul up the ridiculous Nazi show. Lotte would have liked them to have been thwarted.

Eric moved slowly behind his father and Reinhildt, with Horst at his side. While they walked in the direction of the nearby graveyard, photographers snapped more pictures. Off to the right, Eric noticed a small man in a trench coat and a snap-brimmed hat talking to a group of reporters and giving out press releases and directing the photographers. There was something familiar about him, but Eric could not place it. Suddenly the dwarfish form in the too large trench coat pointed to a location for a camera and took a few steps toward it. He limped badly. Eric suddenly recognized him. He was Dr. Joseph Goebbels, the same man who had brought Johann the Nazi Party pin from Hitler. He was clearly in his element—his club foot and diminutive size meant nothing there. If there was anyone who could use the media, it was Goebbels. Eric let his eyes move back to the procession.

The casket had been moved quickly from the church to the cemetery so that it was there ahead of the party. Polished brass rails surrounded the open grave, and the casket was heaped with flowers, which spilled over to conceal the mounds of earth that would be shoveled onto the casket after the mourners had left.

Eric took his place between Reinhildt and Horst, with Johann at the head of the grave. As he looked at the flower-draped casket, he tried to picture his mother. She had been small, shorter than her daughter by more than three inches, but the love and encouragement that she had given the children had been immense. Reinhildt had wanted to study piano and painting, and Lotte had arranged lessons. She had gotten Horst books on architecture and Eric books dealing with the rudiments of anatomy and medicine. She had seen where her children's talents lay, and she had fostered their gifts. Kurt had been her bitter disappointment. She had been unable to reach him, and she had never forgiven herself for it.

Eric's eyes moved up from the casket. He realized that he could feel nothing, at least not then. His medical training had been all-encompassing. The reaction was going to have to wait until later—at a more private time.

His eyes scanned the onlookers. Werner Altenhoff was there, in the second row. He was a law student and a friend of both Eric and Horst. He had once confessed to both of them over too many steins of beer that he was trying to attract Reinhildt's attention—that he was in love with her. Horst and Eric conspiratorially arranged some "accidental" meetings for the two of them, but nothing came of them. Reinhildt simply wasn't interested. Still, Werner remained a friend, and Eric was grateful that the cortege was not entirely made up of political opportunists.

His glance was suddenly drawn to the left. Someone had stepped behind Kurt's chair. Eric saw a long, slender hand snake its way to his brother's shoulder. There was something about the hand and its motion. . . .

Yes.

His eyes snapped upward.

*Anya!*

How many years had it been? Only three?

He turned his head back and stared in the direction of the casket as his memory started to replay something in front of his eyes. . . .


It was the same room that he had left in Frankfurt. She stood across the room. They had made love passionately, fiercely, and he had been surprised when she got to her feet only a minute after they had lain in each other's arms. She stood near the window, nude, and the moonlight silhouetted her as she cast a shadow across the bed.

He lifted himself on his elbow. "Anya? What was it? Was it something—?"

He could see her shake her head quickly in the moonlight. That was all that he could see of her, save the sensuous curves of her body, which, yielding and erotic only moments before, were now still. She was a statue—with a voice.

"No. It was nothing... nothing that you did now. It was something else. We have to speak about something. About two things actually. Perhaps..." she intoned half to herself, "the first will be all that we need speak about."

"What? What is it?" He swung his long, muscular legs across the bed and in a single movement got to his feet. He crossed to the window, but she crossed to the door of the room. He turned in time to see that she was now bathed in moonlight from the upward turn of her small but sensuous breasts to the erotic curve of her hips. The moonlight made her blond hair seem almost white. Her penetrating blue eyes avoided his. He could not be mistaken about that. Her fists were clenched.

"I loved you, Eric. I really did. Make no mistake about that."

"Loved?" He was thunderstruck. All through that year their relationship had seemed more open, deeper, more intense. There had been no question in his mind that he was going to make Anya Forst a von Kleist. Her background—the fact that she was the daughter of a Frankfurt merchant, and that he had met her at a *Fasching* party, did not matter. He loved her. He had since the moment that he had seen her.

"Loved?" He said it again, like a man repeating the words of the judge who has just given him the death sentence.

"Yes." She still avoided his eyes.

"But what... when?"

"It's not important. I think the first time was when you mentioned the kind of medicine that you wanted to practice."

Eric blinked. What did she mean?

"But you knew family practice was what I always wanted. And as far as money is concerned, the trust that I have from my father will provide us with whatever we want. Anya, you know I'm tired of simply being the heir apparent to the von Kleists. I have to do this for myself. And it won't just be a practice. I have other ideas—for clinics and several research foundations. . . ." He stopped. He had allowed himself to drift into the future. "But what does all of that have to do with us?"

Her head drooped in silhouette for a second. Then it rose, and he saw the glint in her eyes. "You are a von Kleist, Eric. That's something that you seem to forget. A von Kleist."

"And you are a Forst. What difference does it make? I have no need to rely on the von Kleists—especially with the politics of my father and my brother."

As he spoke the words, the truth flashed into his mind. The rage that he could feel building was all that he could contain. He remained silent while she spoke.

"You don't see, do you? The von Kleists are power. Perhaps the greatest power in Weimar. You've thrown it all away. Don't you think, ever, that the power of being head of the von Kleist empire would allow you to transcend medicine? It is—" She paused. She had said too much.

And what she had said had confirmed what Eric thought. It was not the man but the name. His guts started to churn, and for a second he thought he might hit her. How had he been gulled? All she wanted was the name—not him.

"And so," he shouted, "you choose to end things because I choose *not* to become an industrial czar!"

"Something like that, Eric. It's over. You are throwing your future away with delivering babies and curing old women's complaints. I'm sorry. I really am. But . . . I cannot let that happen to me."

"So there was no love—not for you? Never?"

"Some, perhaps. Affection. . . . I can't lie about this. I care about you. You may not see that—but there is a part of me that does. Try to understand that."

"I was going to ask you to marry me." He wasn't sure where the words were coming from.

"I know," she said. "That's why we had to talk. I don't want to marry a country doctor. I—" She stopped. Her voice was starting to get shrill.

"Understood," he said icily.

"No. Not understood," she said. There was a tone in her voice that hinted of hysteria. "Not understood *at all*, Herr Pigheaded Eric von Kleist—eventually to be Herr Pigheaded Doktor Eric von Kleist. I do not want the father of my child to be a country doctor. Is that 'understood'?"

He stood there for a moment, numb. "You're—"

"Yes. For something more than two months, now. That was why we had to talk now—not later. Goodbye, Eric."

She moved to the bed and started to gather her clothes. He stood there in front of the moonlit window and watched her.

"I'll marry you," he said. "I love you. I was going to ask you—"

"Shut up, Eric. Just shut up. All of this has not worked out the way I wanted . . . the way I hoped. I—"

"You're carrying my child. We will be married, and that is all there is to it." He passed by the possibility that she was only after the family name. All he could think of was that he loved her.

"There will not be a child after tomorrow morning. That has all been arranged. I will not be the *Putzfrau* of a country doctor. I set out to marry a von Kleist. I still might. But it will not be a country doctor. Is that clear?"

He stood by the window and watched her put on the rest of her clothes. In a matter of moments she was gone. She would attract another von Kleist, if she wished, of that there was no doubt. She was the most beautiful woman that he had ever seen. . . .

Eric's eyes met hers for a split second. She looked away, but Eric continued to stare at her. She wore the uniform of the girls' auxiliary of the Hitler Youth: brown shirt with the familiar swastika arm band. But in place of the round SA hat, there was a black beret. Her hand on Kurt's shoulder seemed a clear indication to Eric that she had found the von Kleist that she had wanted. Yes... she had done it, after all. She was clever. For a second Eric allowed himself to think that perhaps she and Kurt deserved each other. Though even as he thought it, he knew it was a lie. He had been in love with her, and now he could feel the familiar sinking sensation in the pit of his stomach when he looked at her.

After the affair, he had drowned himself in the fleshpots of Frankfurt. It was more than a month later when he came to his senses, realizing that such sex was mechanical and counting himself lucky that he had not contracted anything communicable. From that time on, he had become something of a monk—and had reached the top of the class in medical school. Now, he recognized with more than a touch of alarm, that she was still there, buried in his gut. He pushed the thought away and glanced up at the mourners, who were listening to the words of the minister.

His blue eyes met the dark eyes of Karl Mittenberg. His friend's face held the same look Eric had seen on the steps of the church. He shivered suddenly as the cold November wind whipped rain under the canopy that covered the grave. He glanced at Karl again.

The look.

It was fear.

## 3

Dusk in Germany came early, especially in November. Day simply slipped away.

The cortege had returned to the schloss, and Johann was closeted with Kurt. Eric expected as much.

Going up to his room, he closed the door behind him. After taking off his overcoat, jacket, and tie, he sat down on the edge of the bed and thought about his mother. He didn't know how long he had sat there when he heard a knock at the door.

"Come in."

It was Karl. The haunted look was still there in his eyes.

Eric got up from the bed and crossed to him. The two men said nothing for a minute. They simply shook hands and then embraced. Long ago, as the oldest son in the family, Eric had adopted Karl as a kind of older brother. Karl had spent weeks helping Eric get ready for the medical school entrance exams; more weeks making sure that Eric met the right people on the staff, and days drafting letters of recommendation to the members of the medical school examining board. There had been no doubt in Karl's mind that Eric could have done most of it himself. However, there had been resentment among the medical staff at Goethe, not only a resentment of the von Kleist money or power, but also a wariness that Eric might be less than dedicated, less than fully committed to medicine—a dilettante. Karl's lobbying efforts erased all doubt.

Karl moved to the window that overlooked the sweeping acreage to the rear of the schloss. "There are two things to speak of," he said, his tone surprisingly brisk.

Eric frowned. "Of course," he said tentatively.

"The first is your father."

"I thought so. He didn't look well when I saw him, today." Eric paused for a fraction of a second. "How sick is he?"

Karl shook his head. "His condition has deteriorated recently. He's hypertense—"

"Pressure?"

"It averages two-ten over a hundred. But it's bounced higher than that on occasion. There are times when he goes off his diet, and that tends to drive it up. He won't give up cigars. He likes salty foods—kippers especially. Generally speaking, he's a textbook case. But that's not all. He's . . .

depressed as well. He communicates very little and spends a lot of time locked in that office of his. All he talks about is business and the Nazis."

"None of it sounds fatal—at least not taken alone. He's always lived for the business. That's how he got where he is. Not that I condone his position on the Nazis or his treatment of Mother..."

"That brings me to the second point," Karl said stiffly. "I have to tell you about this. You see, there is no way that I could have told him. Someone must know, and as you are fast getting to be a colleague.... Well... it has to be you."

Eric frowned. "What is it you couldn't tell him? And did it have to do with the hypertension or the depression?"

"Both and neither, Eric. Both and neither." Karl moved to the large wing chair in the corner of the bedroom and sat down. His shoulders were hunched forward like those of a man bearing a crushing weight. "It has to do with Lotte, Eric. It—" He paused for the barest second, searching for the right words.

He shook his head. There were no words, or at least not the right ones. "She didn't die of heart failure, Eric. Or, in a way, I guess we could say that she did. In the end all death is heart failure."

Eric strode to the chair and glared down on Karl. "What do you mean? Say it!"

Karl reached into his jacket pocket and removed an envelope. He opened it and took out a small hypodermic needle. Eric looked at the syringe, which contained a slight blue residue. The plunger had been pushed forward, but the needle was snapped off halfway down the shaft.

"Sniff it, Eric," Karl said, handing him the hypodermic needle.

"What?" Eric was confused.

"I said sniff it."

Eric did. The biting, acrid aroma forced him to pull his head back. He remembered the smell. "Potassium cyanide?"

Karl nodded. "About fifteen milligrams. It would have given her time to dispose of the needle. She didn't do a good job of it, though. I found it just under the bed. Actually, I stepped on the needle as I leaned over to examine her. It was the only way that I could have known, except for a slight distension around the upper part of her left arm. She must have used something in the bedroom to tie off the vein. Whatever it was, she managed to get rid of it, and at about that time, I reason, the poison was starting to take effect. That's why she didn't manage to hide the needle too well. She wanted it to look like heart failure."

Eric could feel himself start to shake. He turned, still holding the needle, and strode uneasily to the bed. He sat carefully on the edge of it, like a man about to faint. After a second he looked at Karl.

"Are you absolutely sure—?"

"That someone didn't . . . murder her? No. But she was alone in the room, and the door was locked from the inside. I don't see any other way. You know how everyone in the schloss felt about her. She was beloved. No. She committed suicide but tried to make it look like natural causes. I don't see that there could be any other way that it could have happened. Klaus Schmidt told me that she had retired at about nine. I placed the time of death about ten. No one had come in or left her room in that time. The next person to see her was Horst . . . but you know about that."

"Why? . . ."

"I'll tell you the same thing that I told Reinhildt. We're doctors—or at least you soon will be. We have to deal in 'hows,' and the whys are best left to God. I'm sorry Eric, but even now I'm breaking professional ethics in not putting it on the death certificate."

Eric stared at his friend for a long time. What was there to forgive? "And you didn't tell Father."

Karl shook his head. "No. I couldn't take the chance. It could kill him. You could tell him, of course. That's your right."

Eric shook his head. No. There was no reason to tell the old man. Karl had been right, things were better left as they were. But why? Why would she do it? He could feel the emotional armor starting to close around him as it had done in the practicum after Reinhildt's call.

"Eric, no conflicts with your father—if there is a way that you can avoid them."

"Of course, Karl. Can—can we speak more later? I mean, I have to sort things out. Kurt and Reinhildt and Horst—?"

"No. You're the only one I've told. Again, you will have to use your judgment about whether to tell them or not."

Eric nodded without looking up. A minute later, when he did look up, Karl had quietly left.

Feeling nothing, he lay back on the bed. He searched inside as a man might search in a dark room for something familiar. But there was nothing there. He got up and started to pace the room. *Why? Why would she?* He stopped and thought automatically of Karl's words; about the "whys" being left to God. But Eric did not have much faith in a god who would allow so much horror in the world. He never really had.

Feeling chilled, he slipped into his jacket, then he left the room and started to wander through the upper halls of the schloss. They were deserted; each member of the family, Eric was sure, had retreated to his or her room, perhaps to grieve alone.

It was sometime later that he found himself standing before the door of his mother's bedroom. It was open, and he entered, then closed the door behind him.

The room was large, with a french window that overlooked the front of the schloss and the long drive. She had loved this room and had had it decorated in French Provincial, with ornate mirrors and a large canopied bed. Now the room had been scrubbed clean. There was no trace of Lotte Gelsen von Kleist. The smell of wood polish and disinfectant was everywhere.

He crossed the room like a zombie, shuffling in the direction of the bed. Sitting on the side of the bed, he dropped his head into his hands. It was minutes later when he started to feel the heat in the pit of his stomach. It seemed to bubble upward. It wasn't fair . . . *she* hadn't been fair. She had been all that he and the others had—the only one to give them the slightest warmth, understanding, compassion. How could she have deserted them this way?

His grief came out as rage.

He got to his feet and grabbed the large porcelain vase that stood on a stand next to the bed. Raising it above his head, he smashed it to the floor. It shattered into hundreds of shards. He stared at it for a minute, feeling himself start to shake. Then he sat back down on the bed like a man finishing a marathon. He never thought that smashing something would help, but oddly it did. He stared at the pieces, feeling sheepish for a second. It was, after all, childish. But still, oddly satisfying.

His eyes again moved to the fragments. It had been one of her favorite pieces. . . .

There was something else on the floor, something that had apparently been *inside* the vase. He reached down and brushed the pieces away.

It was a small, but thick, battered brown notebook.

It was something that he had seen her write in intermittently since childhood.

It was Lotte's diary.

He picked it up and let his surgeon's fingertips run over the inexpensive, imitation leather of the cover. He thought to open it and then hesitated. Perhaps he should not—out of respect for her. But finally he did open it, feeling more curious than guilty.

Her handwriting was neat and precise, and she had carefully dated all of the entries. Eric had only to leaf through some of them to see that the diary was a clear record of the deterioration of her relationship with Johann. Lotte had had no real confidantes; there was no one with whom she could dare share the intimacy of the diary.

He no longer finds me desirable. Is it me? We hardly speak. And he was so passionate, once. Or is it that he feels that the family is large enough? Or was it never a question of me? Was it just that I was

a Gelsen and father owned a steel mill? Did he ever
really love me? And what of the children? What can
I do?

Eric noted with alarm that the entry was dated in the
spring of 1925. He paused for a second but forced himself to
read on. The later entries in the diary were not as neat and
precise as the earlier ones. The handwriting was tense,
pressured. It was clear that the stress of the relationship with
Johann and the conflicts that had raged through the house
concerning the Nazis were starting to have an impact on her.
Eric got to the last entry.

He read it—then read it, again.

*Impossible.*

It was impossible. But there it was, in that same small,
tense handwriting. . . . His mother's reason for taking her own
life.

*Dear God!*

His hands were shaking as he closed the diary and stared at
it. He could feel pain swirl around him like a dark symphony,
and for a moment he wondered if he was going to faint. He
pushed the pain away, forcing himself to think. Reaching into
his jacket pocket, he pulled out a battered pack of cigarettes.
He fished for his lighter and lit a cigarette, inhaling deeply.
The smoke seemed to steady him for a moment.

He stared at the lighter and then at the diary.

Should he?

He snapped the lighter alight and stared at the flame. He
moved it toward the paper. Suddenly he stopped and snapped
the lighter closed. He didn't have the right to burn it: it was
part of Lotte. At the same time, he didn't have the right not
to.

Again, the lighter blazed to life. He would.

There was a knock at the door. "Herr Eric?" It was Klaus
Schmidt.

Eric snapped the lighter shut and turned to the door.
"What is it, Klaus?"

"Herr Eric, Herr von Kleist senior wishes to see you in his

office, as soon as possible." There was a pause on the other side of the door.

"Herr Eric? Is there something wrong, sir? One of the maids said that she heard a crash up here, as if something had fallen. Is everything well, sir?"

"Oh . . . yes, Klaus. I just knocked over a vase."

"Might I come in, sir? I'll clean it up."

Eric looked at the diary, tucked it in his jacket pocket, then took off the jacket and slung it over his arm to conceal the bulge.

Finally—"Yes, Klaus. Come in."

Minutes later, Eric was back in his room staring at himself in the bathroom mirror. His complexion was a pasty gray, and his eyes were circled and deeply hooded. He went to the toilet and promptly threw up.

It was twenty minutes later when Eric headed down the stairs for a meeting with his father. He would later decide that the diary was too important to destroy. It was now hidden in the back of his armoire; next week he would place it in a secret safe deposit box in Frankfurt. There the secret words of Lotte von Kleist would remain for more than three decades.

# 4

Johann von Kleist's office was like a cathedral. Its sixteen-foot-high ceiling vanished in the darkness that the light of the small green shaded desk lamp could not penetrate. The walls were lined with technical and military books. Johann particularly prided himself on his military collection. He even had

first editions of the complete works of Clausewitz, signed by
the author. It was a legacy of studying at Spandau in his
youth.

The old man was sitting behind the huge desk when Eric
entered.

"You wanted to see me, Father?"

"Yes," Johann said, not looking up.

Eric stood there, some ten feet from the desk and stared at
his father. He fought for control. His mother's death; Karl's
revelation and the journal hidden in the vase all conspired to
overwhelm him. But there was no chance that Eric von Kleist
would succumb to such weakness now, not before this stern
old man—his enemy, his father. . . .

"Sit down, Eric," Johann said, gesturing to a chair that
faced the desk. Eric did.

It was clear that the communication was going to be tense.
Johann was cool, distant, businesslike. But Eric was not sure
what the old man was driving at. He was recounting the
history of the von Kleist empire and the necessity for careful
management, especially as Germany moved back to "her
rightful place of leadership in the western world." Eric
remained silent and patient. It took the old man a few more
minutes to get to the point.

"Karl has told me that I have to, as he says, slow down. As
a medical student, I'm sure that you know what he means?"

Eric nodded, wondering if somehow Johann had intuited
what Karl had said less than an hour before.

"Well, then . . . you see, what I need is—how can I say it?
Someone to help me run things—at least for a time. Do you
understand?"

Eric stared at him. He wasn't sure what the old man was
after. "I understand, Father. I just don't know how I might be
of help."

Johann paused and breathed deeply. "I want you to assume
operational control of von Kleist AG for the next year. . . ."
The old man paused and looked down at the table. "Until
your brother Kurt is of an age to assume the reins at
twenty-one."

Eric stared at him. He wondered if the old man was simply trying to play an insulting game with him. The offer was a caretakership, a janitorial service to be maintained only until the resident Nazi could legally take power. He could feel a rage start to build in him. His father could not even look him in the eye when he had asked.

He paused and fought the rage.

The needle Karl had shown him . . . the words in Lotte's diary flashed into his mind. Yes. There was something there . . . something—a weapon? Not yet. . . .

"Of course, I will do anything that I can to help, Father," he said finally. "There is, of course the problem of finishing medical school. I would have to—how shall I say it?—split duties between both. Would you object to that?"

The old man looked up from the table, where it had seemed that he had sought a bit of solace, while at the same time expecting a negative reply. There was a curious look on his face. "You *will* help, then?"

Eric nodded. The old man looked at him with intense, hollow, and slightly sunken eyes that seemed to betray a slight reaction of surprise at Eric's response.

Johann von Kleist, despite his industrial acumen, was a man who knew little of his eldest son. He had half expected that Eric would rebel and walk from the room after the falling out that they had had years before. And he knew that Eric had noted his surprise. He also realized that what he was going to demand of Eric would cause more conflict in the family. Kurt was not going to relish working under the orders of his anti-Nazi older brother for a year until he came of age. Kurt was ambitious and patriotic, and his allegiance to the party eventually would lead him to the highest halls of power in the Reich. Meanwhile, the von Kleist empire must have a leader. Kurt was still too young and inexperienced to deal with the rival industries that would descend on him like sharks on a wounded fish. Eric had all of the qualities that were needed: he was cool, and he kept his temper, whereas Kurt was brash, volatile. And Eric would buy time, Johann thought. He could finish his damned medical school and still help with the management of the von Kleist complexes across Germany. It would allow Kurt to complete his military training.

As the old man ruminated while looking from the desk to the eyes of his eldest son, he felt the impact of all the frustrations he had buried for so long.

Damn him! he thought.

Eric was perfect. He was brilliant. He would have been brilliant in any field that he might have chosen. It was as if the gods themselves had given his firstborn to the von Kleists to lead them to glory. But Eric had fallen into the soporific humanism of Lotte, and she had turned him against his father... as she had turned Horst and Reinhildt. The only one whom she had not been able to seduce was Kurt. And it was Kurt who would eventually be the true leader. For now, Johann would simply have to compromise. He would have Eric run things, no matter how bitter the pill. After all, had his career not been strewn with compromises?

"Yes, Father. I will help. I will try to double up on courses and finish as soon as possible, so that the degree is out of the way. The internship can wait, if need be." Eric tried to sound enthusiastic. Both men knew that the enthusiasm was false.

Only Eric knew the real reason for his acquiesence. He cared nothing about the von Kleist industries. He only sought to be a doctor. The delay that he was about to face was going to imperil that. Still it was worth it—because it was for Lotte.

# 5

**March, 1933**

The winter had been bitter; cold, bleak, and fraught with chilling rains. But in the glory of a freak warm spell, the valley had blossomed into an early spring.

The fine weather had brought a huge number of German voters to the polls, where they voted to more than double the number of Nazi seats in the Reichstag. The result was a stalemate, and a coalition government was formed between Adolf Hitler's Nazi Party and the Democratic war hero Paul von Hindenburg. The balance was delicate, at best. Eric had seen the growing force of the Nazis in Frankfurt, especially in the south part of the city. As Eric drove to the schloss, he knew that his father would be ecstatic about the victory.

Eric forced himself to pay attention to the road. He was near the edge of exhaustion from the stress of the last months. Fitted in with his studies was the management of the von Kleist complexes, which, Eric had to admit, was made easier by the executive staff that his father had assembled. The old man was only seriously working two or three days a week now, and he looked better for it. Kurt was surly, as usual, but his military duties kept him busy, and Eric had little contact with him. Reinhildt and Horst had pitched in to assist, and Eric had managed to double up on his courses, and with the help of Dr. Waldman, his mentor, he had arranged to take his medical boards two months earlier than scheduled.

As Eric drove, he spoke aloud, smiling.

"Herr Doktor von Kleist." He waited a second, as if there would be a response from the sparrows that skittered out of the way of the sports car. "Herr Doktor von Kleist," he said again. It was a triumph. All of the dreams and all of the work had culminated in his finishing months earlier than expected. The medical boards had been a solid week of withering tension, and they were over.

"Herr Doktor von Kleist," he shouted again at the top of his lungs. There was an echo from the distant hills, but the motor noise drowned it.

It was some forty minutes later when Eric swung into the main street of Tübingen. The narrow street was ablaze with red, white, and black banners, bearing the twisted cross of the Nazis. The flags were out in almost every window, and the bunting fluttered in the warm spring breeze. They would make the most of it. They would squeeze out every drop of propaganda from this coup that placed the Austrian corporal in a position close to absolute command of Germany. Eric knew that Hindenburg was weak and malleable. There was little chance that he would be able to resist the onslaught of Hitler when it came to policy decisions. No, Eric thought. It was only a matter of time now, before they had everything. He could only hope that the German people would come to their senses soon and oust Hitler. But Eric knew that that was more a dream than a possibility. He knew his fatherland, and he knew how his countrymen thought of leaders. There had been a parade of strong men from the time of Frederick the Great. It seemed that the Germans needed a father figure. It had been a thought that Eric had pondered since he had first taken a psychology course almost seven years earlier. As he saw his countrymen accepting the Nazis, the possibility of a German patriarchy came ever closer to reality. And where would it all lead?

Lining the streets, along with the flags and the bunting, Eric could see small signs. They had popped up overnight, it seemed: Loyal Germans. Don't Buy from Jews. And, there were others: Jews and Dogs Not Admitted.

So that was the way that it was going to be. He had seen that coming, too. Waldman had spoken of it at the university. There had been pressure to remove some of the Jewish medical staff from their positions. There had been other pressures, too. Among them, to insert Nazi doctors in the places vacated by the Jews. Waldman had said that the pressure was not too great, yet. But, he sensed that there would be more if the Nazis gained control of the Reichstag. Now, it looked as though they were going to do just that.

When Eric reached the schloss, he jumped out of his car quickly, anxious to share his triumph with Reinhildt. He was disappointed to learn that she was out riding with Karl. He asked one of the servants to notify him when she returned, and he went to his room.

Reinhildt, meanwhile, was enjoying her outing with Karl. The gently rolling meadows behind the schloss were the perfect place to ride on a warm spring day. After a lengthy ride, Karl and Reinhildt stopped at a small stream that crossed the meadow and allowed their mounts to drink.

"We'd better let them rest for a few minutes," Karl said as he patted the flank of his bay mare. Reinhildt had begun riding less than a year earlier and now spent a great deal of time in the saddle as well as in the stables, taking care of her Arabian stallion. Karl, too, had taken to riding, though more to see her than to enjoy the pleasures of the saddle.

He looked across at her now. Her black hair was tucked under a riding hat, and her eyes glistened in the sun. It was all that he could do not to sweep her off the horse and make love to her right in the field. A dark thought came to him, suddenly. "Reinhildt?"

She turned to him. "Yes?"

"Do you ride with Werner here?"

"No. He doesn't like to ride, I'm afraid."

Karl smiled inwardly. It pleased him. Werner was a local lawyer, recently taken onto the legal staff of von Kleist. He was rather popular with Johann, despite the fact that he was not a Nazi. Karl was sure that the old man had tried to arrange a number of meetings between Reinhildt and the young lawyer. Clumsy as such encounters were, Reinhildt seemed to like the tall, dark, witty young man. What Werner thought was something that Karl could only speculate on. He was a rival, and Karl knew it. Karl was certain, as only a man in love could be, there was no chance in the world that Werner could love Reinhildt as much as he did. And yet, he couldn't bring himself to tell her how he felt. Each time that he managed to get her alone, the words seemed to freeze in his throat. He felt like a fool. He knew he was going to have to say something soon. Odd, he thought. He had never been a shy man. But, this... this was something else.

"I really wish that he did ride," she said as she moved her horse a step ahead. "But then"—she turned to him—"perhaps I don't. I do like being with you so very much. And you're much more fun at the opera. Besides," she said as she moved the horse another step forward, "I'm not really seeing him—not any more."

Karl blinked. "You're not?"

"No," she said, her eyes studying his.

"Oh." He took a deep breath and smelled the first of the spring wild flowers. He exhaled and did his best to pull himself together.

"Reinhildt?"

She turned and looked at him with the slightest hint of a smile. "Yes?"

"I—" Again, he could feel the words start to catch in his throat. Furious with himself, he took another deep breath. He had to do it. He had to.

"Reinhildt—I—I—"

She gave him a smile that moved to a frown and then quickly back to a smile. She pulled on the reins of the Arabian and moved to a position so that she faced him, the flanks of each mount almost touching.

"What is it, Karl?" Her brown eyes hypnotized him. He could smell the slight hint of perfume in her hair.

"I'm in love with you." He blurted out the words.

She blinked and stared at him for a moment. "I know."

"You *what*?"

"I know, Karl. I've always known."

They sat, staring at one another. "That's why I stopped seeing Werner. I was hoping to get you to say something—anything."

"Then—you?..."

Smiling, she leaned across to him and kissed him gently on the lips. He returned the kiss, slipping a hand around her neck. After a few seconds, she pulled back. "I can't breathe," she whispered.

Reaching out, she touched his face. "Karl, darling... I've loved you for so long."

Too full of emotion to speak, he embraced her awkwardly across the two horses.

Then they spoke for a time, bubbling, excited with the first flush of their mutual revelations. The horses moved slowly forward at a walk as the two talked. Karl grew sober. "I didn't want it to come out this way and not at this time."

"Why? I did," she said, reaching over to take his hand.

"It's the immunology fellowship to the United States. You know it's something that I've always wanted—something that will make a huge jump in my career. If I complete it, I'd be teaching at the university—"

"I know all of that. It's for three years, isn't it?"

"Yes."

"And, you don't leave until the fall?"

"Yes. The late summer, at any rate. I'd have to get things set up at a place in Boston. That is, if I choose to take it. It—"

She reached over and placed her fingers to his lips. "Don't say it, Karl. You don't have to give it up. The fellowship's too important. Eric told me how excited you were when you got the news. I was excited for you. But... I still knew you loved me. I could feel it, and I hoped that you could see that I loved you. But don't say what I knew you were going to say.

Don't offer to reject the grant—not just to be with me, *Liebling*. Don't. You must go."

"But it will be the better part of three years, and now that seems like an eternity. I want to stay here with you."

"We can have the rest of our lives together. Besides, you will come home in the summers, and the time will pass quickly. Let's not talk of it. Not today. I'm too happy."

She cocked her head to the side and smiled broadly at him. "Let's ride." She pulled on the reins of the spirited Arabian, and it snorted, unused to the hard tug. Karl spurred his mare and Reinhildt swung her horse around. It snorted again and snapped its head upward.

It happened too suddenly for Karl to stop it. The stallion reared suddenly upward, and Reinhildt lost the reins, grabbing for the front of the saddle. The stallion, on its hind legs, frantically pawed the air with its front hoofs, and Reinhildt toppled backward over the horse's hindquarters. She lost her riding hat as she fell, and she struck the ground heavily.

Karl leaped from the mare and dashed to her. The stallion bolted, and in a second, the mare, too, was gone, heading back in the direction of the stables.

Reinhildt lay on the grassy slope, unconscious. Karl, with the deftness of a good doctor, checked for broken bones. The back of her head had glanced off a half-buried stone, and her hair was sticky with blood. He had no way of knowing if there was a skull fracture. It seemed that the gash was not too severe but, like all scalp wounds, it bled profusely. He dared not move her for fear of aggravating possible internal injuries. Stripping off his riding jacket he covered her with it. He had to get help—quickly.

The schloss was less than half a mile distant, but he didn't want to leave her. He *couldn't* leave her—and he couldn't stay. His stomach was churning, and his knees started to shake.

Cupping his hands, he bellowed in the direction of the schloss.

"Hello . . . *anyone*. Anyone in the schloss. I need help."

There was no response.

He yelled again, as loud as he could.

Suddenly he could see someone; a squat male figure running in his direction from a copse of trees. It was Klaus Schmidt. Karl waved his hands over his head, and Schmidt waved back as his short, stubby legs pumped furiously.

"What's wrong, Herr Doktor?"

"Fraülein von Kleist fell from her horse. Go back and call for an ambulance—right away. I'll stay with her."

Schmidt ground to a stop and reversed direction, and Karl dashed back to the still motionless form of Reinhildt.

He felt that he had been sitting there holding her for hours, though actually it was only a matter of minutes before he heard the deep-throated sound of an automobile engine. It's too soon, he thought. It would have taken the ambulance from the hospital in the valley much more time to get there. He turned his head back in the direction of the schloss and saw the sun glinting off the shiny finish of Eric's British Laconda. He was driving like a madman down the back road of the schloss. In less than a minute, Eric skidded to a halt a few yards away. He vaulted out from the driver's seat and clawed his way through the bags that he had brought home from Frankfurt. In seconds he found the small black medical bag. He grabbed it and ran to Karl and Reinhildt.

"What happened? I had just gotten back to the schloss and was in my room. Schmidt told me something had happened to Reinhildt." As he spoke, he knelt and removed the jacket.

Karl reached into the bag along with Eric. Eric came out with a stethoscope and Karl with a blood pressure sleeve. Eric was starting to check Reinhildt's pupil reaction as Karl spoke.

"Her horse reared, and she fell. It looks like a severe laceration in the occipital area. Pupil reaction is even bilaterally. Pulse is thready, and her respiration's shallow."

As Karl pumped up the sleeve to get the systaltic reading, Eric had finished listening to her heart. "You're right. Here." He handed over the stethoscope. Karl applied it to her arm near the sleeve to detect the first pulse sound as he started to let the air from the sleeve. Eric looked up. "How the hell did it happen? She was good with horses."

Karl finished the readings and looked across to Eric. "I get a hundred over fifty-five. Not too bad for primary shock. It's that head injury I'm concerned about."

"But how did it—?"

"She was riding the Arabian. It reared up on her, and I couldn't get to her in time."

"I'd shoot that damn horse. She fell in love with it last year. It was always too spirited." He looked to Karl. "Did you palpate that laceration?"

"No. There was nothing that I could have done if I had. Without an X ray... there's nothing we can do."

Eric nodded. Reinhildt needed a spinal puncture and a skull series. There would almost certainly be concussion, perhaps even.... As his thoughts raced through the possibilities, he recalled a lecture given by Doctor Waldman in Eric's second year of medical school. Waldman had warned the prospective doctors about treating members of their own families. He had especially warned about treatment at a time when there was trauma. Of course, he had been right. Clinical objectivity was a vital key in medicine. The closeness of the emotional attachment clouded it, especially in times of stress. But in the meadow with Reinhildt unconscious, Eric found that he could, at least for the moment, push aside his feelings. It was a discovery that would serve him well in later years.

It was some fifteen minutes later when the ambulance, heralded by its warbling siren, arrived at the site. An intern and two attendants dashed out and gently lifted Reinhildt's inert form onto a stretcher.

As Karl climbed into the ambulance, he said to Eric, "Do you want to come with me?"

Eric paused for a second, then nodded. He picked up his bag and climbed in, calling to Klaus Schmidt, who had come out with the ambulance.

"Klaus, take the car back to the garage. I'm going with Dr. Mittenberg."

"Yes, Herr Eric."

The ambulance, again with the siren warbling, sped from the meadow and headed in the direction of the hospital.

Klaus Schmidt watched it for a moment, then looked at the Laconda with the luggage scattered on the meadow. He moved slowly and methodically, picking up the bags and neatly arranging them in the trunk. With the car loaded, he slipped in behind the wheel, studying the plush seats and the exotic instrument display.

He folded his arms. A smile that was almost a sneer crossed his face, and he nodded to himself.

The accident couldn't have happened at a better moment. The time was coming. Yes. It was coming. The time of victory. He had spent a lifetime waiting, and now he had to be patient for only a little while longer. Then, the victory would be his. And it would be sweet.

He laughed aloud, then stopped and looked around, fearing someone might be watching him. Satisfied that no one was there, he started the engine and roared back in the direction of the schloss.

## 6

The hospital room was the best that was available in Tübingen. It was quiet and large, with a superb view of the valley. The shutters, however, had been closed against the light, so the room was dim, with only a small night-light device to provide enough lumination for the nursing staff to minister to Reinhildt. The darkened room had been ordered by Karl in consultation with Dr. Bremmer, the resident neurosurgeon. Despite the fact that there was no apparent fracture, the blow to the back of the head might have had some impact on her vision, and none of the three of the doctors involved wanted to take a chance on bright light impairing her vision any more once she was conscious.

She had been unconscious more than twelve hours, and either Karl or Eric had been at her side the entire time. Her blood pressure and pulse were constantly monitored by nurses. Upon Reinhildt's arrival at the hospital, Dr. Bremmer had thoroughly examined her and had ordered a spinal puncture and X rays. After determining that there was no fracture, he had said that the only course, albeit the most agonizing one, was to wait until she regained consciousness.

The evening hours seemed an eternity. Eric had telephoned the schloss that Reinhildt could not have visitors until she was conscious. There was no sense in having his father or brothers see her this way; all it would do was get them more worried, especially Horst.

Eric had come from the room and was pacing the hall, sipping a cup of coffee that a nurse had given him, when the door to the emergency area swung wide and slammed against the wall. One of the desk nurses jumped. Horst strode down the hall.

His hair was disheveled, and he wore a leather jacket over his white, tieless shirt. His eyes were red rimmed.

"Eric," he called, in a voice too loud for a hospital corridor. Eric said nothing but went to embrace him.

Horst ran a hand through his thick, dark hair. "How is she?"

"Still unconscious."

"Can I see her? I'll be quiet."

Eric shook his head. "There's no sense to it. Wait until she wakes up. I'm sure she'd like to see you then."

"How bad is it? I mean—the injury?"

"No fracture. We have to wait and see, but we're hopeful that everything will be all right."

"I couldn't get to Kurt. He was out on maneuvers with that damn Hitler Youth unit. They said that he was in the Bavarian hills and there was no chance to get to him before tomorrow morning. And they weren't very helpful even at giving me that. The swine!"

Eric could feel Horst's hatred. It had been building almost all of Horst's life, and there was little chance that it would change. Horst and Kurt constantly irritated each other. Eric knew his own dislike for Kurt had grown since their mother's death. He had not wanted it to happen, it was, indeed, something that he abhorred in himself. Hate was not a suitable emotion for a doctor, he told himself. He preferred to call what he felt distaste, but in his heart, he knew it was becoming hatred. During the time Eric had spent working with him, Kurt's attitude had been impatient—an heir apparent waiting until the regent loosed the reins into his care. He had been efficient—Eric credited him with that. Still, his aloofness and cool air of superiority had been something less than helpful, considering that Eric was swamped with both the management responsibilities and the mountainous wave of work at Goethe.

"What about father?" He changed the subject.

Horst shook his head. "He said that he would come in the morning, but that tonight he was tied up and couldn't get away. Fatherly, isn't he?"

Eric shook his head. "There would be nothing that he could do here tonight. There's little that any of us can do. It is simply a matter of waiting."

"Eric!" Karl called from Reinhildt's room.

"Stay here," Eric said firmly. Horst nodded.

Dr. Bremmer and Eric dashed in the direction of the room, and as they opened the door, they had to let their eyes grow accustomed to the dim light.

Karl was hunched over the bed, looking at Reinhildt. He turned in the direction of the door. "I think she's waking up. I saw her eyelids start to flutter."

Reinhildt moaned.

"Thank God," Eric said. He walked closer to the bed and saw that her right leg was moving ever so slightly. If a leg was moving, then the odds were that there was no damage to the spinal column. The chances were that there would be no paralysis.

Eric moved to the right side of the bed as Karl moved to

the left. Both of them watched as Reinhildt swam up from the depths of unconsciousness, and both of them tried to hide the jubilation that they felt behind a mask of professionalism. Neither fully succeeded. One man loved her as a brother and the other was in love with her so deeply that he could barely speak of it.

It was less than an hour later when her eyes flickered again, and this time stayed open. She focused on Karl on the right side of her bed.

"Karl?"

His head snapped in her direction and up from the chart that he had been reading. She started to turn toward him, and he restrained her with a gentle but firm hand.

"No. No, *Liebling*. Don't move. It's too soon. You took quite a bump on the head. Do you remember?"

"In the meadow? The Arabian reared and threw me?"

"Yes. Can you remember what we were talking about before that?"

He leaned closer to the bed. In cases where memory might have been affected, it was standard practice for the doctor to ask the patient to remember incidents just before the injury. But Karl had a far more personal reason for asking the question.

She looked blank for a moment, and Karl held his breath. Then she smiled and said wearily, "Of course. Of course I do, *Liebling*." Her hand reached out and took his.

Eric had been standing, looking out the window, when Reinhildt first regained consciousness. He took a step toward the bed but stopped, hearing a tone of caring in both their voices. He saw Reinhildt take Karl's hand. How long had it been going on? he wondered. He turned back to the window, pretending that he had not seen. But he suspected that the relationship was something new. Surely it had not been going on for any length of time, for Reinhildt would have told him about it. He pondered the fact that Reinhildt had stopped going to the opera with Werner and the fact that Karl had taken a sudden interest in riding. He thanked whatever gods that there might be for the fact that Karl had been riding there in the meadow with her, in any event, and he found himself excited for them.

After a minute, he cleared his throat loudly and headed in the direction of the bed. He watched as Reinhildt extricated her hand from Karl's and Karl moved decorously back from the bed. It was Eric's turn and he leaned over and kissed her. She put a hand on his cheek, which was now stubble-covered from the long hours spent in the hospital.

"Oh, Eric. I knew you'd be here—as I knew that Karl would be. I'm so sorry to have caused you all this trouble."

He smiled and shook his head. "Just wait until you get the bill." He quickly looked to Karl. "It will take her years to pay it, no?"

Karl nodded solemnly. "Absolutely." They laughed, and Reinhildt smiled weakly.

Karl slipped a hand under her head to check the dressing, which was in place. "I think that you had better get some rest now. We can talk more in the morning." He turned to Eric. "What do you think?"

Eric nodded. She would be attended around the clock. He started for the door. "Why don't you two chat for a minute while I get Bremmer? He'll want to have a look at Reinhildt."

Karl looked so grateful that Eric had to smile. He was playing the role of a matchmaker, and it cheered him immensely. Reinhildt would be under observation for several days, but if Eric's guess was correct, Karl would be in the hospital night and day until Reinhildt was released.

Dr. Bremmer was in the hall with Horst, and Eric told them that Reinhildt had regained consciousness. The neurosurgeon went into the room, and Eric turned to Horst, whose young, intense face was registering a mixture of hope and concern. "Well?" Horst asked.

"Things could have been a lot worse. It boils down to a moderate concussion and a few stitches in the back of the head. She was awake and making sense, and I think in a day or two, she'll be all right. She'll have to be watched, of course, and I think that she should get back to the piano rather than the stables for at least a month. But she'll be fine."

Horst put a hand on Eric's shoulder. His fingers were strong. There were the beginnings of tears in his eyes. He closed them and shook his head. Eric reached out and embraced him.

Seconds later, the swinging door of the intensive care ward opened and slammed against the wall. The sound was like a rifle shot in the silence. Eric could hear voices starting to argue at the nurses' station. Turning from Horst, Eric headed for the door. He reached it at the same time that Dr. Bremmer and Karl came from Reinhildt's room. A group of men in trench coats, dripping water on the polished floor, were huddled around the nurses' station. Eric recognized the voices—at least one of them.

"I will see her now!"

It was Kurt, with what appeared to be three other members of the Hitlerjugend detachment.

The nurse was firm but starting to get flustered. "I'm sorry, sir, you're going to have to—"

Kurt looked down at the nameplate. "Slodski. You are Nurse Slodski?"

"That's correct, sir."

"The name is Polish. Are you a Pole?"

"Yes, I am, sir. But I don't see what that has to—"

"Jewish, too, I'm willing to bet. Is that correct. Well?"

Totally rattled now, Nurse Slodski looked down the hall and saw the approaching trio of doctors.

"Oh, doctors. There seems to be a problem. This man—"

Eric was the first to speak as Kurt turned in his direction. "I'm glad that you could get here, Kurt. It seems like Reinhildt is almost out of danger—at least at this time."

Kurt did something odd. He nodded to Eric as if what he had been told had little meaning. Then his head snapped in the direction of the nurse. The woman was clearly intimidated.

"I asked, are you a Jew? Answer me!"

Bremmer moved in the direction of the confrontation, but

Eric stepped in front of him. Eric *knew* that Bremmer was a Jew. There was no sense in putting oil on the fire.

"Perhaps you didn't hear me, Kurt. Reinhildt is doing fine. But she's sleeping, and I'm afraid that Frau Slodski's instructions were to keep visitors at a minimum. They were my orders and Karl's. I'm sure that you understand."

Kurt turned to his older brother. The men's eyes met.

After a second, Kurt averted his gaze. "I'm sorry, Eric. My concern was for Reinhildt. As you know, I don't like to be dealt with by functionaries. All I was told was that Reinhildt was hurt. With the party victory only a day old, there was always that chance that an assassin might have made an attempt on her life. After all, our family is going to be valuable to the party. I brought my colleagues to stand guard by her room. What was the nature of the injury?"

Eric could see Horst coming in their direction. The last thing he wanted was a family squabble at this moment.

"Perhaps we could go into the waiting room and explain things there. There are other patients here, and I'm sure that they require the same quiet that Reinhildt does."

Kurt paused for a second. Eric could see his one-way mind trying to evaluate exactly what the suggestion meant.

"Very well, Eric. Perhaps we were overly zealous. But after all, Reinhildt is one that we all love."

The statement was transparent and both of them knew it. But it would serve long enough for Eric to calm things down. They started in the direction of the waiting room.

Karl excused himself. He didn't really want to be part of this family conference—and he *did* want to get back to Reinhildt.

He stayed with Reinhildt, looking down at her for a long minute. He wanted desperately to hold her, but he knew that a nurse might arrive any moment. There was no sense in starting the rumor mill going in the small hospital.

And indeed, only a few seconds later the nurse came into the room.

It was Frau Slodski.

Karl looked at her curiously. "I thought that you were on duty at the desk?"

She nodded. "I was, Herr Doktor. I switched with Sigrid. She'll cover the rest of the shift on the desk. I'm better at intensive care. It makes her nervous. If something goes wrong, seconds count. Besides, Herr Doktor, I have met Fraülein von Kleist several times in the past. She used to come here with her mother, years ago when her mother was doing volunteer work. She was a lovely little girl, and she's grown into a beautiful woman."

Karl looked at the sleeping form of Reinhildt under the slightly distorting surface of the tent. "She certainly is." He looked at the nurse for a second. "But those weren't the only reasons, were they?"

She thought for a second, before she decided to answer. Eventually, she nodded. "I wanted to get away from those— men at the desk. I am a Pole. And I am a Jew. And I hate them. God help me. It's wrong to hate anyone, but I do so hate them. I came from Warsaw six years ago when my husband died. I had my little boy, and there was no work in Warsaw, especially not for a widowed Jewess in medicine. I entered on a visa, and they told me that I would have to be employed for seven years before I could get citizenship. That was before these"—she gestured in the direction of the hall, as if there were no words she could use to describe them— "these—Nazis came. Now I'm frightened. Have you heard some of the things that they have said about the Jews?"

It was not really a question that needed an answer. Still, Karl nodded. The Nazis had blamed every problem that Germany had on the Jews and many that she didn't even have. The Nazi Streicher's rag *Der Sturmer* had taken the lead and many other papers in Germany had followed suit. More threatened to do so, especially after the Nazis had managed to get a coalition in the Reichstag.

"I'm sorry, Herr Doktor. I didn't mean to—"

He put a hand on her shoulder. "It's all right. Many of us, Jews or not, feel the same way that you do. Keep watch over her. She's very special to all of us."

They exchanged weak but convincing smiles of reassurance, and Karl left, closing the door quietly behind him.

The hall was empty. Eric had cleared the way of Kurt and the others. Karl walked to the utility room, where he poured a mug of hot black coffee from the ever present pot. He stared at it for a moment; his hand was shaking. He tried to take a sip, but it burned his tongue. He put it down to cool—and started to cry, doubled up, with his hands over his mouth so that nothing would be heard from the hall.

Eric left quietly. He walked to the end of the hallway where he saw Karl coming down the adjoining corridor, looking haggard and red eyed. Karl averted his glance, but Eric was not to be put off.

"Everyone occasionally needs a good cry. Even doctors, Karl."

Karl folded his arms against his chest and started to laugh. "Dear God, is it that obvious?"

"Only to one who knows you. Only to a friend, Karl."

Karl laughed again, but the tension had been broken in the first laugh, and now there was only fatigue. "They would have drummed me out of medical school for that slip."

"I think your judgment was a little clouded, Karl. But it's understandable. It's hard trying to treat someone as close as Reinhildt."

"Ah—yes. She's such a good friend."

"She's more than that. You're in love with her, aren't you?"

The look that came over Karl's face was one of initial panic—followed by resolution. "How—?"

"Simple. I saw you look at her when she awoke. I saw her take you by the hand. I just added two and two."

Karl nodded, looking resigned and sheepish at the same time. "Yes. And now that you know? I mean, everything happened so quickly—minutes before. We were both so excited that might even have caused the accident. I feel so guilty. What happens now?"

"You love one another. Enjoy it. I'm delighted for both of you. I knew that she could have done better than Werner Altenhoff, but I never dreamed that it would be my best friend."

## 7

In the waiting room, Eric was explaining things to Kurt.

Kurt, stripped of the rain slicker, stood in his uniform, which to Eric's surprise, was not brown as he remembered. Rather, it was a black tunic, with the familiar swastika on the left sleeve. Though, he noted that not only was the color different, but there was a new circular band worn some inches up the sleeve, it simply said "Adolf Hitler." Eric was sure that it was something of a promotion, though he had no intention of asking.

"So then, do you understand? There is no cause for alarm, and the best thing now is sleep for her."

Kurt nodded. "Of course. But understand me, please. With this new coalition, the Führer has decreed that Jews and Communists will make every effort to stop national socialism from taking its rightful place in the world. Our father has committed us to the struggle. There is always the chance that those same groups of Jews and criminal Communists would try to kill or kidnap the allies of the Führer. As you can see, I have brought two of the best men I have here to guard her. I promise that they will not be obtrusive. I know that you are not fond of my position and the National Socialist movement in general. I only ask that we be allowed to help—at least until she is back at the schloss. How long might that be, Eric?"

Eric took a deep breath. Every word from Kurt's mouth was drawn directly from the diatribes of Goebbels. He wanted to scream in Kurt's face. But he was a prudent man, and he knew it would be fruitless. Not yet... perhaps later, he thought as the beginnings of an idea started to glimmer in the back of his mind.

"I would expect that she would be out of the hospital in a week—ten days at the most. That's assuming that there are no complications."

"Very well, then. I will see Father and accompany him here tomorrow at midday. Will you and Horst be needing a ride back to the schloss?"

Eric looked at Horst. The youngest brother, seventeen and brash, was seething in the corner. Eric did not want to run the risk of his exploding at Kurt.

"Thank you, Kurt. I'll be here awhile, and Horst will also. Karl could drop us off."

"Very well, Eric." He turned to his colleagues, who had also shucked their slickers. They wore the more traditional storm trooper garb; brown shirts, jodhpurs and boots. Their tan caps were cinched under the chin. Eric could not help thinking that they resembled the tin soldiers that Horst had stolen from Kurt after the incident on the beach many years ago. . . .


Horst had waited until Kurt had gone to bed, leaving his collection of cast lead figurines on the floor of the playroom. There must have been a hundred of them. Some were the troops of Frederick the Great. Others were more recent, relics of the Franco-Prussian War. A few more the garb of World War I ground troops.

It was well after midnight when Horst had crept from his bed and into the playroom with a small cloth sack. He collected all of the soldiers and carried them all the way down to the basement, three stories below. The cellar had been dark and musty, Horst had said, when he told Eric days later. Eric had chided him about what he had done, but he himself had had to chuckle. Horst had dropped the lead figurines into the furnace. In minutes they were a small pool of molten lead. He had crept back upstairs and left a small handwritten note on the floor where the soldiers had been scattered. It simply said, "The fortunes of war."

Kurt had never mentioned the incident. It had been a stalemate. . . .

Kurt backed away a step and looked to the other troopers. They snapped up their hands in the Hitler salute, the one that the Austrian corporal had pirated from his Italian counterpart, Il Duce. Kurt snappily returned the salute, turned on his heel, and was gone.

Eric looked at the robots who stood a few feet away. "Coffee, gentlemen? It's going to be a long night."

"No, thank you, Herr von Kleist," the one on the right said.

Eric could see in their eyes the zeal with which they had accepted their assignment. And why shouldn't they? he thought. Everything was going their way. Hitler had been Reich's chancellor for less than ten weeks. Two weeks before, a conflagration had destroyed the Reichstag. They had managed to arrest a semi-illiterate Dutch Communist named Marinus van der Lubbe for the crime, and Eric knew that the odds were that the man would never again see the light of day. The press was ablaze with charges that van der Lubbe was a tool of the Dutch Jewish conspiracy and a tool of Moscow at the same time. Eric would have laughed if it hadn't been so dangerously irrational. The Bolshevists were less fond of the Jews than the Germans and the Poles. But Hitler and Goebbels had pyramided the fire into a national hysteria. *Ruhe und Ordnung* was the rallying cry: Law and Order. Even more frightening was the bill that had been presented to the Reichstag only a week earlier. The law was to be called "The Ordinance for the Protection of People and State." If they managed to jam it through the Reichstag, it would establish a dictatorship and force Hindenburg's weak coalition out. They would have it all.

The brownshirt on the right shuffled for a second before speaking again. It was clear he was unsure of protocol.

"Herr von Kleist, I am SA Obersturmführer Peiper, Joachim Peiper, sir. My colleague is SA Untersturmführer Kraus. We are at your service."

Eric bowed slightly. Kraus, not as seemingly astute as his colleague, broke into a grin and spoke. "Perhaps you did not notice, sir. Your brother's uniform. I am sure congratulations are in order. He just got it as we left the camp. You noticed it's different, of course."

"Of course. I just wasn't sure what that all meant. I don't have much ah . . . touch with the military, you see."

"Of course, Herr von Kleist. I didn't mean to speak out of turn."

Peiper was less reticent. "Kurt is the first in south Germany chosen to wear it. It is the uniform of the *Leibstandarte Adolf Hitler*. They will be the Führer's personal guard, at least they will when their training is completed. We envy him. I envy him perhaps more than the others. I will not be chosen."

Eric wondered if that was because Peiper perhaps had a Jew in his family closet somewhere. But he fought back the urge to ask. "Oh, Herr Peiper, why is that?"

"I graduated from Spandau, sir. I will have a commission in the regular army. I will be in the panzers. However, I hope that if the SS ever involves itself with the army, I will be a part of it."

"That's commendable, Peiper. Thank you both very much. I must warn you that under no circumstances should Fräulein von Kleist be disturbed. She must rest at all costs. You will restrict your activities to the hall and the environs. Understood?"

"Yes, sir." They spoke in unison.

Eric turned and beckoned Horst to the far end of the hall. He spoke quietly as he and Horst paced. "I think you managed to contain yourself quite well out there."

Horst shook his head as he walked. "How can you even be polite to them? I just don't understand," he muttered.

"Diplomacy has many faces, my brother. This is only one of them. Be patient, just be patient. Go down to the commissary and get something to eat. I have to settle some details with Karl about Reinhildt."

"I'm not hungry."

"Go anyway. Just keep away from our brethren—from the master race out there. Now, do as I say. I cannot deal with Reinhildt's condition when I have to be your buffer against the Nazis. Go. Understand?"

Horst took a deep breath and exhaled audibly, like a man who is either about to shoulder a great weight or one who has just released one. Then he strode off in the direction of the small all-night commissary that served the staff of the hospital.

Eric turned and retraced his steps to Reinhildt's room, passing the guards at the door.

The room was still dark save for a small light in the corner, and the only sound was the hiss of the oxygen tent. He crossed quietly to Nurse Slodski. "All's well?"

She looked up, nodded, and silently handed him the chart. The vital signs were holding steady.

# 8

Three days later, Reinhildt was allowed out of bed. Karl and Eric wheeled her to the back veranda of the hospital, where she could look at the early blossoms along the river. The sun was dazzling and sparkled off the water like diamonds.

She took a deep breath and smiled at them both. "You know, I don't want to insult either of you, but I hate the smell of hospitals."

Eric chuckled and lit a cigarette. "So do I. And I think Karl does, too. Perhaps that's why we're in the business—to keep people out of them."

"I don't remember Father being here. Was he?"

Eric frowned. "Long enough to kiss you on the cheek and inquire about your condition. I think Father lavishes as much affection on his pet shepherd as he does on his daughter."

"Eric, that's cruel. But—well, he *is* distant. I don't know if he can help that. I really don't."

"I do, Reinhildt. I was six when you were born, and I remember him playing catch with me and riding piggy-back on him. He was happy and so was Mother. But then things started to change. He started to connect himself to the Nazis, through all of his old friends at Spandau. They had no illusions about Hitler. Do you know what they call him? The Austrian corporal—not to his face, of course. All they saw in him was a way back to militarism. Somehow, father was not as cynical as they. He bought all of it—the whole philosophy. That's what changed him."

Reinhildt shook her head sadly, then smiled. She's a woman in love, Eric thought. She doesn't want to hear these things. Still, there was something that had to be discussed.

"Horst is coming over in a few minutes, and I think that there is something that we all should speak about."

Karl shot a glance to Eric and leaned forward to take Reinhildt's hand.

"Liebling, Eric knows about us." He looked at Eric, who came around to the front of the wheelchair and hunkered down to speak to his sister.

"He didn't tell me, Reinhildt. I saw the way that you two looked at each other the night when you awakened. I could see it in your eyes and I could hear it in your voice." He looked across to Karl. "I've told no one, but I'm happy for you."

Reinhildt smiled. "Oh, Eric. . . ." She leaned forward and embraced him, just as the door to the veranda opened, and Kurt's brownshirted friends entered, carrying boxes of flowers.

Peiper bowed. "Fraülein von Kleist? These came for you late last evening. Herr Doktor Mittenberg requested that we hold them for you until today. I'm afraid that we had to look inside the boxes as a security precaution. We did not, of course, open the cards."

They placed them at her feet, bowed stiffly, and moved off the patio, their boots clicking on the flagstones.

The first, a bouquet of yellow carnations, was from Horst. The next was a single red rose from Karl. She read the card silently, then looked at him with glistening eyes. She opened the third. Pink carnations from Werner Altenhoff.

There would have been a time when flowers from Werner would have made her jubilant. But now, they only reminded her of her newfound love for Karl. She placed them to the side and unwrapped the last box. It was by far the largest and was filled with dozens of African orchids. The card was small, discrete, and shocking.

> *Dear Fraülein von Kleist,*
>
>    *A small offering in the hope that the daughter of one of the finest families in Germany makes a full and speedy recovery.*
>
>                       *Sincerely,*
>                       *A. Hitler*

She stared at the note without comment for a minute before she handed it to Eric. He read it and lifted an eyebrow, then handed it to Karl. The three remained silent for a moment, Reinhildt with her arms folded around her body as one might against a chill breeze.

"It makes you feel that a stranger is leering at you when you are naked. I love orchids, but, dear God, not from *him!*"

Again the door opened, and Eric looked up, still slightly numbed by the note from Hitler.

It was Horst. He wore what had become his habit; casual slacks, a tieless shirt, and a light jacket. It was always a contrast to Eric's dark business suit.

He smiled his greeting, but the smile faded when he read

the card from Hitler. "There's no way that they are going to leave us alone, is there?"

Eric paced away to look at the valley for a minute, then turned back. "No. I don't think that there is a way they will. Kurt will be twenty-one in September and will take over the business. The swastika will fly over everything that we own. They're going to use Father in any way they can to get what they want. And what they can't flatter him into, Kurt will be able to do on his own when he takes control."

"What are they after?" Horst asked.

Eric folded his arms and shook his head. "I can't say for sure, but I can start to guess. It's not hard to see, when one looks at the kind of technical and research visits that they have made to the plants in the last six months. A month ago I was at the shipyard in Bremen. I was told that a party of officials was going to visit. It seemed little more than protocol at the time, but one man was a naval officer and an engineer. He asked a great many questions about the conversion of the plant, from the production of ore carriers and tankers to the production of other priority naval vessels. I asked him what kind of vessels, but he avoided the question, saying that he was interested simply in any kind of conversion. Later, I found out his name was Doenitz—Commander Doenitz—the navy's finest expert on submarines. He was decorated in the last war for commanding them in action against the Allies."

Frowning, Karl looked at Eric. "Are you saying they are rearming?"

Horst gestured impatiently. "Of course they are! And with von Kleist behind them, they'll have the best war machine in the world. And the other companies will simply fall into line."

"Eric?" Reinhildt said. "Are we sure? Really sure?"

"The evidence is building, little sister. Only last week three separate tours of officers moved through the factory at Elmshorn, as well as the steel plant on the Ruhr. They asked about tensile strengths and resistance to rust. They queried about the availability of rubber and a dozen other things that could only relate to tanks and other armaments Germany has been forbidden to have since Versailles.

"You've heard Kurt brag about the glider clubs the Hitler Youth are starting, I'm sure."

She nodded. "Yes. How could one not hear Kurt."

"They're using gliders because the same treaty forbids them having warplanes. It's very clear where things are going."

Reinhildt managed to sit up straight in the chair, wincing slightly from the throbbing pain in the back of her head. "Then we have to find a way to stop them."

Horst was pacing back and forth, occasionally eyeing the door to the veranda. "There are too many of them to stop. They're eating up the government a piece at a time, and soon they'll be able to simply take anything that they want in Germany."

"Perhaps not," Eric said. All of them stared at him for a second, and Karl murmured, "Perhaps I should leave. This is, after all, a family matter. And . . . I'm not a member of the family."

Reinhildt took Karl's hand. "Not yet, my love."

Horst's eyes widened. "What the hell has been going on here?"

Reinhildt, Eric, and Karl laughed at Horst's befuddled expression.

After a second Horst broke into a grin. "Well, that will teach me to keep my nose in architecture books and not look to see what has been going on. When did all of this happen and what about Werner?"

Reinhildt grinned. "Werner will always be a friend. But Karl, if he will have me, will be your brother-in-law. Just when, we don't know."

"Forgive me, Reinhildt," Eric said as he paced back the few feet to the chair, "but that is part of the problem that I've been mentioning."

"How can this connect up to the Nazis?" Reinhildt asked, perplexed.

"I don't believe that the Nazis can begin to prepare for a

war without the industrial leadership of von Kleist. Would you agree?"

"Yes, but—" Reinhildt began.

"Please," Eric interrupted. "You were the one who mentioned that they had to be stopped."

"I don't know that they can," Horst said, dejectedly.

"They can, believe me. In the last six months, I've come to know a great many things about the corporation. I have something to propose. That is why Karl has to be here.

"Reinhildt? How would Father feel about your marrying Karl?"

Reinhildt paused before she answered. It was something she had had no time to think about. "I—I never thought. I—"

"He would not approve," Karl said. "I see what you're after, Eric. It's not too hard to deduce. Johann favored Werner because his father was in industry. The two firms do a great deal of business. I would not be favored. I'm simply a doctor."

Reinhildt was getting angry. "I won't be bartered like a cow or a goat!"

"No, no, Reinhildt, you won't," Eric said. "But you are going to have to be discreet. Remember, it was you who mentioned stopping the Nazis."

"Get to the point, Eric. I don't understand," Horst said.

"I will." He turned to Horst. "What percentage of von Kleist stock has father given to you over the years?"

Horst stared at him for a second. The question baffled him. He had never thought or cared much about finances. "I—I really don't know. I only know that father placed some stock for us in escrow. It was like a trust. At least, that's what I think." He gestured to Eric. "You know I don't really concern myself with such things. What are you after?"

Eric started to pace, a habit he had acquired when he wanted to think.

"Let me tell you how Father has operated on—I suppose I should say—our behalf. He set up five trusts. The first of them was for Mother. The others were initiated for us soon

after each of our births. They were set up so that each of us
would receive a block of stock on each birthday until we were
twenty-one. At that time the legacy would be ours to do with
as we pleased. By the time that we were all of age, the plan
was for all of us to have a majority of the stock in von Kleist
AG. Those four old men who work with Father in the role of
board of directors don't have any power at all, and we know
that. Father controls—or controlled—everything by himself.
We were to get it all.

"Well, that was the way that it was supposed to go, anyway.
Originally ten point two percent was the shares distribution
for each. That would come to exactly fifty-one percent by the
time that Horst was twenty-one. As you know, that never
came to fruition. Father reserved the right to retract any one
or all the trusts before we reached legal age. I'm afraid that I
was the one who caused some problem with that."

"No, you didn't, Eric. Our scheming Nazi brother did,"
Horst said bitterly. It was something that he was going to
have to control, Eric thought, if the plan that he was putting
together was going to have a prayer of succeeding.

"At any rate," Eric went on, "it didn't come to fruition.
However, I was allowed to keep what I already had. I was
sixteen then, and I had just over seven and a half percent of
the stock. When I turned twenty-one, it became legally mine
and I moved it from the bank of Frankfurt to a bank in
Zurich."

Horst was startled. "Why? I mean—"

"I could see it coming, little brother. I don't know how, but
I could see those Nazis in Frankfurt, and I could hear the
rallies and the parades. I just felt it. Anyway, with what
Mother willed to each of us, my percentage comes to eleven
and a fraction. Each of yours will come to almost fourteen
percent by the time that you're both of age. By the time that
Horst is twenty-one, we should have almost forty percent of
the holdings reserved in our names. Father has paid me for
the work that I've done these last months, and I took
payment in the form of stock options. That will amount to
about three percent of the holdings. All in all, within the next

four years, we will then have something on the order of forty-one percent of von Kleist."

Horst shook his head. "Eric, if you're thinking of maneuvering Father and Kurt out of control of von Kleist, I don't think there's a way in the world that you can do it. Father's too smart, and certainly Kurt is."

"I didn't say that we could. But it's better than sitting on our hands and watching everything we have get swastikas painted on it. It's worth a try. Besides, the Gelsen stocks that Mother inherited from her father—the ones that we got in the will—can be liquidated slowly over a period of years, and we can buy more stock from the public sector. We don't really ever have to control fifty-one percent. Something in the high forties with shares in the public sector and perhaps some proxies from the larger private shareholders would be enough for us to influence policy and try to steer things away from the Nazis. It's the best plan that I can think of . . . and I've been thinking about it for a while. There's one huge problem associated with it, though.

"We cannot let what happened to me happen to either one of you. What I mean is that I was caught in the middle of a dispute between our parents. All of the timing was wrong: my wanting to be a doctor, Father's statement about the National Socialists—all of it was wrong. Neither of you must provoke Father, at least until you have both come of age. Then the stock will be irrevocably yours."

"Dear God, Eric," Horst said. "Do you think that I'll be able to play little brother to Kurt for that long? I think I'd kill him first."

"Horst, listen. He will provoke you any way that he can. But you're leaving in the fall. Tübingen's loss will be Yale's gain, right? You will be away for four years, and in that time, except for vacations, you won't be coming in contact with Kurt. While you are away, you will write frequent and cordial letters to Father, and you will bide your time. Meanwhile, Reinhildt gets her legacy in three years. As for me? Between now and September, when Kurt comes of age, I'll continue taking my pay from Father in stock. I'll do my best to squeeze out all of the stock that I can—without letting him get suspicious.

"So there it is. We have to be patient and silent. It won't be easy." He moved across the patio and placed an arm around Horst's shoulders. The younger man stared out across the valley, as if to seek an answer in the rolling Swäbish hills. "Especially for you, my self-righteous and vocal little brother. At least you will be out of harm's way in the United States. You're lucky," he said, smiling. "I hear that American women are very beautiful and they think that foreigners are chic."

Horst managed a smile.

Eric turned back to Reinhildt. "What do you think?"

She shook her head. "I don't know, Eric. It's a long time to wait. Who is to say that the Nazis simply won't take over von Kleist? I mean, the way that they're doing things now, with the rumors of the Reichstag fire going around—the ones that say that the Nazis did it themselves. Well, couldn't they just walk in and take the company over? What do they call that?"

"They call it expropriation, Reinhildt," Karl said. "But with your father's record of support, it is unlikely they would do that. May an outsider and only a prospective member of the family speak?"

Eric nodded and smiled. "Of course, Karl. I was about to ask your opinion, anyway. We need it."

"I think it's a good plan. There are very few complicating factors in this, at least as I see it. It requires almost no action at all. All that has to be done is to wait. Of course, there *is* the chance that Kurt will prevent your father from giving any more stock to either of you. In other words, he might see the plan for what it is—he is not stupid."

Eric's eyes met Karl's. "That's a chance we must take. You know, Karl, there is another aspect to the problem."

Karl nodded. "The problem is me, isn't it, Eric? You wanted me here today so that you could tell me that, didn't you?"

Eric nodded, his eyes downcast. "You always could see through me, Karl. Yes. You're right."

"As I mentioned before, an epidemiologist would not be as

welcome in the family as a captain of industry or a loyal Nazi. Correct?"

"Alas," Eric said.

Karl folded his arms and looked down at Reinhildt and then back to Eric. "Reinhildt and have discussed this. I told her that I was going to cancel the fellowship to Massachusetts General Hospital. She insisted that I take it, and that when it was completed, we could get married." He reached down and put his arm around her shoulder, and she took his hand in his. "That was just before the accident, and I'm not even sure if there was time for one or the other of us to propose. If I understand you, the thing would be to go to the United States and be . . . out of sight for three years? After that, when the legacy is Reinhildt's, we could announce the engagement?"

Eric nodded. "You remember that I said that the plan would not be easy."

Karl moved away a few steps. When he spoke, he directed the words to no one in particular. "I have watched them grow—for years. God, I hate them, and I should not. Hate is not for a doctor. But—" He stopped in mid-phrase and turned back to them with a slightly embarrassed look.

"I'm sorry. These are feelings that I've had for more years than I can say. There is something terrifying about them and their purpose. It is a gut feeling—I can't really define it. I will do anything that I can."

He looked at Reinhildt, who seemed on the verge of tears. "I will wait to marry you. I will—if you will still have me after three years. I—" He turned to Eric and Horst. "Might we—?"

Eric eyed Horst, and they both smiled and nodded. Together they left the veranda.

As they moved down the hall, Horst looked up at his oldest brother. "How long have you know about . . . all of this?" He gestured in the direction of the patio.

Eric shrugged. "About a day or two longer than you have."

"How do you feel about it?"

Eric smiled and clapped Horst on the shoulders. "Short of finding the right woman for myself, I'm ecstatic."

Horst smiled and nodded. "I'm pleased for the both of them. But have you thought about Reinhildt? She'll be here while he's there. It might be harder on her than on all of the rest of us combined. And you'll be here, too. I mean, that puts a great burden on you."

Eric nodded. "I know, but we will have each other to lean on. Don't worry about that. Just you keep control of your temper for the next few months until you leave."


On the second floor of the hospital, a large window overlooked the veranda and the rolling hills. The young Nazi named Kraus lowered a pair of binoculars and turned from the window as Peiper came into the room.

"You are sure that they didn't see you, Kraus?"

"Of course. I stayed in the shadows."

"So what does this skill of yours tell you?"

"Very little. I'm out of practice. It's been six years since I used anything like sign language or lipreading. My mother was the one who was deaf, not me. She was the lipreader."

"So? What did you get? Stop making excuses."

Kraus shrugged. "Mostly, they were faced the other way. I managed to pick up most from the youngest one—what's his name? Horst?"

"Yes."

"He made it clear how much he dislikes Nazis. He said it several times. As far as the rest of the conversation was concerned, I could only catch a snatch or two. It was something about stocks and a trip to the United States. Either or both Mittenberg and Horst are going. That was all that I could get."

"Stocks? Hmmm." Peiper thought for a moment. "There was nothing more than that? Nothing more specific?"

"I couldn't ask them to face the window as they talked, Joachim, could I?"

Peiper folded his arms and laughed. "No, I suppose not. At least, we can mention to Kurt that there was talk of stocks. That might be of some use to him."

"Perhaps it will."

He went back to the glasses and watched Reinhildt and Karl on the veranda, hoping to learn something more.

—————————— 9 ——————————

And so they became shadow puppets like the ones Eric remembered from an Oriental traveling show that had visited the schloss when he was a child. They were only images, projected on a screen with all the deftness Reinhildt and Eric could muster. But, even as they settled into the long game of waiting, things in Germany were moving irrevocably ahead for the National Socialists. It was frightening.

Several months after Reinhildt's accident, Eric noticed that large quantities of materials were starting to flow from the von Kleist plants to Bavaria. He demanded reports from the plant managers and the other administrators and found that the materials were being purchased by the government. There was concrete for foundations and steel for reinforcement. The odd thing about the shipments was that they were all consigned to a small town, a suburb of Munich. The town was called Dachau.

It was on the twenty-seventh of April that a small, squat, spectacled man reported to the office of an old colleague. The man in the office was tall and blond, the image of what the perfect Aryan should be. His name was Reinhard Heydrich. The small man was an old friend, from the days of the Munich Putsch. He was Klaus Schmidt.

Heydrich rose from the leather chair that sat behind a large desk. "Come in, Klaus. How good to see you. A schnapps? A brandy, perhaps?"

Schmidt shook his head. "No, thank you, Herr Gruppenführer."

He came across and shook hands with Heydrich, who smiled and gestured him to a seat. "That's right, Klaus. I'd forgotten. You follow the model of the Führer himself, do you not? You don't smoke or drink, do you?"

"Correct, Herr Gruppenführer. But I do eat meat and the Führer is a vegetarian. They say that it contributes to his sharpness of wit and political skill. At least, I am told that he made an exquisite decision yesterday."

"You sly fox. You've heard already?"

"Congratulations, Herr Gruppenführer. It was a coup for you, or, at least it will be soon."

"Let's call it soon, Klaus. While the Führer signed the *Geheimstadts Polizei* into law as a formal body, he has not made me the official head of it"—he smiled as he poured himself a brandy—"at least . . . not yet."

"The rumor at the Chancellery is that he will appoint you. I'm told Sepp Dietrich is rather miffed at it."

"Sepp wants it all, Klaus. He's not satisfied with commanding the Leibstandarte. He wants to wear both hats. I'm sure that the Führer will see the foolishness of that. All Sepp commands is a showcase unit. The Gestapo has an entirely different mission. Besides, the SD and the SA have been at each other's throats recently. I think that will all come to a head soon. And our chicken farmer friend, Himmler, will come out the winner. He's already plotting against Ernst Roehm. I'll get the appointment eventually, I think. But it won't be until things settle down among the old guard of hotheads that the Führer keeps around him.

"I do know this, though—and this relates directly to you. Sepp has a fair-haired boy. He's mentioned him to the Führer several times."

"Kurt von Kleist."

"Exactly. He would be a prize."

"Sir?"

"If I could steal him from Sepp and put him in the Gestapo. The trouble is that his face is too well known for the kind of work we do."

Klaus shook his head and folded his arms. "I don't think there's a chance of getting him in any event, sir. It won't be long before Sepp Dietrich loses him, too. He and his friends, Peiper and some of the Junkers see the SS taking to the field with the Wehrmacht eventually. They are starting to talk about the *Waffen* SS."

Heydrich nodded. "Weapons SS, huh? Catchy name. But why would they need weapons? Besides, the Wehrmacht would never stand for an independent army working under Himmler. But then again, anything's possible. Now, what of the von Kleists?"

"My position is still secure. They know nothing. The youngest boy...a man now, Horst, is violently antiparty. Kurt, of course, you know about. Eric and Reinhildt's views are shadowy. They say nothing, though they have been against us in the past. There are three Jewish servants in the house. I keep track of them, but they have been with the family longer than I have. They are no problem."

"What of this oldest brother, Eric? He's running a great deal of the corporation now, is he not?"

"That's correct, sir. From what I hear, he's doing a rather good job, too."

"His politics?"

"Hard to read. Certainly not a member of the party. He seems to be rather apolitical. That's really all that I could tell. He says very little."

Heydrich went to the window.

"Quiet men bear watching, Klaus. The loud ones are easy to understand. Make sure that you keep an eye on this Eric von Kleist."

As Schmidt walked slowly down the street, he could see some children playing. They had bright, freshly scrubbed, cheerful faces; not like the starving urchins he had seen in the street when he was growing up in Bremerhaven. Hitler was bringing good things to Germany and slicing out the bad.

The children, absorbed in their play, seemed to take no note of his passing. Klaus was used to it. He had practiced becoming invisible over the years. It was part of his job. All that he asked of Heydrich or any other superior was that he be allowed to stay with the von Kleists. How long would it take, he wondered? Five years? Perhaps ten? It didn't matter. He had committed his life to a task, and he would see it through to the end. He chuckled to himself as he realized that Heydrich and all of the others would never realize what the true nature of that task was. The Gestapo and the party and the Führer himself were only incidental. As they used him for information, he also used them.

He was the only one who really knew why.


It was a warm night in June when Reinhildt's small roadster pulled into the private entrance of the clinic on the mountainside. She drove it into the open garage and turned off the engine. After a moment she got out and smoothed her dress. Her hands were perspiring, and she was a bit shaky. She told herself it was stupid to be edgy. She had been with Karl before. Nevertheless, the secrecy, the excuses were unnerving her. She always had to make sure that she had a cover and that there was no one following. She felt like a spy or a criminal. Still, she knew that it all would evaporate like morning dew under a warm sun when she was in Karl's arms. In all of her younger years, reading romances and fantasies, she had never guessed that she could love with such abandon. She liked to think that it was Karl's touch that did it. And yet, there was something that remained buried in Karl, despite the intimacy that had grown between them. She had seen it in his face and felt it in his body. There was something that he was holding in reserve, a barrier between them that she was determined to tear down. But, with him going abroad soon. . . . She tried not to think of it. Though she had been adamant about his going, she now wondered how she would bear it. She had thought more than once in the last spring of asking him to cancel the grant and not go. But it would have been far too selfish; the work that he would do in the United States could make him a famous name in medicine. Besides, there was Eric's plan to consider. . . . There was no way that she could reverse her position now.

But as she stood in the semidarkened garage and stared out into the twilight, the von Kleist stock and the empire and the Nazis and the plan dwindled into insignificance. All that was really important was Karl and the love that they shared and the small amount of time that they had left.

She moved quietly up the winding stairs to the private apartment. The door swung open, and Karl stood there looking down at her. He was wearing a cardigan and slacks and smelled of cologne. He swept her in through the door and closed it behind him.

"Karl . . . I—"

He shook his head and stroked her cheek. She reached up to be kissed. His lips were warm, and his mouth was hungry. They probed each other's mouths, delicately. . . then passionately.

"Karl . . . darling, I—"

"Don't speak." He picked her up and carried her to the bedroom, gently placing her on the large four-poster. He kissed her again and slowly undid the buttons of her blouse, slipping her clothes off so deftly that she had the feeling they were falling away from her, that everything was falling away from her . . . except him.

She lay staring up at him from the bed. She was nude, and the first rays of a rising moon silhouetted her body. She could feel her nipples, hard and erect. He got out of his slacks, and in a moment she could feel his body pressing against hers. He fondled a breast and pinched the nipple of the other. She moaned. Her body was screaming for him. His mouth flicked across one of her nipples, and he moved slowly, inexorably to her smooth, flat stomach . . . then lower. She thought that she was going to die as he lingered there.

It might have been centuries later when he entered her. Reaching up, she dug her fingers into the muscles of his strong back.

She exploded. Once...twice....She lost count. He increased his speed, driving into her again and again. At last he climaxed, exploding deep inside of her, and in minutes, they were an exhausted tangle of arms and legs lying in the disheveled bed.

Reaching down, he pulled a blanket over them. She propped her head against his chest and started to drift to sleep.

She did not know how long she had been asleep when she felt him move. Opening her eyes, she saw him go to the curtained window, from which a ray of the now high moon washed across his body. She watched as he folded his arms and breathed deeply, exhaling with a deep sigh.

"Darling?"

He turned from the window startled, as if he had been shaken awake from a dream. "Oh. I thought you were asleep." He moved in the direction of the bed and sat on the side. She inched closer to him and propped a hand under her head. Her other hand gripped his firm thigh.

"What is it?"

"What's what, love?"

"What you were thinking at the window?"

He shrugged. "Nothing, really. Just the thought that in less than two months I'm going to be more than five thousand miles away. And . . . I don't like this secrecy. It has to be, but I don't like it—not a bit."

She stared up at him for a moment. "Is that all? I can't help feeling that there's something else. Is there?"

He thought for a second, then shrugged. "Nothing that would be important to you. Just that I love you and I don't want to go to America now. But I must."

She could feel deep inside that there was something more, but there seemed to be no sense in pushing the point. She didn't want to ruin the precious little time they had left.

"Then we have to use the time the best way we can, don't we?" Her hand reached down and fondled him.


Horst tapped at Eric's door in the schloss late the following afternoon. "Eric? It's Horst."

Eric came to the door in his shirt-sleeves. His room was piled with books and ledgers and a sea of papers and folders.

Horst looked at all of it and shook his head. "How do you make sense of all this?"

Eric laughed and lit a cigarette. "Corporate affairs are in yellow folders. Medical materials are in the blue ones. All of the folders are labeled, and I manage to make sense of all of it—adequately. They used to say at Goethe that a doctor was memory and that he could be defined by that one word if with no other. I have a good memory. Beyond that, Kurt helps, when he's not running off with his soldier friends to wherever it is that they go. Klaus helps, and so does the management at the plant in Stuttgart. I don't like to work down in Father's office, so I got this." He pointed in the direction of the desk that had been set up in the corner of the large bedroom. There were two phones on it, along with several pads and scribbled notes. "Working here lets me stay near Father and sort of prevents him from feeling that he has to go out and tour the plants. That's what Karl wants him to do—stay close, that is."

He scanned the working papers and the files. "You know, Horst, I have to admire him. He's pulled it all together, and he's run it like a taut ship."

"Yes. And will Kurt?" There was an edge to Horst's tone.

"Part of me hopes that he does—for the family. The other part hopes that he will fail utterly and take his Nazi friends with him. In medicine, we call that schizophrenia." He laughed again, this time with a sardonic edge. "Dear God. There are times that I don't know what I want anymore. Except to set up a practice after I manage to get through internship." Suddenly he remembered something. "Oh, look." He went to the desk and pulled an envelope from some other correspondence.

"Look. It came in the mail today."

The envelope bore the crest of the prestigious Heidelberg Hospital. Horst did not need to open it; Eric's broad smile told him what was inside. "They accepted you, didn't they?"

Eric nodded. "Absolutely, and they are going to let me start late so that I can get a chance to transfer all of this to Kurt."

"Oh, fantastic!" Horst grabbed his brother by the shoulders, and the two men embraced. "Now, if I can only achieve what you have achieved. Except, you are at the end of things, and I'm just beginning in architecture. It seems like a long, twisting road, especially in the United States."

"Americans are interesting people, Horst. At least the ones I met at Goethe University were. They're open—perhaps too open. Father thinks that. He doesn't really respect them. He thinks that they are naive children. I don't. I think you'll like them. At any rate, you'll have four years to get used to them. Have you been practicing your English?"

Horst shrugged. "Some," he said in English. "I can understand and write—" He paused and looked for the right phrase. "But of the speaking of it I am not yet sure. There are so many rules that exceptions have to them? Is right?"

Eric laughed. "You mean that have exceptions to them. Perhaps we should work on that this summer. You don't want to seem like a rich immigrant when you get to Yale."

"Why is it that you seem to know everything?" Horst grumbled good-naturedly, this time in German.

Eric chuckled. "Having to learn to speak English was one of the better things that Father foisted on me. As I was the oldest and to be the inheritor of all of this"—he swept his hand around the room in a grand gesture—"I had to learn English because, despite the fact that Father dislikes Americans, a great deal of his business was with them. I'm glad Kurt's English is worse than yours. Since he can't speak the language, perhaps he won't insult American clients." He thought for a second. "Then again, perhaps that would help to sabotage Kurt. It's as I said—schizophrenia."

"Oh. That's why I came," Horst said glumly. "I'd almost forgotten. Have you seen this?"

He pulled a small engraved envelope from his jacket pocket and handed it to Eric. It was an invitation to a formal dinner at the schloss. Eric read it and looked at the calendar.

"The eighth—that's tomorrow. Why weren't we told? Are we not to be there?"

"I think we're going to have to be. Klaus mentioned it to me this morning. I'd rather that he hadn't. Do you know who's going to be there?"

"No," Eric said warily.

"Have you ever heard of Sepp Dietrich?"

"No."

"He is the head of the Leibstandarte Adolf Hitler. It's the unit that Kurt is in now. They are the ones with the black uniforms. That's why I would just as soon have passed this dinner."

"Do you think it's a test, Horst?"

"I don't know—and I really don't care." Horst moved to the window. "Oh, damn it, Eric. I'm thinking with my glands again. I don't mean to. I'll just have to—how do you put that?"

"Maintain a low profile. Yes, you are going to have to do just that, and so am I. Reinhildt will, too. Though she doesn't bother me as much as you do."

"Well," Horst quipped, turning from the window with an insincere smile, "perhaps I'll manage to enjoy the meal and play the game pretending to be deaf. Hilda and the kitchen staff say that Kurt and Father have laid on quite a feast. Veal, trout, beef, truffles, caviar, several bottles of vintage Rothschild. It seems as though both Father and Kurt are doing everything they can to impress this man."

"Who else on the guest list?" Eric asked, cautiously.

Horst turned to him, and his eyes narrowed in thought. "Karl will be there—and of course, Reinhildt. This man Dietrich might or might not be bringing someone, and—"

"And who?"

"Oh, and Kurt's girlfriend. You've met her, I think. Her name is Anya Forst."

Eric nodded, not wanting to believe what he heard. The evening was going to be hard enough without that. But Horst had no way of knowing what Eric's relationship had been with Anya. "Well," he said, summoning up the best mask that he could, "I'm sure we'll manage to handle things well. Just don't lose your temper."

Horst clapped Eric on the shoulder. "I'll smile if it kills me."

Eric pointed to the files. "Now get out of here. I have to get back to work. Tomorrow night, I'll smile, too—if it kills me."

After Horst left, Eric moved to the desk. Sitting in the swivel chair, he looked at the papers on the desk. He took a piece of yellow note paper from a pad and slowly, methodically crushed it into a small, tortured ball. He hurled the ball with all his strength in the direction of the window. It thumped harmlessly off the pane and dropped to the Persian rug on the floor.

"Yes," he hissed, "if it kills me."

## 10

The next afternoon, a thunderstorm slashed across the Neckar Valley, dropping the June temperature from the high seventies to the mid-sixties. Eric watched the rain as he adjusted the bow tie that went with his white dinner jacket. He heard the squeal of tires on the driveway and looked at his watch. It would be Kurt leaving to get Anya at her apartment in town. He took a deep breath and looked at himself in the mirror that lined the back of the closet door. Yes, he would manage; he would pull things off. He always had. After donning the dinner jacket, he headed off to the drawing room, where cocktails would be served.

Sepp Dietrich arrived alone and a few minutes early,

alighting from a black Mercedes that bore swastika flags on the fenders. His driver ran around the back of the car and opened the door, snapping his heels together and giving the Nazi salute. Dietrich returned the salute and came up the steps to greet Johann.

Eric watched the two speak as they exchanged a long handshake. Then, they turned and walked down the hallway. Eric approached them.

Dietrich was smaller than Eric, but strongly built. He had deeply set brown eyes and a strong, straight nose. The smile that flashed below the thin mustache could have been that of a film star. He wore the black uniform of the Leibstandarte with silver collar "s" flashes. The uniform hat displayed an insignia Eric had not taken note of before, a silver skull with two crossed bones below it. Eric tried not to chuckle. Were they saying that these men were like the pirates of old?

"This is my oldest son, Eric," Johann said.

"Eric, this is Obergruppenführer Sepp Dietrich of the Leibstandarte."

Dietrich flashed a smile that Eric immediately recognized as well practiced. The man was no stranger to politics. "What a pleasure to meet you, Herr Doktor von Kleist. I understand that you have been helping with the operation of the conglomerate. Kurt tells me that you are something of a Renaissance man."

Eric smiled and shook hands. Dietrich's grasp was firm and his eyes clear. "Not really, Herr Dietrich. I manage to help, and I get a lot of help in that helping, if you know what I mean."

"You're too modest, Herr Doktor. Kurt says that you have taken the reins with professionalism. After all, von Kleist is a symbol of the fatherland. And, in helping it, you help your country." Again, Dietrich flashed the practiced smile.

They moved to the drawing room, where Johann introduced Reinhildt, whose beige evening dress made her eyes seem even darker. Karl stood next to her, in a black tuxedo, and on the end of the receiving line Horst stood, attired like Eric and apparently keeping his temper under control.

Klaus and the staff served cocktails, and Eric noted that Horst simply had a fruit juice. He breathed a sign of relief. He had worried that Horst might have a drink or two and lose the forced calm that he had assumed for the night. Under the watchful eye of Karl, Johann had a small glass of superb Rhine wine from the cellar. That and a single brandy after the dinner were his ration. Dietrich and Eric drank a fine old English scotch whiskey. Eric planned on having at least two before dinner. He considered it an anesthetic.

Moments later, Kurt swept in with Anya on his arm. She was stunning with her blond hair set off by a black evening gown. As they stopped at the door to the drawing room, her eyes met Eric's, for a second, before the introductions forced her to turn away.

There seemed to be no emotion in her eyes, Eric noted. Perhaps the years had dimmed the anger that she had expressed for him that night, long ago. He found that he could look at her without too much of a knot in his stomach. The two scotches allowed him the distance that he needed to deal with his feelings for Anya. Had she ever loved him? And had he loved her? He wasn't sure about Anya's feelings, but he knew that *he* had loved her. She had been the first real love of his life. . . . Well, there were many bottles of schnapps to help get him through the evening.

Oh, but she was stunning. Her black gown outlined her beautiful figure. . . . She had marvelous breasts, he remembered. He thought of Kurt fondling them, and for a split second he got upset. Then he allowed himself an internal laugh. They deserved each other; they were both enormous opportunists. And there was no returning to the past. He remembered the words of a Russian poet, he could not recall the name: "Time turns the greatest hurts to poetry." Appropriate, he thought. It was a fitting epitaph for a dead relationship.

"Meinen Damen und Herren?" All heads turned in the direction of the door. Klaus Schmidt, in his cutaway stood there, doing his best to smile.

"Thank you, Klaus."

The dining table was magnificent. It glittered with silver and crystal. The courses were endless, and by the time that the servants had cleared the table and the Viennese pastry cart had been rolled from the room, Eric felt as if he had been at a Roman feast for more than a month.

"So then, what exactly is this Leibstandarte unit, Herr Dietrich?" Johann asked, with flattering interest.

"We are a number of things, Herr von Kleist, though we were formed formally just a few months ago. Essentially our mission is to guard the person of the Führer and his entourage wherever he might be or choose to go. Needless to say, this requires the best of German manhood and the most rigorous training. But I'm sure that your son has mentioned the strenuous discipline."

"It is difficult, but vitally important. And a great honor to even be chosen as a candidate." Kurt beamed as he put down his coffee cup.

Anya placed a hand on Kurt's. Eric recognized the familiar gesture and felt a slight twinge. "Kurt has told me how exciting all of it is. It's too bad that there is no place for women in the organization."

There was a moment of silence before Dietrich's face beamed his practiced smile. "Oh, Fraülein Forst, many of the things that the Leibstandarte is involved in require great risk, and the Führer is opposed to such beautiful German women as yourself being endangered. I'm sure that you understand?"

"Are we then to understand that the unit is an honor guard of sorts? For official functions?" Horst asked from the other end of the table.

"Well, it is that and more, Herr von Kleist." It was clear from the tone of the answer that Dietrich had been briefed that Horst would not be the most appreciative dinner conversationalist. "The chances are that as time goes by and the size of the organization increases, Herr Himmler will find a number of additional duties for us. For now, we must train and build a cadre that will allow our ranks to grow as they are needed."

"What kind of additional duties, Herr Dietrich? Do they have anything to do with that new insignia on your cap?"

"How observant of you, Herr von Kleist." Again, there was the smile. Eric looked to his younger brother. He was hoping that Horst would not proceed to bait Dietrich. "Actually, the Todteskopf, or death's head, insignia tells all that we are prepared to fight to the death for the Führer and the fatherland. It will go hand in hand with our motto, Führer Commands... We Follow. I find that appropriate, don't you, Herr von Kleist?"

Horst forced a smile. "Of course, Herr Dietrich."

"It's so wonderful to have Kurt be honored so," Anya said, again with her hand clasped over Kurt's.

"I agree," Johann said. "Shall we adjourn? I for one am anxious to get to that one snifter of brandy that my watchdog there, Doktor Mittenberg, allows me to have. I have been looking forward to that all night."

They moved back to the drawing room, where three huge, deep sofas surrounded a low, glistening mahogany coffee table that had been set with decanters of cognac, a box of cigars, and a steaming coffee service. Reinhildt served the cognac, making sure that her father had only the tiniest bit in a snifter.

"Well, Herr Dietrich," Johann said expansively, "what has the rest of the party been doing since the installation of Herr Hitler as chancellor?"

"Many things, Herr von Kleist. The first, of course, is to get the working force back to work. And this requires a lowered inflation rate, more productivity in the private sector. As I say, many things."

"You have given yourselves quite a task," old Johann quipped as he sniffed at the cognac. "With Germany's current economic condition in the world market, foreign markets are going to have to be increased."

Dietrich crossed his legs and sat back. "Well, to that point, Herr von Ribbentrop has been negotiating a number of international trade agreements with various markets. We feel sure that when these negotiations are completed, there will be literally dozens of new contracts that the government will make available to domestic conglomerates. Also, there is a considerable amount of new construction under consideration. The Führer himself is in the midst of designing a number of new buildings for Berlin, and he has hired a bright young architect, Speer, I think his name is, to construct a large sports arena in Nürnberg. It's an exciting time."

A glimmer of an idea flickered through Eric's mind for a second, but he let it pass. Then, overcome by his curiosity, he summoned it back.

"Excuse me, Herr Dietrich? Is there another sports stadium being constructed near Munich? I think it would be in the suburbs somewhere?"

Dietrich turned and eyed Eric coolly for a second. It was clear that he was not prepared for the question. Then his face again broke into the movie star's smile. "Ah . . . no, not exactly, Herr Eric, if I may call you that?"

Eric smiled and nodded. "Of course. You see, I've noticed that a lot of building materials and heavy construction equipment has been consigned there recently. Of course, we are pleased to make the sale to the government. I was just curious as to the nature of the project. If we knew, we might be able to plan on a longer term program of development."

Dietrich paused and folded his arms, and Eric could see that a dozen thoughts were racing through the man's mind. He moved his eyes from Dietrich and took a cigarette from the silver holder on the table. As he did, he glanced at Kurt. His brother's eyes were aflame. Something was terribly wrong. Was it the question about the construction? It had to be. If there was any alarm in Dietrich, the man was a professional at concealing it. Kurt, however, had no such guile. Yes, there was something there, and Eric had touched a nerve. It was, ironically, the one thing that he did not want to do—not that night. It was, indeed, the thing that he had warned Horst against doing. He wondered if perhaps there was a gentle way of getting out of the predicament.

He spoke while Dietrich was apparently still trying to form an answer.

"Perhaps, Sepp, if I may call you that, the remainder of this project is one that is supposed to go to the Farbens or the Krupps. In which case, the question is retracted."

Dietrich laughed as did Johann. Even Kurt, still fiery-eyed, made an attempt at a chuckle.

"Not at all, Eric. Not at all. No. All of the companies who have been loyal to the fatherland in this struggle will be given a chance to bid on all of the projects that are being considered. Actually, we had hoped that Von Kleist A.G. would get this project in its entirety. I only paused because the project deals with security and other things. I can tell you this much: the facility will be a detention area for many of the criminal element that still try to oppose the National Socialist efforts. There is a large Communist element in the state. Surely all of you here know that. You also know of the Führer's promise to establish law and order as soon as possible. It is hoped that this facility will be a detention area and a transit point for such individuals as might be rehabilitated or deported. It will be a place where they might be allowed to concentrate on the behaviors that have been antisocial and to rectify them. While that is happening, they will not molder in cells but will, rather, be allowed to work in the open air, beautifying the environment and working in construction.

"Of course, there will always be those who are hardened criminals and will never be rehabilitated. I'm afraid that many of them will eventually be deported."

"Where would they be sent?" Eric asked.

"To a variety of locations, Herr Eric. If they were immigrant aliens, they would be sent to their country of origin, for example."

"It is a work camp, then?" Horst asked.

"Something like that, Herr Horst, something like that. There is no sense in creating huge correctional facilities such as . . . oh, Landsburg prison, for example. The nature of the labor camp is transitory. We are sure that as soon as the criminal element is gone, there will be no further need of

them. They might then become something on the order of
military training camps."

"They?" Horst jumped on the word.

"Did I say 'they'?"

"Yes, you did, Herr Dietrich."

Kurt turned to his brother. "I think what the Obergruppenführer means is that there are several of these under
consideration now. Though, the one outside Munich will be a
model camp."

"Yes, and—" Dietrich hitchhiked on Kurt's words—"the
Führer does not like the term labor camp. He says that it
sounds too much like the ghastly places that the Bolsheviks
send their political prisoners. He prefers to call them places
where through work and concentration on the patterns of
thought that have opposed national socialism, people can be
made free. Concentration camps are what they will be called,
and there are several being planned for various places in the
Reich. There won't be a need for too many of them, and as I
say, their nature is transitory."

"Well," Johann said, taking a sip of his brandy, "it sounds
like a noble effort. It will clean things up from the corruption
that used to dirty Germany. Let us drink—to Adolf Hitler,
our new leader." He raised his glass. Eric watched as Reinhildt
hesitated and then raised her glass. Karl breathed deeply and
did the same. Kurt and Anya's glasses were already poised.
Only Horst still hesitated. Finally, he raised his glass but did
not drink with the others, and to Eric's chagrin, Kurt saw the
gesture.

"You don't drink, Horst? Is the brandy not to your liking?"

It was a trap. Kurt was baiting him. The best thing that
could have happened in that moment, as far as Kurt was
concerned, was to have Horst fly into a rage and ruin the
evening in the presence of his father and Sepp Dietrich.

Horst managed a smile. "I pause only to propose a second
toast, dear brother. I ask that we drink to Germany."

"Here . . . here," said Dietrich, again flashing the smile.
He was a master diplomat, Eric thought.

They drank.

# 11

**August, 1933**

Eric looked out on the long row of Bessemer furnaces that dotted the horizon of Frankfurt-Höchst. The office in which he stood had been designed for his father, to overlook the factories and the various processing plants and marshaling yards that dotted the horizon of the industrial complex. He thought back on the dinner with Sepp Dietrich and wondered at what the man's smile concealed. There had been massive orders for materials since that time, and many of them had gone to different locations: some to Silesia; others to an area south of Berlin called Sachsenberg. Still others had been sent southeast. The names had been odd, many of them simply small towns in the general vicinity of the construction. He had no way of knowing exactly where the construction sites were. All he knew was that von Kleist was being given millions of marks in contracts to supply materials for the entities that Sepp Dietrich and Adolf Hitler were calling concentration camps.

The intercom buzzed, and Eric snapped the lever on it.

"Herr von Kleist, your brother is here to see you. He says that it is urgent."

"Which brother?"

"Herr Sturmbahnführer von Kleist, sir."

"Very well. Tell him to come in." Eric took a deep breath and exhaled audibly, not wanting to deal with Kurt. He was sure that it would be a repeat of the last visit more than a month before.

Kurt strode into the room and slammed the door. He was furious, and Eric knew why.

"Eric, what is the reason for this?"

"For what, Kurt?"

"You know what I mean. We spoke of it before—last month. Don't play dumb. It's the fucking Jewish engineers—that's who. They were to be dismissed then, in accordance with the party's request. Soon, it will be a law. Right now, we have the chance to comply with the party's wishes before it becomes a law. How dense are you?"

Eric could feel the blood rush to his face. He wanted to rush from behind the desk and smash his brother and his imposing black uniform onto the carpet, but he resisted the temptation, and, instead, sat down. There would be no sense in it, he reminded himself of the agreement with Horst and Reinhildt. As head of that secret combine of relatives, there was no chance that he would compromise that. "Sit down, Kurt. There are realities that you and your colleagues are going to have to face in this matter."

"What realities?" Kurt, still blustering, took off his peaked cap and sat in the chair reserved for visitors.

Eric moved from behind the desk and started to pace. As he moved, he thought. He had delayed as long as he could in the firing of the Jewish engineers and technicians. There were his own reasons for the actions, and then there were the reasons that he would give to Kurt. The latter were more than valid, as far as the industrial complex was concerned.

"You don't seem to understand, Kurt. Nor do your colleagues. Something over twenty percent of the employees of the entire von Kleist organization are Jews. Most of them are in crucial technical or engineering positions. They are the best educated and skilled of the lot. To fire them en masse would be to cripple what we are doing—for the family and for the people that you represent. That is the reality of the matter. In another month you can wrestle with that. But, now, I have to handle it, along with Father. If you do not want the entire production here and at the other plants to fall off to nothing, then the National Socialists have to provide skilled engineers to replace these Jews, or they have to simply back off."

He paused, remembering the meeting that he had had the month before with more than fifty Jews in high-level technical positions with von Kleist. . . .

The room was silent when he arrived. He had tried to pass the word through the grapevine rather than sending a memo, which would have been a dead giveaway for his intentions. To his surprise, the room was full to capacity. Not all of them were there, but he was pleased to see that all of the men present were of the rank of department head, and he wondered if that had been done by design.

They looked at him expectantly.

"Gentlemen, I know that there have been a great number of rumors flying through the organization, and I wanted to talk to you about them."

"Are they true, Herr von Kleist?" asked Albert Greenwald, who was the quality control manager for the rolling mill.

"Are which ones true, Albert?" Eric asked in return.

"We all know that the Nazis want us out so that they can put their own flunkies in our jobs."

"That part is true. I have to be honest about it. But there are other things, too."

"What of Meister von Kleist? He was fair with us in the old days."

"I know," Eric said. There was a slight hint of sadness in his voice.

"He doesn't seem to feel that way any more." The voice was that of a young man in the front of the room. Eric had forgotten his name, but he remembered that the man was a chemical engineer from the nitrate plant at Elmshorn.

"I'm afraid that there is more than a grain of truth in what you say, sir. My father has become a rather ardent supporter of national socialism. And, along those lines, I'm afraid that we have our differences."

"So do we, Herr von Kleist. So do we." It was the chemist again, and his comment started a small buzz in the room.

"Let me mention this," Eric said. "None of you is blind or deaf. You have seen the attitude of the Nazis regarding Jews. I am sure that many of you have felt the sting already. So there is no sense in creating too much of a reassuring atmosphere in this meeting. I will go on record as saying that as far as I am concerned, you are loyal and skilled employees of the company. And I for one don't really care on what day of the week you worship. But I am only the caretaker of all of this. There will be a time when someone else runs von Kleist. I can guarantee that"—he stopped short of mentioning Kurt by name—"he will have views that coincide more with the National Socialists and those of my father than mine. So, despite the fact that I will maintain things as they are for as long as possible, in the long run, I'm afraid that you are going to have to look to yourselves.

"On the bright side, the Nazis do not have a wealth of skilled professionals—"

"Farmers and Bavarian bullies." The comment came from the back of the room. The voice was shushed to allow Eric to continue.

"As I was saying, the chances are that they will not be able to replace you with their people for some time, due to your technical expertise. Still, the weeding out process is something that I believe is inevitable. All I can do is to stave it off for as long as possible—and I will do the best that I can at that."

Albert Greenwald called from the back of the room. "Thank you, Herr von Kleist. You are a fair man."

Eric smiled and told them to go. . . .


"To answer your question, Kurt, I am not dense enough to know that steel cannot be produced by ghosts and there have been no attempts to send any Nazi geniuses to this plant and only a few to the other operations. The Jews must be kept on. Father hired them years ago for their skills. Now they are—how shall I say it?—out of fashion. But steel is still in fashion and will be in great demand soon by those friends of yours in the party. And if they want steel and nitrates and all of the other things that von Kleist can give them, then they will have to put up with these 'out of fashion' Jews."

"We will not have to put up with them for long, Eric. The Ministry of Production will be in touch with you, today." Kurt grabbed his hat and stormed from the office.

Eric clasped his hands behind his back and headed to the large window that overlooked the complex. Several stories below, he saw the swastika flag fluttering in the summer breeze in front of the administration building. In the distance sprawled the huge open-hearth plant, with more than a mile of open-topped railroad cars leading to it. Above the chimneys belched black smoke. Eric looked at the clock on the wall. It was just past three, and in minutes, the oven slag plugs would be battered open by grimy men, who for more than two decades had called themselves "Kleistlings," the children of von Kleist. At the other end of the plant was the rolling mill that would take the cooled steel and batter it into sheets. Eric guessed that in a matter of time, those sheets would be used for tank bodies and gun tubes. He would have failed them, these, his father's other children. He sighed. There was nothing he could do.

The intercom buzzed. "Yes?"

"Herr von Kleist, a Herr Trost from the Ministry of Production is here to see you?"

Eric wondered if Kurt had planned to have the visits set so closely together. "Send him in."

Eric moved behind the desk as a small, slender man in his fifties came into the office. He was fair and fine featured, with blue, penetrating eyes. Eric thought for a second that he was facing a shy schoolmaster.

"Herr von Kleist, I am Walter Trost." He presented his card, which stated that he was the associate director for heavy industry for the Ministry of Production. Eric gestured the man to a seat and took his own behind the desk.

"What is it that I can do for you, Herr Trost?"

The conversation was a relief from the harangue that had come from Kurt. Trost was soft-spoken, and he laid out a number of production and delivery problems that the government was facing in several areas. He indicated that a number of other firms had fallen behind in their delivery commitments. It seemed that the problem was something to do with a shortage of skilled engineers.

Eric laughed in spite of himself.

Trost seemed confused. "I'm sorry, Herr von Kleist. Was there something that I said—"

Eric stopped laughing and shook his head. "I'm sorry, Herr Trost, but I wish that you had been here when my brother was a few minutes ago."

"Oh—you mean the young Sturmbahnführer?"

"Exactly, Herr Trost. He was fighting with me about the firing of the Jewish engineers that I have. I'm sure that the other firms that have fallen behind in their commitments have done so for that very reason."

Trost gestured equivocatingly with his hands. "Well, that's the political side of things, Herr von Kleist. I have nothing to do with that kind of politics or racial policies. My job is simply production."

Eric noticed a small gold Nazi Party pin in the lapel of the man's blue jacket.

"Still, you are a Nazi."

"Yes. I am a member of the party. There is no way that anyone could be in the position that I am in now and not be a member of the party, Herr von Kleist. It is as simple as that."

So, it was pragmatic. Eric wondered whom he hated more, the rabid idealists or the pragmatic men who simply went along for position. He took a deep breath.

"I am sorry, Herr Trost. I didn't mean to be testy. If the other firms are falling behind, von Kleist will take up the slack in government contracts and subcontracts. But we can only do that as long as our operational staff is left intact. After my caretakership of this organization is over, that policy might change, but until that time, we will do the best that we can."

Trost nodded. "Believe me, we understand the problems, Herr von Kleist."

"I am sure that my father could brief you more fully on the exact operational concerns and delivery times that are going to be needed in this matter. After all, I am only a doctor, filling in, as it were."

Again Trost nodded, and his hands fluttered for a second. Then he got to his feet and looked around the room with a degree of care. Eric, confused, got to his feet, and Trost held up a hand in a gesture that was reassuring.

"Herr von Kleist," he said in a hushed tone, "keep my card and contact me in the ministry whenever you need to." He pointed to the swastika pin in the lapel and shook his head. When he spoke again, his voice was just above a whisper.

"Remember, Herr von Kleist...not all of us Nazis—are Nazis." They were eye to eye. "There are some of us who are still—Germans."

He shook Eric's hand and smiled, then turned and strode from the office.

Eric sat back down in the chair. What the hell did that mean? He mused over the statement for a few minutes until the roar of the tapped hearths brought him from his seat and to the window. Huge plumes of sparks exploded from the furnaces, followed by the roar of molten steel pouring into the great holding ladles. The blast was deafening even behind the thick glass of the office window.

The thought struck him like a fist.

Dear God! It did really exist. All the time that he had been watching the Nazis grow in power, he had thought that it was only a myth, something that they used to build paranoia in the population.

It *did* exist.

There *was* an underground...and Trost was a part of it!

# 12

The Frankfurt Opera was the envy of Covent Garden, Albert Hall, the New York Met and the Bolshoi together. Its five balconies and hundreds of side boxes soared to a hundred feet above the stage. The looming proscenium dwarfed the singers; it was a theater perfectly suited to the titanic scale of Wagner. On this night in August, its capabilities would be taxed to the limit. The gods would gather in Valhalla, and in the thunderous climax of the final act, the production would simulate the utter cataclysm that symbolized *Die Götterdämmerung*... The Twilight of the Gods.

On the drive from Tübingen, Karl and Reinhildt had said little. She had watched the rain pepper the windshield as he managed to negotiate the mountain's slippery curves, dangerously slick with late summer rain.

It was the last night that they would share for two years, and the thought of it weighed on each of them. He had tried to be lighthearted, but, in the face of her desolation, he retreated into the interior part of himself that Reinhildt had never succeeded in penetrating. It was this that frightened her most, this reserve in his behavior. All through the summer, she had hoped that he would mention the things that were troubling him, but he had failed to do so. Despite the passion of the relationship, there was the ever present barrier that prevented him from sharing himself with her. Now, with the time for his departure so near, her fear was starting to turn to a strange form of paranoia.

Over and over she had asked herself in the dark of the night: is this just a summer fling? Is there someone waiting in the United States? Will he write to me when he gets there? Will it all be over? But she had no answers.

She had planned the evening carefully, making sure that the Frankfurt townhouse was in order and that they could spend a secluded night there. In the morning Horst and Eric would join them, Horst to join Karl on the train to Bremerhaven, where they would board a ship for the United States. She had spent the entire day promising herself that she would not mar this last evening with tears—though she couldn't be sure that there would be none on the following morning at the train.

The outer lobby of the opera was jammed for this last night of the Ring series. Germany had long enjoyed a love affair with Wagner, and since the advent of national socialism, the relationship had grown ever more passionate. Good Nazis, hoping to emulate the tastes of their Führer, flocked to the opera houses in droves.

The lobby was a sea of uniforms, swirling in dark colors; the browns of the SA, the deathly black uniforms of the SS, and sprinkled between them, the gray green of the career military, the graduates of Spandau, the old Hanoverian families who accepted any of the political movements that came along, so long as the army would prosper. Five years before, the tails that Karl wore would have made him totally anonymous, but here amid the uniforms, he clearly stood out.

He took Reinhildt's arm and moved her in the direction of the grand staircase that led to the private box that Johann had retained for the family and guests.

"Let's get to the box," he said, quietly. "They give me the feeling that I'm at a masquerade ball."

She smiled and gripped his arm. "If there were any more uniforms here tonight, they would be taking you for one of the ushers."

They laughed quietly at the small joke and proceeded up the stairs. Holding hands, they sat in the first row of the spacious box that bore the von Kleist family crest.

Below them, the orchestra seats were filling with the sea of uniforms. Several rows had been blocked off with a red rope, but neither Reinhildt nor Karl took special notice of it. She was leaning close to him, whispering, "I love you."

He squeezed her hand. "And I, you."

"Will you do something for me . . . while you're away?"

"What? Anything."

"Write every day—or close to every day. Tell me anything. Talk about the weather, the fashions—just write."

"Of course. And will you?"

She laughed quietly, almost to herself. "I think I have the first fifty of them in my head already."

"That's the famed von Kleist efficiency. Your father would be proud of you."

"I doubt it." She smiled tentatively. "There's something else, darling."

"More? Such demands and we're not married yet?"

"No. I'm serious."

"Again. Anything."

"It's Horst. You won't be too far from him. You said that Boston wasn't too far from—where is it? New Haven?"

"Yes. A few hours' drive. Not far."

"Look after him. You know what I mean. Make sure that he does the things that he must and that he stays out of trouble. You know how impetuous he can be."

"Get him out of prison; see that he wears his scarf in the winter; keep him from the clutches of American girls who are after his money. I'll do all of it."

They moved their attention to the stage as the orchestra began the first notes of the haunting overture.

Reinhildt was glad that the opera had begun. The music was a respite from thoughts of what she must face at the train station in the morning.

During the first intermission Karl got two glasses of wine, which they sipped quietly as they watched the men in uniform move about, many of them seeking superiors so that their presence at a cultural event would be registered. How bourgeois they are, Reinhildt thought. Yet, these were the people who had changed the face of Germany for good or bad, and they all would have to live with it.

The last act was starting, the music building slowly. Karl leaned close to Reinhildt and started to say something, then stopped and drew back. She could see that same veil of reticence descend, and she could have wept with frustration.

"What is it?" she whispered.

He shook his head, his eyes on the stage.

A few minutes later he leaned close again. "Let's go to the back of the box. There's something that I have to say—now."

She was puzzled. There was a look of dread in his eyes.

She quietly slipped from her seat, and together, they moved to the sheltered rear of the box.

In the darkness he took her in his arms and kissed her gently, then drew back and looked into her dark eyes. His own were still uncertain, but there was also a look of urgency.

Suddenly the music stopped. There was a cheer and a burst of applause. Drawn by the sounds, they moved to the front of the box. The main aisles had filled with a stream of black uniforms. Throughout the opera house, a forest of arms snapped up in the Nazi salute. On the stage, the performers, suddenly devoid of their characters and ludicrously comic now in their horned helmets and shields, broke into a chorus of "Deutschland über Alles." Surrounded by an elite corps of bodyguards, Adolf Hitler moved slowly down the center aisle, stopping here and there to greet an old friend or a political contact.

Karl guessed that these "safe" people had been planted there by the "Merlin" of national socialism, Goebbels, who, limping markedly, followed the Führer by a few feet.

At the Führer's right side was Sepp Dietrich. To his left was another officer in the imposing uniform of Leibstandarte —Kurt von Kleist.

He knew that Reinhildt had seen her brother at about the same time that he had. But he was sure that the sight was not as great a shock for her as for him. Karl was a rational man, with all the tenacity and common sense that a man needed to get through one of the toughest medical schools in the world.

Still, there was something about seeing the brother of the woman that he loved at the side of Adolf Hitler that made his blood run cold. The things that he had planned to tell her only seconds earlier were trapped inside again, and he began to think that there was no way that they would ever come out.

The grand entrance and the ovation went on for more than half an hour, after which the performers tried to compose themselves for the remainder of the opera.

Reinhildt leaned close to Karl. "What was it? What you were going to say before?"

He shook his head, as if the thought was no longer there.

She drew back and watched the rest of the opera through a haze of tears.

They did not make love that last night, and the farewell, next day at the train station, was chilly, the unspoken words creating a chasm between them.

## 13

For weeks, Reinhildt was haunted by the farewell at the train station. It was something that awakened her in the middle of the night, and it was something that forced her to rekindle the excitement that she'd had earlier for playing the piano. She dove back into practicing with a vigor that she hoped would still the raging emotions deep inside her. She had never guessed that being in love could cause such pain. But then, Karl was the first man she had ever really loved. . . .

Oh, why didn't he write? She had made a dozen excuses to herself: he wasn't settled in an address yet; the trans-Atlantic mail service was slow and unreliable; he didn't love her any more—the chill of the last night together at the opera had driven him away, and now, he was simply trying to find the words to write her a farewell letter. This thought filled her with dread, for she feared it might actually be the right reason.

One rainy afternoon in September, she sat at the piano in the small studio at the back of the schloss. She was working her way through a difficult passage in a Liszt etude when the door opened, startling her. "Fraülein Reinhildt?"

She turned suddenly, pulled from her thoughts. "Yes?"

It was Sarah, the downstairs maid. She was a slender, older woman, quiet and almost frail. She had been with the family for more than thirty years, and except for an occasional visit to a brother down in the town, the schloss was her entire life. Reinhildt had always liked her, as had Lotte. She was observant, and Reinhildt suspected that she had an inkling about the affair between Karl and herself. Well, if someone at the schloss knew about the relationship, she was glad it was Sarah.

"I am sorry to interrupt, Fräulein. Would you wish me to return at another time?"

Reinhildt smiled. "No. Not at all, Sarah. What is it?"

Sarah handed Reinhildt an envelope, covered with postage. "It came in just a short time ago. I—thought you would like to see it right away, as it came from the United States."

Reinhildt took the envelope and stared at it for a second. Yes. It was from the US. Yes, it was from Karl. She tried not to let the combination of fear and excitement show. Sarah had taken a step back but was still staring at Reinhildt.

Was she looking for a reaction? "Yes, Sarah? Was there something else?"

Sarah shuffled for a second, trying to find the words. She looked down and clasped her hands in front of her. "Well, I don't know if I should mention this . . . but I feel that I've known you so long Fräulein Reinhildt . . . since you were such a little one. And—"

Reinhildt got to her feet and crossed the few steps that

separated her from Sarah. She looked eye to eye with the older woman.

"What is it, Sarah? You can speak openly. We are the only two here. Is there something that is bothering you?"

"Well—" Sarah took a deep breath. "It's probably nothing, but you know how meticulous Herr Schmidt is with the mail. He sees it as soon as it is dropped, and he sorts everything carefully into folders for the business and the members of the family?"

"Yes, of course. Why?"

"Well, I came to his office to get the mail—for you and the doctor, and he was in the midst of sorting it."

"Get to the point."

"I was just surprised to see that he had misfiled this letter. It was not like him. I have never known him to do that."

"I'm sure that it was just an oversight, Sarah." Reinhildt placed an arm lightly on the woman's shoulder. "I mean, even the perfectionist Klaus Schmidt *can* occasionally make a mistake. Where was it—the letter I mean?"

"It had been placed in Herr Kurt's file."

Reinhildt caught her breath, then composed herself, hoping the maid had not noticed. "Well, the error was rectified," she said smoothly. "I wouldn't worry about it—not a bit."

Sarah managed a smile and a small apology before she left.

Reinhildt went back to the piano and sat on the stool. Placing the letter on the music stand in front of the Liszt piece, she stared at it.

Was there a reason that it had been in Kurt's file? Indeed, she had not *ever* known Klaus to make such a mistake. She pushed the thought away. No matter what the contents of the letter, which she was for the moment, too frightened to open, at least Kurt had not seen it. In any case, she found it difficult to believe that her brother would have opened anything that had been addressed to her. Not even Kurt could be that crude.

It took her a full minute before she got up the courage to open it. If everything was over, then it was better to know than to sit and wonder.

She opened it and unfolded the paper.

*My love,*

*Forgive me. If you can forgive me. I relived that last
night all through the crossing, hating myself for my
cowardice and the wrong I did you. There was no
reason for it, except perhaps seeing Kurt, so much a
part of them, posturing in his uniform. Perhaps it
was seeing the others en masse, there in the opera.
I'm not sure, except that suddenly I couldn't face
leaving you. Even the plans you've made with Horst
and Eric didn't seem to make sense any more. All I
wanted was to get out of the theater with you...forget
the fellowship, the family, everything. I know now I
was being selfish. It's you, after all, who will have to
stay there and face that sort of spectacle for the next
two years.*

*Forgive the foolish man who loves you—please?
I've gotten settled in an apartment in Cambridge.
It's just a short trolley ride to the university and
the hospital. The seminars are interesting, and the
work schedule is exhausting. Horst tells me that he
is getting a small apartment in New Haven. He
says he wants something off the campus so that he
will not be distracted. He seems so serious about
his work for one so young. I will call him often and
chide him when he fails to write. He joked about
that on the ship, saying that "architects don't have
to write—all they have to do is calculate and
sketch."*

*Again—I love you, and forgive me.*

*Always,
Karl*

She read the letter three times before she folded it and
placed it gently back in the envelope. Liszt forgotten, she got
up and moved from the small room and headed up the stairs
to her own.

She closed the door and went immediately to the writing

desk, forming in her head the words of the letter that she would write to Karl.

In the office off the pantry, Klaus Schmidt was in a black mood. That Sarah should walk in on him like that, before he had a chance to read the letter! He had suspected that there was something between Mittenberg and Reinhildt, but there had been no evidence that he might be able to present to Kurt. He had had it all planned, but needed proof—some correspondence that associated Reinhildt and Karl romantically, which he could use to illustrate to Kurt how badly he needed Klaus. It would also be a prod for Kurt to use with his father, who did not really consider Karl was a suitable match for Reinhildt. That chance was lost now.

Klaus opened the drawer and pulled out a sheet that was a roster of all of the employees of the schloss. The name was close to the top. *Blume, Sarah—Juden*.

The last note was in his own handwriting. He placed a check mark next to it and placed it back in the drawer. It would, he thought, only be a short time before she could be dispensed with—at least if everything that Heydrich had said was true. He would be patient. Meanwhile, there were other things to do.

# 14

**September 18, 1933**

Johann had spared no expense. The schloss had been decorated, and an enormous amount of food had been shipped

from the most exotic locations. There had been lamb from
Australia, the best British trout, the finest Russian caviar, and
the most magnificent veal for schnitzel. There was little more
that Johann could do for the birthday of a son who was about
to inherit one of the largest empires in western Europe.

Kurt reveled in it. All the work of the last seven years was
about to come to fruition. He knew that his father had spared
nothing for his birthday. It was something out of ancient
Rome—at least that was what Anya had said. The sensation
was more than heady.

He took great care that evening to make the SS dress
uniform all that it should be. His boots were glistening, and
the bright flashes on the collar of the uniform had been
polished for hours by one of the servants. Proper appearance
was mandatory. It was something that he had learned in
leadership school. The training had been hard, but like his
older brother, he had remained at the head of his class.
Perhaps the image of leadership was something that was
important, no matter what the field.

There was a knock at the door.

"Come in."

Anya entered and stood in the doorway. She was in a pale
blue, floor-length gown that accentuated the long, lean lines
of her figure. Her blond hair was piled on top of her head in a
manner that Kurt could only figure had been designed by an
engineer. The blue sapphire earrings that he had given her
only the day before hung from her ears. She stared at him for
a moment.

"You are magnificent," she said breathlessly.

"And you, my love." He moved to her and took her in his
arms, feeling the long, sinuous lines of her body mold
themselves to him.

She was tall, nearly his height, and there was no need to
lean down to kiss her. Somehow, that excited him, and she
knew it. They kissed. But though it began as a light caress, in
seconds his tongue was slipping between her warm, moist
lips.

She backed away. "No, Kurt. No. Not now—not tonight. We have to wait a bit—just a few hours. No more."

He stepped back and grinned. There was no rebuff in her words, simply the promise of more later. He nodded.

"Not to muss the pretty hair, *Liebling*?"

She smiled and gave him a slight wink. "Not to muss the pretty anything. Remember, tonight is the most important of our lives—at least until now, that is."

"Yes, it is. Indeed, it is." Dutifully he headed back to the mirror in order to make sure that the uniform was entirely correct. It was. Everything was.

Eric stood in his room and looked at Reinhildt. She was stunning in white. "You are magnificent, Reinhildt."

"Do you think I have a chance to eclipse that harpy Kurt will have at his arm?"

She looked at him, and he could see that there was a flash of anger in her look, and something else that he could not fully define. He crossed the room to embrace her.

She pulled away. There was still anger in her eyes, and the embrace seemed to heighten rather than diminish it. "Is there something with Karl?" he asked in a subdued tone.

She shook her head and turned to the window. "No, Eric, nothing like that. He writes every day, or at least every other day, and the mail has started to catch up with him."

"Then, what?"

She turned to face him. "Sarah was fired today—along with two of the other servants." She shook her head and sat on the edge of the bed.

"Sarah?" Eric said incredulously. "But she has been here forever!"

"I know, Eric, I know. She came to me in tears this afternoon. The whole thing wrecked my day, and I'm sure that it will wreck the evening."

"Who—?"

"Kurt—or Klaus at the orders of Kurt and Father. It seems that Sarah is Jewish. I knew it, and I daresay that you did, too, not that it mattered to either of us. It seems to matter to Father and Kurt, though. I tried to mention it to Father, and he didn't have the time to see me about it. I tried to get to Kurt, and he was away with that woman of his. Sarah is desolate. She said that Schmidt simply called her into the office, gave her two weeks' pay, and told her to leave as soon as possible. That was it—the culmination of thirty years with the family."

"Well—"

"There's more, Eric. Ludwig and Anna are also being let go in the same way. They are the only other Jews on the staff." She folded her arms and rocked slowly backward and forward on the edge of the bed.

Eric came and sat next to her, reaching a hand across and stroking her shining, dark hair. "What if I ask Klaus about it, Reinhildt? Is there a chance that things might be reversed?"

"Not a chance, Eric. It's Kurt and Father, and this is the right time for them to be starting all of this. You know how they feel about Jews. Sarah knew it. I don't think that there's anything that we can do about it. Not now."

She stayed on the side of the bed and thought for a moment. "This was not a day that I was looking forward to, what with Kurt and Anya and this party. But this was just the final straw." Another thought suddenly struck her. "Oh, I completely forgot. At least one good thing happened today— we got a letter from Horst." She went to the small writing desk in the corner of the bedroom and pulled an envelope from the top drawer.

Eric opened it and unfolded the paper.

> *My Dearest Reinhildt and Eric,*
>
> *I love New Haven. There is something about Americans that attracts me. True, the college students are not at all the same as we see in Germany. They are a bit more light-hearted and—perhaps foolish. Though, I cannot say the latter with assurance until I get a better grasp of the language.*
>
> *Oh, Eric, you were right. I should have practiced*

*more. Though, I think that in a month or so, I will
be able to manage the lectures in the freshman class
without any real difficulty.*

*On the other side of things, the Americans whom
I've been speaking to (mostly teenagers) seem rather
ambivalent about the political developments in
Germany. Perhaps the distance is too great for them
to see any substantial impact on their lives. There is
some poverty here, though the students at Yale are
hardly in touch with it. Then again, at home we are
not too closely in touch with it either, are we?*

*I'll be seeing Karl in a week or two, and I'll write
again as soon as I can get the time. Now, I am
working on getting registered.*

> *My love to you both,*
> *Horst*

Eric folded the note and placed it back in the envelope,
then smiled warmly to Reinhildt. "I suppose that our brother
will spend a lot of the time out sowing oats and running
around with American girls?"

Reinhildt shook her head. "I don't know. He is so bookish
and shy."

"Well, I'm willing to guess that in a matter of weeks or
months, that will disappear. He'll get into the swing of things.
Mother was always too protective of him. He needed to get
on his own, and now he's doing that. I'm glad to see it.
Besides, I'm sure that you instructed Karl to watch over
him—or something like that. Didn't you?"

She laughed. "You've read my mind or Karl's letters to me.
Which?"

"Neither. I just know you, little one." He hugged her.
"Now, we're going to have to get our armor in place to face
our dear brother's party." He looked at his watch. "We should
be going now."

"Eric?" She stopped at the door and turned to him, her
face serious. "Is there something about this Forst girl that
bothers you?"

He stopped suddenly, and she could see his eyes narrow a trifle. He didn't have to answer. It was something that she had seen before when he had been in the presence of Anya. There was a hint of excess formality. Anya would attempt to flirt, and he would not react. It was out of character for Eric, for, as long as he had been an adult, he had always succeeded in being charming, even gallant.

"She's an attractive woman, isn't she? I mean except for her politics," Eric said, giving Reinhildt a smile that she could not possibly believe.

"Yes, Eric. She is. But that's all right—you don't have to answer the question. I didn't have the right to ask it in the first place."

He looked at her and thought for a moment. She didn't have the right to ask. But then again, she was his only sister, and the question came from love as well as curiosity. So, she had seen something between him and Anya. Was it something that anyone else could see?

He cocked his head to the side and looked at her. "You're observant. Anya and I were close friends for a time my first year of medical school."

She paused and looked at his expression. "You were more than that."

He nodded slowly and said nothing.

"I was sure of it. I could see something in your eyes. The only reason I asked was that I wondered if there was anything of that left. I don't want you hurt, Eric."

"I don't think I will be." He took her hand and moved to the door.

The party was small but elegant. Kurt and Johann were beaming, and Anya was regal and radiant. The dinner proceeded with ease, and a large cake crowned the evening. It stood like a wedding cake, more than two feet high, the top adorned with the von Kleist family crest, Kurt's name, and a small swastika. Johann made a speech.

"This is more than the coming of age of my son. Indeed, it

marks the total alliance of von Kleist with the National Socialists."

Eric noticed that his father, taking advantage of the absence of Karl, had poured a second glass of wine. He had seen his father slip into this kind of mood in the past, and it meant that the old man was going to wax poetic. All Eric and Reinhildt could do was to sit tight and weather it.

"Kurt said that he didn't want a party. He's going to celebrate, I know, with those brave comrades of his. But it seemed fitting that he celebrate with the family as well... because of other things that must be discussed tonight. Eric?"

Eric snapped his head in the direction of his father. He had not expected to be addressed. "Yes, sir?"

"Eric, I have to thank you for all of the help that you have been to the corporation in the last months. I am pleased that now a large part of the burden can be removed from your shoulders. I know that for you, medicine is primary. And we now let you go to that profession. You have my thanks."

Eric nodded. "Thank you, Father." He looked at Reinhildt. Her face betrayed nothing, but her hands were knit into a tortured, white-knuckled knot. She had had several glasses of wine, much more than she was used to. He hoped she would keep her composure.

"And there is more," the old man continued. "There is something very special this evening in addition to a birthday."

He looked to Kurt as if to cue him. Kurt got to his feet and smiled thinly. He raised his glass. "Thank you, Father—thank you all." His glance passed over Reinhildt quickly and over Eric with equal speed. They settled on Anya. She smiled broadly and nodded. It was coming, and Eric could see it a split second ahead. He was glad for the warning.

"I wish," Kurt continued, "to announce my engagement to Anya Forst."

And, there it was. Eric could not say that it had come as a surprise, and he managed a smile. He wondered how much she had told Kurt about her relationship with the oldest von Kleist son. He felt sure that she had done a lot of editing.

He could feel Reinhildt's eyes on him as Johann cleared his throat and got to his feet. "I toast the happy couple." His smile was jolly, though this last glass of wine flushed his face. Eric rose and drank the toast. Reinhildt did the same, though she remained sitting. Her fingers were strangling the glass, and Eric was starting to worry.

The toasts continued. Kurt drank to his father and the rest of the family, then toasted the Führer, which caused Reinhildt's hands to tighten more on the glass.

"Kurt, if I may?" Reinhildt was on her feet. Kurt looked at her warily. It was clearly something that he had not expected. "Of course, Reinhildt."

"I would like to toast Lotte Gelsen von Kleist, our mother. May she rest in peace."

There was silence for a second. Then Kurt nodded. "Of course. To Mutte."

They drank, and Eric sighed with relief. The dinner table had not become a battlefield.

Anya cut the cake, and each member of the family took a piece, served by a new servant. Reinhildt suspected that he had been hired to replace one of the three who had been fired during the day. She finished her wine and took a deep breath. "Kurt?"

"Yes?" His smile was starting to widen under the influence of the wine that he had been consuming throughout dinner. "Yes, Reinhildt? What is it?"

"Did you know that Sarah, Anna, and Ludwig were fired today?"

Kurt's smile faded. "Yes, I knew." Yet something, a slight twitch of an eye, told Eric he was lying.

"I was wondering. . . ."

"You were wondering what, Reinhildt?"

"Why they were fired? I mean was something stolen, or were the books not in order or something?"

"No, Reinhildt."

He didn't attempt to explain. He was being cautious, unsure where she was headed.

"Well, then, I was wondering what the reason was?"

"It is the new policy at the schloss and the corporation in general—in keeping with the wishes of the Führer. They were Jews, and soon all of the Jews in the von Kleist system will be gone."

Reinhildt started to get to her feet and then thought better of it, preferring to sit and discuss rather than to stand and scream. Eric could see her restraint and prayed that she didn't carry this discussion further.

When she spoke again, her voice had a forced calm. "Sarah has been with the family more than thirty years. Was it fair to throw her out like that?"

"As fair as one can be with Jews, Reinhildt. Remember, they are the ones who have been behind the Communist plot to drive the country into anarchy. Why the Führer himself said that it was a direct threat to the autonomy of the Reich to have Jews in places of power in the new Germany. Certainly you can understand that?"

Reinhildt's hands were in her lap again. Eric could see them twisting a napkin. "I'm afraid I cannot agree, Kurt. It's cruel. I don't know about the Communists but I also don't see where Sarah or the others were in any position of power. What I *can* see is that among them, Sarah, Ludwig, and Anna represent more than a century of service to the von Kleists, and I think that we've treated them shabbily."

"I think we've been more than fair, Reinhildt." Kurt's tone was impatient now, and Eric moved to avoid a full-scale argument.

He reached for the wine and got to his feet. "It's a night to celebrate. We should be as happy as possible. I will be happy, for one, to get back to medicine. And that makes me think of family and friends not here. Let's drink to Horst and to my dearest friend Karl, whose current studies in the United States I envy. I wish that they could both be here on this festive evening."

As he moved to Reinhildt to fill her glass, he smiled, though his eyes held a warning to calm down. He had hoped that the mention of Horst and Karl would remind her of the plan that the four of them had developed months before. She looked at him, giving the slightest nod, and he knew he had gotten the message through.

They drank the final toast, and Reinhildt got to her feet. "I'm afraid that the wine has given me a slight headache." She turned to Johann. "Father, I'd like to be excused, if I may. I don't want to spoil the celebration. Kurt and Miss Forst seem so happy."

Johann nodded, though clearly annoyed.

Eric got to his feet. "Is it anything that I can help with? After all, you have a doctor in the family now."

She shook off the gesture with a thank you and another apology, and left the dining room.

Johann moved in the direction of the drawing room arm in arm with his future daughter-in-law. Eric followed, but Kurt excused himself for a moment, heading for the rear hall. He had not gone far when he found Klaus Schmidt.

"Good evening, Herr von Kleist. And how is the Untersturmführer this evening?" Schmidt inquired politely, though he could sense Kurt's anger.

"You fired three people today without my knowing it. It should not have happened. I had to react too quickly. . . ."

"That is understood, sir, of course," Schmidt answered smoothly. "But it was necessary. Sarah Blume was most assuredly a spy in the household. And she had great influence upon your sister." He paused, evaluating the effect of this statement: Kurt was well aware of the stock shares Reinhildt controlled. He added soothingly, "After all, sir, they are only Jews. I can guarantee that the replacements will be as efficient—*and* loyal."

Kurt looked at him uncertainly. "The unit you said you worked for? . . ."

"Yes, Herr Untersturmführer?"

"I am sure that in the weeks and months to come, you will be able to prove it."

"I can do it now, sir."

"Now?"

"Of course, sir. Simply call this number tonight—now if you wish."

Kurt looked at the handwritten number and then at Klaus Schmidt. The man's face was hard to read. Still, the call had to be valid. His curiosity overwhelmed him, and he strode to the phone in the hall. Kurt waited while the call was placed by an operator from Tübingen. It took more than five minutes.

When the last of the clicks and whistles was finished, it took only two rings before there was an answer at the other end.

"Oberstgruppenführer Heydrich."

Kurt drew a sharp breath. He had not anticipated that Schmidt was that well placed. A thousand thoughts flashed through his head in the second of silence on the phone. Still, he had to play the call in the right way.

"Sir, this is Sturmbahnführer Kurt von Kleist. Please forgive this intrusion, however, I am forced to ask about the identity of an individual."

"Who is that, Lieutenant?"

"That, sir, is Herr Klaus Schmidt. Do you know him, sir?" There was a pause on the phone, and Kurt knew in an instant that he was holding his entire career in the pause. To deal with a man of such rank, to call him apparently at his home—a man who conversed socially with Himmler regularly—all was lost unless the answer came back right . . . with the right words and in the right tone of voice. He waited.

"Of course, von Kleist. He has many good things to say about you. In fact, your allegiance and that of your father to national socialism is something that the Führer himself is proud of. Sepp Dietrich tells me that you are doing a fine job in leadership school."

Heydrich paused, waiting for the measured response that he wanted. He got it.

"Yes, sir. Thank you. Forgive the call. I had to check this or be remiss in my duties. Forgive the call at your home?"

"Of course, young man. An excess of zeal is laudable. I will mention it to Sepp when I see him next week. Good night."

"Good night, sir."

Kurt took a long time hanging the phone back on the cradle. He looked at Schmidt. "I am sorry that I doubted you."

Klaus averted his eyes. "There is a great deal more that I can feed you in terms of information, Herr Kurt. Remember that, please. Do not forget, when you climb to the top of this empire, who helped you?"

Kurt stared at the small, balding man and saw a new partner. Perhaps not a member of the family, but there were enemies in the family, too. No, this man could be valuable, especially with his acquaintanceship with Heydrich.

"I won't forget, Klaus. I promise. I must get back now." He turned and left Klaus Schmidt standing in the back hall.

Schmidt watched him go. He was another—like her. It didn't matter. Not really. There was time. There was always time. All he had to do was be patient. Everything he wanted was only a short time away.

He would wait.

## 15

**March 8, 1936**

Eric toyed with the envelope in his hands as he watched Reinhildt finish her dessert. They were having dinner in his apartment, which adjoined the clinic he had opened in Tübingen. It had become their custom in the past two and a half years to get away from the schloss at least once a week. It allowed Reinhildt to avoid Anya who, since her marriage to Kurt more than a year before, had assumed more and more the command of the schloss, with the full consent of her husband and Johann. Eric and Reinhildt said nothing, knowing that there was little that could be done, so Eric had set up these nights out to create a safety valve for Reinhildt, who was growing more tense as the antipathy built between her and Anya. There would have been little chance that either of them could have become friends, even under ordinary circumstances. And circumstances at the schloss were far from normal. Johann withdrew more each day, and Kurt, as expected, was assuming more and more responsibility in the management of von Kleist. A year before, all of the Jewish professionals in Von Kleist AG had been summarily dismissed, following in the steps of Sarah, Ludwig, and Anna. Indeed, almost daily new German laws were promulgated. They were euphemistically called the Laws for the Protection of German Blood and Heritage, and they barred Jewish professionals from many positions. Waldman was gone from the university, Frau Slodski from the hospital. The power had fallen to the opportunists and they were making the most of it.

Eric sighed. There was little any of them could do. He fingered the envelope again and looked at Reinhildt—but obviously her thoughts were far away. With Karl, he was certain. . . .

Karl had been home only twice since his departure for the United States. Each had been a summer visit to Tübingen that lasted merely ten days. Still, the two visits had reassured both Karl and Reinhildt and become the anchors between which a serpentine chain of correspondence kept them close. If anything, their love had deepened and matured, though the maturity that it had gained seemed to have no impact on their passion. . . .

The sun created shadows as it shone through the large stand of trees at the west end of the estate. The horses Karl and Reinhildt rode were old and swayback, her concession to his worries about her accident the previous year. They moved at a walk through the trees until they came to a small clearing.

He climbed down from his mount, looped the reins around a branch, and walked to her horse to help her.

"When was the last time you rode, Karl?"

He smiled and reached back to massage his rump. "Too long ago. I think the last time was the day that you fell."

"It shows." She giggled.

He reached up and lifted her down, then pulled her close to him. He could feel the warmth of her breasts pressing against the thin fabric of her blouse. They kissed, gently at first, then passionately. She pulled back and stroked his face with her hand. "I love you."

Then she turned, tied the reins of her horse, and started to unload the saddlebags. They had a bottle of wine, a blanket, bread, cheese, and a large wurst. He watched her, chuckling to himself. "How much more have you stuffed in there? No wonder the old nag is swayback."

"I was going to pack the dining room furniture, but I didn't want to burden the horse any more than was necessary."

They laughed and spread the feast on the plaid blanket near the base of a fallen tree. "Will you tell me about Boston?" she asked. "Or, shall I tell you?"

"Pardon?"

"Your letters described it so well. Then I bought a map so that I could find the things and the places that you mentioned. The Commons sounds wonderful—with all of those swan boats. And, there are so many colleges. How many is it— eleven of them?"

"I think—if you count the ones that are on the outskirts of the city. I don't get much of a chance to see them, though. The schedule at the hospital tends to be something like twelve hours a day, six days a week. When I get time off, I go back to the apartment and collapse. But I'm learning so much. And I've gained a great deal of respect for Americans. They are very informal—they tend to call you by your first name as soon as they meet you—they think I'm too formal, too stiff. Still, they're very bright, and I'm pleased to be working with them.

"Now, what's been happening here?"

"Oh, not much. I spend most of my time writing letters to a friend, and I'm sure that he knows more about the schloss than I do." They laughed, and he pointed to the food.

"Well, in that case, do we talk and then eat, or do we eat and then talk?"

She moved across the blanket to him and slipped an arm around his back.

"Neither . . . for now."

They were like two nervous teenagers. He fumbled with the buttons on her blouse as she managed to undo his belt. After they were undressed, she slipped beneath him and pulled him down to her. Their mouths met hungrily and his hands moved across her body like fire. She reached down and touched him—he was large and firm.

His hands moved down from her belly to her moist pubic hair. His fingers slipped inside of her, probing, massaging.

"No. No, Karl. Do it now. Come to me—please, now."

He moved astride her and entered her with a firm thrust. She made a small whimpering sound, but he knew that it was not one of pain. It seemed that they exploded together in an instant.

Later, they dressed. Watching her pull on the riding boots that she had shucked earlier, he said, "I know now," he said.

"I know, too, darling," she said as she pulled at a boot.

"What do you know?"

"How much I love you."

"Oh. I was going to say I knew why you'd brought the food. It was to make sure that I kept my strength up."

"You're impossible. How can a woman in love be romantic when you talk about food?"

He shrugged. "Well, isn't that why you brought it?"

"Maybe it was to keep *my* strength up."

"I think we'd better get to it soon, or the ants will discover it."

They laughed and opened the bottle of wine. . . .


The meeting in the second summer was much like the first. And, now, in those early days of March, 1936, Reinhildt was already looking forward to June, when Karl would come home for good. . . .

Reinhildt looked up from the table and pushed away the dessert plate. "Oh. I'm sorry, Eric. I'm afraid I was drifting."

Eric was smiling. "I know. How long will it be before he comes back?"

She didn't hesitate. "Eight weeks and a few days."

"I'm happy for you both. Meanwhile, I have a present for you."

Her eyes grew wide. "Another one? You gave me that beautiful bracelet, and now there's something else? You're quite the spendthrift of the von Kleists, considering that you're only a country doctor."

As playful as it had been meant, the phrase rang in his ears. They were the words that Anya had used years before, and they had stayed with him. As Anya had stayed.

In her new role as mistress of the schloss, there was no way to avoid her. She prepared the activities for her father-in-law, saw to the weekly menus, did most of the things that Reinhildt had done before Kurt's marriage. In general Anya had taken over.

It was for that reason that the envelope that he held gave him such pleasure. He handed it across to her.

"What is it?"

"Open it."

She did. They were a series of legal papers, replete with stamps and countersignatures, which officially turned control of her trust fund to her.

She looked up from the papers.

"Why didn't Father give them to me himself?"

"You know Father. He called me into the office yesterday and asked me when the best time and place would be to give you this. He said you told him you didn't want a party. Did you?"

"Yes. Anya would have arranged it, and I can't stand her!" Recalling Eric's involvement, Reinhildt tried to soften her words. "Believe me, I've tried to get to know her, but all she ever seems to think about is Kurt and the party. So I stopped. There was just no sense to it. But,"—she fingered the documents—"I hadn't thought of this from father. I guess I'm getting to be too much of a hermit, even to my own family."

"How do you feel about this?" He gestured to the papers.

"I don't know. Three years ago, I was so fired up about things, it would have been a huge victory. But now.... Oh, Eric, all I want to be is Karl's wife. Take this and put it in that trust fund of yours, or whatever it is. I know it's important to you. It was to me, but I have other priorities now."

"Are you sure? You can have Karl and still help us keep those swine from taking over the company."

She shook her head. "I am always with you, and I agree about them. But I don't know if we can win. Every time I see Anya, I realize how much influence she has over father and how much she is amassing over the corporation. Take the stock. I'll sign a power of attorney or whatever it is that has to be signed, and you can do with it what you wish." She passed the envelope back across the table to him.

"You're sure?"

She nodded.

"It will always be yours, little sister. Always. Don't worry about that. I'll place it, with my account in Zurich, then later I can add Horst's to it. Don't give up—there might be a way. And speaking of our little brother, when is your wedding date—and will Horst be home for it?"

"We don't have a date yet. We were going to wait until Karl got back. But one way or another, we'll be sure that Horst is there, even if we have to go to the United States and get married in New Haven."

Eric raised his glass. "To my little sister and the addition of another doctor to the family."

# 16

Boston, March 9, 1936

Karl stood at the counter of the Western Union office and stared at the yellow message pad. He had started to write the same thing three times and then torn each of the papers from the pad, balled them up, and thrown them in the wastebasket. He could see that the woman behind the counter was starting to grow impatient with the foreigner who seemed to be having so much trouble. Despite the fact that his English was fluent, there was an accent that would tell any American that he was a foreigner.

"Can I help you, mister?" She asked.

"Thank you, no. Perhaps I'll wait before I send this."

"Where were you sending it?"

"Tübingen, Germany."

She glanced at the clock. It was just past three. "Well, if you get it to us before four, your party would have it—let me see." She opened a rate book. "Before four tomorrow in the Berlin office. They would phone it from there."

"They would phone it?"

"That's right."

He thought for a moment, then shook his head. "Thank you, but perhaps I'll put it into a letter."

He turned and left the office, pulling his scarf around his throat against the cold wind that wafted from the Charles River.

He walked a long time, lost in the darkness of his thoughts, some thoughts that had nagged at him since he had first declared his love for Reinhildt. At first, he had buried himself in his work rather than think about it. But it was there as he tried to sleep at night, and it would not go away. He was going to have to do something. Soon.

Why had he not told her that night at the opera? Why not before, or during the summer weeks that they had spent together? He was a coward—a weakling. He stopped and looked across the river. The last ice floes were melting in the river. It was a reminder of the vicious winter that had laced Boston with more than two feet of snow. He took a deep breath and took off the Irish tam that he had bought in the coldest weeks of winter. Such hats were plentiful and cheap in Boston with its huge Irish community. He hated hats, but he'd needed this one on the trolley ride to the hospital. But the weather was warming and. . . . On an impulse, he tossed the hat far out across the chilly waters and watched it hit the current. It floated downstream. Eventually it would sweep into the bay, and if it survived the churning props of the merchant ships, it would end in the Atlantic.

He *would* tell her. He would go back to the apartment and put it all into a letter. Then he would wait for an answer. It was the only fair thing to do. Everyone was allowed a measure of fear, he thought—and his was the fear of losing Reinhildt.

He took the trolley and got off at the stop three blocks from his Cambridge apartment, then walked the rest of the distance. He heard the shrill cry of the newsboy almost a block away. The voice was very Irish, very Boston.

"Read it here. Hitler moves on Rhineland. League of Nations protests."

Karl bought a paper and stared at the headlines, shuddered, and tucked the paper under his arm.

As he reached the steps of his apartment, he stopped dead in his tracks. Horst was sitting there, waiting for him.

"Surprised, Karl?"

He had grown: older, larger, more confident. He had less

of an accent than Karl had, and yet he had been the one who had had to practice English! As Karl looked at him, he saw a young American rather than the youngest son of a German industrial tycoon. Horst wore a turtleneck and a parka and a Yale button that screamed from the mouth of the Yale bulldog for them to beat Harvard in the annual spring baseball game with the Crimson.

"Surprised?"

Karl grinned. "Yes. Aren't you in the middle of midterm exams?"

"Finished, yesterday."

Karl struggled with his own inner turmoil. He liked Horst a great deal, but with the problem that he wrestled with, at the moment Horst was the last person in the world he wanted to see.

He gestured toward the button. "You know, you could be killed up here for wearing a button like that?"

"I'll dare it. I had to see you."

"How did you get up here?"

"By car—*my* car. One of my classmates at the architecture school was short of money. I bought it from him. See?" He pointed in the direction of the curb, where a battered 1931 Ford was parked.

"It's colorful," Karl said.

"You're tactful. It's a wreck. I did a lot of work on it myself. But I made it here, and I think I'll make it back—if the water pump holds out. Otherwise, I think it's in good shape. Of course, there's bodywork to be done. It had been in a share of accidents, as my friend, Ted, likes to drive after too many drinks."

Karl sat next to him on the cold stone stoop. "What's new with the family, Horst?"

"Not much. Reinhildt wrote that she got her trust fund and gave it to Eric for the account in Switzerland. As far as I know, everything is fine. Father is well, Reinhildt says. As for the rest of it, it looks like Kurt is becoming the darling of the SS." He gestured toward the newspaper Karl held. "You've heard about the Rhineland?"

Karl nodded soberly. "Yes. It doesn't look good. They've thrown the Versailles Treaty out the window. But enough about that. What about you? You mentioned that you were dating an American girl. Let me see.... She was from Radcliffe? Was it?"

"Smith. I met her a few months ago at a mixer. She's fascinated by architecture." He shrugged.

Karl laughed. "It would seem that she is more fascinated by male architecture than by anything made of stone, from the look on your face." He clapped an arm around Horst's shoulder.

The younger man smiled shyly. "Perhaps," he said, dreamily. Then, defensively, "But she does know architecture. She discusses the Bauhaus artists with the same breath as she talks of the American, Frank Lloyd Wright. She's really quite intelligent. She's one of only ten Smith women majoring in engineering. Isn't that impressive?"

"Absolutely." Karl paused for a moment. The look in Horst's eyes reminded him of the look he had had three years before. Indeed, he was sure that it was the look he still had.

"Did you drive all the way up here to tell me about this girlfriend? You haven't even mentioned her name."

"Oh. It's Diana. Diana Lassiter. Karl, she's really wonderful."

The name registered in Karl's mind. He couldn't place it, but there was something....

"The name sounds familiar."

"Oh. Her father's in the steel business. He's had some dealings with Father in the past, I believe. I'm not sure how well-known his name is in Europe; but he's famous here. Do you know them?"

Karl shook his head. "It was just that the name sounded familiar."

Horst pulled his wallet from his jacket pocket and handed a snapshot to Karl.

The girl was wearing a long gown, and she was stunning: tall and lean, with striking eyes. He could not tell from the snapshot whether her hair was blond or auburn, but she was beautiful. He told Horst so.

"Thank you, Karl. I hope you get the chance to meet her before you have to go back."

Suddenly Karl knew why Horst had come to Boston. It struck him with the clarity of a lightning bolt. He was contemplating an important step—Karl thought he knew what it was—and he needed to talk to someone on this side of the Atlantic before he made the decision.

"I'd like that. But I'll be leaving in less than two months. Perhaps we could get together before I go? I'd like to meet her. Or will you be coming back to Tübingen for the summer vacation? Reinhildt and I will probably—" He stopped in mid-sentence. It was something that he couldn't be sure of—not until he had written her and she had responded. The fear that had gnawed at him at the river returned.

"At the wedding, you mean?"

Karl nodded. "Yes. At the wedding."

"I'd like to be. . . ." There was hesitation in the statement. Karl realized that the apartment steps were not the place to discuss such matters. He suggested that they get an early supper at a local restaurant, an Irish pub that he frequented. Horst agreed, seemingly relieved at not having to complete the thought that he had just started, at least for the moment.

O'Reilly's was a classic Irish pub. They served the finest corned beef and cabbage in all of the city, as far as Karl was concerned, and the prices fitted his budget. The beer was excellent too, though both men agreed that it could not compare to German beer, especially from the tap. A waiter in a huge white apron took their order as they sat at a rear table. Minutes later, he returned with steins of beer, then left the two to talk.

"Are you afraid that you won't be there for the wedding, Horst? You really should be, you know. Your sister would want you there."

Horst nodded solemnly. "I know, Karl, I know. It bothers me. But I've decided not to go back. Not for the wedding— not ever. I'm going to become an American citizen and stay here. If I have two more years of continuous residence, I can apply for citizenship. I plan to do that. I like it here, it's open and free. I can make my way as an architect, and that's what I want to do."

Karl sipped his beer. There seemed to be none of the rashness of youth in the statement. It was obviously something that had been thought out over a period of time. "I don't have to ask if you're sure, do I?"

Horst shook his head. "Not at all. But I know all of this is going to ruin the plans that the four of us discussed that day at the hospital. You remember?"

"I remember well."

"What do you think my father will do? And what will Eric think of me?"

"Your father will have a fit, Horst. Eric. . . . Well, Eric will understand, I am sure. Besides"—he pointed in the direction of the headline of the newspaper, which was on the table between them—"I'm not sure if the small conspiracy that the four of us put together will have much bearing on where Germany is headed at this time or for the foreseeable future. Perhaps it was silly of us to even consider that it would be possible to stop Kurt and your father from giving so much support to the Nazis. We tried, at any rate. The try was important."

Again he sipped his beer. Horst took an envelope from his pocket.

"There is at least one thing that I can do. I can give you this. If things work out for me, then it will not matter. If they do not, then in a manner of speaking, it will not matter also."

At that moment the waiter returned with steaming plates of corned beef and cabbage.

"How can you serve such huge portions?" Horst asked the waiter incredulously.

The waiter looked at Horst, and winking slightly at Karl he said, "What's the matter, lad? Don't they serve man-sized portions where you come from?"

Horst looked at the waiter for a second, then his face broke into a grin. "They serve man-sized portions in New Haven—but not Irish-sized portions."

The waiter guffawed.

"Well, lad, for that, you and the doc here get the next beer on the house."

He left, and Karl felt that he was looking at a young American rather than a temporary German transplant. He was impressed. It had taken Karl more than two months of steady dining at the small bar-restaurant to make friends there, and Horst had done it in less than a minute. Clearly, he was now far more an American than a German.

Horst, still laughing, handed the envelope to Karl.

"I want you to give that to Eric. It's the paperwork about my trust fund. I hope that it will help, though I fear that it won't. Father will, as you said, have a fit and break the trust. He can, you know. I'm not of age, yet."

"How will you—manage?"

"I'll do all right. I've summer employment lined up as a draftsman with Lassiter Steel. Diana helped with that. Then, there is the money that mother left me. Together, all of those things will help me to manage. I'm not worried."

"You're sure about everything?"

"About everything."

Karl was humbled by the courage of this young man. It shamed him. Suddenly he found himself speaking.

"There are some things that you should know—things that I've never managed to tell anyone. I—tried to tell Reinhildt many times, but, to be honest, I was too frightened. I tried the last time that we were together, and I still couldn't manage. I want to tell her. I tried to send a cable today, and I simply couldn't do it." He stopped and drank some beer. Now, he would have to say it. He had cornered himself, and there was no way to slip away.

"Horst, I'm a Jew."

Horst blinked.

"My parents were both Jewish. They converted to Christianity soon after I was born. It was before my father founded the clinic. They were never very devout. I doubt that my father ever saw the inside of a synagogue—except perhaps when he was a child. I have no idea why the conversion took place. But they proceeded to bury their old religion and become good Methodists. I never told Reinhildt or anyone until now—except you." He paused.

Horst simply stared back across the table. "This is the deep secret?"

Karl nodded and ran a hand through his hair. "Yes."

"Well," Horst said, "I can see your problem, what with Father and Kurt and the Nazis so cozy."

"I knew if word of it got out, your father would disinherit her and forbid us to marry."

Horst reached across the table and placed a firm hand on Karl's sleeve. "I can see the reasons. I really can. But did you think that the secret wouldn't be safe with me or Eric or most of all, Reinhildt? If there is any surprise in me, it's that you did not trust your friends—and Reinhildt."

"I know. It's been sitting in my stomach like a cancer for years now."

"Dear God. You two claim to love one another. You are going to get married—when?—in the summer? Tell her. Tell her now. If she isn't too hurt by the fact that you failed to trust her, then marry her and bring her back here. Make a new life. That's what I'm doing. You have no close family, no one to tie you to Germany. Write her."

"How—how do you think that she will react?"

"I don't know, Karl. But if Reinhildt loves you half as much as she seems to, she wouldn't care if you were green and had two heads."

Karl managed a smile followed by a deep breath. "I will."

Horst looked around the restaurant, which was rapidly filling with laborers, men in coveralls and heavy boots. "You don't suppose that they have any schnapps here?"

Karl shook his head. "They wouldn't even buy it for me. But they do have fine Irish whiskey."

"Good, let's get some. Both of us need it."

It was late that night when Karl finished the letter. He had labored over every sentence and agonized over each phrase.

Satisfied that it was the best that he could do, he sealed the envelope and addressed it. He would send it by the new trans-Atlantic air mail service. It would take only days that way, rather than the weeks that boat mail would take.

As an afterthought, he wrote *Most Personal* on the envelope.

Though Karl could not know it, the afterthought was a terrible mistake.

## 17

A week later, Klaus Schmidt stared at the pile of envelopes and parcels that were heaped on the desk of his small back room office. He sighed and sipped hot black coffee from a delicate Dresden cup. The steam from the cup wafted up and fogged the bottoms of his rimless spectacles, forcing him to take them off to clean them. He was in no hurry to get to the mail for the day. He had worked late into the night clearing up after the party, one of the many that Kurt was currently giving for the officials of the Leibstandarte. There had been more than a hundred guests. As Klaus had moved through the huge ballroom, checking on the food and drinks, he had come face to face with Heydrich. The two men had stared at one another for a minute, then Klaus had nodded politely and moved on. Heydrich had made no attempt at a greeting, which was as it should have been. But the experience had rattled Klaus. He had gone back to the kitchen and barked at two of the servers for not getting enough champagne glasses out to the party.

Under normal conditions the meeting would not have had much of an impact on him. But after so many years of being undercover, the chance that Heydrich might have said something that could have compromised him was something that he dared not risk. He was angry with himself for not realizing Heydrich's name had been on the guest list. After all, he had sent out the invitations. It had been a minor slip, but something that his normally precise mind should not have done.

Then another thought occurred to him. Perhaps Kurt had invited Heydrich at the last minute. Yes, that had to be it.

He grunted and looked again at the mountain of mail. Resigned, he started to sort it.

He was three-quarters of the way through the file when he came to a letter for Reinhildt. He set it aside, as was his custom. She was the only one left whose mail he monitored. Horst was in the United States, and Eric was receiving his mail at his clinic. Kurt, of course, was something different. Klaus had to take much care in examining Kurt's mail, lest he suspect. For Kurt was well aware that Klaus was monitoring Reinhildt's correspondence and had given his tacit approval.

Klaus sorted the rest of the mail and then got up from the desk and crossed to lock the door. He felt this to be necessary ever since Sarah Blume had walked in on him that one time, unannounced.

Letter in hand, he went to a small table near the window. This was going to be easy. The corners had not been fully pasted down. The outgoing mail was always harder. Reinhildt usually managed to seal everything tightly. At times like that, he had to loosen the edges with the steam that rose from the coffee cup. Often, he would have the kitchen staff bring in a steaming pot of coffee—and he demanded that it be steaming. He would then slowly loosen the glue with the rising steam. This letter, however, would require no such work.

He paused for a moment and wondered if he should even bother. When he was busy, he sometimes didn't; Karl's letters were trivia. He thought for a minute and started to put the letter aside.

*Most personal.*

He looked at the words. It was the first time that he had

seen them on a letter from the doctor. Perhaps there would be something special in it. He decided to take the time to open it.

He took a small leather pouch from his jacket pocket. Inside, there were a series of lock picks, a passkey for the schloss, and several gleaming, slender stilettolike blades. Each one had been honed to the sharpness of a scalpel. Placing the envelope flat on the worktable, he inserted the thinnest of the blades under the open space of the flap. Gingerly he pried up the edge. The technique was to slice through the glue rather than the paper. Then, in the resealing process, he would simply reapply a new layer of glue and close it back up. The person who eventually opened the letter would never notice that the envelope had been tampered with.

He slipped the blade through the rest of the glue and opened the flap. It was a single piece of writing paper. He started to read. Halfway through the letter, he stopped.

*Dear God!*

He went back and read it again, this time finishing the rest of the letter. His hands began shaking as he realized the enormity of the contents. Should it go to Heydrich or to Kurt? he wondered. What a wonderful choice to have to make. Which of them would serve his long-term goals best? There was no real question. It would have to be Kurt. He took the envelope and the letter to the desk and cleared away a space. He pulled a bright reading light down close to the paper and then unlocked the bottom drawer of the desk. The camera was small but powerful. He had made excellent photocopies with it in the past. He snapped three exposures of each side of the letter and then three shots of the envelope.

After resealing the envelope, he returned it to the pile that would go to Reinhildt. Now, he would have to find Kurt. He wondered what the young man's reaction would be.

The first thing that Reinhildt felt was surprise, though she couldn't be sure what the nature of the surprise was. It wasn't anything akin to shock. It was more a reaction to the intensity of the letter. She could sense the agony it must have caused him in the time they were apart. More than that, she could feel what it must have been like for him during the times they were together. All the puzzling things about their relationship became suddenly clear. His reserve, the things that seemed to be locked painfully inside. He *had* been ready to tell her on that last night at the opera. It had been the presence of Hitler and Kurt and all of the Nazis that had bottled the secret up again.

She was not without a feeling of pain. He *should* have told her, it was something important to him. It was a part of the mutual honesty that they were going to have to develop if they were going to be married. And under ordinary circumstances, she told herself, she was sure that he would have gotten it out front immediately.

She tried to sort out the rest of her feelings. How would this affect things? What would happen to Eric's plans now, if she went to the United States with Karl? She would have to speak to Eric; he would have to know as soon as possible. The secret would be safe with him. But first, there was the letter back to Karl. She went to the writing desk and started to compose it. Yes, she would marry him. Yes, she would go to the United States. But why had he not told her before? Why had he caused himself so much pain? The very fact that he had not mentioned it was more hurtful to both of them than the mere fact that he was a Jew.

She stopped and crossed out the last sentences, then threw the paper away and started over. She didn't want to mention the revelation at all.

After finishing the letter, she gave it to one of the maids. The maid, in turn, placed it on Klaus Schmidt's desk.

# 18

May 28, 1936

It was the last Saturday in May, and Frankfurt was ablaze
with spring. Flower sellers lined the banks of the Main River,
and shoppers filled the Zeil. On the south side of the river,
near the old city, Eric and Reinhildt sat, sipping coffee at one
of the cafés that sat on barges that dotted the river bank.
Across the river, the carillon was starting to play at the
cathedral, and the sound of it blended with the barge horns
and the churning motors of the passing tour boats.

Reinhildt was wearing a white dress that seemed to radiate
against her dark features and flashing eyes. She was beaming,
Eric observed, and fidgeting at the same time. Eric's mood
was more somber. Too many things had hit him at once. The
grand design of the past three years had been shattered.
Perhaps he had been foolish to keep the hope that von Kleist
could be kept from the Nazis. Now, it was academic. Despite
Reinhildt's stock and his own, Horst's stock was lost. There
was no way that Horst would get his full trust. His decision to
stay in the United States—a country Johann had despised
since the end of the Great War—would enrage the old man.
The remainder of the stock would fall into the hands of Kurt
and Anya. The plan would have to be abandoned.

With Horst not returning and Reinhildt and Karl gone, or
soon to be gone, Eric had entertained the thought of also
going to the US. He had his trust. All he had to do was to go

to Zurich and claim it. He toyed with the idea of opening a practice there—perhaps even getting married. He had had little resembling a romantic life in years, and felt a twinge of jealousy toward Reinhildt and Karl. After Anya, he had managed to dive into his work, shunning all personal entanglements. He often wondered to himself if it had simply been a buffer against the pain that Anya had caused. He had thought of going into analysis, looking for the deep-seated Freudian root of the problem, but eventually he dismissed the idea. He did not need an analyst to explain the love-hate relationship with his father—the need for fatherly approval in childhood. That would be what they would tell him, and that was information he had already deduced for himself.

But what if he did go to the United States? Would a change of scenery alter his outlook? He decided that it would not. He was comfortable in Germany, despite the Nazis. He was still a German . . . still a German. He turned the phrase over several times in his mind. They were the words that Trost had spoken those years ago—a lifetime ago—at the factory. They had made him realize that there was something else to stay in Germany for. There *was* a group of Germans who could do something about the Nazis, and as long as Eric stayed in some degree of proximity to Von Kleist AG, there was the chance that he could work with them to toss the Nazis from power. It was something of a dream, slender but nevertheless enough to tip the scales in favor of his staying in Germany. In addition, he thought to himself, he loved his practice. He sensed that both staff and patients were loyal friends. It was something that buoyed him up.

"Eric?"

"Oh—what? I'm sorry."

"Wherever you were, you were being very serious about things." Reinhildt sipped her tea.

"I'm always serious about things. That's the trouble with me."

"Right. And the answer is to come with Karl and me."

He shook his head ruefully. "No. We've been through all of

that before. I thank you both, but there's no way I could do it. I've given you all of the whys."

She looked across the river. The carillon had stopped.

"Shouldn't we be getting to the station? The train will—"

"We have almost an hour, and it's only a five-minute taxi ride across the river."

"But what if the train gets in early?" Her tone was that of a petulant child.

"Reinhildt, my dear, wonderful sister. Have you ever known the Reich *Bundesbahn* to be early? Have you ever known it to be late? If the arrival time is ten minutes after two, that's when it will arrive. If the prior train is not out of the station when it gets there, the trainmen will be on the tracks pushing the blasted thing. Relax."

"Do I look all right?"

"You look radiant. He will fall at your feet."

"Oh, Eric. Don't tease. Do I really look all right?"

"I am serious, remember—always too serious. And you do. But there is something that we have to discuss."

"Hmmm? What?"

"Have you told Karl about what's happening with Jews in Germany? I mean these Nürnberg laws? They're banning Jews from everything. They can't go to German schools; can't get into professions. In some places, I'm told they can't even patronize German shops, except on certain days. But, Reinhildt, most specifically they forbid a Jew to marry an Aryan! You may not have much time, little sister. There is no guarantee that Karl's heritage won't be discovered—the Nazis are fanatics about ferreting out Jews. Get married as quickly as possible—then leave!"

The urgency in his tone frightened Reinhildt for a moment. "I—I was thinking that we could make the announcement in a week and then get married toward the end of June. I've gotten my passport, and we are going to say that we would go to the United States for our honeymoon. Then we would just stay."

Eric nodded, then asked, grinning wryly, "Were you thinking of getting married at the schloss?"

"Of *course*, Eric, and we were going to invite Himmler and all the rest of the party." She laughed, relieved by his lighter mood.

"Seriously," he said.

"You must be serious again?" she asked impatiently.

"I surrender. Where will it be?"

"I thought at the chapel at Bebanhausen. It's beautiful and close to the place that mother is buried. I don't think that Karl would mind."

"I don't think so, either."

"The only thing that bothers me is that Horst will not be here." She stopped, suddenly confronted with another thought. "Does anyone know—?"

"No. There's no sense in mentioning it until after you two are married and safely in the United States. Then, I'll break the news to Kurt and to Father. Father will sputter and fly into a rage, and Kurt will start counting the shares of stock he'll inherit."

They spent the rest of the hour talking of the future. Karl had written that he might get a position with the United States government, something in immunology. It might speed up the process of naturalization, and there were any number of friends at the hospital who would be willing to sponsor him for both the job and citizenship.

Reinhildt mentioned that Karl had written about the new girl—almost the first girl—in Horst's life. "Horst in love! I didn't think I'd ever see it," she said. "Karl says that her father is in steel, rather big in the United States, and that he also would be willing to sponsor Karl. Though I think if things develop correctly, Horst will be the first one that he will sponsor."

"What is she like, this Diana? Did Karl say anything?"

"Little. Just that Horst seemed in love and that that was something he had never seen before."

"None of us have." He looked at his watch. "We'd better go." He paid the check, and they moved from the barge to the street, where he flagged a cab.

The station was crowded. It took them a full ten minutes to

work their way to the track, where the train was just pulling in. The announcement of the arrival echoed from the huge glass-domed ceiling of the station.

"Reinhildt?" It was Karl, lugging a bag and heading in the direction of the gate. He swung her into his arms as Eric took the bag. After a moment he put her down, and he and Eric embraced. They moved to the small outdoor café at the side of the terminal and sat at one of the tables, waiting for the larger bags to be unloaded.

They didn't see the two men who followed and sat carefully a few tables away. One was tall and blond. The other was portly.

After a few minutes, the tall one glanced at a photo he had pulled from his pocket and handed it discreetly to the other man.

"The man on the right is the Jew?"

The other nodded. "Correct."

---

## 19

For the first week, they ravaged each other on every occasion they could manage alone. Reinhildt had never known such passion. On the second afternoon in his apartment, she almost screamed.

"Are you all right?" he asked anxiously. She looked up at him, allowing her eyes to focus for a minute. "Oh, God, yes. It's all right. More than all right." She stopped talking and dug her fingers deeper into the small of his back, trying to tell him to simply take her and not be so careful. She had never felt like this before—not in the summer interludes that they had shared—never. Perhaps it was that the secret had been revealed. The tension of whether they really loved each other had been resolved. She was beyond caring. She had never made love with such abandon in her life, and she was beginning to worry that she might be a nymphomaniac until she reminded herself that such a woman would take any man and she could see no other than Karl.

Afterward, they lay in each other's arms, both of them sated, beaded with perspiration. He rested his head on his hand and looked at her nude body, let his glance move over the contours. She reached down and pulled the sheet over her.

"Oh, God," she said. "How can you be so brazen and so shy at the same time?"

He started to laugh. "You amaze me. Did you know what Schiller said of women?"

"I'm afraid to think."

"He said that women should be madonnas in child rearing, gourmets in the kitchen, and harlots in bed."

"And?" she asked.

He thought for several seconds, then turned to her, smiling broadly. "Well . . . we can always get someone to cook and to help raise the children."

"You beast." She grabbed the pillow from under his head and hit him with it. It exploded, filling the room with a blizzard of down. They both laughed, despite the mess.

In the middle of the laughter, he said, "I'll have the cook or the nanny clean up things."

"Will you, really?" she asked, barely able to speak. Feathers wafted throughout the room.

"No. I'll have Olga, that ancient Putzfrau, clean things. I know her. She'll get every feather in the room and she won't ask a thing about how it has happened."

"Has she done it so many times before?" There was the slightest tone of trepidation in her voice. And he caught it.

"Of course. All through the orgies when I was a resident here, she had to clean up. You know . . . whipped cream, strawberry jam, whips, chains—all of it. After all, I *have* been to Berlin."

This time he stopped her before she could throw another down pillow.

"Stop!" he yelled as he grabbed her wrist. "Even Olga cannot deal with two pillows." They rolled into each other's arms, laughing.

By the time that they parted late that afternoon, they had decided on two weeks for the announcement of the wedding. That would give them time to make their plans without the harassment that was certain to follow. Not that Reinhildt cared any longer how her father would react. She was going to give up her name. She was going to become Reinhildt Mittenberg!

They were getting dressed when Karl said, "You should have guessed that I was a Jew."

She stopped putting on her dress and flushed. After a minute she turned to him. "I know. I finally figured it out. But women in love are stupid. I never considered it. If I had, would you have thought me a whore?"

He shrugged. "No." Still naked, he crossed the room to take her in his arms. "But I'm flattered. It told me how little experience you had."

She pulled back for a second, in mock defensiveness. "Besides, Eric told me that circumcision was getting more common among all infants, not only Jews. I—" She stopped trying to find the words. "I—gave you the benefit of the doubt."

They both broke into gales of laughter.

The second week, they managed to meet three times in his apartment. On the third night, Reinhildt was running late. She had gotten a late start, trying to find the dress that she wanted to wear. A storm had slicked the roads, and she was driving through the town at a speed that she would not have dared only a week before. On the road that wound through the hills to the research clinic on the mountain, she forced herself to slow down, not wanting to risk an accident. She was supposedly going to a piano lesson across town. Her father had wondered why she did not have the teacher come to the schloss, concerned that she might be denigrating the power of the von Kleists by going for the lesson. She had explained that the teacher was brilliant, but confined to a wheelchair. She managed to keep a straight face throughout the explanation. Fortunately, Kurt and Anya were not there, for certainly they would have seen through the flimsy excuse. But she had grown far more daring in the last week. She would dare almost anything for Karl.

She turned the last corner and braked to a stop. There were two cars parked on the road in front of the foundation. As she got out of the car and pulled her trench coat up around her neck, the cars took off at a rapid speed. Something was wrong.

She walked ahead to the main entrance of the clinic, only to see two of the nurses standing there watching the cars speed off in the darkness. Both of the women appeared as though they were in a state of shock.

She approached them directly, with a sense of foreboding starting to grip her stomach.

"What happened?"

"It's Doktor Mittenberg. The men from the Gestapo came and took him."

Reinhildt felt the rain hit her face, and she could see flashes of lightning across the valley. She tried to concentrate on them for a second, not wanting to believe what the women had said.

After a minute she managed to say, "What did you say?"

The older of the two women in white uniforms turned to her. She was holding a handkerchief to her right cheek. She lowered it as she started to speak, and there was an ugly red welt on her cheek. "I told one of them that a wretched mistake had been made. I told them that the doctor was not a Jew—but, Fräulein, they took him. And the man hit me in the face. He said that the entire clinic could be arrested for hiding a Jew who had come into the country illegally."

Reinhildt looked at the woman in stunned silence. She could hear a sound like the roaring ocean in her ears, and the lightning streaks that crossed the sky seemed, for the moment, to be in back of her eyes.

"They have to be wrong," the woman continued. "He's not a Jew."

The other nurse placed an arm around the drooping shoulder of the first. "Don't worry, Gretchen. It will all be put right. The doctor will be back in hours. All they will do is make sure that he is not a Jew."

"Thank you," Reinhildt said hypnotically. She headed back toward her car.

She did not remember the drive back to the schloss. The first thing that she did remember was calling Eric and asking him in a clear, calm tone to come to the schloss. She said that she had not been feeling well and that since Karl was no longer available, could he come and help her?

He was there in less than fifteen minutes. He came into the main hall and headed immediately for the stairs. He was surprised to see that Johann was there, in the main foyer, with Klaus Schmidt.

"Eric," Johann asked, "is there something wrong with Reinhildt? Klaus here said that she looked ill when she came in. She was not due from that piano lesson of hers until much later. Is she all right? Did she call you for treatment?"

Eric could hardly deny it. He had his bag in his hand, and he was sure he had a harried look on his face. He tried to appear calm, but, it was difficult. What had she meant? *Karl was no longer available?*

"She called about a stomach ache. It was nothing serious. I thought that I would check in on her and then steal a glass of cognac from you, Father."

"So, nothing serious then?" Klaus asked.

"I don't know. But from what she said on the phone, I would guess not. I'll go up and check her."

"Eric?" The voice came from behind him, and he knew who it was without looking. The timbre of the voice was one that he remembered all too well, though the tone tried to convey a sense of false concern.

"Yes, Anya?"

"Is everything all right?"

"As far as I know. I'll know better when I see her. Is she in her room?"

"Yes, sir," Klaus snapped.

"Well, let me check, and I'll come down and let you know. Let me be with her alone. You know how she likes her privacy."

They all nodded, and Eric headed up the stairs, trying to look calm and only routinely concerned.

He got to the top of the stairs and speeded up as he headed for her room. He stopped before the closed door and knocked softly. "Reinhildt?"

"Eric?" There was a note of hysteria in the voice from the other side of the door.

"Yes. Let me in."

As the door swung open, he could see that she was indeed on the edge of hysteria. He put a supporting arm under her and moved her to the bed. He propped a pillow under her head and looked at her face. Her mascara had traced jagged lines of tears across her cheeks. Her pupils were mere pinpoints as she looked at him wildly. He recognized the symptoms: she was on the edge of deep shock or sliding into it.

"Th-th-they took him. They *took him*!!" Her voice started to rise, and that was what he had wanted to avoid. He took one of her hands in his and squeezed it. Then he placed a fingertip across her lips.

"Who took who?" He tried to remain calm, all the time haunted by the phrase that she had used on the phone. *Karl is no longer available.*

"They... took him... Karl. They took him."

"Take a deep breath and try to think. Who are they?" He slipped an index finger to her wrist and started to take her pulse as she tried to form the words. He didn't need to feel the vein for more than a few seconds to realize that his initial assumption had been correct. It was too rapid: she was slipping into shock. He was going to have to get as much information as he could before he had to sedate her. His mind raced to find a plausible excuse to give Johann and Anya: food poisoning—anything.

He leaned close to her. "Who took him?"

"Th-the Gestapo. They—they said that he was a Jew who had illegally come into the country. They said that he might be a spy."

Eric could feel the cold chill of fear blend with the heat of anger. "Where? Where did they take him?" He hoped that a phone call would settle everything.

"Stuttgart. They took him to Stuttgart."

She started to shiver, and Eric wrapped a blanket around her, then dug into his bag. He found the syringe in its sterile container and then managed to fish the small bottle of morphine from the side of the case. He gave her an eighth of a grain intravenously. In a matter of seconds, her breathing became regular, her pupils began to dilate. He checked her pulse. It was slower than it had been, and it would be slower still. Her body had been burning up endocrine reserves with the speed of an express train, and he had just shut down the mechanism. He placed another blanket on her and sat by the side of the bed.

What the hell was going on with Karl?

## 20

The night that Karl was arrested was something of an anniversary. It was exactly two years less two weeks since the *Putsch* of Ernst Roehm had attempted, and failed, to wrest power from Hitler himself and Himmler's SS with the help of the old guard of the storm troopers. Hitler's control was such that he managed to turn the uprising around in less than three days. Then he turned the "death's head" units of

Heydrich and Himmler loose on the corps of Bavarian cronies who had once supported him. It was the beginning of the rise of the SS as a political and military force. There was little that they could not do on their own authority. They had the power to arrest and imprison, to confiscate and to murder. It was their practice to move in to arrest a suspect at night. They would whisk the wretch off so quickly that it would be thought that he had vanished into the "night and the fog."

With his hands cuffed behind him, Karl was tossed in the back of the sedan, which roared off in the direction of Stuttgart. He knew better than to ask questions. The hulking men who surrounded him seemed ready to smash him with their truncheons at the slightest provocation. It was several hours before they arrived at SS/Gestapo headquarters on the outskirts of the city. As they got out of the car, Karl could see a large truck in front of them disgorging a number of civilians. There were a few women among them, but most seemed to be rather well-dressed men in business suits. Some were injured, and Karl guessed that the injuries must have occurred when they were arrested. There were cuts and bruises, missing teeth, and a few men were doubled up, moaning with pain. The group was formed into rag-tag ranks and marched through a side door in the headquarters. The long, dark hall led to what seemed to be a series of pens, the first of which was jammed to capacity with what had been another group of arrivals. The men who had arrested Karl had been in civilian clothes, but those inside the building wore the characteristic black uniform of the SS. Karl was surprised to see several of them wearing the circular Adolf Hitler band on their left sleeves. They were members of the Leibstandarte—Kurt's unit.

"Inside," a voice commanded, and hands grabbed Karl from behind. He did not see who had grabbed his wrists to unlock the cuffs, but he was grateful. He moved into the cell with the others, and soon there was barely enough room for any of them to sit. The door was slammed shut and locked by a guard. The terrified crowd, silent all the way to the cell, started to whisper among themselves. "Who are you?" "Where are you from?" "Why have they arrested you?" The whispers buzzed through the cells that adjoined one another. There were many Jews, some political opponents of national socialism, and several felons. They had all been rounded up in one night. None of them had been told the reason for the arrest.

Karl saw a tall, thin man with graying hair in a corner of the cell bending over one of the prisoners, apparently checking the man's ribs for injuries. It took Karl a few minutes to work his way through the mass of people to get to the other side of the cell.

"You are a doctor?"

The man nodded, never looking up from the supine figure on the concrete floor. "Kern—Dr. Ludwig Kern."

"I'm Dr. Karl Mittenberg." He hunched down and looked at the man. "What is it?"

For the first time, Kern looked at Karl. Kern's face was wrinkled and creased, but it did not look like he had been abused.

"It looks like the floating rib on the right side. Palpate that. Tell me what you think." Karl did. "Agreed. It doesn't feel like a vertical break. It might be a lateral split." Karl checked the man's pulse and respiration. "Shock. He's going to need attention." He got to his feet and looked down the hall. As far as he could see in the dim light, there were no guards there. And all he could hear were the moans of the injured in the other cell.

Kern grabbed him by the sleeve. "Don't. Don't ask for anything. This man was in the truck with me." He pointed to the unconscious form on the floor. "He made the mistake of asking the reason for his arrest. That's what caused this. They hit him with a rifle. So don't ask."

Karl looked down at the man, who was short, dark, and in his twenties.

"We have to stabilize it. Otherwise, he might puncture a lung." He took off his wide belt and slipped it under the man's back. As he pulled it tight, the man moaned. Kern, seeing what Karl was doing, slipped a finger under the belt at the point of the suspected fracture. Karl hooked up the belt when Kern was satisfied that the rib would not move.

"Why did they arrest you?" he asked Kern.

"I and the members of my family are Socialists."

"But that—"

"No. Not their kind of socialist. Real socialists. They will probably call me a Communist—if they decide to call me anything at all."

"You see," Kern continued in a hushed tone, "I did a foolish thing. My wife and children and most of my other relatives had already left Germany. I sent them to Norway. I have good friends in Oslo, at the university. I was going to follow them when I got my practice settled and my house sold. It was stupid of me. I know that they would get me sooner or later. I should have left earlier. What of you?"

"I am a Jew."

Eric stayed with Reinhildt far into the night. He called the clinic and had one of his best nurses come to the schloss, instructing her to keep Reinhildt sedated and to keep her on a liquid diet for the balance of the day. The latter was nothing more than a smokescreen, for he had told Johann that Reinhildt had a slight case of food poisoning. He sped to the clinic and locked himself in his office.

After fifteen minutes of concentrated thought, he realized that he didn't know where to begin. He thought of Trost but knew this could not be handled over the phone, and Eric simply did not have time to get to Frankfurt. Speed was essential. He could not let too much time pass, or Karl would have been moved to God only knew where. There was no time for Trost.

Kurt! His brother's name haunted him. Each time that he came up with another possible solution and dismissed it, the thought of Kurt in his SS uniform flashed into his mind. He tried to push it away, but the logical side of him kept coming back to it. He was going to have to ask a favor of Kurt. He thought of Reinhildt and of Karl. Yes. He would do it. He reached for the phone.

"SS Headquarters, Stuttgart. May I help you?"

"Yes. This is Doktor Eric von Kleist. I wish to speak with Untersturmführer Kurt von Kleist. He is my brother."

"Is he on the staff here, Doktor?"

"Yes. He has been for several months. He is in a group called the Leibstandarte."

"One moment, please."

Eric waited for what seemed more like five.

"Herr Doktor von Kleist?" It was another voice that had come back on the phone.

"Yes?"

"Herr Doktor, I'm afraid that your brother is not here. He has taken a detachment to the railroad station and is not due to report back for more than three hours. You could call him here then. I will be sure that he gets the message."

"Well, you see, this is something of an emergency, and I have to get in touch with him as soon as possible. Is there a way that I could get him at the station?"

There was another pause on the other end of the phone. The man had placed a hand on the speaker, and all that Eric could hear were muffled voices. In a minute the voice returned.

"Sir? You could reach him at our liaison office at the station." He gave Eric the number.

Eric got up from the desk and ran both hands through his hair. It was something that he still did not want to do. He went to the door and then into the hall, where he poured a cup of coffee and came back. He took several sips of the hot black coffee, then put the cup down. There was no sense in putting it off. He picked up the phone and dialed the number.

"Von Kleist."

"Kurt. It's Eric."

"Eric? What a surprise. Why do you call me here? There's nothing wrong, is there? Father? Anya?"

"No, Kurt. Nothing of that kind. There is something else, though."

"Yes?"

"It's Karl Mittenberg. He was arrested last night—by the Gestapo."

"I see." He said nothing more. He was not going to make it easy for Eric.

"Is there any inquiry that you can make about all of this?"

"Perhaps, Eric. Then again. . . . You said that the Gestapo had arrested him?"

"That's what I was told."

"Well, despite the fact that we work closely with the Gestapo, they have their own methods and act on arrests independently. Did you know what the charge was?"

*Is he feeling me out? How much does he really know?*

"I believe they said that he was a Jew and that he had illegally entered the country."

A pause.

"That's quite a charge, Eric. It's very serious. Is it true?"

"I know that his papers were in order when he came back from the United States. Otherwise, why would he not have been questioned at Bremen when the ship docked?"

"That's *not* the point, Eric. Is he a Jew?"

"I don't think so. I believe that he is a Methodist. As far as I know, he has been all of his life. All of this seems preposterous."

"Let me tell you something, Eric." There was a firmness in Kurt's distant voice. "When the Gestapo makes an arrest, you can be sure that the case has been thoroughly researched and investigated. They simply don't make random arrests."

"Kurt, he's an old friend of the family—the man who helped get me into and through medical school. He treated Father for years. The least that he can receive at our hands is an inquiry at this miscarriage of justice. Is there anything that you can do?"

There was a knock at the door of Kurt's office. "Can you hold a minute, Eric?"

"Yes."

"Come in." An SS sergeant came through the door and

snapped to attention. Kurt nodded and reached for the manifest that the man had in his hand. The sergeant clicked his heels and left, shouldering the rifle that he had been carrying.

Kurt looked from the window to the siding, where a ragged file of prisoners was being driven in the direction of a freight train. He saw the SS guards push them into the cars. He thought for a second that he saw the tall, lean form of Karl going into the second car. He looked carefully through the manifest until he came to the entry he sought.

*Mittenberg, Karl—Jew—illegal entry.*

He circled the entry with a pencil, then got back to the phone.

"I'm sorry, Eric. There was something that had to be attended to. Now, you were asking about Karl. Let me say this. I've worked, as you know, very hard to get to the position that I have now."

"Yes, I know."

"Well, it's a serious thing to interfere with the Gestapo, even for a member of the Leibstandarte. They are the security arm. We simply enforce. To inquire about a Jew who has been arrested by a senior branch of the SS is to, quite clearly, place one's career in peril. After all, you have an independent career. You are a doctor. My career hinges on the political structure. The Leibstandarte is more than an honor guard. They are closely linked to both the political and the military operation. To make an untoward inquiry on behalf of a Jew would be taken as suspect. It might be seen as a conspiracy. It could all too easily wreck my career. I'm sure that you understand?"

"Kurt, Karl was a doctor, too. He had a career. He was a close friend, damn it, Kurt. All of this is wrong." Eric fought to hold his temper.

"I understand, believe me, Eric. I know how you feel. But there is a great deal of personal risk in all of this for me. Would you risk losing your practice or your license without some assurances?"

Eric paused. He sensed Kurt was starting to get to the point. "What kind of assurances?"

"Well, as I said, I am putting my career in peril to do this. I have to ask that you be prepared to compensate me for the risk. That's fair, isn't it?"

"Of course, Kurt. What kind of compensation would you consider?"

"As a guarantee against what might be interpreted as a conspiracy, I would require . . . all of the von Kleist holdings that you and Reinhildt currently have in your names!"

Eric was silent. So that was it. But, he wondered, why Reinhildt? What did Kurt know of this, really? He bluffed.

"What has Reinhildt to do with all of this, Kurt? This is a favor that I am asking as brother to brother. She has no part in it. I am asking the favor."

On the other end of the line, Kurt grimaced. He was suddenly furious with himself. He had overreached. To implicate Reinhildt at this time might expose his own part in the arrest and perhaps even implicate Klaus Schmidt as a Gestapo agent. It was something that he could not afford.

"Of course, you're right. It is a favor from brother to brother. Still, I would have to have the assurance that you would sign a power of attorney for *your* portion of the stock. After all, you have said that you understand the nature of the risk here?"

Eric thought for a moment. He hit upon an idea. "I will assign my stock to you without reservation—when Karl is released and allowed to leave the country unimpeded. Is that sufficient?"

"Will you sign a paper to that effect?"

Eric tried to quell the rage that gripped him. But they were bargaining for the life of the man who Reinhildt loved. There was little else that he could do. Besides, he had written off the possibility of wresting back the corporation from Kurt and Anya. "I will draw up and sign such a paper. Remember, though, I must have real assurance that Karl has gotten out of the country. Is that clear?"

Kurt thought for a long moment. He was indeed on the

horns of a dilemma. To get the release of a Jew was next to impossible. And he had been telling Eric the truth when he had said that interference in the operation of the Gestapo was dangerous.

"I'm sorry, Eric. It's too risky. I would have to have the stocks in advance. That's the only way that I could do it."

Eric knew his brother. He was sure that he would get hold of the stocks and then insure that Karl was dead. He had lived too many years with Kurt not to know how his mind operated.

"I can't do it that way, Kurt. The offer as I stated it stands, though. Can we compromise on that?"

"I'm sorry, Eric. It's too much of a chance to take. How do I know that you wouldn't renege as soon as Karl was out of Germany?"

"You have my word, Kurt."

"I'm sorry, Eric. Without the immediate stock commitment, there is little that I can do. I'm sure that you understand."

Kurt hung up.

He looked at the railroad cars. They were almost filled now. The train would be heading south in a matter of minutes. He looked for the name on the manifest. Finding it, he penned a note on all three copies.

*Important Jew—Special Treatment!!*

In the serpentine coding of the SS, the message was clear. Karl would be killed as soon as the train reached its destination.

## 21

The cattle car was jammed. There was barely room to stand, and only the few who managed to get to the outer walls of the car were able to sit or stretch out, at all. Kern had been dragged to the corner by Karl. The older doctor had been injured while boarding the car. He had not moved quickly enough to suit the guard, who had swung a rifle butt and smashed it into Kern's left side. The doctor had screamed, and Karl had managed to pull him aboard the train before he was hit again.

Kern was half unconscious and moaning. Karl huddled over him, so that he would not be trampled by the mass of people. The old doctor's left side was raw. Karl touched it gingerly. Kern yelped. It only took that first palpation to see what had happened. His spleen had been ruptured; he needed immediate attention—but how? Karl looked at the crush of bodies in the car. He had no idea where they were going or how long the trip would take, though he guessed it would be a short ride as there was no food in the car and no sanitary facilities. Even the Nazis would not want to risk the possibility of an epidemic by having the journey go too far without sanitation. He was sure that it would only be a matter of hours. He slipped the old man out of his coat, making sure that he did not agitate the wound any further. He balled up the coat as a pillow and made Kern as comfortable as possible against the wall of the car. Through the slats, he could see that they had cleared the station and were heading out into the countryside. He was not sure what direction they were taking, but it took the train more than half an hour to get to full speed. He sat next to Kern and pulled the man's knees up so that they would not be stepped on.

They had been traveling for more than four hours when Karl felt the train start to slow. A murmur of excitement ran through the car. Perhaps they were at the destination; perhaps they were going to be fed. They were wrong.

The train stopped at a siding and stayed there for more than an hour. There was no attempt to open the doors or to provide any food or water for the passengers. The train simply stood there. As long as it had been moving, there had been a breeze. It was not until they stopped that the heat hit them, and with it had come the smell of human waste. Soon it became intolerable. Karl left Kern where he was and threaded his way through the car to the other end. There, he found the cause of the smell. An old woman propped against the side of the car had filthied herself. At first Karl simply thought that she had gotten frightened and lost her bowels. But a quick check showed dehydration. It could be dysentery, typhus, almost anything. He spoke to two men cramped together in the far corner.

"Is there anything that we can clean her up with? I'm a doctor. If this goes on, we're all going to be sick." They shook their heads and said nothing. He noticed that one of the men wore a business suit, ironically decorated with a flowered handkerchief in his pocket.

"Let me have that." He reached out and grabbed the handkerchief. The man said nothing; he was numb with fear. Karl looked to the other man. "Have you got one?"

He managed to gather five or six handkerchiefs and small rags with which he did his best to clean the woman. Then, balling up the handkerchiefs, he pushed them through the slats and out of the car. He didn't think it would do much good, but at least it would keep the smell down some.

He worked his way back through the car. But the word that he was a doctor had preceded him. He was stopped by five or six people, all with cuts and bruises. There was little that he could do for them or for the other more seriously injured. There were at least two fractures and God knew how many internal injuries, but he was helpless.

The trip *had* to end soon.

He was wrong. The trip took more than two days. Kern died the second night. There was nothing that Karl could do for the man, except make him as comfortable as possible. He had needed surgery. Karl rubbed his tired eyes, telling himself all of this was not going to bring the man back from the dead. After that, he restricted his activity in the car. He was getting giddy from hunger and thirst. The woman he had cleaned up had died on the second afternoon. He was sure that there were others in the car who were also dead. But there was nothing he could do . . . nothing.

It was late the second night when a small, dark man managed to work his way through the pile of moaning humanity to get to where Karl sat, peering through the slats. The train swerved, and the man tumbled into Karl.

"Sorry," he whispered.

"That's all right," Karl whispered back, his throat dry from lack of water. "I want to find out where we're going."

"You don't know?"

"No. You mean you do?"

The man nodded. "Dachau."

Suddenly Karl remembered the words of Sepp Dietrich at that dinner, so long ago. *Places of concentration and hard work.*

"And what will happen there?"

"There are a lot of rumors. We've been sorted and categorized. You can tell by these." He pointed to the ink stencil on his jacket and his shirt. It was a Star of David, the same as had been stenciled on the jacket and shirt that Karl wore. "You are a doctor, are you not?"

Karl, saving his voice, managed a nod.

"You see, Doktor, they will assign us different jobs when we get to the camp. The rumor is that if you work hard, they will free you. That's why I'm told that they have a large sign over the entrance: Work Makes You Free."

"Does it?"

"I wouldn't count on it, Doktor. I have heard what happens on the inside. A star means kaput. As soon as you are off the train. What you should do is what I'm trying to do." He pulled a jacket and a shirt from the tight roll that he held under his arm and unfolded them. Neither man could see well in the dark, and Karl could not make sense of what the man was doing.

"You see, this stencil says *P* on it. That means political prisoner. The word is that they will get better treatment than the Jews in the camp."

"Where did you get that?"

"From one of the bodies out there on the floor. He was

about my size. I suggest that you do the same thing with your friend here."

He saw Karl's eyes flick around the car, at the forms huddled miserably in the darkness, and added hastily, "None of them realizes what's ahead. It would do no good to tell them. They can do nothing. Save yourself."

"Why would you tell me this?"

"The old woman at the other end of the car was my aunt. I saw that you tried to help her. I wanted you to know."

"How do you know so much about Dachau?"

The man cupped a hand and spoke quietly into Karl's ear. "I am a child of Zion. Someday, we will all be. We will go to Palestine. We have to live for that, even if it means that we deny the fact that we are Jews, for a time. We have to live to tell the outside world what is happening here."

As Karl watched, the man took off the jacket and shirt and put on the new ones. Karl paused, then took the shirt from Ludwig Kern. He changed clothes and replaced Ludwig's with his own. The man, whose name he had never gotten, slipped back into the crowded, stinking darkness of the car. Karl imagined that he would be putting his own jacket and shirt on the corpse, forcing himself to dress Kern's corpse in his own incriminating clothes. He wished that he had asked the man's name.

It was less than an hour later when the train started to slow and eventually came to a halt. It was night, but as the door was flung open the car suddenly seemed to be bathed in sunlight. Karl just had time to register that bright searchlights were being aimed at the cars, before twenty men in striped clothes, obviously prisoners, leaped into the car, shouting at the passengers.

"Out—out! Move quickly." Those who could not get to their feet were beaten with truncheons and tossed to the siding. Karl moved quickly, avoiding getting hit, and jumped to the gravel siding. The searchlights were blinding; he tried to shield his agonized eyes from the glare, but he could still see little. Behind him, the prisoners who had emptied the train, were removing the bodies of the dead. There were a huge number of them. They laid them out side by side on the gravel and started to check their stenciled clothes against what appeared to be a manifest. Nearby, an SS captain supervised, checking their count against his own copy of the list.

The process seemed to go on indefinitely. Karl stood where a guard had told him, with a group all also wearing the *P* stencil on their clothes. He noticed that all of the passengers who had worn the Star of David were moved far off to the left end of the siding. Perhaps the man had been right.

A guard ordered Karl's column to march quickly. Karl could barely walk, but he managed when he saw a man fall several yards ahead. The man was battered by rifle butts, and Karl was sure that several bones were broken. The guard ordered two other prisoners to help the injured man, and they did, fearing that they might get the same treatment. Karl tried to move quickly, hoping to remain as anonymous as possible. Some distance from the train, they were herded into a large stockade area, surrounded by guard towers and more blinding searchlights. Karl's cramped muscles were screaming with pain by the time the guard at the front of the column ordered it to halt.

They stood there for what seemed like an hour, while the front of the column was split into two parts. Each rank was marched to a small desk lit from behind by bright lights at the top of a distant building. The structure was long and low and looked something like an army barracks. Karl's rank moved faster than the other, and soon he could see that each of the new prisoners was being stopped at the table and interrogated by a man who appeared to be a high-ranking SS officer. Karl tried to listen as the prisoners in front of him were asked the same series of questions that he was going to have to answer. After the first desk, they were stopped at a second. At the second desk, there were two clerks, who, themselves prisoners in striped uniforms, frantically scribbled things on cards, which he assumed were for the camp records.

Suddenly Karl stopped in his tracks. His blood chilled at what he heard.

In the distance, far to the other side of the train, he could hear a volley of shots. It sounded like machine-gun fire. It came from the direction where the separate column of Jews had been marched. He craned his neck back and forth to see if he could find that anonymous man from the train. He could not. Had the man been right? Had all of the Jews just died? He shivered and moved on.

The line moved faster now, and in a matter of minutes, Karl was face to face with the bored officer at the first desk. The man had a copy of the manifest in front of him.

"Your name?"

"Ludwig Kern, sir."

"Your crime?"

Karl thought quickly. "Political, sir. I was a Socialist." He tried to keep his eyes averted as he spoke. The officer looked at the list for a few minutes and nodded. "Your profession?"

"I am a doctor, sir."

"Very well, move on. Next?"

Karl moved to the second table. Oddly, the prisoner clerks asked the same last question. "Trade or profession?"

"Doctor."

The clerk looked up, his eyes hollow and deep. Karl noticed that the man's prisoner uniform bore the letter *K*. He did not know what it meant, probably some kind of superior in the hierarchy of the prison population.

"We have no more need of doctors. We'll get you some exercise. You can treat the rocks in the quarry. Perhaps they will thank you for it." He turned to the other prisoner who was writing out a card. "Labor commando," he barked. The clerk scribbled.

Karl was issued a thin cotton uniform but allowed to keep his own shoes. "You'll need them in the quarry," he was told. He was also issued a wooden soup bowl and told to carry it with him at all times. To lose it was to fail to get a ration. "People don't live long without rations," the clerk told him. After these insane three days since he was arrested, Karl listened and said nothing. He and some other prisoners were assigned a barracks, where they slept on wooden racks, three jammed into the space meant for one.

Only an hour after Karl had crawled gratefully into his rack, a whistle blew at the end of the barracks. Prisoners dove from their racks and lined up at attention. Karl followed, groggily trying to imitate their movements. Some of the thinner, older prisoners who were too slow getting out of the racks were slapped and prodded by a man with the now familiar *K* on his chest.

This man strode to the end of the barracks, looking down the line of prisoners. There were about a hundred prisoners in the line. "Who are the new ones among you? Raise your hands."

Karl and a dozen or so others did.

"Very well. Lower them," the man said. "I am Georg. I am the Kapo of Block Twenty-one. Is that clear?"

The prisoners nodded. Kapo meant leader.

"Answer me. When you answer, you will say, 'Yes, Kapo.' Is that clear?"

"Yes, Kapo." Their voices were a ragged chain.

"Louder."

"YES, KAPO!" Karl bellowed with the rest.

"You are lucky to be here. You are alive, and you are not Jews. Things are a lot worse over there on the Jewish side. Roll call will be in fifteen minutes. After that, you will assemble at the front of the block, and you will be marched to work. You all have been given assignments." He pulled a small pack of cards from the pocket of his uniform. Karl noticed that *he* did not have the luxury of a pocket. There had to be some prestige in being a Kapo.

"Remember this. The SS runs this camp. But Georg the Kapo runs this block. You are in my hands. If I say for them to kill you, they will. Do not forget that. Following roll call, you will be given a ration. You will get another after you have come back from your jobs." He stopped and leafed through the pack of cards. He stopped, glanced down the bay, then to the cards again.

"Kern, Ludwig—one step forward."

Karl was suddenly terrified. Had they discovered the ruse? Were they going to kill him? He stepped forward, as ordered. "Here, Kapo."

"Come with me." Georg turned and headed toward the rear of the barracks. Karl dutifully followed. Georg led him into a small room, with a desk, many files, and a bed in the corner. A young boy, no more than twelve, lay nude on the bed.

"Take care of him," Georg barked.

Karl approached, got down on one knee, and looked carefully at the sleeping child. Gently, he shook him awake. The boy's eyes went wide for a second. "Don't worry. Georg has asked me to look at you. I'm a doctor." The boy said nothing but seemed calmer. The right side of his head had been gashed, and caked blood had run down toward his ear. Karl palpated the area, and the boy moaned. There didn't seem to be a fracture, though he had taken a nasty blow.

Karl turned to Georg, who stood a few feet away. "Is it permitted to ask a few questions, Kapo?"

"Yes. What?"

"When did this happen?"

"Yesterday. One of the other leaders hit him. The bastard will pay, too. No one messes with Georg's—little friend."

Karl nodded, trying to hide his gush of nausea, his loathing. A twelve year old used like this! "I want him well again," the Kapo growled. "How serious is it?"

"I don't think it's a fracture, but it's almost impossible to tell without the right equipment. There are many things that I would have to check."

Georg strode past Karl and grabbed a parcel from the floor, which he placed at Karl's feet. "See if this will help—and mind that you don't breathe a word of this, or you're a dead man. Is that clear?"

"Quite clear, Kapo. Quite." Karl ripped open the carton and saw that it contained dressings and iodine, a stethoscope, an examining light, and some other paraphernalia that he was sure was quite rare in Dachau.

It took him fifteen minutes to examine the boy. He cleaned

the wound and dressed it. "He should be kept quiet for three days, Kapo."

"Why?"

"It is impossible to determine, without further equipment, the severity of the head wound. If the boy is kept from too much movement for several days, we can be sure that he will be relatively free of danger."

Georg, a tall, broad-chested man with arms like a butcher, folded his thick arms and stared at Karl. "Put that stuff back into the box and put the box back in the corner." Karl did as he was told.

"All right. You stay here with him for the rest of the day. You will be answered for at roll call. Consider yourself lucky that you have been spared a day in the quarry. The other newcomers are about to be baptized about what 'work makes you free' really means."

"Kapo?" Karl didn't understand.

"It gets you free of life, Doktor—what was your name?"

"Kern, Kapo. Doktor Ludwig Kern."

## 22

A week after Karl arrived at Dachau, a report was routed back through SS channels to Kurt in Stuttgart. The wording was simple: "Prisoner Karl Mittenberg died in transit."

Kurt called Eric at the clinic some hours after receiving the news and simply relayed the message.

"What was the cause of death?" Eric asked, numbed, though he half expected something like this.

"The message does not state. It simply says that he died in

transit. He might have fallen ill—it could have been any-thing. The chances were, Eric, that even if I had tried to do something, there would not have been time. I checked the shipping dispatches. He was on the train to Dachau at the time that you called me. He might have been dead already. There is, of course, no real way of telling. My condolences."

"Thank you for calling, Kurt."

"Oh, Eric. There is some good news amid all of this trouble."

"Is there?" There was ice in Eric's voice.

"Anya and I are going to have a child. We just found out."

"Congratulations. How far along is she?"

"Six weeks, we think."

"Who is the gynecologist?"

"His name is Waldrup. Ernst Waldrup. Do you know him?"

"Yes. He's said to be quite good. Congratulations."

"Thank you, Eric. I'm sorry about the Mittenberg affair. As I mentioned, there was nothing that I could have done, given when he died."

"Understood, Kurt. Again, congratulations."

"Oh, Eric. Please don't tell Father. We would like to do that ourselves."

"Certainly." He hung up, then sat perfectly still for what seemed like a long time. He looked at his coffee mug, drained after he had seen his last patient of the day. Karl had given it to him some years earlier. Dr. Eric von Kleist had been engraved on it in anticipation of his finishing medical school.

With a scream that reverberated through the halls of the clinic, Eric hurled the mug through the closed window. Shattered glass flew onto the lawn of the clinic.

Seconds later, Greta Heidril dashed into the office. She was a small, fat woman in a white uniform. But her frumpiness was only a disguise. She was the finest nurse that Eric had.

"Herr Doktor? Are you all right?"

He was back behind the desk again. He looked up at her.

"Yes, Greta." His voice was quiet and calm. "It seems that

someone threw a rock through the window. I got angry and threw it back. See to the repair of the window, will you? I am going to my apartment." He got to his feet and without another word, left the office.

Eric wondered where he would find the words to tell Reinhildt about Karl. He told himself he would wait for the right time.

Ironically, that time came the day after Kurt and Anya announced to Johann that they were expecting a baby.

Eric sat behind the desk, studying the test results Reinhildt had handed him.

He looked at her, so pale, so fragile—yet so brave.

"You are pregnant. About six weeks, I think."

Reinhildt nodded. "I was sure," she said. "It was something that I knew as sure as—" She stopped in mid-sentence.

"As sure as what?"

She looked away.

"As sure as what, Reinhildt?"

"As sure as many things. As sure as that I am unhappy. As sure as many things."

"There is something else, Reinhildt...." He stared at her across the desk, his heart aching for her.

"I know," she said.

"You know what?" He was startled. What strange game were they playing?

"I know that Karl is dead."

He stared across the desk at her. How could she know? He pushed the thought aside. There were too many things he could not explain... too many questions that might never be answered.

They sat there for a long time, in silence. Eric felt the need to speak first. "What do you want to do about it?"

There were tears in her dark eyes as she looked at him. "I

don't really know. It's Karl's child. All that I will ever have of him. Does that limit the choices?"

"Considerably. You want to keep it."

She nodded, on the edge of breaking into tears.

"Well, then . . ." He thought. If there was a choice, at least in the past, it would have been between abortion and marriage. If Karl were alive, there would have been no question. They would have simply married and had a slightly premature child. But that was no longer in their hands. What they had to consider now was the possibility of someone figuring out the parentage of the child. If Karl were known to be the father, the child would, by the latest edict of the Nürnberg Laws, be called a *Mischling*—a half-breed Jew, his paternity would threaten his survival, at least if what had happened to Karl was any indication.

There was, of course, the possibility of marriage, so that Reinhildt could still produce a premature child—one who could pass as fully Aryan. He thought of it but didn't dare mention it to Reinhildt at the moment.

"There are several other possibilities," he continued. "I don't know all of them, but at least one is to have it and raise it. Of course, you would be subject to all of the scorn and abuse that comes with this sort of thing. You understand how difficult that might be?"

He looked at her as she sat there, silent and stoic. She nodded. Her eyes were misty and distant. She had been through more than any human being should be asked to go through, and she had survived it. She had exhibited more strength than anyone he had ever seen. He was sure that the nod meant that she, too, had considered all of the ramifications of the decision that she had made. Part of him wanted to convince her to get an abortion. Still, he was sure he would never be able to convince her to undergo it. She was right; the child would be all that she ever would have of Karl.

In that long moment that they sat quietly across the desk from one another, he could feel another emotion. It was anger—perhaps even remorse, but certainly anger. Why had he not acceded to Kurt's demand? Might there have been a chance? Could he have gotten him out of the hands of the Gestapo? Could there have been another way to do it? He pushed the questions to the back of his mind. He would never know the answers. Yet, there was one nagging question he could not dismiss: who had betrayed Karl? Who could have known that he was a Jew? That was something that he would not forget. He would find out in time and deal with the traitor. Now, there was the immediate problem to be resolved.

"I'll give you a diet and several kinds of vitamins. I want you to start taking them immediately. Get a lot of rest and no more horseback riding. Understand?"

"Yes, Eric."

"I'll handle the first two trimesters of the pregnancy. As we get close to the third, I'll have someone else come in on the case."

"Who?" she asked, for the moment insecure about trusting anyone but her brother.

"There are several good gynecologists in Tübingen. Leave it to me. Do you want me to drive you back to the schloss?"

She shook her head. "I'll drive back. I'm fine. Really I am." She started to get up, and Eric came around the desk to her. He embraced her. "Oh, little sister. My dearest Reinhildt. There has been so much placed on you. Is there anything more that I can do?"

She pulled back and looked at him, her eyes still misted but strong. "Just let me talk to you from time to time? I'll have to have that."

"Of course."

"You know, I'm glad of it, Eric. I'm very glad. If it had to happen this way, what better thing could Karl have left me than his child?"

He couldn't answer. He simply embraced her again, and then she turned to leave.

"Reinhildt?" His voice stopped her.

"Yes?"

"I still think that there is another solution to all of this—

though I can't be sure what it is. Might I just continue to think about it?"

She shrugged. "You can think all that you want, Eric. I doubt that there's anything that I haven't considered. But think about it. I might be wrong."

After she left, Eric sat behind the desk, turning the problem over in his mind. Was there a way that the child could be given a name? A thought flashed through his mind, but he dismissed it as too preposterous.

He finished with the last patients of the day, then set out for his apartment. Not wanting to cook, he stopped at the small restaurant where he and Reinhildt had gone for lunch. He ordered *jäger schnitzel*, his favorite and the speciality of the house. After he was served, he barely picked at the veal and mushrooms. Instead, he ordered a beer and then several schnapps. By the time that he left the restaurant, he was feeling lightheaded.

In the apartment he snapped on the radio and listened to a Swiss station report on the debate that the League of Nations was having about censuring Germany for retaking the Rhineland. With all of the bluster, he knew that there was nothing that they could do about it. The German stations, carefully orchestrated the story according to the party line that Goebbels had dictated. According to them, the Rhineland was rightfully and historically German and the Allies had robbed her of it in 1918. According to the glib announcer, it was the American Jews behind that, as well as the killing reparations that had strangled Germany and driven her into an economic depression worse than in any other country in the world.

Eric switched back to the Swiss station. There was something almost comic about it. He could snap from station to station and listen to two entirely different versions of the same story. He allowed himself the luxury of another schnapps and then glanced at his office schedule for the following day. He had a full slate of early appointments. He downed the glass of schnapps, took a hot shower, and went to bed.

It was perhaps three hours later when he came awake in bed and sat bolt upright.

"It wasn't preposterous. It wasn't!"

He sat there for a long moment again going over the idea that had come to him at the office. It was the compromise that he had been looking for. The child would have a name, and the pressure would be taken from Reinhildt. But until this moment, he hadn't known who.

Now he did. He knew who the man would be!

## 23

The knock at Johann von Kleist's office door was crisp.

"Come in."

The wide door swung open, and a tall, well-built man entered. He wore a blue business suit and carried a slender briefcase.

"Good morning, Johann. You're looking well." The man smiled and moved in the direction of the desk, his hand stretched out.

Johann got up from the chair with difficulty. "I wish I felt well, or at least as well as you say I look. I can't eat the things I like. I'm rationed to one cigar a day, and I can't even drink anymore. What else is there left to me but to work?"

"Well, Johann, you can look forward to becoming a grandfather."

"Oh, yes. Isn't that wonderful?" He sat back in the chair and folded his arms. "Imagine, Kurt and Anya having the first von Kleist grandchild. But they only mentioned it to me last week. How did you know?"

"News travels quickly in Tübingen—especially when it emanates from Schloss von Kleist. The reason that I came over was to see if you wanted to make any arrangements, legal ones, concerning this little von Kleist?"

The old man shrugged. "There is time. Kurt tells me that the baby isn't to be born until—let me see. February, I think it was." The old man fell silent for a minute, then his penetrating blue eyes fixed on those of Werner Altenhoff, personal attorney to the von Kleists.

"Perhaps you are right, Werner. After all, there is the chance that I might not be alive to see the child."

"Don't be silly, Johann. You look better than you have in years. And that was not the reason that I came over here so soon. I just think that the details of this can be gotten out of the way early, so that there is no need to rush things later. You know me. I like to be efficient in such matters."

"Indeed, Werner. You always have." He pressed a button on his desk, and the reply came immediately.

"Bring some coffee for Herr Altenhoff—or," he took his finger from the button, "would you prefer a drink?"

"No. Coffee will be fine."

Werner opened his case. "I have taken the liberty of setting up something tentative. It resembles the trusts that my firm set up for your children. My father's files gave me a format."

"Your father was an excellent lawyer and a good friend. I think of him a great deal these days. It's been six years now, hasn't it? Since—?"

"It will be seven, this month."

"Dear God. Wolf Altenhoff dead almost seven years. When you get old, the time moves quickly. Well, show me those papers."

Werner passed them across the table.

It took them less than half an hour to work out all of the details of the trust. Werner carefully replaced the papers in the case. He would draw them up in final form and bring them back the following day.

"Johann, there was something else that I wanted to speak to you about. It was something more personal."

"Certainly, Werner. Certainly."

"It concerns Reinhildt." He fidgeted.

"Oh, yes." Johann smiled, wistfully. "The fortunes of love and war are about the same, aren't they, Werner? It looked like you two were getting close a few years ago. I was very happy about that. But, well, things don't always work out, do they? I am sorry."

"Don't be sorry, Johann." He paused and wiped his brow with a handkerchief. "Reinhildt and I got—ah—reacquainted while I was settling the details of her trust, almost two months ago."

"Oh," he chuckled. "You never gave up, did you? Not after all of these years. You are like Kurt—tenacious! Then you have been wooing my little one?"

"Yes, Johann. We are in love, sir. We want to get married."

"What? Married?" The old man sat back in the chair and laughed deeply. "Married, you say. Fantastic. Wonderful for the both of you. But all this was so quick. A whirlwind courtship, no? But, why has Reinhildt not come here with you? When is all this to come about?"

"Reinhildt is not here for reasons that I can explain in a minute. In fact, she does not know that I am here. As for the date of the wedding, we would like to have it as soon as possible and make it a small, intimate affair. Perhaps—within the month?"

"So soon? There will be much to plan. I want her to have a large wedding, but then again, I'm only the father, and the bride gets what she wants, doesn't she?"

"Yes, I guess she will."

"But how is it that she doesn't know that you are here?"

"That was the other thing that I had to talk to you about, Johann. She didn't know that I was coming here because we only recently discussed things. This is something that it's very hard to speak about, Johann. Please be patient with me."

The old man leaned forward, sensing something awry. "What is it, Werner?"

"Well, Johann—you are going to be a grandfather a second time."

"What?"

"You are going to be a grandfather a second time. Reinhildt is pregnant."

"I see." Johann's hands knitted tightly into one another. His eyes narrowed, and he peered across the desk in silence for a minute. "And when will this—blessed event occur?"

"About the same time that Kurt and Anya have their child. It's ironic. It was something that I had to tell you man to man. We were planning to get married in any event. This— simply hastened the procedure."

"Reinhildt pregnant? Reinhildt pregnant!" There was no way to read what the old man was thinking through the opaque mask that his face had become. His eyes burned into Werner's. Werner looked down.

"I'm sorry about the way that things happened, Johann. But I do love her, and she loves me. We simply let our passions run away with us. . . ."

The old man said nothing but got up from the chair, again with difficulty, and crossed to where Werner sat. He said nothing but simply looked down at him.

"I do not approve of all of this. I am sure that you know that?"

"I know, Johann, and I know it comes as a shock. But I assure you that we would have been married in any event. I also felt that I rather than Reinhildt had to be the one to tell you—so that you would have no doubts as to my love for her. I hoped that you might be able to feel some joy at the fact that you were going to be a grandfather for the second time. Perhaps I should not have put it that way?"

"And you *do* love one another?" The old man said, as he moved in the direction of the door.

"We do. I can assure you of that."

"This, then is a fait accompli. There is nothing that I can do except assent. Perhaps, Werner, I can be more cordial about the whole thing when the shock of this announcement wears off. For now, thank you for telling me, and would you please leave?"

"Of course, Johann." Werner moved silently to the door and then through it, closing it behind him.

Johann went back to the desk and sat down in the chair. He turned the chair until it faced the window, then looked out on the rolling acres. She was, after all, a woman now. At twenty-one, Lotte had already had two children. Of course, the two of them were married. He shrugged the thought away. There was no changing things. They would do what they would do, in any event. There was no sense in objecting to the inevitable. He had learned that in business many years ago.

He would play the role of the pleased father of the bride. And what of the child's "early" birth? Well, he supposed that they could call it premature. After all, families in such situations had been doing such things as this for centuries.

After a few moments a smile creased his face. Another grandchild. To be sure not carrying the von Kleist name, but—another grandchild.

He reached over and pressed the intercom.

"Yes, sir?"

"Bring me a cognac—a large one. There is something that I am celebrating."

Eric had played a daring game and won. He had approached Reinhildt first with the idea. She had been resistant until Eric had explained all of the positive things that the arrangement could do for the child—Karl's child. He told her that his intent was not to trap Werner, rather to create a business arrangement with him. It was perhaps this latter point that Reinhildt hated most. She was being bartered into a marriage of convenience that was not at all fair to Werner—or in many ways to her. But Eric guessed why Werner had not married, although he wasn't certain until he arranged a meeting with the lawyer. Telling Werner was one of the most difficult tasks he had ever undertaken.

"Pregnant, you say, Eric?" The lawyer clasped his hands behind his back as the two men strolled on the riverside path that wound along the lazy Neckar.

"Yes."

"And who is the father of the child?"

"Reinhildt says that he was a college student whom she met while he was on a summer trip. They were only together for two nights, and then he went back to Holland. Reinhildt has not heard from him since. She is not sure what college he is in. In fact, she is not sure that he even mentioned the right name. It was, of course, foolish of her."

"Has she considered an abortion?"

"We spoke of it, Werner."

"I would assume that with you being a doctor?..."

"Of course. It would be easy to arrange. But she will have none of it. She wants to go ahead and have the child. You know how stubborn she can be."

Werner sighed. "Yes, Eric, I do." He glanced at Eric as they walked. "And now I assume that you want me to marry her to legitimize her ba—her child?"

Eric nodded. "Yes."

"Well," he said, as the two men stopped and sat on a bench, "it's not at all the way I wanted things to happen."

"I know. But, well, you see, I was the one who suggested the possibility of a marriage, and she was the one who, after some consideration about the idea in general, thought of you. There's some small compliment in that, I guess."

"I guess. I don't know, Eric. I have to think about it. I really do."

"Take your time, Werner. Understand that I know the sacrifice that you would be making, if you decided to go through with it."

"I know that, Eric, and I know how hard it was for you to broach it in the first place. There can't be many men whom you could feel close enough to to speak to in this way."

"That's true. And, Werner, if you choose to go through with this, I would like to present you and Reinhildt with a wedding present. Something that would be useful in the raising of the child."

"What's that?"

"Half a million Reichsmarks, placed in escrow in Zurich.

Though it would be in the child's name, you and Reinhildt would be able to draw on it as needed."

Werner looked at him, his eyes narrowing in anger.

"Is that a bribe, Eric?"

"Not in the least. As I said, it's something for the child and all of the years that you would be raising him or her as your own. It's nothing more or less than that. Believe me, Werner."

"Well, if I choose to go through with it, the money will not be necessary. My law practice is doing quite well."

"If you choose to go through with it, I'm afraid that I would have to insist that you take it. I care for you deeply as a friend, Werner, but understand me, this is something that is important to me and to my sister's child. It is something that she does not know about, and I want you never to tell her, no matter what you decide. I wouldn't want her to think that I was bribing you, either." Eric stood up. "I'll let you think about it. Goodbye, Werner. Call me, please, at the clinic, if you want to speak about it again."


The following day Werner called Eric.

"I love her, Eric. I always hoped to marry her—and I still do. But you must step out of it now. This is something Reinhildt and I must handle between us from now on."

Relieved, Eric was only too happy to relinquish his role, especially as he was now certain he had done the right thing. Reinhildt would never forget Karl, but neither would she be able to resist the enormous gift of love Werner was offering her.

Reinhildt and Werner spent a long afternoon in the garden of the schloss. It was he who suggested the way to approach Johann, arguing that the old man was no fool, and even if the "premature" birth did slip by him, certainly Anya and Kurt would pick up on it. When they explained it to Eric, he had to agree.

Weeks later, Eric presented the papers to Werner. An account had been opened at the Kaiserbank in Zurich. A large portion of von Kleist stock had been negotiated in the deal, but Eric felt it was no longer necessary to worry about stock. Reinhildt's and Karl's child was an investment in the future.

## 24

February, 1937

The wedding had gone as Reinhildt wanted it. It had been in the church at Bebenhausen with just a few members of the family present. Happily, Anya was in Berlin with Kurt at the time, attending a party function.

After a small honeymoon, Reinhildt and Werner moved into his modest estate on the far side of Tübingen. Reinhildt felt both grateful and humble when she discovered that Werner had arranged for them to have separate bedrooms. While they were in public, they appeared an idyllic couple, but when they were alone, she was acutely aware of how he strived not to impose himself on her. Gradually, she came to realize how tender and very caring he really was. And, being Reinhildt, she turned to him with warmth and affection. But she never could bring herself to give him her love. That was something she was sure she would never be able to give to anyone again, save to the baby.

Reinhildt's son was born on the first of February, healthy in all respects, with Reinhildt's flashing eyes, and a shock of dark brown hair so like Karl's it brought tears to her eyes. Fortunately, Werner's hair was also dark.

He was christened Ernst Christoph von Kleist Altenhoff. Less than two weeks later, Anya gave birth to her son.

Named Heinrich Johann von Kleist, after his great-grandfather and his grandfather, this child was as fair as Ernst was dark. The children were opposites, and history would prove that that was true in more ways than appearance.

Reinhildt took the call herself. She had been watching Ernst for the afternoon, it being the day that the nurse was allowed a bit of free time to go into town to shop.

"Reinhildt? This is your father."

She paused for a second, startled. It was not like her father to place a call himself. She was used to a domestic announcing him and keeping her waiting until he got on the line. In fact, it was unlike her father to call her at all, unless there was something very wrong.

"Yes, Father. What a wonderful treat, to hear from you this way. What can I do for you?"

"You have heard about Anya and her little one?"

"Yes, I have. It's—wonderful, Father. I'm so happy for her."

She remembered the time, less than a week in the past, when Johann had first seen *her* son. He had remarked that he had looked like his mother and that was all.

"Well, I would like to get both of my grandchildren together at the schloss. I hope that that will suit you and Werner. I have already spoken to Kurt and Anya. Will the Sunday after next be all right?"

"Yes, Father, of course. Whatever you decide."

"Fine. I will get to you with the details. Goodbye, Reinhildt."

"Goodbye, Father."

She sat in the living room and felt like a fraud. The last thing she wanted to do was go to the schloss—especially with having to face Anya and Kurt. Still, it was something she had to do. At least Werner would be there. She had come to depend on him—yes, to care for him over these last months. He had made no demands on her, and though they had never shared a bed, he had been a devoted husband. She wondered if, perhaps, he had a mistress in the town. It wouldn't have mattered to her earlier. But now . . . she began to think that it might be another matter. She could look at Karl's son in the nursery crib and still love his father. But, Werner was becoming very dear to her. His gentleness and quiet stability had comforted her deeply. She could not explain it, but a part of her was starting to love the man. The love was nothing that defiled the feelings that she had for Karl. Rather, it complimented them and enhanced them. He had been as excited as if the child had been his own. He could not have postured that—not at least in front of her. She would have known.

She could hear the front door open, and she went to meet Werner, to greet her husband with a happy new resolution in her heart.

It was two weeks later that the gathering at the schloss took place, with all of the pomp and luxury that Johann could muster. Two small cribs had been set up in one corner of the drawing room, which had been festooned with blue crepe paper, in the opposite corner was a buffet, magnificently appointed for a Sunday brunch. Eric noticed that Kurt was in his civilian clothes, which was unusual for him. Anya was in a slightly matronly white dress, while Reinhildt wore green, also matronly, to cover the figure that would take time to reemerge from pregnancy.

Werner and Reinhildt were greeted politely by Anya and Kurt. Eric watched the proceedings and wondered what his father had in mind: this already was no casual family get-together. Klaus Schmidt served champagne, and Johann proposed a toast.

"If I may." He raised a glass. "To both of the von Kleist grandchildren; Heinrich Johann von Kleist and Ernst Christoph von Kleist Altenhoff."

His smile was broad and genuine. Eric had not remembered a time that his father had seemed so genuinely happy.

As the toast was drunk, Eric noticed that Klaus Schmidt passed a note to Kurt. His brother looked at it for only a split second and then crumpled it into a ball and tucked it into his pocket.

"Father?" Kurt's voice was firm, confident. Eric could sense something ominous in it.

"Yes, Kurt?" The old man was beaming.

"There is something you must know. I am sorry that it has come up now. But perhaps it is something that the family should hear together."

Johann paused, part of the happiness draining from his face. "Very well. What is it?"

"More than anything, I would have hoped that my brother Horst could be here on this day. So I sent him a cable. I have just received the response. It seems that Horst could not be here—and not because of his studies. Rather, he has informed me by cable that he is not returning to Germany—ever."

There was a stunned silence in the room. Reinhildt turned to Eric, shock and urgency in her eyes. She crossed to him and spoke quietly. "You never told him?"

"He sent me a cable asking me to say nothing—yet. I honored that. There's something wrong here. Kurt would never have sent a cable to Horst. We know him too well. And Horst would not have sent such a message back. No. That's not like Horst at all. If he was going to make a pronouncement, he would have communicated it to me or to you first. There is something wrong with all of this. Kurt's timing is too dramatic—too pat."

Whatever the nature of the timing, it seemed to have the planned effect.

Johann turned, striding off in the direction of the huge fireplace. Finally, he turned back to the small group that stood silently, awaiting a reaction from him. He still held the champagne glass in his hand. Before he spoke, he drained the glass, then suddenly turned and smashed it into the fireplace. "It is done. My—" He paused, and for a second, Eric worried about his father. He seemed suddenly tired and frail.

"My—" Again, he paused, staring for a second at the hand that had held the glass. He balled the hand into a fist.

"My . . . youngest son . . . is dead. He is dead. DEAD!" His voice rose in shrillness until Ernst woke crying and Heinrich started to stir. Both mothers went to their children, and Eric took a step in the direction of his father. He stopped and turned to Kurt, who was standing quietly next to Klaus Schmidt.

Eric had never been one to trust his intuition. His medical training had belied it all too often. Still, the sudden revelation he had now was too clear to be denied. The betrayal of Karl, the firing of all the Jewish servants, and so many other things that had managed to slip into Kurt's hands—they had something to do with Klaus Schmidt. But how? The man had been with the family long before there were such things as Nazis. He had spent the better part of his adult life with Lotte and the children, caring for the details of the schloss with a feverish tenacity. Now he was allied with Kurt against the rest of them. Of that Eric was certain. But why? How?

Johann was dangerously livid. "His name will not be mentioned in this house again—not as long as I live. Is that perfectly clear?" The five in the room dared not say anything. They simply nodded. Johann strode across the room and stopped at the two cradles in the corner. "They," he said, "*they* will be the new heirs." His voice awakened Heinrich, who started to cry. The old man looked confused and crossed back to Kurt and Eric. He pointed back in the direction of the cradles. "They," he said in a quieter tone, "*they* will get the inheritance that Horst would have gotten. They will share in it—the two of them, my two grandsons."

Both mothers were trying to quiet their crying children. Eric and Kurt kept a discreet distance between them. Johann's voice was broken now, almost pleading. "You, my sons, you understand why I must do this? Even at the hardest times— even when you, Eric, decided to go into medicine—none of you deserted his family or his country. Neither of you did. Now Horst has done just that. It is unforgivable. Absolutely intolerable. I will not hear his name again."

Eric saw that the old man was quivering, obviously weak at

the knees. Moving forward, he took his father by the arm. "Perhaps you'd better sit down, Father—just for a moment."

Johann looked through Eric for a long moment, as if trying to focus his eyes on his eldest son. "Yes, Eric . . . perhaps I'd better."

The gathering dissolved into polite, quiet conversation, and in less than half an hour they left. Except Eric, who had gotten his bag from the car and proceeded to take his father's blood pressure. The systolic reading was just above two hundred and the diastolic was a fraction over one hundred. He gave the old man a mild sedative and saw him to his bed.

What had been the purpose of it all? he wondered as he drove back to his apartment. Why now? Certainly, there was a liaison between Kurt and Schmidt. But if a letter or other communication from Horst had been intercepted, why wait till now? The truth struck him like a mailed fist. He pulled the car to the side of the road, watching as the clouds swept a winter storm across the valley. The rain or snow would come hard on its heels. He got out of the small sports car and pulled the top up. When he got back inside, he sat and thought. It had to be. Somehow, Kurt and Schmidt had discovered that Karl was a Jew. There was a good chance that they also knew that Karl was Ernst's father. Even if they weren't sure, Werner's speedy courtship and the premature birth of the child would tip them off.

But what were they trying now? Why announce Horst's defection at that precise moment? Had they simply waited for a moment when the old man was happy and off guard, knowing that he was in danger of a stroke or a coronary if he got too upset?

Eric tried to dismiss the suspicion, but it clung to him like the cold on a January morning. Could his brother be so callous?

He shuddered and started the car. The first wet snowflakes were spattering across the windshield as he got to his apartment. He went inside and sat looking outside at the weather. He would have none of it, he thought. No more intrigue, no more trying to control anything. He would hurl himself into medicine with a renewed vigor. Perhaps it would be for the next generation to solve things. His stomach felt like there had been a stone planted in it. He tried to think when the stone had not been there. He remembered that the feeling had started with the decision to go to medical school. It had been there in one way or another ever since. It was not fair. He reached for the bottle of schnapps in the liquor cabinet. It was empty. He had forgotten that he had finished it the past week. He put the empty bottle in the trash. He had dramatically increased his consumption of alcohol, and he knew it. Anesthetic, he had called it. But now he had to wonder if it had become more than that. He determined to limit himself to one glass of wine with dinner and to refrain from keeping alcohol in the house.

He went back to the window and looked out to a mix of wet snow and rain that pelted at the pane. Yes, he thought. He would let the next generation settle things—if there was to be a next generation. Let Kurt and Anya have it. Reinhildt had adjusted and seemed to be making the best of things. She even seemed a bit happy with Werner. There was no reason for Eric to worry about anything except his own happiness. He laughed. It had been so long since he had truly been happy that he wondered if he remembered what it was.

## 25

*From the Journal of Eric von Kleist*

*November 9, 1938*

*I visited Reinhildt today, as I do about twice a month. There seems to be a warm and meaningful*

*relationship between Werner and her now. He has
accepted Ernst as a son. And there are times that I
feel that he has forgotten the arrangement that we
made more than two years ago, though, deep inside I
am sure that this is not so.*

*A letter from Horst arrived last week, and what a
joy it was. He graduated third in his class and was
offered a scholarship to graduate school. He says
that he took it and that he is deep in study. He
mentioned Diana Lassiter again and enclosed a snap
of the two of them. They were on a beach, somewhere, arm in arm. She's beautiful, and he looks
happy. Despite my anger at him when he wrote that
he wasn't coming home, I am beginning to think that
he might have made the right decision. Things are
going mad in Europe. Hitler has managed to gobble
up Austria, and the Sudetenland Czechs are suddenly
Germans after the fool Chamberlain simply handed
the land over at Munich. I can only see it ending in a
conflagration that will consume all of us. Perhaps I
should go to the United States? I've thought of it
more and more in the last year.*

He closed the journal, which was little more than a small
loose-leaf notebook, and locked it in the bottom drawer of his
desk. He sipped at the coffee in the mug. It was cold. He
could not remember how long it had been sitting there. The
day had been long, hard. It had begun just past five in the
morning with an emergency appendectomy on a child of
seven. The mother had brought the child to the clinic in the
middle of the night. Had she waited, the chances were that
the swollen organ would have burst and filled the entire gut
with poison. Instead, Eric's quick, deft hands had removed
it, and now the child had a scar that he could show off to his
schoolmates.

He looked out the window to see a real rain pounding at
the valley, with jagged streaks of lightning illuminating the

area for seconds at a time in the early darkness. It was unusual for the mid-fall. Luckily, he had had the top of the sports car up when he came in during the early morning chill.

As he watched the storm, the door burst open. Greta Heidrich stood there, eyes wide, beside herself.

"Herr Doktor! On th-the main road . . . there has been an accident. . . . We just got the call. You must go there quickly."

He got to his feet and again looked out into the rain. The day was going to get longer still, he thought.

"All right, Greta. Where is it? Do they know how many were injured? Why couldn't they get someone else?" The last was said, sotto voce.

"But, Doktor—it was Herr Altenhoff and your sister."

"What?"

"Yes—yes. Herr Altenhoff and your sister on the mountain road."

"Get my bag." He grabbed his jacket and topcoat, after tearing off the white hospital jacket. Greta gave him his bag, and he dashed out the door, heading for the parking lot in the downpour.

Though the traffic was blessedly sparse at that time of night, Eric still managed to skid several times on the narrow streets. It had been a dry fall, and this was the first real rain in weeks. As such, the first few minutes of the storm had mixed rainwater with the road dirt and tar that had deposited itself on the roads. They were as slick as if they had been ice covered.

Eric turned from the main street area off to the right and started to the east. They would have to be up ahead on the winding few miles of Bergstrasse. It was narrow and treacherous even when it was dry and visibility was good. As it was, Eric's windshield wipers could barely keep up with the flow of water that battered them. He could see less than fifty feet in front of him. A glance in his rear-view mirror told him that the ambulance that he had asked Greta to call was only a few hundred yards behind him. The red lights were a glow in the distance, and he could hear the warble of the siren.

Ahead, he could see the glow of flares in the road. He slowed and slipped the car inside the protection of the last flare, left the engine running and the headlights on, grabbed his bag, ran in the direction of the other flares. The police car was some fifteen yards behind the battered Mercedes sedan. The car had skidded to the left and hit a poplar tree broadside. It looked as if the impact had been right at the driver's door, for the frame was fractured and bent around the tree at a grotesque angle. Two policemen were shining lights into what was left of the interior of the car.

Eric, slipping as he ran, almost collided with one of the officers.

"Be careful. You'll hurt yourself," the man said.

"I'm a doctor. I am Eric von Kleist."

The policeman shined the light into Eric's face for a second. "Oh, very well, Doctor. Perhaps you can help." He moved the light to the interior of the car. "But I'm afraid that we'll need a wrecker to cut him out of this." Eric looked into the car. Werner was slumped across the driver's seat, with his head resting on the passenger side. The impact would have hit him on the left side.

"Bring the light," Eric said as he trotted around the back of the car. The passenger's door was open, and he hunched down, trying to see what injuries Werner had suffered.

He searched for a pulse. Nothing. He ripped the stethoscope from the bag and placed it against the man's back. Again, nothing.

"You!" he shouted to the other officer. "Point your light into this bag." The man did as he was told, and Eric grabbed for one of the longer, sharper scalpels. He sliced away the jacket that Werner wore and then the shirt, exposing the man's back and neck. He was about to slide a hand under him and turn him over when he saw it.

Werner's head was twisted at a strange angle, off to the right. Eric palpated the neck until he could feel the lump. There was no question about it; Werner's neck was broken. It had to have happened on impact. He looked at the face. The eyes were opened and starting to glaze. There was a look of surprise in them. Werner must have been killed on impact. His body would have been thrown across the car into...

"Where is my sister? Where is she?"

The policeman waved his light toward the cruiser only a few yards away. Its red light still spun, coloring the rain with great swatches of crimson.

He ran to the car. Reinhildt was in the right seat, holding Ernst in her arms. Eric ripped open the right door and knelt in the rain beside her.

"Reinhildt?"

She didn't say anything, simply turned and looked blankly at him.

"Reinhildt," he said, more firmly this time.

She only nodded but said nothing.

There were some cuts on her face and a large bruise on the right side of her head.

"Did you walk to this car? Or did they have to help you?"

"She came under her own power, Doktor." A policeman had come up behind him. Eric was peering intensely into her face as the policeman shone his light on it. He could see her pupils suddenly contract. It was a good sign.

"We don't know about the child, sir. She wouldn't let him go."

Reinhildt's grip around Ernst was viselike. Eric was afraid that in her state of shock, her grasp alone might hurt the toddler. He leaned close to his sister. "Reinhildt, let me take him. I have to."

She shook her head.

"I have to take him to see that he is all right."

She paused as the words started to sink in through the numbing shock. She loosened her grip, and Eric took Ernst from her. Quickly he probed, palpated, and checked every major bone and organ. As far as he could see, the child was all right. Still holding the child, he again knelt down in the rain, next to the door. "He's going to be all right, Reinhildt. Ernst is going to be fine. And you were very lucky. It looks as if you are going to be all right, too."

For the first time, she looked at him, her head slowly turning to the right. "Werner?"

"We're not sure yet." Eric lied. He hated it, but there was no sense in breaking the news in this setting.

"Yes . . . yes, you are . . . E-Eric," she stammered.

"They're going to have to get some tools to get him out, that's all."

"Don't lie, Eric. Don't. He's dead. I know it."

He said nothing but lifted her from the car, while one of the policemen carried Ernst, who had started to cry.

Eric got her into the ambulance and handed the child to her again. "We're going to take you to the main hospital. There might be a need for more treatment than I can give in the clinic. I'll follow in my car and meet the ambulance there."

"What about Werner?"

"As I said, they're going to need equipment to get him out of there. We'll do the best that we can. Once I get you to the hospital, I'll come back and check on things here."

It seemed to mollify her.

They only had to stay at the hospital for a few hours. The staff of doctors, many of them acquaintances of Eric's, ran every test imaginable on Reinhildt and the boy. Their injuries were minor. Eric thought it best to take them to the schloss, and he called ahead, getting Klaus Schmidt, whom he ordered to prepare a room for Reinhildt and an adjoining one for the child.

Klaus sent a car, and it was close to ten when they got to the schloss. The rain had ended, and the sky had cleared, but it was chilly. Schmidt and two of the other servants helped Reinhildt and the child up to their rooms, and Eric managed to get her stretched out on the bed.

Klaus Schmidt stood a discreet distance behind, with one of the upstairs maids. "Is there anything else that I can do, sir?" he asked.

"Is my father here?"

"Yes, sir, but he has retired. I thought it best to wait and ask you if you wanted him awakened."

"Don't. I'll stay the night and see him in the morning. Meanwhile, there are other arrangements that are going to have to be made. Wait outside, and I'll speak to you about them."

Schmidt bowed and glanced at the maid, who curtsied. They quietly left the room.

Eric went back to Reinhildt, who was sitting up on the bed. "Where is Ernst?"

"He's in the next room. There is someone with him. Lie back and rest."

"And Werner, Eric. Why did you lie about Werner?"

"I'm sorry, Reinhildt. I'm sorry." He sat on the edge of the bed and held her.

She pulled away, not in anger, rather because she needed room to speak to him. "I know he's dead. I know it."

"How would you know?"

"As the car skidded into the tree, he dove to the right, trying to cover us with his body. As it hit, he was snapped backward and slammed into the door. He fell back on top of us. He didn't move or speak after that. I thought that he might have broken his neck. We were there for almost fifteen minutes before the police arrived. They had been called by a passing motorist. I knew that he was dead by the time that you arrived."

She was dry eyed and calm, or so it seemed.

"Is there something that I can get you—something that might help you sleep?"

She shook her head. "No. I'll be all right. I want to look in on Ernst, that's all." She started to get up from the bed, and Eric tried to help her. "No, Eric. I'll be fine." There was something deeply wrong. It was a kind of shock that he had not seen before. He could only wait for her to shatter. He stood in the hall as she went into Ernst's room and came out a few minutes later. She headed back to her bedroom. "Good night, Eric. Thank you for all of the help."

Two steps into the room, she fainted. Eric was just behind her. He carried her to the bed and slipped her under the covers, then gave her an injection. He thought back to the time when he had had to do all of it before—when Karl died. *She's had enough,* he thought. There were only so many things that should befall anyone in a lifetime. Reinhildt had had more than enough for several. Thank God Ernst was all right.

He turned out the light and left the room. Klaus Schmidt was passing in the hall as he closed the door. "Is Frau Altenhoff all right, sir?"

Eric stared at the small, squat man. For some strange reason, he wanted to hit him, but he resisted the temptation. "She's well—as anyone could expect, Klaus. Get a room prepared for me. You mentioned Anya and Kurt were not here?"

"That's correct, sir. They are on an inspection tour at the Weser plant. It was something about shipbuilding alterations, I think. They went with some officials."

"They will need to be contacted. So will the Altenhoff family, in Stuttgart."

"Sir?"

"Werner Altenhoff is dead, Klaus. His neck was broken when the car hit the tree."

"I'm so sorry, sir. I'll make the arrangements." He waddled off along the hall before Eric could say anything more. Eric stared after him, ever more sure that this was the man who, along with Kurt, had betrayed Karl.

He went down to the drawing room, opened the liquor cabinet, poured a schnapps, then sat in the chair near the picture window, which overlooked the city below.

There was something wrong.

The sky. . . . It was red, like the rain-soaked mountain road had been in the glare of the police car's light.

The door opened, and a maid came in. She stopped in her tracks when she saw Eric. "Oh, I'm sorry, sir. I didn't know anyone was here. Please forgive my intrusion?" She turned and started to scurry out. Eric stopped her with his voice. "Excuse me. Do you know what the trouble is down there in the town? There seems to be a rather large fire in the middle of the city."

"No, sir. I'm afraid that I don't. Shall I inquire for you?"

He turned and again looked at the glow. The fire was a large one, and it seemed to be spreading.

The girl returned in a few minutes. "Sir?"

"Yes?"

"Well, it's rather complicated. It seems that the ambassador to France was killed in Paris. I believe his name was Von Rath?" Eric vaguely knew the name, though little more than that. "Yes? How does that connect to the fire in the town?"

"Well, sir, it appears that the man who killed him was a Zionist. They caught him—it was on the radio in the servants' quarters—but now there are mobs in the streets. They are destroying the Jewish shops, breaking the glass windows and throwing torches. A terrible thing, sir."

"What, the burning?"

"No, sir. I'm sure that it is all deserved. I meant the death of the ambassador."

"I see. That will be all."

"Yes, sir."

She left, closing the door behind her. Eric looked out the window. The glow was still in the sky, and Eric was sure that the police and fire units of the city would be "unavailable" to go to the aid of the Jews.

Perhaps, he thought, it was better that Karl was dead.

The thoughts that he'd written in the journal late in the afternoon drifted into his memory. He had been thinking of leaving Germany. Suddenly the thought evaporated, dancing away like a drop of water on a hot griddle. There was no chance that he would leave now, not with Ernst and Reinhildt alone. He would have to take the role of Karl—and of Werner. He would have to become Uncle Eric.

He watched the glow in the sky and sipped the drink that he had poured. It was a long time before he went to bed.

# 26

Mrs. Judith Tilly was widowed for just over a year before her friends convinced her to leave Des Moines for a vacation. Charles had died of a coronary after they had been married for twenty-six years, and he had left her more than comfortable. So, after some convincing, she decided to visit Europe. She was just arriving at Basel, Switzerland, when she realized that she had grown tired of the tour. She had seen more castles on the Rhine than she would be able to remember for the rest of her life.

They had said when they had left Munich that there would be a half-hour stop in Basel. Part of it was to get through two sets of customs. And part was to change engines. Something about the size of the rails, or was it the electric power? Judith Tilly couldn't remember. It was enough that they were going to be in the station for a time. She could walk a bit. After weeks of sitting on tour buses, she welcomed the freedom.

She stepped to the door and clung to the handrail as she came down the four iron steps that led to the platform. Looking down, she saw that steam was coming from the underpinning of the train. And there was something else.

She screamed.

What she had seen was a hand clinging to one of the steel rods. The hand let go of the rod after her scream, and a body tumbled out from the rods to the tracks.

Train personnel were coming from all directions. Two of the trainmen grabbed the body and pulled it to the platform.

It was a man, dressed in rags, incredibly thin. He was half frozen but still alive, and the trainmen pulled blankets from the train to put around him, while yelling to the others in the station to get a doctor and an ambulance. While they waited, they tried to pull the man back to consciousness with hot coffee from the train's dining car.

He was shivering, despite the blanket, and barely conscious when the police and the ambulance arrived. The policeman hunkered down next to the man. "What is your name? Where do you come from?"

The man's lips moved, but there were no words.

"Can you hear me? What is your name, and where do you come from?"

Even as the policeman asked the questions, a commotion was building down the track on the German side of the Swiss frontier.

The German border guards, realizing that something had escaped their attention in their search of the train as it crossed the border, went right to the gates, where they were confronted by their Swiss counterparts, who refused them entrance. After a few minutes of haggling, the head German customs official was allowed to cross the border alone. He glanced at the man who lay prostrate on the platform. It only took him a second to recognize the tattered uniform.

"He is German. He came over on the train. We have to take him back."

The policeman ignored him, listening as the shivering form whispered something in his ear. Then, "No. You can't take him. Not now, at any rate. He is sick, and besides, he has said that he seeks political asylum. This will have to be decided by the politicians—not you and me."

"He is still a German and must come back with us." The German official insisted.

"He is no one now, no one but a man on Swiss soil. Lodge a complaint through your embassy in Geneva. That is all that I can tell you. If he'd fallen from the train on your side of the border, then he would be your problem. On this side, he's ours. That's just the way it is. Now, get back on your side, before we start an international incident."

Reluctantly the German went back across the fence that marked the division between the two customs areas of the station.

The man was whispering again. The policeman leaned down.

"I . . . am Mittenberg . . . Karl Mittenberg. . . . I am a doctor . . . a German. . . . I ask political asylum."

They took him to the central hospital in Basel, where they treated him for exposure and malnutrition. He slept the better part of the first day and night. When he awoke, he thought back to what had happened to him. . . .

Georg had lasted more than a year and a half before he swindled an SS guard of some loot taken from prisoners. The guard had shot him in the head and made Karl the new Kapo. He was not proud of the things that he had done then. He had been harsh with prisoners when the guards were in sight and helped them where he could when there were no black uniforms in the area. He had stolen food and started a black-market operation to get supplies to the sick in the block. Each day that they were marched to the quarry, they managed to produce the quota that they had been allotted. This kept them from the truncheons of the SS. The food was barely adequate to sustain life, not to mention twelve hours' daily in the quarry.

It was then that the typhus epidemic broke out in the camp. Karl was pulled from the Kapo job in the quarry and put into the hospital, where he treated the staff that had come down with the disease. The prisoners were forced to fend for themselves.

Hundreds died. The bodies, Karl warned the SS doctors, would have to be incinerated as soon as possible. They gave him the task of overseeing the operation. A detachment of prisoners was detailed to move the corpses from the barracks each morning after roll call. They were piled on wagons that

were drawn by hand to the railroad siding. They were
dumped in the cars and moved to a spot some three miles
distant from the camp. It was the first time that Karl had seen
the burning pits. He had smelled them at a distance, and he
had seen the glow of their fires in the night sky. But it was
something that Georg, while he was still alive, warned Karl
never to ask about. Confidentially, he had whispered, the
smoke and the stench came from Jews. The bodies were
being disposed of in the pits. "Jews burn well," Georg
quipped.

The pit was perhaps two hundred feet across. The bodies
were dragged to the edge and thrown in. In the hellish
bottom of the pit, Jewish prisoners, barely more than skele-
tons themselves, dragged the bodies into a line and probed in
the mouths of the cadavers, yanking gold teeth and dropping
them into a bucket, held by a Kapo. Finally, they scrambled
from the pit, and the bodies were soaked with a mix of
benzine and fuel oil. The fire was lit, and the corpses started
to burn.

The process went on most of the day. Karl was heading
back across the field to supervise the unloading of another
batch when, passing the engineers and firemen from the
train, he heard one of them mention that they were going to
have to move back to the siding as the engine was needed to
haul a passenger rig to Munich and then to Basel.

Now that he thought back on it, he was amazed how calmly
he had acted. He had not hesitated, had not stopped to think.
He merely walked to the engine and, glancing around to be
sure he hadn't been spotted in the failing light, had climbed
under the huge machine and swung himself onto the support
rods. There he clung as the train moved to Munich. In the
yards he waited until it was coupled with the passenger train,
and then he wove his way through the maze of rods and
suspension systems into a position where he was near a steam
jet from the interior heating system. After the chill of the
night air in the thin prisoner's uniform, the warmth of the
steel apparatus made him giddy. He ripped strips from his

uniform and strapped himself into position. And held on until he knew that the train was in Switzerland.


"Good morning, Herr Doktor Mittenberg."

The doctor who came to his room was small and slender, his white coat was starched and pressed. Karl had not seen such cleanliness in over two years.

"Good morning," Karl said. He was still exhausted, but he willed himself to be alert: the officious man with the doctor had the smell of a bureaucrat.

"We are glad to see you well."

Karl listened to the man's accent. Thank God he was not German. The man was a Swiss, but, even so, Karl could not allow himself to relax. There was a chance that they might not believe him. They might think that he was a German spy or a criminal.

"Were you aware, Doctor, that when you arrived, you weighed only a hundred and five pounds?"

"Yes, sir. I was on a restricted diet where I came from."

"And, where was that, Doctor?" It was the official.

"Dachau, sir. It's a small town outside of Munich. There is a concentration camp there. There were perhaps forty thousand prisoners there when I escaped."

"What crime were you convicted of, Doctor?"

"I am a Jew, sir. That is crime enough in Germany, these days."

"How is it that the Germans do not have a record of a Doctor Karl Mittenberg?"

"They have a record of his death in 1936. I was there under the name of Doctor Ludwig Kern. He died on the train to the camp." He explained the rest.

The official was making notes. When Karl finished his story, the official, who had never introduced himself, slipped the papers back into his case and snapped it shut.

"You understand, Doctor, that anyone asking for political asylum, especially in my country, has to be checked thoroughly."

"Of course, sir. But, understand that I am a professional

and would be a contributing member of society. I also have some funds here, in an account in Zurich. I would have to arrange to validate my identity before I could get hold of them, but I am not a vagrant."

"Thank you, Doctor. You have been very helpful."

After the Swiss doctor checked Karl's chart, the two men left, and Karl fell back onto the bed. He had no idea what the disposition of his petition would be. But he was sure of one thing. He would take a scalpel to his throat before he would let them send him back.

Still, there was something else haunting him. He knew that by the time that the train had left the switching yards at Munich, the barracks would be in the middle of roll call. Thousands would be standing in the freezing air, waiting through the methodical calling of the names from each of the blocks. He would be noted as missing immediately.

Then, the SS would have waited twenty-four hours while search teams plied the environs of the camp. After that . . . the hundred men in block twenty-six would be shot. It was the terror they lived with night and day. The entire block would be dead if there was a successful escape. If it were unsuccessful, then the escapee would be brought back and crucified on one of the poplars that lined the parade ground borders. The body would be allowed to stay there as the prisoners were marched by.

They were all dead, now, because he had escaped. He pushed the thought from his mind and tried to close his eyes.

A few minutes later, the door opened and pulled him from the beginnings of sleep. He sat up with difficulty as a white-coated orderly came in with an armful of bedding.

The man looked at him and nodded, then went to the closet and started replenishing the supplies. There was something unusual about the man's actions, something that said that he was only going through the motions. Karl looked to the bedside table on the right and saw the water pitcher. If necessary, he could grab the pitcher and bash the man with it. He propped himself on an elbow and waited.

The man simply kept folding and stacking bedding. Finally,

he looked to Karl. He turned back to the closet, pulling the ragged uniform from the hook and staring quizzically at Karl. He started to approach the bed. Karl allowed his right hand to move in the direction of the pitcher. The man stopped.

"You don't need the pitcher. I'm not going to attack." The accent was clearly German.

"You're German."

"Yes. And so are you, Doctor. I know a great deal about you."

"How?"

"You were in block twenty-six. A lunatic named Georg was the Kapo. He liked little boys."

Karl froze. "How?..."

The man came closer to the bed. Karl's hand came closer to the pitcher.

"No. Don't go for it. Remember the train. The man who told you that a Star of David was a death mark? Would you kill a son of Zion?"

"Dear God." Karl stared slack-jawed at the man for a long moment. Could he have been the same one? Was it possible? He had to be cautious. "Tell me more about the train."

"Not convinced, eh? You helped my aunt. She had dysentery. She died. You were with another man—another doctor, I think. He had been hurt, and I think it was his clothes that you took, in the same way that I took mine from another political prisoner in the car. Convinced now?" The man rolled up the sleeve of the left arm where Karl saw the five-digit number like the one that he bore.

He nodded. "Yes. I'm sorry. Now what?"

"The Germans are going to push hard to get you back. They don't like to advertise what goes on in places like Dachau."

"Places? There are many of them now?"

"You must have heard of them in the camp. I did."

Karl managed to sweep back into the rear areas of his memory. Yes. There was something there. There were names...Buchenwald...Sachsenhausen. There were, indeed, many of them.

"But," Karl said, "there were those with different designations. What were they called? Vernichtungslagern... extermination camps."

"Yes. They are for the Jews. And they are building them all across Germany. It is thought that if there *is* a war, they will spring up all across Europe. Unless we stop it."

"How?"

"You will do it—and I will. Zion, brother, Zion."

"What do you mean?"

The man went to the closet and took out some bedding. Clothing had been neatly placed between each piece. It was the uniform of an orderly. From the corner of the closet, he took a pair of shoes. "I could only guess at the size. Get dressed. The first step is to get you out of the hospital before the Swiss come back with the German consul and ship you back. We think that they will do that—and soon."

"We?"

"Yes. We are a large group, and we get Jews out of Europe."

"To where?"

"To Palestine. Get dressed quickly. I don't want to have to kill anyone to get you out of here."

They moved through the halls of the hospital, and though Karl was still painfully thin, he managed to keep up with the cart full of laundry that his unnamed benefactor pushed. They got to the loading gate and into a car. The driver sped off in the direction of the suburbs. There were more clothes waiting in the car, and the benefactor, who introduced himself as Isaac Ben Aram, told Karl to change into them. After that, there followed a series of intrigues that took them to many parts of the countryside. Karl figured that there were a dozen or more in the group, moving from place to place at night, always farther south. They took a train and got off before the Italian frontier. On the coast they were met by a boat and from there transferred to a ship. Five weeks later, Karl Mittenberg, late of Dachau, stepped onto the warm sand of a beach south of Haifa.

Still, there were several days more where they were on the run. They ended in a camp in the area of Galilee.

Karl was beginning to realize that he had been exfiltrated with speed for a number of reasons. The first, and most important, was that there was a dire shortage of doctors in the movement, which, he had learned, was called the Hagannah. In addition, he had valuable first-hand knowledge of what the Germans were doing to the Jews of Europe. There had been many rumors about the extermination camps, but nothing specific. Now, there were others coming through the pipeline from Europe, and Karl and other doctors were needed to treat them. He had been there; he would know the kinds of injuries to expect. He laughed when Isaac Ben Aram had mentioned that, and Isaac laughed in return. He was one of the few who understood the bitter laugh. There were too many ways to die in a concentration camp to be concerned with or specialize in.

Less than a day after he had arrived, Karl had been told of the almost legendary status of Isaac. He had been in and out of Europe more than five times in a year and a half, gathering information, getting photos of the camps, smuggling Jews out. He had never come close to being caught.

It was dusk on the third night that he was there that Karl stood outside the barracks and looked at the mountains in the distance. He turned suddenly, then relaxed when he realized that it was only Isaac approaching.

"Calm down, Doctor. Though I should not say that. Those are good reflexes to have here. The Arabs have little more love for us than the Germans do. Still, it's good to be home." He took a few steps out into the sand. "For you, I know it's still alien. But for me it's home."

"You were born here?"

"Yes, Doctor. I am what they call a Sabra—a native here."

"I don't know much about those things."

"Understood. Your family converted to Christianity when you were small, I heard." Karl reacted with a mix of surprise and anger at the remark, seeing it as an invasion of privacy. "Wait a minute. I—"

"Don't get all upset, Doctor. If we did not have a complete dossier on you, we would not have risked so much to get you out. We have confidence. There are others who knew you in Dachau, and they have testified to your reliability. We simply had to be certain that you were what you claimed to be. We cannot afford to be wrong about such things. Besides, don't worry about it. You, too, are about to become a Sabra. They are making your passport downstairs."

"They are?"

"Yes. That's why I came up."

Karl looked up at the flat-topped mountain in the distance that caught the rays of the late afternoon sun. "Is there a name for that mountain?"

"That one? Oh, that's famous. But, then again, you would not be expected to know about that." He held a hand up. "No offense, but unless you knew your Old Testament well, you wouldn't have heard of it. That is Mount Tabor, where the forces of Deborah, led by Barak, destroyed their enemies with the help of God. You must read it sometime. It's a very inspiring story. I come here many times in the early evening to look at the mountain.

"Which reminds me. There is another reason that I'm here."

"What?"

"You need a name."

"I have one."

"You need a new one. You are about to become a Sabra. You need a Hebrew name."

Karl thought a moment, then pointed at the mountain again. "What about something to do with that?"

"Excellent. You will be son of the mountain. Ben Tabor—Uri Ben Tabor." Isaac went back inside to tell the engraver the name to put on the passport and other documents.

Karl watched the last of the sun's rays curl in the crevasses of the mountain. For a flickering second a thought crossed his mind. It was something that he had not thought of in more than a year . . . something distant . . . part of a dead past.

Reinhildt.

He let the thought pass. It was something of the dead Karl—not something that the newly born Uri Ben Tabor could be concerned with.

He slowly went back inside.

## 27

*From the Journal of Eric von Kleist*

*September 5, 1939*

*And so, it has begun at last. The true insanity that Hitler wanted for Germany since the time that he took power. We invaded Poland last week. And I wonder why I said "we?" Perhaps, because it is that I, too, am a German. But I do not want to be classed with them.*

*Reinhildt has moved to the schloss. They say that it will be safer there if there are air raids. Goering has said on national radio that if a single bomb falls on German soil, the public could call him "Meyer." It was an obvious slur at the Jews, but despite the fact that the Poles seem to have no air force, I have asked Reinhildt to move back to the schloss with Ernst. It is on the far side of town from the industrial area. Besides, the schloss is more sturdily built than the old Altenhoff estate buildings.*

*Kurt has been away for more than two months. The last letter that Anya got from him said that he was "somewhere in the east." We all expect that he is charging across Poland with his panzer unit. Anya has, at least for the time being, gotten what she always wanted—operational control of Von Kleist A.G. Goebbels has made the most of this, arriving yesterday for films and still pictures of Anya signing papers with Father and Klaus Schmidt, who has been assigned to help her, by Father. Nazis were at the schloss the better part of the day. They even took pictures of her holding little Heinrich. I'm sure that the caption will say something like "Special German mother helps the war effort."*

*Heinrich and Ernst have become a real study in contrast. Heinrich is fair and blue eyed—every inch his father. He tears through the schloss like a little hellion, aggravating his mother. Ernst is painfully shy—like his father, and like his mother for that matter. He clings to her, perhaps too closely, although it's not for me to say. For now, I am glad that Reinhildt is back at the schloss. I spend as much time with her and the little one as I can.*

*Father has asked me to help with inspection of the medical facilities of the plants. He claims that I should not mind as it is not a part of the war effort. I have agreed, to keep peace in the family. It will let me see what kind of reaction there is to the war on the part of the workers. I can't say why I am interested in their attitudes, except that for myself, I loathe it and wonder at the people like my brother and father.*

Attached to Army Group A, Kurt's Waffen SS Panzer unit smashed ahead as one of the lead elements. Using what Goering had called airborne artillery, in the form of the Stuka dive bomber, Kurt's unit and the four divisions that followed it sliced through the entire Lodz Army Group, and in less than ten days was only twenty miles from Warsaw. Weeks later, after the capitol fell, Hitler visited the front line units and promoted Kurt to Sturmbahnführer—major—also awarding him an Iron Cross Second Class. Eric saw the publicity photos when he visited the Saar to inspect one of the plants. He noted that the photos were also sent abroad—or so the captions read—and wondered if Horst would see them—and what he would think. As he moved from complex to complex, he could see that the transition to a wartime production mode was going on with great speed. The Von Kleist Fabrik on the Weser River was producing U-boat hulls, while the Elmshorn factory had been converted totally to the production of two new models of panzers. The huge chemical complex at Höchst had gone over totally to munitions, or so Eric had been told. It was to be his last stop on the tour of plant medical facilities.

He drove through the main gate and slowed as he wound his way through the buildings heading in the direction of the administration area. He remembered that the complex manager's name was Gunther and that the man had a taste for scotch whiskey. He chuckled to himself. Gunther was going to have a hard time getting it now that England and France had entered the war on the side of Poland.

Suddenly something caught his eye off to the right. One of the smaller buildings looked as if it had sustained damage— an explosion of some sort. Or had it been an air raid? There had been several, according to rumor, though it had been officially denied. He thought of Goering's remark and wondered if anyone dared call the air minister "Meyer." But it was not the damage that held his attention, so much as the people working on the repairs. They were clearly not the "Kleistlings" that he had grown accustomed to seeing. They were in rags, some limped, and there were two gray-uniformed guards with rifles nearby. Eric got out of the car and walked across to the group, only to be stopped by a guard before he reached them.

"I am sorry, sir. It is not permitted to go any closer than this."

Eric looked at the man with the rifle. He was young, perhaps in his late teens, and he was unsure of himself.

"Who are those men?"

"Workers, sir."

"Are they in the employ of von Kleist?"

"They are simply workers, sir. I don't know any more than that."

"I want to speak to them."

The guard fidgeted but answered promptly. "I am sorry, sir. But you can't go any closer than this."

"I certainly can. Some of those men look like they need medical attention, and I am a doctor. Let me check them."

"Impossible, sir. I must insist."

None of the workers looked up from their shovels and picks, but Eric could see that another guard was starting to move in his direction. He would get nowhere with these two, and he knew it. "Very well." He turned and strode back to his car.

"Well, who are they, Gunther? I have never seen workers in poorer physical condition."

Gunther, slight and small, a man whose hands were always aflutter, looked away to the window as he spoke. "They are Poles."

"Poles? What are they doing here?"

"The army shipped them here. It seems that their prisoner of war camps were getting overcrowded. After all, there were something like six hundred thousand Polish prisoners in the campaign. The first of them got here about three weeks ago."

"And what happened to that building?"

"The newspapers said that it was an explosion, Herr Doktor."

"And what was it really?"

"An explosion."

"An air attack?"

Gunther turned back to Eric and smiled nervously. "A tiny one, yes. Since then, we have made arrangements for bomb shelters."

"About the workers."

"Guest workers is what they are being called by the government, sir."

"They are in terrible condition. They look underfed and in need of medical attention. The guard out there told me that I could not approach them. I won't have that. If they are working for the company, then they are to be treated like the other workers here. Is that clear?"

"I would like to accommodate you, sir. I was shocked by their condition when they got here, but—" Gunther's hands fluttered.

"But what?"

"They are in the charge of the military. They are kept in a camp near here and shipped in by truck every day with a military guard. Aside from giving them jobs to do, we have no control over them."

"Find out who is in charge of the camp. I want to know, and soon. If I do nothing else for the corporation, I have some control of medical conditions for the workers, and I don't care if they are called guest workers or Martians. Is that clear?"

"I will do the very best that I can, sir. Oh, and there is something else. We are expecting some newsmen in here soon. They will be wanting to take your picture as you inspect the medical facilities. I took the liberty of telling them that it would be all right. Will it be, sir?"

Eric shrugged. "All right. Just don't let them get in the way. Now, let's get to the medical facility."


For the better part of the day, Gunther and Eric roamed the massive complex. In spite of himself, Eric was awed by the size of the empire that his father had assembled in less than thirty years. It chilled him to think of all of it being geared into the Nazi war machine. As far as the medical inspection was concerned, Eric was as methodical as the staff at Goethe had trained him to be. He checked the equipment, the supplies, the carefully controlled drugs, and spoke at length to the medical personnel. He peppered Gunther with questions about the complex in general as well as the medical area. While the answers were immediate and efficient, Gunther feigned ignorance each time that anything related to the war was mentioned.

It was early afternoon when they stopped the tour, and at the invitation of Gunther, Eric ate lunch in the large workers' cafeteria. It was simple fare; wurst, rolls, and beer. Gunther introduced Eric to various administrators and managers, none of whom Eric had ever seen before. As he shook their hands, photographers snapped shots. Eric assumed that a number of them would eventually appear in the von Kleist archives, and he was also sure that several would find their way into Goebbels's hands for propaganda. The latter thought disturbed him, but there was little that he could do about it.

It was late afternoon, and the shifts were changing before Eric and Gunther finally went back to the office. Eric watched from the window as the hordes of workers moved out through the main gate only to be passed by others, who would take up the work until midnight. He noted that there seemed to be no change of shift for the "guest workers." It disturbed him, but he decided to wait and see what kind of information filtered back about it. He was looking out the window and pondering the drive back to Tübingen when Gunther cleared his throat to attract Eric's attention.

"Sir, I would be honored if you would have dinner with me. My wife is an excellent cook. Will your schedule allow for this?"

Eric thought for a moment. He *was* tired from the day. Perhaps he would have dinner with the man, then drive to his apartment in Frankfurt. Then, he could get an early start back to the schloss in the morning.

"We only live two miles down the road—in the town proper. And, sir, the executive suite here in the building is at your disposal, should you wish to spend the night. Or, we would be honored if you would spend the night with us?"

Eric had forgotten the suite. It was the one that Johann had built so that he could be close to the plant operation during the times of difficult projects. It would save him even the drive to Frankfurt. "Yes, Gunther. I would be pleased. We'll take your car, and you can bring me back here afterward. I'll spend the night in the suite. Besides, there are a few more things that we can clear up about the plant, then."

Gunther looked both elated at the prospect of his dinner guest and crestfallen at having to come back to the plant after supper.

Frau Gunther was short, blond, and plump, as were the three boys who sat around the dinner table in the Gunther home. Eric found the dinner table conversation banal, but he was pleasantly surprised at how good a cook Frau Gunther was. He was glad that he had decided to stay rather than try to drive to Frankfurt or Tübingen. After a polite round of after-dinner conversation in the living room, Gunther drove Eric back to the plant.

The two of them worked over some of the findings of the inspection tour, with Eric speaking from his notes and Gunther making more notes for a follow-up check.

It was just after dark when Eric was startled by the warble of a siren.

"What's that? Another change in shift?"

Gunther was on his feet, the color draining from his face. "It's an air raid, sir—like the one that *didn't* happen a week ago. This is another one that is about to *not happen,* I think. We will have to go to the basement. They have just put a shelter down there."

"No, not yet. How close could they be? Turn out the lights, and I'll watch for a few minutes. You can go to the basement if you wish."

Gunther fidgeted but stayed. He turned out the lights, and Eric watched out the window.

In the distance, he could see a few searchlights sweeping the sky in the direction of Frankfurt. He could start to hear the thin crump of anti-aircraft batteries trying to fix the range to the planes.

Above Frankfurt, heading in the direction of Höchst, a few British Hudson bombers, at the limit of their fuel range and launched from bases in France, moved toward the plant, which was starting to black itself out. It was futile, Eric thought, the light from the furnaces would be a beacon, no matter how many of the electric lights in the plant were extinguished.

As they flew closer, he could hear their engines.

"Sir? It's perhaps best that we go to the shelter now?"

Eric nodded, and they headed to the stairs.

The basement had a low ceiling that made Eric hunker down so as not to bash his head, and it was crowded with night staff. They had been there for less than half an hour when Eric started to feel the impact of a few hits on the plant. It was terrifying. He wondered why he had stayed in the office for so long before coming down. He also wondered at how Kurt could revel so in war. It was half an hour later when the all clear sounded and the crowd started to pile out of the basement.

He went back up to the office and looked at some smoke that was coming from the extreme end of the plant. There was little damage—Eric knew the British planes carried only small bomb loads. It was more of a harassment raid than anything else; in a matter of two hours, everything was under control. Nevertheless, when Eric went to the suite that had been prepared for him, he drank a cognac, for he was still shaken from the air raid. It was a long time before he could get to sleep.

In the morning he showered and shaved, then realized that there were no clothes that fit him in the closet of the suite. All of them were Johann's, who was shorter and stouter. He shrugged, and feeling something less than comfortable in the previous day's clothes, he went to the office. Then, with Gunther trailing along, he headed to his car and was pleased to see that it had not been damaged. The courtyard of the administration building was jammed with photographers; some were Goebbels's men; others were from neutral countries. They were following up on the raid of the night before. They took both newsreel and still shots of Eric in front of the building while he again queried Gunther about the "guest workers." Gunther waffled, promising to get him information as soon as possible.

Finally climbing into his car, Eric put the key in the ignition and stopped to find a cigarette. Next to the cigarette pack, in the side pocket of his coat, he found a small, wadded piece of paper. He was about to throw it away when he realized that it had not been there before.

He unwadded it and looked at the hurried handwriting.

> We know what you are doing. We will contact you when the time is right. Remember: some Germans are still Germans. Burn this.

He placed the paper back in his pocket, and barely able to contain himself, he drove some twenty miles in the direction of Tübingen before he pulled to the side of the road and read it again. *Remember: some Germans are still Germans.*

They had been Trost's words, years before. There *was* an underground, despite the madness of the Nazis. He debated calling Trost. No. They said they would contact him. Perhaps there was still hope.

One of the Swedish journalists sold his story and pictures to an American news service. It included a film clip of Eric moving through the factory. A large American newsreel chain purchased the film, and an editor recalled the pictures of Kurt von Kleist getting his Iron Cross from Hitler at the close of the Polish campaign. The man, an ardent interventionist, with a shrewd eye for a story, managed to get the film clip into the newsreels. The title ran: *Head of the von Kleist Empire . . . Czar of the Nazi War Machine!*

It was not something that Eric would take note of, even if he had been informed of it. It would not make a difference in his life until years later.

# 28

**Brest-Litovsk (Poland), June 22, 1941**

Kurt sat with the hatch of the panzer open, smelling the air of the warm summer night. He knew that they had more than an hour before the order to cross the Bug River would come down from Guderian at the head of Panzergruppe Two. North and south of him, on a fifteen-hundred-mile front, more than a hundred thirty divisions waited for the signal. It was to be the largest land invasion ever mounted, this Operation Barbarossa. Kurt had been singularly honored by the position he had been assigned in the order of battle. He had learned his trade with Guderian in France and the low Countries. The battalion he commanded was fast becoming known as "Panzer Group von Kleist," and the German press at home was making the most of it. The letters he received from Anya glowed with the reports of his exploits. He was exactly where he had wanted to be since he had been a child.

The order came at exactly three in the morning, precisely on schedule.

Kurt barked a command into his microphone, and his tank started to rumble across the bridge. As the last tank crossed, he moved into high speed and ordered his column to move into a wedge formation. He had done it. His unit had been the first to cross into "Mother Russia."

In the nine weeks that followed, Kurt's column roared eastward for almost six hundred miles. The Russians were retreating in disorder, and resistance was laughable. By the first of September, Kurt's lead unit had stopped to consolidate near Bobryusk. It was on the second night in the small field camp that his officers surprised Kurt with a belated birthday party.

They drank captured vodka and schnapps that had been sent to them by Guderian himself. There was a makeshift cake, gleaned from what the cooks could put together from the field rations. A toast to the Führer was drunk, followed by one to Kurt. The revels were at their peak at about ten in the evening when a messenger arrived on a motorcycle. The man was mud spattered and weary.

"Sturmbahnführer von Kleist?"

"Yes?" Kurt said, putting down his glass and crossing the tent to the man.

"This is for you, sir. Most secret and personal."

Kurt took it, returned the man's salute, and looked up. A silence had fallen across the officers. He smiled. "I expect it's from Guderian. He'll want to know what to do next."

Amid the roar of laughter, Kurt retreated to the corner of the field tent and opened the seals on the letter.

> *Herr Sturmbahnführer von Kleist,*
>
> *At the direct request of Reichsführer Himmler and with my personal approval, you are to be transferred to an alternate unit for the duration of Operation Barbarossa. It is believed that the heir of such a prestigious family should merit a more challenging and meaningful wartime assignment. Therefore, you are to be assigned to a Totenkopf unit, under the direction of Herr Himmler's RSHA division.*
>
> *I have every confidence that you will serve the fatherland with distinction in that position. The mission that you will undertake is sacred and has been personally ordered by me.*
>
> *A. Hitler*

Kurt was flabbergasted at first. A letter handwritten by the Führer himself and sent by messenger more than six hundred miles into Russia. But in a few minutes the shock wore off, and it was replaced by a flush of anger and a slight feeling of resentment. What was this RSHA? Why under Himmler personally? What kind of unit could give him more prestige than he was getting in this one? He couldn't piece it together.

He frowned. So he would not be in the first tank to enter Moscow, after all. He downed a vodka and told his men. The glitter wore suddenly from the evening as his officers wondered who the new commander might be and where von Kleist was headed next. It would be a week before Kurt himself would find out.

He was flown to Warsaw, where he was driven to the temporary RSHA headquarters. Without delay, he was ushered into the presence of Obergruppenführer Reinhard Heydrich.

"Please be seated, Kurt? If I may call you that?"

"Of course, sir." After months spent at the front, Kurt was amazed at the luxury of the rear area.

"I'm sure that you must be bewildered about the speed with which we moved you?"

"A bit, sir."

"Well, we have an important mission to discuss. Cognac?"

"Yes, thank you, sir."

Heydrich poured the liqueur, then sat behind his desk and savored the cognac before he spoke.

"Kurt, the RSHA is the security arm of the SS. Our job is to apprehend the criminal and undesirable elements in the populations of the conquered countries. You will be a part of that operation. You have been recommended for it because of the zeal with which you attack every mission that you are given. I must tell you that General Guderian was rather upset to lose you, but the Führer himself overruled him."

"I am honored by that, sir," Kurt said glumly. Security elements. Crap. They were going to turn him into a policeman.

Heydrich got up and uncovered a map on the wall. "There are currently three Einsatzgruppen, or special operations groups, working in Russia. We are going to need a fourth. I want you to command it. Your unit will be of a strength of two thousand, and your mission will be to round up and eliminate the subversive elements in this area." His hand swept across a part of the map Kurt was familiar with. Indeed, his units had been there only weeks before.

"Kurt, we are sending you there because you have been through the area before and know many of the villages."

"What are the other specifics, sir?"

"Bluntly, you will round up all of the Jews in each of the towns in the area. You will inform them that they are to be resettled elsewhere. Use the Jewish community groups to help you. Then you will take them outside town and shoot them. A special group will be with you to bury them. Oberst Neeb will brief you on the other specifics. Is all of that clear?"

Kurt sat silently for a second. "Yes, sir," he answered, more from his training than from the comprehension of the task.

It was not until the next day, in the subsequent briefings by other officials of the RSHA, that Kurt realized the gravity of the mission. Together, all of the Einsatzgruppen were to dispose of a million and a half Russian Jews.

The task, Kurt thought, would be indeed staggering. He wondered how much it would detract from the real war effort—how much of Guderian's ammunition and petrol would go into chasing down Jews. It didn't matter, though. It was at the direct order of the Führer, and the order was sacred.

Kurt hurled himself into the task.

# 29

**New Haven, 1941**

"Horst von Kleist—master's in architecture." There was a
polite scattering of applause as the name was read. Horst
ascended the stage and took the scroll from the president of
the graduate school. He looked into the audience and for a
second caught sight of Diana—her flaming red hair marked
her like a beacon. Next to her, Horst could glimpse Richard
Lassiter, the Back Bay Republican industrialist, who had
built, as Johann von Kleist had, an empire from a single small
steel plant. Horst liked the older man. He was firm but
warm, and Horst thought that it was Diana that was responsible for the latter quality. She was an only child whose
mother had died giving her life, and her father had, in his
own words, spoiled her rotten. He could never have guessed
that his daughter would go to college and emerge a wild-eyed
Roosevelt Democrat. Horst had been at their summer home
on Cape Cod many times when Diana and her father had
crossed political swords. Their debates had been fierce, but
there had always been an undertone of love between them.
Diana was given her head, and she took it. She was an avid
horsewoman, sailor, and professional gadfly. She would try
anything on a dare. In fact, she had been the one who
seduced Horst, after they had been out only a few times.
When they had discussed it afterward, she said that he
simply looked as if he "needed a push."

She was what an earlier generation would have called "fast"—and she was dazzling. They had been together five years before Horst managed to summon up the courage to propose. Her reply was that it was "about time."

Three days later, following a large party for Horst at the Cape Cod Lassiter home, Richard and Horst went for a walk along the beach. The elder man had shucked his jacket in the warm June sun. Horst, in his characteristic shirt-sleeves, was sweating with worry: he knew why the old man had asked him to come along on the walk.

"This has been a fortunate week for you, my boy. Citizenship and a graduate degree all at the same time."

Horst nodded and smiled. "I have never been able to thank you enough for the help that you gave me with the citizenship, Mr. Lassiter."

"Why don't you start calling me Richard? Mister makes me feel old." He clapped Horst on the shoulder.

"A habit I'll have to break. My family is formal, to say the least."

"Well, we're not. And, you've made some strides in that direction. The first time that Diana brought you home, I thought that all I would have to say was 'jump' and you'd say 'how high'?"

Horst laughed. "Was it that bad, Richard?"

"It was worse. But the more you call me Richard, the better things get. Now, there's something else that we have to discuss."

"I thought there might be. You normally like to take these walks alone. Although, the last time that I was here, you took one with your board chairman. So, when you don't walk alone, you want to discuss business. Correct?"

"Am I that transparent, or are you that observant?"

"If I say you're transparent, I'll insult you. If I say I'm observant, I'll be arrogant. Let's just say that we both are creatures of habit. It's safer that way."

Lassiter shook his head. "With a daughter like I've got and you as an about-to-be son-in-law, I'll have to be on my toes. But I admit it, it *is* business. Have you considered what you will be doing with this wealth of knowledge you've amassed on industrial architecture?"

Horst clasped his hands behind his back as he walked. Both men stopped to watch a small hermit crab scurrying into a tide pool left by the retreating Atlantic. "Diana hinted that you might ask that question, Richard."

"Good God. And I didn't even mention it to her. Creature of habit again?"

"Perhaps."

"Well, what did she say?"

"She said you'd offer me a job with Lassiter Steel. She said that there was no way in the world you'd let a—these are her words and not mine—'brilliant architect get into the family and not into the company.' I'm afraid that she also said something about the name von Kleist not exactly hurting the situation."

Lassiter threw his head back and laughed. "She's done it again. Right on all counts. Here's what I'm interested in. Oh, and by the way, that other walk that you observed me take on the beach, the one that I took with my board chairman?"

"Yes."

"Well, that was to discuss the same thing. He was the one who approved the offer that I am prepared to make now. Ironic, that you noticed that one."

"I'm afraid that I didn't manage to divine the purpose—and neither did Diana."

"Well, here's the proposition. As much as I don't like the idea, I think it's only a matter of time before we get into this damn European war. If we start to send raw materials across the Atlantic, they'll be sitting ducks for U-boats, and that's for sure. We've been working for some time on an idea for a plant on the other side of the ocean. It's to be a large complex, and there should be little need to ship raw materials to or from it. We want it in reach of the Allies, without risking convoys and transport. The board agrees with me on this. Incidentally, don't mention this to Diana. I'm always ribbing her about us getting into Mr. Roosevelt's war. Besides, she'll know soon enough.

"At any rate, we want to design a plant on some land that we've bought in Sweden, near Stockholm. The Swedes are neutral, of course, but they were happy at the possibility of a plant. What do you think?"

Horst nodded. "It sounds interesting. What exactly would be my job?"

"Senior design architect."

"That's a great deal of responsibility for one who has so little experience."

"That's right. But that's the way I operate, Horst. It's the sink or swim method."

"When would the project start?"

"Well," he said, scratching his chin, "I was kind of hoping that you and Diana might spend your honeymoon in Stockholm, if you take my meaning."

"That soon? I've seen Stockholm. I was hoping to see the Grand Canyon."

"All I can say is that the board is anxious to get the plant started before—well, before real hostilities break out between Germany and the United States."

So. It had been said. At last.

There was a long pause as Horst watched the small hermit crab slip from the tide pool and skitter across the sand in the direction of the ocean.

"Of course. What business would a young architect have refusing such an offer? My colleagues at Yale would stone me for refusing. Not to mention my wife-to-be, who would be in the first rank with the largest stones."

Lassiter laughed.

Having agreed on the deal, the two headed back across the sand. Money was never mentioned. Horst had learned one thing from his father. There was no need to haggle. Such things were dealt with by others. He was sure that the salary would be more than sufficient for a Lassiter son-in-law.

Diana watched from an upstairs window, anxious to see the look on Horst's face when he got close enough to the house for her to see his features. Her father's face would also tell her things.

Yes! They were smiling, and Horst was talking animatedly. She ran from her room and dashed down the stairs. Stopping at the landing, consciously affecting nonchalance, she strolled down the last few steps in time to see her father and Horst come into the hall.

"Did you two have a nice walk?" she asked casually.

The men looked at one another and then at her. Richard Lassiter started to laugh, and Horst followed. For a minute, Diana stared at them dumbfounded.

"Pardon my asking, gentlemen, but just what the hell is going on?"

Her question started another peal of laughter. "I'm sorry, darling," Horst said. "Yes, we had a wonderful walk."

He trotted up to the landing and hugged her.

"What *is* it?" she said, aggravation edging into her voice.

Richard pointed to the door. "We saw you at the window for a second, then as we got to the door, we heard you charging down the stairs. . . ." He doubled up, laughing again.

Horst turned to her. "Before all of this gets too insane, yes, your father did offer me the Sweden job. Yes, I did take it. Yes, we will honeymoon there. Although I warn you, wait until you see a Stockholm winter. You'll have to give up horses for skis."

"I'll learn."

They were married in July and sailed for Sweden in August.

The S.S. *Queen Christiana* was certainly not the *Queen Mary*. But while the latter was fair game for German U-boats, the Swedish liner, her flanks painted with the huge yellow and blue emblem of the Swedish flag, screamed that she was a neutral. Still, for Horst, much of the crossing was tense. He knew the Nazis in a way that Diana never would; at least he hoped she never would.

It was late in the afternoon of the fourth day at sea when they stood together on the deck and looked out at the chill Atlantic, which in these northern latitudes never fully warmed in the summer.

"What are those, Horst?" she asked, looking south.

He squinted and strained his eyes in the direction that she pointed. Finally he could see them. They were small dots on the horizon, regularly spaced and many miles away.

"Not sure. If you want, I'll go back to the cabin and get the binoculars for a closer look."

"Yes. Do. I'm very curious."

In a few minutes, he was back with a pair of binoculars. He picked out the dots on the horizon and adjusted the focus.

"It's a convoy. British, no doubt. Headed for England. They're less than two days out, now."

She peered at it for a long time, then handed the binoculars back to him.

"It feels so strange. The war is on the horizon, and we're here. It's odd."

He put the glasses back in the case. "In Sweden we'll be even closer. That's something that you will have to get used to."

"How, Horst?"

"You have a new last name. A well-known one, especially in Europe. It may not be the most popular name in the world, what with von Kleist feeding the German war machine."

"Oh. Is that why you shy away from speaking about your family? You've done that since I've known you. What I mean is, I know about them, but I don't know *about* them."

He looked at her and smiled. "Would you care to check the logic of that statement?"

"Oh, you know what I mean. They're my in-laws, and I'd just like to meet them once. But the way things are going, the world may blow up before I get the chance. You understand, don't you, darling? All I ever had was my father and no brother or sisters. I'd like to feel that there was family out there."

He shook his head. "I know what you're saying, Diana, and I understand the need that you have. But just let's get settled in Stockholm first, shall we? And let me think about how to proceed from there." He took her by the shoulders and kissed her. Her mouth was warm and pliant against his. After a minute she pulled away. "Are you trying to change the subject, my immigrant husband?"

"Ha! In Sweden we'll both be immigrants. So much for calling me names!"

Behind them, the dinner chime rang.

"Let's eat," she said. "After all, we have two more nights in the cabin—we have to keep your strength up!"

Laughing, they walked off, arm in arm to the dining room.

In the distance one of the small dots that they had been watching blossomed into a plume of flame. After a minute, another followed suit.

A wolf pack had found the convoy.

## 30

**Near Lvov, USSR, November, 1941**

Kurt was drinking more but he never seemed able to get really drunk. The pressure was relentless, the task of the Einsatzgruppen was mountainous. It seemed that everywhere he went there were more and more Jews. In seven weeks with the new unit, he had accounted for the elimination of just over eight thousand Jews. Still, Neeb and Heydrich demanded that the processing go faster. One bullet per Jew was the order; there could be no waste of ammunition, which was needed for the front—which, Kurt noted with chagrin, was racing in the direction of Moscow.

He couldn't remember the name of this town, simply that he had been through it before on the drive east; it seemed a century ago. The standard procedure was to be followed, though, and that was a relief.

His staff car stopped in the small main square. Off to one

side was a small, onion-topped church, and Kurt knew there would be a small synagogue down the road. On the far side of the square there was a town hall, and the young sergeant with Kurt leaped from the car to locate someone in charge. In a few minutes the mayor came from the town hall. He was little more than a peasant, and it was clear from the fear in his eyes that he had dealt with Germans before.

Kurt stood up in the staff car and looked down at the little man. "You are the mayor?" he asked in broken Russian.

"Yes, sir."

"All of the Jews in this town are to be assembled here as quickly as possible. You have records of the number and names of the Jewish families?"

"Yes, sir. We have complete records."

"Bring them out here at once. When the Jews are assembled, we will have roll call."

The mayor scurried back into the town hall. Behind Kurt four trucks pulled up, two of them disgorging soldiers who fanned out, scouring each of the town's houses. In the square a German soldier, fluent in Russian, started to repeat Kurt's orders using a bull horn.

"The Jewish population of this town is to be resettled to the west, where they will join other Jews who are also being resettled from this area. All Jews are to report to the square in thirty minutes. Bring only the personal possessions that you can carry and food for one day." He repeated the message, this time in Yiddish.

Everything seemed to go smoothly, at least at the outset. The mayor's list of names was tallied against the people, and they seemed to match. Families straggled to the square, and the numbers were double-checked again as the Jews, mostly woman and children with a scattering of old, gray-bearded men in black, were loaded on the empty trucks.

List in hand, a young soldier approached Kurt and saluted. "Sir, the tally doesn't work. We seem to be missing sixteen."

Kurt nodded. "Get me that mayor."

In minutes the small, cowering man was again in front of Kurt.

"Where are the rest of them?"

"I don't know, sir. I don't keep track of them from day to day. Some might be in another town for the day. They could be out in the fields. They could be anywhere, sir."

Kurt stepped down from the car and took his pistol from his holster. He slammed a round into the chamber and placed the gun to the man's head. His Russian was good enough for this speech; he had made it before. "You will take a roll call and find out who exactly is missing. You will get them here in fifteen minutes or determine their exact locations. Otherwise, we will have to assume that you are harboring Jews. That would mean that the entire town would be burned, and all of you, Jews and everyone else, would be shot. Do I make myself clear?"

The man nodded, took the list, and started to call the names.

It only took a few minutes for the count to be finished. "Well?" Kurt said to the mayor.

"There are fifteen, sir. We miscounted. Three of them are out of town for at least a week. Eleven are in the hospital, and one is the nurse who runs it. We have no doctor, you see. They all went with the army."

"Where is the hospital?"

The man directed Kurt to the small building on the outskirts of the town. It was a small place, wood frame and tarpaper. It had only one ward, and Kurt strode through it to the far end. A woman in a white smock awaited him there. She was young; perhaps in her early twenties. She was tall, dark eyed and clear featured, far from the farm drudges that Kurt had seen in the past weeks. There was an arrogance in her look that both attracted and angered him.

"Please come into the office, sir."

She ushered him into an office that also served as an examining room. A soldier with a machine gun came to guard the door. There were two small windows at the corner of the room. The place was little more than papier-mâché, and in the medicine cabinets he could see little that might have been made use of in a hospital.

"Your name?"

"Tonisha Durov, sir. I am in charge of the hospital since the doctors left."

"How many patients do you have here?"

"Twenty-two, sir. I can break them down by ailments if you wish?"

"I don't have time for that. How many of them are Jews?"

She stiffened visibly. "There are . . . eleven, sir."

"There are twelve, are there not?"

"No, sir. Eleven."

"You forgot yourself, didn't you, Durov?"

"Of course, sir. But you asked about patients. With me, there are twelve."

"Get them to the town square, and you join them. All of the Jews in this town are being resettled. Bring the possessions that you can carry and food for one day. Do that immediately."

She shook her head. "But, sir, there are patients here who cannot be moved. One has a broken leg, and there are five or six women close to delivering babies."

"You don't seem to understand, Durov. In a half hour everyone in the hospital will be in the square. That includes you."

"But, sir—"

Kurt took a step toward her and slapped her across the face with the back of his hand. She staggered and then recovered, her hand covering the searing welt on the left side of her face.

Kurt grabbed her by the throat. "You Jewish bitch, get them out of here now. If you don't, I will lock the doors and burn this fucking place to the ground with you and them in it. You hear me?"

"Oh, sir, please." She came close to him, placing her hands on his uniform tunic. "Please . . . let them stay. I'll go . . . just let them stay."

She dropped to her knees. Kurt stared down at her for a moment, then he looked to the guard. "All right—get the gasoline cans. This is going to have to be done the hard w—"

The rest happened too fast for Kurt to react. From the

position on her knees, the woman's hands lashed out. She
yanked Kurt's pistol from his holster and slipped to the side.
She fired once at the guard in the doorway, and the bullet
slammed into the man's chest, knocking him back into the
hall.

Kurt lunged for her, and she raised the pistol again. She
fired.

The shot ripped a slash up and toward the right shoulder of
Kurt's uniform tunic. The bullet entered through his right
shoulder and exited through his back. The impact spun him
around, and he fell to the floor. She scrambled to her feet and
aimed at Kurt's head.

She pulled the trigger.

Nothing happened. She dropped the gun and dashed for
the rear window. She was out the window and into the back
alleys, headed in the direction of the fields, before Kurt could
yell for help.

Minutes later, soldiers arrived at the hospital. They helped
Kurt, who was still conscious, to the car.

"Burn it! Burn the fucker down—burn all of it," he shrieked.

The hospital doors were barred shut from the outside, and
gasoline was spattered across the walls. When it was lit, a ball
of orange flame towered upward, a pyre for the patients,
whose screams were masked by the roar of the flames.

Reinforcements were called in, and all of the population of
the town was herded into the town hall. It, too, was set
alight. Three hundred Russians perished. Kurt watched the
fire from a distance, as a medical officer tended to his wound.

"You are lucky, Herr Sturmbahnführer. The wound is slight,
though there is a dangerous tear in one of the muscles. I
daresay you might get home for a couple of weeks. Better
than being out here with us, eh?"

"I want that woman found, the one who shot me. I want
her found."

"I am told, sir, that they located her home address. It's
over twenty kilometers from here."

"Is someone being sent?"

"Absolutely, sir. They are en route at this very moment."

"Good."

Alexandra Durov stood in the small kitchen of the house where she had grown up. Typhus had taken both her parents the previous winter. Now, she and Tonisha managed as best they could with the small vegetable garden and Tonisha's salary from the hospital. Alexandra was twelve, but she did the job of several men. She was dark and sharp featured like her older sister, and her figure was already starting to blossom.

As the truck roared up and screeched to a halt, she stopped slicing the turnips and wiped her hands on her apron. She headed for the door, but it was smashed in before she could get to it. She jumped back and screamed.

The three men who came in through the broken remains of the door wore German uniforms. All of them had rifles. They barked at her in German, though she tried to indicate she couldn't understand. Then, one of them came to her and spoke in Russian.

"This is the home of the Durov family?"

"Yes. What is it that you want?"

"Your sister. Where is she?"

"Tonisha? She's at the hospital."

"She is not at the hospital. Where is she?"

"The last time I saw her, she was headed for the hospital this morning."

The man gave a command, and the others started to search the house, overturning furniture and breaking crockery. In a few minutes they returned.

"She's not here, sir."

"Well," said the leader, "I doubt that she would have had the time to get this far on foot, in any case. Chances are she is somewhere between here and the town." He looked at his watch. "We'll not be able to wait. The best we can do is leave her a calling card. The major would be happy with that. Take care of her." He pointed in the direction of the young girl, who did not understand what was being said. "Then we'll burn the place."

The younger of the other two soldiers looked at the girl.

"Sir, do we have any time at all? I mean?..."

The leader looked at the two men, then nodded. "Very well. The major won't know anything about it, not from me, at least. But be quick about it."

He went out the front door, or rather through the remains of it.

One of the two remaining soldiers grabbed Alexandra from behind, while the other ripped off her blouse and skirt. She screamed and tried to pull loose, but she was tiny, and they were huge. They picked her up and spread-eagled her across the kitchen table. One held her down while the other dropped his pistol belt and unbuttoned his pants. He spread her legs across the sides of the table so that he could take her standing. He rammed into her like hot steel. She screamed again, and the soldier who stood above her head slapped her across the mouth.

When the first one was finished, they changed positions, and the second one took her. She went limp, unconscious. After the second soldier finished, the two gathered their equipment. As they were ready to go, the first man to have raped her pulled his pistol and placed it against her temple. He fired. The right side of her head was blown away, and a swatch of blood and brain tissue spattered the kitchen wall.

They soaked the house with gasoline and set it ablaze, then returned to the town to report to Kurt von Kleist.


A mile distant, in a small hillock of trees that marked the border of the neighboring farm, Tonisha huddled. She could see the farmhouse in flames. She had heard the shot. She knew the Germans, and she knew what had happened to her sister. There was no sense even going back.

She waited until the nightfall covered her movements and headed off to the north. She would find a partisan unit and join them. One thing that she was sure of: she would never

forget the face of the blond officer she had wounded. If there
was a God, she would find that man and kill him.

---

# 31

**Schloss von Kleist, early December, 1941**

She had managed to convince him. It took several months to
do it, but Diana got her way. She convinced Horst to get in
touch with Eric, and together, they arranged a meeting.
Much to Eric's surprise, Johann did not fly into a rage when
he mentioned the possibility. Rather, he calmly suggested
that the meeting be at the schloss and that Anya host the
affair. It was not until much later that Eric found out that
Kurt, too, would be there. Anya mentioned it, saying Kurt's
wound was not serious but that they wanted to send him
home to have it checked in a proper hospital.

Diana and Horst flew from Stockholm to Berlin and then
on to Stuttgart, where they arrived late on a blustery Sunday
afternoon. They were met at the plane by Eric.

When they arrived, the schloss was decorated for Christ-
mas, though there were no exterior lights, a necessity of the
war. As Eric introduced Diana around, he noticed Horst's
grimace at Kurt's black SS uniform.

Soon after the introductions, Eric showed Horst and Diana
to their room. The arrangement had been that they would
stay the evening and leave from Stuttgart in the mid-morning
of the following day.

As Eric opened the door, Diana exclaimed, "Oh, Horst,
what a magnificent room."

"Yes, it's beautiful. I guess you only appreciate such things when you haven't seen them for a while."

One of the staff followed Diana into the room and set the bags down.

Eric looked to his brother, and for a second, they spoke in German.

"You have a stunning woman there."

"I know. How is it you didn't tell me that Kurt was going to be here? I thought he was off somewhere in the army."

"The news that he had been wounded came after Father and I had made the arrangements. There was no point in changing things then. After all, this is so that Diana can meet the family, isn't it? Well, she'll get a chance to meet all of them at once."

"I guess you're right. But Kurt still gets to me."

"Just steer things clear of politics. There's less and less room for discussion with Father as the years pass. He's not at all well. Don't start a row."

Horst affected a broad, mock grin. "I'll be as amiable as an American. Reinhildt looks fantastic, considering all that she's been through. And the child looks like—"

Eric shook his head. "Not to be mentioned, even in jest."

Horst nodded. "Not a word. But then again, Heinrich looks like his father, too."

"Indeed. You two get changed and come down for cocktails. It should be an interesting evening."

"It certainly should."

Eric headed downstairs, and Horst followed Diana into the guest room.

She looked around again. "You know, I thought that the Lassiters lived well. But this is incredible. When was it built?"

"Father had it built just before the last war. I think he wanted it to be a monument to him after he was dead. I suspect it will be."

She took a long green gown from the dress bag and held it up against herself. "What do you think?"

"Exquisite. Unfortunately, I'll be forced to wear that damn

tuxedo. I don't even like ties, let alone dealing with bow ties."

She put the dress down and came over to him. "You, my love, are looking at the world's foremost expert in the art of bow tie tying. Would you care to use my services?"

He slipped his arms around her waist. "Well, I'd rather have another service, if that's possible."

She pushed away from him. "Why, sir, what do you mean?"

He shrugged. "Just a little help with the studs."

She frowned, and he laughed. "I'll take a raincheck for the rest of it. We have to be something less than bedraggled for Father and the rest."


"Horst, you were right about Eric," Diana said as they were about to go downstairs. "He's charming. And Reinhildt is stunning. What a horrible thing to have been widowed at such a young age."

He thought of the irony of the comment. He had not told Diana about Karl and the revelation that Eric had made to him more than a year before. It was something, he told himself, that he would tell her in due time, and only if the circumstances permitted. He wondered what Diana would say if she was to know that Reinhildt had been, in effect, widowed twice.

"Yes, it was. They were only lucky that Reinhildt and the boy were unhurt."

"I have to say that you're right about Kurt, though. He does look a bit sinister."

"He's changed. There's something different about him than I remembered from years ago. He's quieter for one thing. Ordinarily, Kurt would be spouting propaganda like a phonograph at high speed. Perhaps it's the war. Oh, love, take this in the spirit in which it's intended. Eric asks that we avoid discussions of things as politics. I'm sure you know why."

"Keep my American mouth shut, right?"

"I didn't say that. Perhaps you could discuss film stars or something other than Mr. Roosevelt. That would trigger my father into one of his longer tirades, and I'm not up for one of those."

"I've never seen one of those."

"Don't tease. I've seen too many of them, and besides, Eric says Father is not in good health."

"Very well. No politics. I promise."


Eric watched as Horst and Diana came down the main staircase. She was in a deep green gown, and her shimmering auburn hair was piled high on her head, held in place by a small tiara. He envied Horst.

Cocktails and small talk followed in the drawing room. Anya was playing the role of perfect hostess, and Horst was surprised to see that Reinhildt was not really challenging her for the roll. Horst crossed to where she was sitting, watching Ernst and Heinrich playing on the floor.

"Our little Nazi princess is stealing all of the spotlight," he murmured.

Reinhildt nodded. "She can have it."

"How long has this been going on?"

"For a while. She maneuvers Father and manages the empire, and that's what she always wanted. I have Ernst." She looked down to the little boy, whom she had dressed in an American sailor suit. By contrast, Anya had decked Heinrich out in lederhosen.

Horst reached down and scooped the boy up. "He never really knew his father, did he?"

Their eyes met for a second. "No. He didn't. He has his uncle Eric now and, at least for a day or two, Uncle Horst." She looked across the room to where Diana was speaking to Kurt. "What a beautiful woman has finally managed to catch my little brother. I don't know which of you is luckier."

"I keep telling her that she is, but I'm not sure that she believes me."

Reinhildt laughed, then stopped suddenly and murmured, "Look at Anya, Horst."

He turned to look, and all he saw was what he has seen a moment before.

"What do you mean?"

"The way she brushes her hair from her face. She's getting ready to move in for the kill. Perhaps you should warn Diana."

"Well, Kurt, that's a nasty-looking sling. How did you get the wound?" Diana was asking.

"Combat, in the east."

"Russia?"

"Yes."

Perhaps it was the fact that his English was poor that limited the conversation, Diana thought. But she thought also that even if her German were fluent, he wouldn't be much of a conversationalist.

"Kurt is one of the youngest—how do you say it in English? —yes, one of the youngest majors in the service," Anya intervened.

"Oh, I'm very impressed," Diana chirped.

"I'm sure, Diana, that they don't have such young, experienced officers in the American service, do they?"

"I don't know much about the military."

Dinner was announced. Diana felt as though she'd been liberated.

Johann dominated the dinner conversation, with an occasional side comment by Anya, always in agreement. He spoke animatedly about Germany's dream of expansion, of breathing space, and of the eradication of the mongrel races of eastern Europe and the development of a great hegemony that reached to the Pacific. On occasion, Eric managed to interrupt with other topics, but Johann would not be deterred. By the time that dinner was over, Horst could see that Diana was sorry she ever came, despite how much she seemed to like Eric and Reinhildt. Things were starting to wear thin.

"Shall we adjourn to the drawing room for liqueurs? I'm sure that Diana would like that," Anya said, watching her guest carefully.

"I am always in favor of liqueur," Diana responded. Horst noticed that she had managed to keep her best social mask on. He was proud of her.

Kurt moved arm in arm with his father, helping the old man in the direction of the drawing room. Horst and Diana followed, with Kurt and Anya bringing up the rear. The boys had been put to bed by the servants as it was by now well past eleven.

Johann looked weary and lapsed into silence. Diana seemed grateful for the respite. She looked at Horst and whispered, "You were right. And I didn't say a word about politics. Not a word."

"I know. And you didn't get up and scream. I'm proud of you."

The cognac was from before 1914, and Diana, who enjoyed a cognac after dinner, estimated that she would need at least three to come down from the emotional high that she was on. She had never felt more frustrated in her life. As soon as they got back to the room, she was going to confess to Horst that he was right about his family.

The first of the brandy was poured into snifters, and Johann stirred himself to propose a toast.

"If I may, family, and I think that I might call all of you that, I propose a toast—the first for this cognac of the evening. I propose a toast to the Third Reich and its leader, Adolf Hitler."

There was a moment of silence. Diana clutched her glass tightly. So did Horst. They were waiting for the others. Eric and Reinhildt did not move. Kurt's eyes moved to all of them.

Anya stepped forward and raised her glass. "Yes—to Adolf Hitler."

Kurt followed suit. "Here—here."

They paused, Kurt, Anya, and Johann looking at the other three.

Suddenly the door to the drawing room opened, and Klaus Schmidt, florid-faced and excited, dashed in. He went immediately to Johann and whispered in his ear. Whatever he said animated the old man, who immediately turned to the rest of the group. He raised the glass and drained it, then as he had at the announcement of Horst's becoming an American citizen, hurled the glass into the fireplace, which this time, contained a roaring fire. "And so, it has begun. . . . After all of the waiting, the glorious mission has begun."

Horst stepped forward. "What mission?" There was no deference in his tone. He was tired of the evening, of his father's harangue, of the insipid conversation of Kurt and Anya, and, indeed, of the forced silence of Reinhildt.

"I said, what mission?"

Johann looked at him. A sneer curled his lip. "And so the thankless son might well ask. And so might my other thankless son." He jabbed a finger at Eric, who was watching him carefully.

"It is avenged—all of it. All of the humiliation of nineteen eighteen. Everything will be made new again—on a worldwide scale.

"The Japanese have sunk the American fleet at Pearl Harbor. We will be at war with America within hours. The Japanese have already declared war."

Horst and Diana looked at one another incredulously. Eric went to Reinhildt. Anya and Kurt, as if by some silent bidding, moved toward Johann.

"It will all be Germany's . . . her manifest destiny . . . ruling all ru—"

The old man's right hand moved in the direction of his temple. The other hand seemed to flutter and flap without direction.

Only Eric recognized what was happening. He moved swiftly, but Johann pitched forward and before Eric could reach him, fell to the carpet.

Eric looked up at Klaus Schmidt, who stood in the doorway dumbly. "Klaus!" he roared. "Get my bag. It's in my car. And call an ambulance immediately."

"Yes, sir." Klaus raced off in the direction of the driveway.

Reinhildt, watching her brother take care of their father, while Anya and Kurt still stood inert, was the first to break the ominous silence that followed. She strode across the drawing room and went directly to Horst and Diana.

"Listen to me, both of you." Diana was still staring at Johann and Reinhildt grabbed her by the shoulder. "Listen to *me*," she hissed. Diana turned. "You will have to get out of Germany immediately. Tonight. Do you understand? Otherwise, you will be considered illegal enemy aliens. That will mean at least a concentration camp—perhaps worse. I know what that 'worse' can mean." Diana stared at her, not being able to understand the last remark. Horst nodded. He certainly knew.

"I'm serious. Let me try this. Follow my lead."

She walked swiftly out of the room and to the hall phone. She picked it up and swiftly dialed a number.

"This is Reinhildt von Kleist. I want the von Kleist plane ready at the Stuttgart Airport as soon as possible. I don't care if that means bringing a crew in at night. Get it done immediately."

Horst could not remember ever hearing such power in his sister's voice.

"Yes. And, my brother and his wife will be leaving from the schloss momentarily. I would expect that they will be there in something over an hour. . . . Where? Oh . . . Stockholm. Understand? Yes. I know that it would be via Berlin for fuel. What? The authorization? Kurt von Kleist. Sturmbahnführer, SS. Is that understood?"

She turned back to them as they stood a few feet away. "You have to get your things together as soon as you can. I will drive you to the—" She stopped suddenly as she stared beyond them. Kurt stood there, his feet spread apart. He looked like a man swaggering, despite the fact that he was standing still, his one arm in a sling.

"You have just committed treason, my sister. Do you know that?"

"How? We are not at war with the Americans yet?"

"You used my name as verification for the plane. By the time that they are halfway to Stockholm, we will be at war. As I said—treason."

In the distance they could hear the siren of an ambulance, working its way up through the snow-covered Bergstrasse.

Eric, shorn of the dinner jacket that he had placed over his father and having done all that he could do for the old man, came to the doorway.

"What the hell is going on? Father has just had a stroke, and you're arguing out here?"

"Be quiet, Eric. We're not arguing. We're negotiating," Kurt said as he turned to his brother.

"For what, in God's name?"

"For the lives of your sister, your brother, and his wife."

"What are you talking about?"

Kurt explained what Reinhildt had done and how the government would view it, if not by morning, in a day or two.

As he spoke, Klaus Schmidt came in through the front door, bag in hand, and crossed the hall to Eric. "The bag, sir."

"Take it in and put it next to my father. And stay with him. If he awakens or moves at all, call me."

Schmidt moved to the drawing room at a run.

"Now, what is this all about, really?" Eric asked, his voice showing his anger.

"It's about the family, Eric. It's about negotiations. It's about stock. It's about the thing that we tried and failed to negotiate five years ago, when you tried to buy the life of the Jew doctor friend of yours."

Reinhildt's eyes went wide. Eric forced himself not to look at her.

"What the hell do you want?"

"The stock. Yours and Reinhildt's, that's what I want—placed in my name. Otherwise, these three get sent off somewhere. You might care to guess where."

"I don't care to guess, Kurt—you animal!"

Eric took a step in Kurt's direction, and the only thing that stopped him was Horst, who stepped between them. "No. Eric, no. That's what he wants you to do. If you hit him, he can find a way to get you arrested, too. Don't."

Eric backed away, feeling an almost explosive rage. "I am

in there trying to see to our father, and you are out here threatening your brother's life. He should be conscious to see the son that he raised and the—creature that he married."

Anya moved to Kurt's side. "Remember, Eric, this creature gave you up as a lover years ago."

Reinhildt, still numb from the revelation about Eric's try to negotiate Karl's release, was too stunned to react. It was Horst who suddenly found himself staring at Anya. Lovers? They had been lovers?

Eric himself was startled. So Anya *had* told Kurt about their affair. His glance flicked to his brother: there was nothing in his face but a cold, smug smile. He turned back to Anya.

"We all make our mistakes, Anya. You were one of the bigger ones I made. I am pleased that everything was over as soon as it was. You did what you said you would do. You married another von Kleist—one with more prestige and greater possibilities. Congratulations."

His eyes moved to Kurt's. "Now what kind of deal were you after?"

"Exactly what I said. All of the stock that you and Reinhildt hold. If I get that, I will see that these two get to Stockholm."

Eric looked to Reinhildt, who had sat down on the bottom of the stairs.

She looked up at him and nodded. He had no way of telling what was in her thoughts.

"Very well, Kurt. You shall have it. But only after my death. It is in a neutral country and cannot be gotten by anyone but Reinhildt and me. I will sign a paper turning it over to you if and when I die. I repeat, there is no other way that you can get it."

Kurt thought for a moment. "Very well. We will draw up the document."

The ambulance skidded to a halt in the snow outside, and two attendants rushed in. Eric led them to his father and helped them move the old man to the stretcher.

As they moved him to the steps, Eric grabbed Kurt by his good arm. "I will go with them to the airport along with you.

Draw up your document. I will sign it as soon as I know that they have gotten to Sweden. Remember, I said that there was no other way that you could get the stock."

Kurt watched the stretcher being moved down the stairs. "Very well." He went off to the side of the hall and gave some quiet orders to Klaus, who rushed off in the direction of the office. It was clear that he was going to be the one to draw up the agreement.

Reinhildt got up from the stairs and, shaking away the shock of Kurt's remark, forced herself to move to Horst and Diana. "Do as I told you. Get your things together. Change into traveling clothes—quickly. Minutes could count."

They dashed up the stairs and ran to the guest room.

Eric went to the phone and called the hospital. He got hold of the resident and gave him a hurried diagnosis.

By the time that Eric was off the phone, Diana and Horst were back from the upstairs room, with their bags in their hands. Reinhildt hugged them and then hurried them into the sedan that waited at the foot of the steps, with Kurt in the driver's seat.

The plane was waiting at the runway in Stuttgart. Kurt stayed in the car as Eric and the two passengers headed across the windblown, snow-covered field. They were a few yards from the rear door when Eric stopped and embraced both of them. He took a small card from his pocket and slipped it into Horst's hand as he shook it. "The name is Trost. He is a high official in the ministry of war production—and a member of the underground. I will be working with him. Find a way to contact him from Sweden. Memorize the name and the number and then burn this."

Diana grabbed Eric by the shoulders and kissed him. "Isn't there a way that you can get out, too?"

"Five years ago, perhaps. I thought of it. Not now. Who would look after Reinhildt? Go now. Quickly!"

In a few minutes the plane was in the air, and Kurt and Eric rode silently back to the schloss, where the paper waited to be signed.

It was late the next morning when the call came from

Stockholm. The message, simply stated, was that they had arrived safely. Nothing seemed amiss with the call. Eric signed the paper and headed for the hospital. He had only been in his father's room for a few minutes when three SS officers entered.

"You are Doktor Eric von Kleist?"

"Yes," Eric said.

"You are under arrest for assisting the flight of enemy aliens to Sweden."

---

## 32

*From the Journal of Eric von Kleist*

*February 1, 1942*

*In my haste I obviously made a foolish bargain with Kurt. He must have notified his colleagues immediately after I signed the document. I was arrested and placed in a cell in the Stuttgart SS Headquarters. It was two days later when two men visited me. The first was from Goebbels's office and the second was a Wehrmacht medical officer. Goebbels's dupe wrung his hands and told me that anything involving such a charge against the family of von Kleist was not only absurd but was a disaster for the morale of Germany. The medical officer said that all of the charges would be dropped if I exhibited a gesture of faith in the Reich. The gesture, as I later found out, was volunteering for medical service with the Wehrmacht.*

*And so, here I am at Luga, fifty miles south of the frigid Gulf of Finland. I am attached to the Fourth Panzergruppe of the Sixteenth Army. Leeb's Army Group North is driving on Leningrad. Their goal, or so it seems, is to cut off Leningrad from Lake Ladoga, its supply line, and breach across the Gulf of Finland, to link up with the Finns, who are attacking south. All of the strategy seems very distant in the bitter cold of this medical camp. The reality at the camp is the wounded. They come in all varieties: frostbite, gunshot, and shrapnel wounds, food poisoning—everything. There are hundreds coming every day, now.*

*How clever Kurt was. If there was one place in the world that he could have sent me, where the chances were good that I might die, it would have been here. He was generous to allow me to stay for Father's funeral. I was instructed to wear the uniform of a Wehrmacht captain (medical) at the service. I did as I was ordered rather than go back to the cell. The funeral was a circus. Nazis abounded and cameras whirred. Himmler turned up for the SS and Ribbentrop for the party. I left for the front less than three days after that. I've written Reinhildt, but as yet, there has been no answer. I want so to explain to her about the remark Kurt made concerning Karl. I should have told her sooner—fool that I am. But, I dare not put it in a letter. I will have to find some other way.*

**Stockholm, March, 1942**

The manipulations by which Horst and Diana escaped internment in Sweden as American aliens were legion. In the United States Richard Lassiter arranged with the Swedish government, with whom he had numerous contracts, to nationalize the Lassiter steel complex, changing its name to Swensk Fabrik. The agreement was that Horst and Diana would be given Swedish citizenship for the duration of the war. Following that, they would renounce it and reapply for American citizenship. Meanwhile, Horst would continue work on the steel plant, selling the largest portion of the ultimate product to Swensk Fabrik. Lassiter had managed to massage a great deal of the arrangement through his friends at the State Department, whose only requirement was that the US be allowed to buy some of the more delicate machine parts through other neutral countries. Sweden, Lassiter, and the State Department agreed; and Horst, along with Diana, became Swedish subjects for the duration.

It was on an evening late in March when their doorbell rang. Horst answered it himself.

Two men stood in the doorway, hunched over to avoid the cold rain that whipped in from the Nørd Kanal. One was tall and dapper, with quick, dark eyes that seemed to assess everything. The other was short and squat, with huge glasses and owlish eyes.

The tall man smiled. "Mr. von Kleist?"

"Yes?"

"I'm Clifford Hurley. We spoke on the phone today?"

"Oh, yes, Mr. Hurley."

"And this is my associate, Karl Weatherow."

Horst moved them into his small library office and offered them coffee. Both declined.

Hurley did most of the talking.

"Mr. von Kleist, we represent the United States government. Unfortunately, if you repeat that to anyone, we will have to deny it, and so will our—ah—your government. You have a rare distinction, sir. You are both a Swedish national and an American citizen. On behalf of the American government, we want to ask your help."

"In what way, sir?"

"I'll be blunt, sir. The war is not going well. I'm sure you know that. The British are struggling in North Africa as well as at home. America is doing badly in the Pacific. A second front is some time away. So, for the present, an air war is what is envisioned."

"Why tell me this? I design steel plants."

"It is perhaps for the very reason that you do, that we come to you—that and the fact that you are a von Kleist."

"Mr. Hurley, please get to the point."

"We want your help. The von Kleist factory operations are the backbone of the German war effort. We need to know how they operate. We need to know what they are producing and how. In effect, we need to know anything and everything that you can tell us about Von Kleist Fabrik."

Horst thought. He tried to weigh the dangers and the benefits. There were far too many factors to be considered in the moment. His initial reaction was negative.

"Gentlemen, if I cooperated with you and the slightest word leaked about that cooperation, Diana and I would be interned immediately—not to mention the fact that the entire arrangement that my father-in-law has with the Swedish government would be compromised. Aside from that, any leak of information would threaten both my sister and my brother in Germany, as well as my nephew. I don't mean to be abrupt. But I hope that I am clear about this?"

"We assure you," Weatherow interrupted, "that the utmost secrecy would be maintained in this matter."

"I understand your assurance, and I do not wish to malign your what is it called—OSS? But, all security systems have leaks. In any case, there really isn't too much that I know about von Kleist war production. I have spent most of the last eight years in the United States. I'm sorry, gentlemen. I would like to help you, but I am sure that I can't."

After a formal goodbye, Horst headed moodily back to the living room where Diana waited.

"Why won't you help them?" she said as he came in.

"You were listening?"

"Of course."

"Then, you know why—for the reasons that I said."

"Your help could end the war faster."

"It could get Reinhildt killed, too. No, it took your father too much work to get us into this position. I won't compromise it."

She got to her feet. "Horst, you're being an ass." She stormed out and headed for the bedroom.

The division over the matter lay between them like a deepening chasm. In the months that followed, it was lightly glossed over, but each time that the topic of the war was brought up, it was there again. Both of them wondered whether it would spell the end of their relationship. It was almost a year later that two unrelated incidents in Russia helped to resolve it.

Kurt fired a single shot. It was all that was necessary for the target, a boy of ten, who was kneeling in front of him. A few feet away, the boy's father witnessed his son's death. The body pitched forward into the ditch. Kurt approached the father. "Now will you tell us where the other Jews are?" He pointed to the edge of the ditch, where the man's wife and two daughters were perched as their brother had been. "Don't make me turn my troops loose on them. They've been in the field a long time, and your wife and daughters are attractive. You wouldn't want to watch that, would you?"

The man, battered and with his hands bound behind him, simply looked down.

Kurt knelt down next to him. "I'll make you a deal. I'll let you and the rest of your family go free if you tell me where the other Jews are. You have my word as an officer."

The man looked incredulously at Kurt for a moment and then looked back to the frozen ground.

Kurt turned and looked over his shoulder. "All right, tell the first squad that they can have all three of them. We can sit here and watch the fun."

"Nooo!" the man shrieked. In the distance the wife and daughters were starting to whimper, as seven or eight laughing members of the SS troops advanced on them. "Papa— please?" one of the girls screamed.

The old man caved in. "Ahead . . . ten kilometers. . . . Perhaps twenty of them."

"You're lying." Kurt said. He waved to the soldiers.

"No. I swear, I swear. It's true."

Kurt was convinced. "Thank you, old man." Kurt put his pistol to the man's head and fired, blowing the back of his head off. He got to his feet and holstered the pistol. He called to another officer. "I'll go alone with my driver and herd them back. You finish up here."

As he drove away, he could hear the screams of the women in the background.

It was twelve kilometers up the road that the command-detonated mine went off some five feet from the front of his car. The driver was killed instantly, and Kurt was thrown clear and knocked unconscious. He awakened spread-eagled and lashed to a tree. His uniform and his boots were gone, and he was freezing in his underwear. A tall Russian partisan was standing in front of him.

"So, we have the blond beast," the man said. A chill ran through Kurt. He knew that he had been identified. Intelligence reports over the last months had indicated that that was the Russians' name for him.

"We are so glad that you could join us, Herr Sturmbahnführer. We have been waiting for you for a long time."

The man drew a long, thin knife from his tunic. It looked to have the sharpness of a scalpel. "Do you know what we do with these?"

Kurt's eyes went wide, and his stomach tightened.

"We neuter sheep. Like this."

A searing pain ripped into his groin, and Kurt screamed for at least a minute before he passed out. The partisans doused him with gasoline and set him on fire. They saw it as a kind of poetic justice.


It was five days later and far to the north when the message reached Eric. The casualties were coming by the thousands now, as unit after unit had been hurled against Leningrad, which still held. Eric had come from more than twelve hours in surgery and gone to his tent. Out of habit, he opened the small pocket journal that he always kept in his tunic and prepared to write. The journal, he mused, had become a constant companion; something that helped him keep his sanity. Before he could start, a messenger came in through the tent flap. He saluted and handed Eric the cable.

*Herr Hauptmann von Kleist:*

*Be advised that Sturmbahnführer Kurt von Kleist died heroically on January 12, while subduing partisans in the operating area of Army Group Center. His remains have been returned to Germany for a funeral with full military honors. Special leave has been arranged for you to return to Tübingen for the service. Transport will be arranged through this headquarters. You have my sincerest condolences.*

*Heil Hitler.*
*A. Neeb*
*Colonel General*
*Army Group North*
*Commanding*

He stared at it for a long time. Kurt had gotten what he had always subconsciously wished for—a hero's death.

Eric got to his feet and tucked the journal back into his pocket, then left the tent and headed for the command shack. He was fifty feet away when the mortar round landed behind him. Eric pitched forward into the snow, the world spinning into blackness around him.

## 33

**From the Journal of Eric von Kleist**

*Late January, 1943*

Well, at least I am alive. I am told by one of the comrades that ten men near me were killed. The artillery was something new, a Soviet 122mm mortar. They make no noise coming in, as do bombs. Rather, they rain death silently, until they hit. The barrage was followed by an infantry assault, which caught the unit by surprise. Of the three hundred of us, there were no more than fifty to take prisoner, not that the Soviets were anxious. My orderly loaded aboard a truck with me, though he did not survive the journey. He tried to escape, though I would not know where he would have run to. He was shot by a Soviet guard. The rest of us were driven to Leningrad.

I was unconscious off and on for more than three days. I was taken to a military prison in Leningrad, where I was interrogated by a Red Army colonel. Once he was sure that I was a medical officer, he assigned me as a prisoner doctor to the central military hospital in the city. I remained there for two days before I got any treatment. I had been placed in a cell, and when I awoke there, I found that there was a water pitcher and a bucket for a toilet. My *wound was bandaged. The water seemed clean, so I set about a self-examination. A mortar fragment had entered through my back and exited through my right side, bypassing the kidney and the liver. The exit wound seemed clean, though there was no way of seeing the entry wound, short of having a mirror. By palpation, it seemed that there had been no infection. The one thing that I have learned about combat wounds is that the hot metal cauterizes itself as it passes through, assuming that it hits nothing vital. I had been more than lucky. I washed out the wound, scrubbed the bandages, and tried to rewrap it, using scraps from my torn tunic to hold it in place. It took all of the energy that I had. I fell back on the steel cot and into sleep.*

*Sometime later, I was awakened by the door of the cell opening. Two Russian officers came in and sat on stools next to the bed. One of them spoke fluent German. He was the one who interrogated me.*

"Your name?"

"Eric von Kleist. Captain, Wehrmacht Medical Corps."

"You're a doctor?"

Eric nodded.

The two talked together for a few minutes before the first officer again looked to Eric.

"What do you specialize in, as a doctor?"

Eric shrugged. "General practice. Some surgery. Many things."

This remark seemed to impress the Russian officer. The second officer said something to the first, and Eric could tell that it was something negative simply by the tone.

The officer who spoke German paused to phrase the question.

"You are a Fascist? A Nazi?"

Eric blinked. If he told the truth, would they believe him? These men whose nation had been raped by Nazi hordes? He shook his head. "Conscript. Forced to serve or go to prison:

Sobibor, Treblinka. Only a doctor." He had named the two concentration camps that the Soviets would have been most familiar with, and he was sure that it would have some impact.

"You are Socialist? Communist?"

He paused. Was he playing into the trap? He had to be honest. "No. Nothing. No politics. Only a doctor, sir."

"A Jew?"

"No."

There was a long conversation between the two in Russian, but it was too fast for Eric to understand. It was clear that there was a disagreement developing between them. Thank goodness, he thought, that they wore the same rank, though one had purple piping on his sleeve and the other had green. The one with green was the one who spoke German, and the one with purple was pushing him to ask more, as he held the clipboard.

"Where are you from in Germany?"

Eric was not supposed to answer, according to the rules that he had been taught, though he saw no damage in answering. "Tübingen."

The two looked at one another and spoke again. The German-speaking one looked at him and smiled. "You are, of course, not of the industrial family, von Kleist?"

Eric had to think. What would the answer mean? The chances were that it could mean a firing squad. There was no way of telling. But as he thought about it, he decided that he might as well die with his right name as with any other.

"Yes."

Again, they talked. This time the conversation was more animated and faster than it had been before.

The German-speaking one looked at the other's clipboard and then to Eric. "Can you prove this?"

Eric would have laughed if he could, without the pain in his side. How could he prove that to two Russians?

"How?"

Both of them laughed, though there was little humor in their laughter. There was more an air of frustration.

They stayed for more than an hour, asking the details of his life, which were slavishly copied by the German-speaking officer, whom Eric took to be the military member of the team. The one with the purple piping seemed more political. As it turned out, he was right. They finished rather abruptly and left, before Eric had a chance to ask for water or food. However, in less than half an hour, a team of doctors and orderlies came into the cell, dressed the wound, gave him some pills that turned out to be painkillers, and left a bowl of watery soup and a fresh pitcher of water. He assumed that his answers to the two officers had proved satisfactory.

The next morning, his cell door opened, and a nurse entered silently. She watched him in sleep and then tapped the end of the bed. Eric came awake, bolt upright and frightened. She took a step back and then stopped. They looked for a long minute at one another as Eric realized where he was. He spread his arms in a conciliatory gesture.

She nodded. "Don't be afraid, Captain. We are not going to shoot you. At least, that is what I hear. Otherwise, dressings would not be wasted on you. They are precious in Leningrad. I'm sure that they have something else planned for you."

Her German was fluent. He was amazed. And more than that, she was a beautiful woman. He had seen so few in Russia. Her long dark hair was pulled back from her face, which seemed not a bit Slavic. Her eyes were dark and piercing, and there was something of an aristocratic quality to her bearing. He wondered for a second if the Bolsheviks had managed to get all of the Romanoffs after all. He managed his best smile as he tried to sit up, propped on one arm.

"I thank you. I'd like to know what that something else is, though?"

She shrugged. "They don't tell me such things. That is for the GPO to decide. Let me change that."

She changed the dressing, quickly and efficiently, like a woman used to dealing with the speed necessary for a field hospital.

When she finished, she turned to go.

"Excuse me." He said. "Might I know your name?"
She looked back at him coolly. "You might not."

My Dearest Horst,

    *I dare to write this letter, as I am going to post it myself. I have learned that Eric was taken as a prisoner of war only a week after Kurt was killed in combat. They say that Eric is alive, though there is little more from the Swiss Red Cross than that. Is there any information that you can get about him through Sweden? Please try. Of all of us, he was the one who wanted all of this least. All he wanted was medicine, to help people. As for myself, I manage, here in the schloss, though food is starting to be rationed, and so is gasoline. Ernst grows bigger every day and, blessedly, continues to look like his father. The corporation has been placed under the managership of Anya and, of all people, Klaus Schmidt. They run the schloss like it was a fortress, and that is why I do not trust this letter to be posted by the staff, who are now all Nazis. We are well, and remain so, but please, inquire about our brother.*

My love,
Reinhildt

Horst read the battered letter several times before placing it back in the dog-eared envelope. How could he help Eric? Or indeed, find out anything about him, except the most perfunctory information from the Swedish Red Cross, who might have less information than the Swiss. He pondered the idea as he sat on the side of the bed. He looked at Diana and handed her the letter. After she read it, she looked up at him.

"At the risk of starting a fight, can I suggest something?"
He looked at her quizzically. "What?"
"Who would know more about Eric than the people who are holding him prisoner?"

"The Russians? What will I do, get a boat and sail to Leningrad and ask about him?"

She folded her arms. "Your sarcasm underwhelms me, my love. Of course you can't go to the Russians. But who can? Their allies, right? The Americans are their allies. Remember the two men who called last year? They left a card, correct? Call them. Perhaps there is something they can do."

She watched him closely. It was something that had started many fights between the two of them. Though this time, she thought, there was a vested interest for him.

He looked at her and frowned. "Perhaps."

In the morning he called Hurley.


"What do you propose, Mr. von Kleist?"

Hurley had come alone this time. His tone was considerably cooler than it had been the year before. Perhaps it was because the tide of the war had started to turn in favor of the Allies.

"I am prepared to assist you in any way I can, vis-à-vis what was discussed last year."

Hurley sat back and folded his arms. "I would then assume that there is something more important than the compromise of your sister or the possible internment for yourself and your wife that you mentioned on my last visit?"

"Are you asking me if I want something in return?"

"I know you do, Mr. von Kleist. Otherwise, there would have been little reason for your getting in touch with me."

"Of course, Mr. Hurley. You are a professional at this, are you not?"

Hurley nodded. "I know my job. I know that you now need us in the same way that we needed you."

"You use the past tense. Am I to assume that my help is no longer needed? Or is that a ploy? If it were not still needed, you would not have bothered to come here. You would have simply failed to respond to the message that I left you. But the fact that you are here, and so promptly, says that the information that I might provide for you would be valuable.

"The tables aren't exactly turned, are they? Despite the

recent Allied victories, there is still a need for the air war. A great need, I would say. And von Kleist still feeds the German war machine as it did last year. I would think that the Allies would be looking to something like strategic bombing to precede the opening of a second front. To do that, they would have to cripple the German armaments industry. Perhaps use new bombers—perhaps use more of the old ones. At any rate, the Farbens and the von Kleists and the Krupps will have to go before there is anything like the opening of a second front—unless I am sadly mistaken. So, Mr. Hurley, you still need what I can provide, and I in turn will ask payment from you and your—what do I call them? Operatives?"

"The term will serve, Mr. von Kleist."

"Well, then, shall we have a drink and get to business?"

Hurley smiled for the first time. "Certainly."

They sipped aquavit and started to shape the needs of the Allies as posed by Hurley. As Horst listened, he realized that he might have overextended himself. There was a great deal that he didn't know about the wartime von Kleist operation. But, Hurley must know that. Horst had mentioned that the year before, and he was sure that Hurley was a man who never forgot a comment. When Hurley finished, Horst knew that it was his turn to state his demands—or rather, petitions.

"Mr. Hurley, my brother Eric is a prisoner of the Russians—"

"Yes, we know."

"You—?"

"Yes."

"How?"

"Please, Mr. von Kleist. We know." Hurley opened his briefcase and pulled out a folder marked with a red border. Horst assumed that it was something classified. "He was taken prisoner in the first week of February. There was a wound, though it was not serious. He was transported to the central hospital in Leningrad. As far as we know, he is alive and well there. . . . Oh, the date of this report is two weeks old, you understand."

"Then you understand what my request is?"

"No. Perhaps you'd better explain."

"I want him freed."

Hurley laughed. "Mr. von Kleist, surely you don't think that you are back in prewar Germany, where the family name could move mountains? What you ask borders on the absurd. Do you know how the Russians operate concerning prisoners of war? Their procedures make Genghis Khan look like a Franciscan monk. No. I can keep you up to date on his status, conditions permitting. But, more than that—I'm sorry."

"Then, Mr. Hurley, I don't think that we have anything to speak about. Thank you for the information that you have given me. Oh, and by the way, if you anticipated that I would ask about my brother and you brought the file for that purpose, why are you so perfunctory in saying no to my request?"

Hurley smiled as he placed the file back in the case. "There is no way to underestimate you, is there, Mr. von Kleist?"

"Thank you, Mr. Hurley. But I can't really banter. Oh, we could, if you wish. However, I assume that we are both men of business. There is something to be traded here. My brother for information and assistance. Why was my request absurd? Why are the Russians like Genghis Khan?"

"Perhaps that was an overstatement. They are tough-minded and pragmatic. Otherwise, they would not be turning the Nazis back at Stalingrad—and they have all but broken the siege of Leningrad. To them, everything in the world breaks down into two categories: economic and political. If it serves their purpose to keep your brother for political reasons, then there is no power on earth that will move them. If economics is their game, then, perhaps, there is a chance."

"What is your estimate of the situation?"

"I can't say at this time."

"What you are saying is that you need something from me so that we can discuss this more."

"I was not going to be so direct."

"Please, Mr. Hurley. Spare me your diplomacy. Be direct."

"Your estimate is correct."

"What exactly do you want?"

"My colleagues would like something on the order of a gesture of good faith. If we get that and further information, there are inquiries that could be made concerning your brother."

Horst was expecting it, and he responded briskly. "The man's name is Trost. He contacted my brother several years ago—twice, I believe. He established a liaison. When my brother got my wife and me out of Germany, he mentioned Trost and said that the man could be of some help. He works in the ministry of War Production. I have never met him directly, though I am sure that he could be reached by operatives in the country. I believe that he should be approached indirectly. My brother mentioned the phrase, 'Some Germans are still Germans,' and I think that it was a sign of recognition. Is that sufficient?"

"It will do for now, Mr. von Kleist. I will be getting back to you."

### From the Journal of Eric von Kleist

*February, 1943*

*She has been here each day for three weeks now. I find myself looking forward to her visits. She says little, and when she answers my questions, she is usually sarcastic. Still, there is something in her eyes. I don't know. The wound is healing well enough, though part of me wishes that the procedure would go slower, for the chances are that when the wound is fully healed, I won't see her again. I don't even know her name. I have not asked again. The doctors seem to treat her little better than a prisoner, and yet she is a skilled nurse. It's very confusing. Still, her visits are the highlights of my day. There is nothing to read or do.*

She entered the cell with a tray of dressings. The guard slammed the door behind her as usual.

"Good morning," she said, placing the tray on the bedside table.

"Good morning."

She worked in silence, taking the dressing off, painting the area with antiseptic, and replacing the dressing with a clean one. When she finished, she got to her feet and stared down at Eric. "You appear to be well enough."

"Well enough for what?"

"Well enough to take care of the other prisoner patients. We have few doctors to spare, and you will be ordered to help other wounded Germans. I expect that you will start in the morning."

"You mean that I can get out of this cell?"

"You will wish that you had the time to stay in it. They will have you on an eighteen-hour-a-day schedule—like the rest of us."

He managed a smile. "I'll take it. I need the work. I was going crazy in here."

"Well, you won't have that problem now." She turned and started to to go.

"Wait." She stopped and turned, surprised that he called her back.

"Yes? Is there something wrong with the dressing?"

"No. I just wanted to say that you're an exceptional nurse." Her expression did not change. "Thank you, Doctor."

"Might I know your name? You know mine."

"My name is Tonisha Durov."

## 34

It was as Tonisha had said it would be. Most of the time, Eric was a zombie, working hour after hour with the German prisoners and occasionally being allowed to treat Russian wounded, under the watchful eye of a Russian doctor. In a matter of weeks in the hospital, the supervision was ever so slightly decreased. Strangely and fortuitously for Eric, it seemed that they assigned Tonisha to be his jailer. Perhaps, it was because she spoke German, perhaps it was because she was spying on the German prisoners and trying to get information—Eric didn't know and didn't care. All he knew was that he was happy when she was nearby and depressed when she wasn't. He found it hard to admit, even ludicrous to consider, that he might be falling in love with her.

It was well past four in the morning when they finished with the burn victim. He was a Russian tank commander, and he had sustained third-degree burns on the upper half of his body when his tank was hit by a German antitank round. After giving the man a shot, Eric backed off, brushing his hair back from his forehead as he looked down at the unconscious patient, swathed in bandages.

Then he turned from the bed and staggered a step to the left, steadying himself on the next bedpost.

Tonisha took a step to steady him, then stopped. "Perhaps that should be all for this evening, Doctor."

He gave her an exhausted smile. "Perhaps. You are, after all, the jailer." He looked back at the man in the bed and shook his head. "He won't live. I'd say three days at the most before psuedomonas sets in. After that there will be renal failure, coma, and he'll be gone," he said quietly.

She nodded. "I know. It happens that way with most of the seriously burned. One need not be a doctor to tell that." She strode off in the direction of the ward door. "Come."

Eric followed, half asleep on his feet.

They went from the third floor to the first and headed in the direction of the detention cells. Eric, almost sleepwalking, barely noticed that she took a right turn where she should have taken a left. He suddenly found himself in front of a room door rather than a cell. She opened it. "Come in."

He did, a bit bewildered.

The room was small, though far more comfortably furnished

than his cell. There was a small bureau, a desk, and a bed. And there was actually an outside window, with curtains.

Without saying a word, she went to the bureau, took out a small bottle, and handed it to him. "Take some of this. Not too much. Just a swallow. It's very strong."

He drank and nearly choked. It was vodka. Coughing, he handed the bottle back to her, his eyes watering and throat burning. She was laughing.

She replaced the bottle in the drawer and still laughing, came to him. He could feel the vodka hit his stomach and start to spread warmth slowly outward.

"You will have to go back on duty in five hours," she said.

He nodded glumly.

She passed him and went to the door. He turned toward it and was surprised when she didn't open it. She simply threw the bolt. Turning back to him, she pulled off the white babushka that covered her long raven hair. It cascaded down across her shoulders.

She came across the room to him and stood close to him . . . so close. . . .

"Make love to me, Eric."

It was lunacy, and they both knew it. Getting caught in a romantic liaison would mean Siberia for her and a firing squad for him. Still, they risked it.

She slowly unbuttoned her dress and let it slip to the floor. Her full, round breasts sprung free. His mouth moved to find hers as his fingertips lightly brushed her nipples. She could feel the crinkly blond hair on his chest against her. He moved a hand to the small of her back and another down to the backs of her legs. He lifted her effortlessly and laid her gently on the bed.

He lay beside her, his hands exploring her body; the firmness of her stomach . . . lower.

In only a minute, she pulled him to her, her hands on the small of her back. He moved inside of her, with an incredible gentleness . . . and an agonizing slowness. Her fingertips started to dig into his back, and he grinned, then suddenly started to move faster . . . faster . . . faster.

Afterward, they lay, with their long legs intertwined, her head resting against his chest. It took a moment for him to realize that she was crying. He said nothing, only pulled her closer to him. In moments she was engulfed by great sobs. After a time, they subsided, and she got up and went to the bureau. After a minute she turned back to the bed. Her eyes were red rimmed as she stood there naked, looking at him.

"What will we do?"

He shook his head. There was no answer.

"It would seem that there is something that might be done, Mr. von Kleist. I emphasize *might*, you understand."

"We have been at this for ten months, Hurley. You have made contact with Trost. You are getting good bombing information. I am giving you all of the expertise that I can on the recon photos." Horst got up from the table and moved across the large living room of Hurley's flat. The walls were covered with maps, and the tables were strewn with glossy photos. Some showed before air strike views and some showed the same scene after a B-17 or British Lancaster raid. "So, don't be coy. Just where do we stand with Eric?"

Hurley chewed his lip and went back to his desk. He pulled a file from the drawer. "They took all of this time to do it, but they have come back with a proposal. They will release him, if we follow their procedures and meet their terms."

"What exactly are the terms?"

"Half a million American dollars in gold, delivered to the Soviet embassy, here in Stockholm."

Horst whistled. There was no way in the world that he could lay hands on that kind of sum—especially in gold. Still, he said nothing. "What are the conditions?"

"A neutral transfer point. But there are some arrangements still to be settled with regard to that. Can you raise the funds?"

He knew that there was only one way to do it. "Yes. It might take a little time . . . but yes."

*    *    *

The cell door opened suddenly, and a bright light was flashed in Eric's eyes. A hand grabbed him by the shoulder. "You. You dress. Come—be quick."

He stumbled to his feet in the darkness. Grabbing for his shoes, he almost fell over his own feet. The light in the cell snapped on, and a second man entered carrying a shirt, a light jacket, and trousers. He spoke better German than the first.

"Put these on. Be quick." Eric knew better than to ask questions. He simply did what he was told.

They moved him out of the cell and then out of the hospital. On the street he could hear the distant sound of artillery. There was a car waiting with the motor running. The chilly air awakened Eric fully. What the hell was going on?

The car, lit only by small, square blackout lights, sped through the bombed-out streets as if the driver knew them by Braille. In a few minutes they were in the area of the docks. Eric was pulled from the car by two other men, who seemed even more impatient than the first two. He was transferred to a Russian torpedo boat and told to get below. In minutes the boat roared out of the harbor. The trip took just over an hour. It was then that he could hear the din of the motors lessen, and he could start to feel a ground swell. There were voices above, but only some of them talking in Russian. He could not make out the other language. One of the Russian sailors came below and beckoned him on deck.

The torpedo boat was bobbing up and down near the hull of a high-riding freighter. A jacob's ladder hung from the side. The sailors prodded him, indicating that he should climb, and he made a grab for the ladder. He seemed to climb forever, eventually reaching the deck. Two sets of hands pulled him over the rail. He looked around dumbly. After a few seconds, he could make out a man standing a few feet away. The man took a few steps toward him and addressed him in English. "Welcome aboard, Mr. von Kleist."

Eric had to think for a second. It was a language he had not heard in several years. "Ah . . . thank you?"

"My name is Hurley. Clifford Hurley. There is someone here whom I think you might wish to see." The figure came from the far end of the deck.

"Hello, Eric."

"Horst?"

They ran together and embraced. Both of their faces were streaked with tears.

"How? I mean . . . oh, God . . . I don't know what I mean."

They stood on the deck holding on to each other's arms and saying nothing for some time before Eric noticed that the ship was getting under way.

"Where are we going?"

"Stockholm. You're about to become a Swede, for the duration . . . or if nothing else, a German national."

The first smudges of gray were behind Eric in the east, and he turned to look. Suddenly he gripped the rail.

*Tonisha!*

Later, they sat in a small inboard cabin as the ship moved swiftly through the Gulf of Finland. Eric reached up and rubbed his temples with his fingertips like a man not sure of the border between dream and reality. He was exhausted, and excited, teetering between laughter and tears. He was sure that someone would pound on the cell door in a minute and tell him to get out to the ward.

*Tonisha. How could he—would there be a way?*

"Come back. You're really here. It's all right." Horst noticed that his brother's hands were starting to shake. "Here." He got up and went to the small bar in the corner. He poured a strong shot of schnapps and gave it to Eric, who had to hold it with two hands to steady it. He bolted the drink and handed back the glass. "Another, I think."

Horst poured another, and Eric drank it, more slowly. His hands were starting to steady.

He forced his eyes to focus on Horst. "How did you manage all of this?"

"A little money changed hands and so did a little information. It took about a year to do."

"Horst? Ah . . . about Kurt, I—"

"We heard. It was about the time that you were captured."

"How did you know?"

"The gentleman who met you at the rail? Hurley? He knows a lot of things like that. Oh, I have some good news for you."

Eric held out his glass. "Dear God . . . more. Let me get used to this. *That* will take about a month."

"No. This I have to tell you. There is another von Kleist."

Eric was starting to feel befuddled. The schnaaps was working.

"Wha—who?"

"His name is Manfred Richard, and he is just short of twelve weeks old."

"Yours?"

"Well, he's not yours."

Eric grinned and weaved slightly. The—then all of the von Kleists are . . . free?"

Horst shook his head. "No. Reinhildt and Ernst are still in Germany . . . at the schloss."

---

## 35

**July, 1944**

In the east the field armies of Zhukov were slashing toward the Vistula, driving armored wedges through the German lines. In the west the British and Americans were driving across the hedgerows of France. It was on the twentieth of July, at eleven in the morning, when General Klaus von

Stauffenberg carried his briefcase into the briefing room at Wolfsschanze, the Führer's headquarters in a forest in East Prussia. Moments later, the general was called away. He made sure to tip the briefcase on its side as he left the room. Two minutes later the blast shattered the briefing room.

Reinhildt was living on a razor's edge. She and Ernst shared the schloss with Anya and Heinrich—if share was the right word. The fuel shortage had forced them to close down much of the house. Most of the servants were gone, many of them conscripted. Only one maid and Klaus Schmidt remained. Reinhildt could never fathom why the man stayed. Was it simply that he had no other place to go?

Tall weeds had overgrown the gardens, and the once neatly trimmed shrubs grew wild along the long drive. Blackout curtains covered the windows and in the closed-off portions of the schloss, furniture sat, shrouded in white dust covers... cadaverous.

Despite the fact that a warm July sun brightened Tübingen, Reinhildt could see little joy in the faces of the townspeople. With most of the servants gone, she had assumed the role of food shopper for the schloss. It gave her something to do, and it was a weekly outing for Ernst: they could make the trip only once a week because of fuel rationing.

Food was getting as scarce as fuel at this point in the war. The weekly ration of meat was less than half a kilo per person. Mostly, the butcher sold horse meat, though he never tried to pass it off as beef, for that would have led him to arrest and instant execution at the hands of the Gestapo. Still, there was a line in front of the shop that stretched to the end of the block. Women waited patiently, their expressions grim as they clutched blue ration books in their hands. Reinhildt carried the ration books for everyone in the schloss.

As she moved through the line, she mused at how things had changed. Meat and fuel were not the only things that were in short supply. Vegetables were hard to get, though she hoped that they would be more plentiful in the fall, with the harvest. However, a larger quota would probably go to the front. Coffee had been nonexistent for the better part of the last year. What the stores were selling was a strange substitute made of chicory and other seeds. Whatever it was, it was repulsive, and Reinhildt simply could not drink it. There were a number of other things that had vanished. Pens, light bulbs, tires, silk for stockings and underwear—the list stretched on and on. There were fewer men on the streets and in the shops as the universal conscription both raised and lowered on each end to provide replacements since the collapse of Paulus's Sixth Army at Stalingrad. Reinhildt had heard rumors that in the last days and weeks of the fighting for the vital city on the Volga, the German and Rumanian armies were sustaining twenty thousand casualties a week. There was no way that she could fathom such loss of life. She could only see the truth in the thin, gaunt faces of the women in the lines.

There was little left by the time that Reinhildt got to the shop counter. But she managed the best deal that she could, getting some gristle-filled beef and as much wurst as the ration cards would cover. The trip to the vegetable market was similar, though there were several stalls there to choose from. She filled her large shopping bag and started back to the car.

Dinner was bleak. Anya, just returned from Berlin, sat with Heinrich at one end of the table, with Reinhildt and Ernst at the other. Klaus and the one remaining maid served the food, a pitiful amount of wurst and potatoes. Anya looked at it with disdain. Then she looked to Reinhildt.

"This was the best that you could do? I don't understand why. There is a much greater selection in Berlin. Why just last night at the Ministry—"

"This is not Berlin, Anya. This is Tübingen. I'm sure the bureaucrats in Berlin have more cooperative butchers...."

Anya's eyes flashed. "All of Germany must make sacrifices, Reinhildt. We have to support our troops at the front."

"Fronts, Anya. That's plural. Don't forget the Americans and the British in France. I think soon we will have to live on more of Goebbels's promises and less of this food. At least we have the two cows so that the children have milk. We have them, that is, until a bureaucrat comes and requisitions them."

"Are you saying that the rationing is unfair?"

"No. Just that it is fruitless."

"It is not fruitless, and your comment borders on treason. I would warn you to watch your words. If you remember, I run von Kleist, now. You are a guest here. You don't contribute to the war effort at all. You are tolerated."

Reinhildt caught herself before she got up. She managed a smile. "You are not even a von Kleist, Anya. I am."

"It is you who are not a von Kleist," Anya snapped back. "You are an Altenhoff—by marriage. I am the widow of a von Kleist who was one of the greatest war heroes that the Reich has ever seen."

Reinhildt's eyes moved to the two boys. She would not insult Heinrich's dead father in front of the child. "I won't debate the military prowess of Kurt in front of his son, Anya. Suffice it to say that when you look at the food situation in the town, you have to wonder how the war is really going."

Anya pushed her plate away. "What would you know about it? I am the one who goes to the plants and to the conferences in Berlin. There are magnificent new weapons on the drawing boards, ones that will change the entire picture of—"

"Oh, I've heard of the 'Wunder Waffen.' There are rumors of them. But I don't see that there is any way that they can change the course of this two-front war, not since the Allies are in France."

"They will be thrown into the sea," Anya snapped.

Reinhildt shrugged; the conversation was pointless as always. They finished the meal in tense silence, and Reinhildt took Ernst for a walk in the early evening twilight.

When she returned, Klaus Schmidt told her that Anya had again left for Berlin, taking Heinrich with her. Reinhildt smiled to herself: it was a long trip for a good meal.

\*    \*    \*

Near midnight the phone rang, tearing Reinhildt from a sound sleep. For a second the ring terrified her. The phone in her room was one of the only two left in the house, and the service was intermittent. She never received calls—there was no one left to call her.

She grabbed for it before it rang a second time, fearful that it might wake Ernst, who was curled under a blanket in the bed on the other side of the room.

"Yes?"

"Reinhildt von Kleist?" It was a man's voice, barely above a whisper.

"Yes."

"This is Trost. Walter Trost. There are Germans who are still Germans. Do you understand?"

The words flashed through her like an electric shock, triggering the memory of what Eric had told her years before.

"I—I understand."

"Eric is alive and well in Stockholm. You must get out of Germany—now. Go to Frankfurt, number seven Grüneberg-weg. Can you remember that?"

"Yes. Number seven Grünebergweg, Frankfurt."

"See my daughter Erika there. She will help. You must go now—tonight. You *must*. The plot has failed, it has failed. Go to—"

There was a buzz as the connection was broken.

Reinhildt held the phone to her ear for a second, hoping that Trost could get back on the line. Then she decided that it was no use.

Then she heard it, another click. Somewhere in the schloss, another phone was being hung up.

Her stomach was suddenly knotted in steel, and her feet would not move. Ernst, she told herself. Get Ernst out.

She switched on the bedside lamp, just enough illumination to get some things together in a train bag. She grabbed riding pants and then discarded them. Instead, she took a pair of slacks, a sweater, and a pair of hiking boots. She grabbed two sets of sturdy outfits for Ernst and then emptied her jewel case into the small bag. It took only a few minutes to wake and dress Ernst, who yawned and followed her as if in a dream.

They got to the bottom of the main staircase and were headed for the front door, when she saw him silhouetted against the dim blackout lights.

"A small trip, Reinhildt?"

The hall exploded into light as Klaus Schmidt threw the switch that controlled the huge chandelier.

Reinhildt covered her eyes with her hand as the light stabbed at them. Ernst started to cry, and she set down the suitcase and picked him up.

With her eyes adjusted to the light, she stared at Klaus, who stood with his head cocked to the side and a strange, crooked smile curling his lips. It was a look that she had never seen before, and it terrified her. In his right hand, Klaus held a luger. He gestured with it as he spoke.

"The British or the Americans will be bombing Frankfurt again tonight. Listen."

In the distance Reinhildt could hear the sound of planes and sirens in the town.

"From the sound of that, they'll probably hit Stuttgart, too. It would be a dangerous drive to Frankfurt, no matter what Trost said."

"Klaus . . . just please . . . *please* get out of my way."

He shook his head and laughed. It was a strange, high-pitched giggle.

"I'm sorry, Reinhildt. But you will have to stay here, you and that little half-Jewish bastard in your arms. They'll be here for you soon."

"Oh, sweet Jesus." She dropped to her knees and pulled the terrified Ernst close to her. "What did we do to you? What did we do? Can you be that much of a Nazi? For God's sake, can't you just let us go? Please?" She could feel tears starting to pour down her cheeks. She fought back hysteria.

"A *Nazi?*" His voice was a shriek. "A *Nazi?* I never was

much of one. Do you think I gave a fuck about their little Austrian corporal? Ha! I used them, used them, and all the time Heydrich and the rest thought that they were using me. I got what I wanted... or I am about to. Aren't you going to ask what it was?"

She was too terrified to even speak. She could only shake her head.

"Have you ever heard of Wolf Schmidt?"

"N-no."

"He was my father. He was *my* father. He was a well-to-do man, with his own steel mill. Another man drove him out of business, while I was still a child. I was ten when that happened. My father hanged himself. I was the one who found him in the office that night, hanging there, his eyes wide and his tongue black. . . . I found . . . I did." He stopped and breathed heavily. "The man who drove him out of business was Johann von Kleist. I swore then, that if it took the rest of my life, I would finish the von Kleists."

It was an insane nightmare. She was not hearing it.

"Your brothers are gone. Russia, Sweden—gone. You, you, are the only one left—you and the little Jew bastard there. Did you know that Kurt sent your Jew over to Dachau? He did. He did. . . . We did. . . ."

In the distance the drone of aircraft engines grew louder.

"They tried to kill Hitler today at Wolfsschanze. They failed, and from what I heard on the phone, the man Trost was involved. They'll get him, and they'll twist his balls until he tells them about you. But I'll call them first! You will become a conspirator in the plot to kill Hitler. And you will be shielding a half-Jewish child from deportation—if that's what they're still calling it. Both of you will go to a camp. And when that stupid bitch Anya gets back with her idiot son, I will make sure that they are implicated too. The witch-hunt will be on, and they'll go where you go. And then everything will be complete. You see. It took forty years— forty years. Hanging there . . . staring at me. . . . Papa hanging there . . ."

She managed to get to her feet, after pushing Ernst behind

the banister. She took a step in Klaus's direction, and then a second.

He raised the gun and then leveled it at her head. "Stop, there." His voice was low, guttural. "There's more . . . more. Once, I was starting to lose patience. I'd decided to kill all of you, one at a time. I'll wait, I thought. And now, it's come." Again, he giggled.

She could almost see him flashing back and forth from madness to sanity like a flickering light bulb. She took a deep breath, and though she could feel her stomach shudder, she was starting to build a resolve from somewhere deep inside. She would never go to a camp, nor would she let Ernst. Karl had died in a camp. She and his son would live, she decided, or else they would die right here in the foyer of their home.

The sound of the plane engines was a deep-throated, roaring drone now. In the distance, the British Lancaster bombers were starting their turns. They would make the long run into Stuttgart from the east, where the flak guns were more distantly spaced than in the west.

"No, Klaus. No. We are not going to a camp."

"You are. You are." His voice was a manic shriek, like a small child in the midst of a tantrum.

"We are not. You are going to have to kill us, both of us right here. Otherwise, we're going to walk out that door and drive away from here."

"No. They'll come and take you—drag you out."

"I'm going to make you kill us. I'm going to walk back to Ernst and pick him up and go out the door, and to stop us, you will have to kill us. And do you know what will happen then, Klaus? You won't be able to prove that I have a half-Jewish son. The weapon that you were going to discredit the family with will be gone. Anya will have control, and her son, another von Kleist, will rebuild the empire." She moved to her right as she spoke. He followed her with the pistol but did not say anything to stop her. It was as if he were a man listening to a foreign language, barely catching a word in ten. She kept moving. In a moment she managed to inch her way to the huge hall window, shrouded by the thick blackout curtain.

"Shoot me now, Klaus. Shoot both of us. Do it now, or we're leaving."

Klaus looked quizzically at her. Then he nodded. "I'll shoot him first." He turned in the direction of Ernst, who huddled behind the thick banister. "That way, you can watch him die."

His head turning away was what she had been waiting for. She spun, and yanking with all her strength, she pulled the blackout curtain from the window. The chandelier's brilliant light spilled outward into the inky, moonless night.

"White flare," the bombardier called into the microphone in the nose of the Lancaster, some fifteen thousand feet above. He thumbed a small stud on the panel. "Sighting bomb gone."

Forty feet behind him, a single five-hundred-pound bomb released itself from its rack and started to fall lazily earthward.

"Abort! Abort!" cried the voice in his headset. "That's not a white bombing flare. Repeat: not a bombing flare. Flight commander to flight. Do not drop on that light. We are still five minutes from target."

The bomb accelerated as it fell forward and down, toward the white light that the bombardier saw in the crossed hairs of his bombsight.

"Go ahead, Klaus. Go on, shoot. Then you and Ernst and I and the schloss will all go at the same time. Go on." Her voice was a scream. She could start to hear the whistle of the bomb.

He screamed and dashed at her, forgetting that he had the gun.

She dove to the floor as the bomb hit, some thirty yards in front of the schloss.

The thick stone walls of the building shielded her from the blast that blew in the thick front doors and turned the picture window into thousands of deadly shards of glass, which roared into the great hall.

Klaus Schmidt was blown some ten feet backward by the impact. The speeding glass ripped through him, killing him instantly.

It was a few minutes before Reinhildt could manage to get to her feet. Her ears were ringing, and her nose was bleeding. Mortar dust created a thick fog in the dark hall. She slipped and fell several times on glass before she managed to feel her way to the stairs.

"M-mommy?"

She could hear Ernst sobbing. She groped for him in the dark, finally managing to get a hand on him. He seemed to be all right. The curve of the staircase had protected him from the blast. She grabbed him by the hand, picked up the suitcase, then staggered and half crawled to the door. They ran in the direction of the garage, and she opened the door. She took the small Mercedes sedan and tucked Ernst in the backseat. She looked around the garage until she found two partially full gas cans. One she placed in the trunk of the Mercedes with her suitcase, and the other she lugged to the house. She moved back inside the door, into the thick fog of dust, and emptied the can into the hall. Choking from the dust, she went back outside and fished in her purse for her lighter. Finding it, she flicked it into life and tossed it far into the hall.

There was a whoosh of flame, and in an instant, the hall was a pyre for Klaus Schmidt. She was hoping that if and when the SS arrived, they would think that it was also a pyre for her.

She dashed back to the garage, drove the car out, and shut the door behind her, reasoning that it would be better not to advertise that a car had been taken. It might delay them further.

She roared down the Bergstrasse, driving one-handed and feeling for her papers in her purse. Yes, they were there. If there had been no general alarm given, there was a chance that she could get to Frankfurt. She ran over the address in her mind and the woman's name: Erika Trost...number seven...Grünebergweg. She knew where it was, it was not far from the place where Eric had stayed in medical school.

The sun was nearly up as she got into the southern outskirts of the city. For the last twenty miles, he had seen the city as a smudge of black smoke rising skyward. The air raid had caused fires all over the downtown industrial area. She prayed that the bridges were intact because to get to her destination, she was going to have to cross the Main.

Luckily, two of the car bridges were still standing. She managed to get into the city and skirt the bombed areas. It was seven-thirty in the morning when she got to Grüneberg-weg. She found number seven. It was a small apartment house, and the mailbox indicated that Trost lived on the ground floor. Carrying Ernst, who grumbled sleepily, she rang the bell, and a woman in her early twenties opened the door a crack.

"Yes?"

"Fraülein Trost? There are some Germans who are still Germans," she whispered.

The young woman nodded tersely, then opened the door and waved the two of them in.

She closed and locked the door behind them.

"Who are you?"

"Reinhildt von Kleist."

"You are the sister of the doctor?"

"Yes."

"Did my father give you any information about him?"

"Yes. He said that he was in Stockholm."

"Good." The woman took a pistol from where she had it concealed behind her back. "I'm sorry. We can no longer be sure about the passwords. Everything is madness now. The Gestapo is everywhere, searching for the ones who plotted to kill Hitler. My father is in Köln. If he hasn't been arrested already, there is a good chance that he will be soon. I know him, though. He won't be taken alive."

"I'm sorry."

"How did you get here?"

"Can I find a place to put my son?"

"Oh, I'm sorry. Of course." They put Ernst on the sofa, where he fell back to sleep.

"I got here by car."

"Have you got fuel?"

"Yes. An extra can."

"Good. We will have to leave as soon as possible. We will head to Saarbrücken. We have friends there. They will help get us across to France."

"What will we do, then?"

"Keep moving west. The Allies are moving east out of Normandy. The BBC says that they are flying across France and the Wehrmacht is retreating. With God's help we can get through to them. . . . Where is your car?"

"I parked it in the alley next to the building."

"Good. It will be out of sight there. I'll get a bag and some food."

"There's no one else? But you, I mean?"

"There was my fiancé. He was conscripted and died in Russia."

"I'm so sorry."

"My father told that you are a widow."

"Yes."

"We both understand then, don't we?"

"I guess we do, Fraülein Trost."

In less than an hour, they were driving out of the city and heading westward on the back roads.

They made it to Saarbrücken without incident, and Erika's underground friends produced papers to get them across the French border. They were a hundred miles inside France when the motor sputtered and died. They had to leave the car and travel on foot, Reinhildt leading Ernst until he tired and had to be carried, and Erika lugging their bags.

It took them four agonizing weeks, moving with refugee columns in the daytime and at night alone, to reach the lines. They could hear the firing of distant guns. They were outside Troyes, huddled in an abandoned farmhouse, when Reinhildt fell ill. She was burning with fever and racked with coughing. Erika wrapped her in a blanket she found in the farmhouse and tried to stay awake while Reinhildt slept. But she herself nodded off at about six in the morning.

When she woke, Reinhildt was no better; the fever seemed as high as it had been before, and she was coughing in her sleep. Erika looked to the corner of the room.

The child. He was gone!

She got to her feet ' started to the door, then froze. She could hear truck motors in the distance. And voices...

Suddenly the door flew open, and Ernst ran in.

"Look, Erika. They gave me this."

The brown-wrapped package said... HERSHEY.

The Americans had liberated Troyes. In less than half a day, Reinhildt was in an American field hospital, and Erika with Ernst were in a barracks for displaced persons.

## 36

It was two weeks before Reinhildt was well enough to be questioned by US officials, and then her interrogators were reluctant to believe who she was; it seemed too insane that the daughter of one of the most staunchly Nazi families in Germany would have to flee the country. In the end it was only because of Erika's testimony—and her father's connections with the underground—that the officials accepted Reinhildt's story.

It took another two weeks of red tape, and waiting in a DP barracks near Paris, before Reinhildt was able to make contact with Eric in Stockholm. It was the last Saturday in October when Reinhildt and Ernst stepped off a plane in Stockholm and were greeted by Eric, Horst, and Diana. The internment laws, slackened as the war was ebbing, allowed Horst and Diana to accept responsibility for Reinhildt, as they had for Eric. For the duration, she was allowed to work in the same hospital that Eric had been assigned to.

At last, on a warm evening in May, 1945, the four of them gathered around the radio, to listen to the English language news broadcast that the Germans had surrendered unconditionally.

The nightmare had ended. Later there would be the question of where to go and what to do, but for now Eric poured champagne for all of them, even Ernst, who sniffed it, sipped, and made a funny face, asking for juice. Diana laughed and headed off to the kitchen to get him some.

Eric looked across the living room to his younger brother.

"Horst, you never mentioned how much money changed hands to get me out of Leningrad."

Horst sat back on the couch. "That's right, Eric, I didn't, did I?"

Eric cocked his head to the side. "Well?"

"Well what?"

"How much was it?"

"It's a military secret."

"Horst, I'm serious. I must owe you—all of you—a great deal of money."

"Poor older brother, still so serious about everything. The amount is meaningless. You ended up in Russia because you got us out of Germany in 1941. Let's call it even. Now, more important—with the war over, what are you going to do?"

Eric did not hesitate. "I'm going back to Germany."

Horst sat forward on the sofa. "What? Why, for God's sake? There's nothing but rubble in the cities and poverty in the streets. It will be years before Germany recovers, and at that, the chances are that the Russians will control half of the country. Why would you want to go back when all that was keeping you there from the beginning was Reinhildt?"

Eric spread his hands in an expansive gesture. "Because I'm a German, Horst. I'm still a German. It's my country, and I love it, despite the lunatics who have been running it for the past twelve years.

"There are a great many things that I want to do, that I've wanted all along. Clinics. I want to try and accomplish some of the things that Karl was working toward when"—he glanced at Reinhildt—"he was killed. I would like to start a research foundation. There are a hundred things to do."

"And where will the funds for all that come from? You no longer have the corporation. Anya does, I expect, if she's alive. Where will the money come from?"

"I have my account—plus the original stock—in Zurich. In addition, there are some other investments that I made before the war. There's not much, but there's enough to make a start. When the banks get back in operation, they will be able to finance things to a point. There will be a great need for cheap medical care in Germany in the years to come. And besides, how do we know who will control the old corporation now? Anya was a Nazi. Surely, she won't have much of a claim, now that the war is lost? The Americans, the British, and the Russians will be hanging Nazis from trees as soon as they get the chance. I know. I saw what the Nazis did to Russia—Russian wounded shot where they fell. Not that the Russians did much better to us.... There was only one Russian I ever met who— Well, that's not important now. What I mean is, there is a chance that the corporation might be available to us."

"You're really serious about all of this, aren't you?"

"Totally serious—too serious as usual."

"Who's too serious? No one should be. This is a party," Diana said as she came back in the living room with a glass of apple juice for Ernst.

"Eric here. He's set on going back to Germany."

"And why shouldn't he? After all, he's a German."

Eric laughed loudly, and Horst shook his head.

"Leave it to my wife." He turned to his sister, who sat next to him. "And you, Reinhildt? What will you do?"

"I think I'll go back, too, Horst."

"For the same reasons?"

"Yes. For the same reasons. I want to do something productive with the rest of my life. But I won't go back to Tübingen. It would always make me think of... too many things that I want to forget. I'll go to Frankfurt, perhaps, and look into starting a business. I'll have a lot to learn, of course. All that Father ever prepared me for was playing concert piano and marrying the right man—the one that he chose. But as Eric says, there is a great deal to be done, and the opportunities will be there as Germany rebuilds. Have you forgotten that that was the way that Father made *his* fortune? Much of it, anyway? And what are you two going to do—you Swedish-American Germans?"

"Back home, I think," said Diana. "It will be at least another year, though, before the complex is finished. Is that right, Horst?"

"Yes. Perhaps a year and a half. Then back to the US." He turned to Diana. "You know, we should get them to visit, especially the Cape in the summer. Then they would be seduced into staying. Could your father use a doctor on the staff?"

She nodded. "Oh, I'm sure he could find room. I remember that he said once, years ago, that he was contemplating funding a hospital. Would you like that, Eric? Is that seduction enough?"

Eric got to his feet and waved his glass, smiling. "What I think I would like is another drink."

After an hour, Eric got up to leave, saying that he had early rounds at the hospital. Reinhildt did not have to work the following day, but she walked Eric to the street corner, where he would wait for a trolley back to his tiny apartment.

"There was something that you said back there, Eric. It puzzled me."

"What's that?" he asked, peering down the street and checking his watch for the trolley.

"You mentioned a Russian—and there was something in your face, something that I never saw there before."

"What was that?" He didn't look at her.

"I'm not really sure. It was just something strange, something distant in your face."

"Oh, little sister. Stop seeing signs and portents in everything."

"I'm serious." She stopped and backed away a step. "Eric? Was there a woman in Russia? Was there someone special?"

He seemed not to hear the question at first. He looked again down the street, hoping for the trolley, and then again at his watch. She waited.

"Yes," he said finally.

"What was she like?"

"She was a Russian Jewess. And . . . we loved each other. It couldn't have happened at a worse time or place. We stole moments for more than a year under the noses of the doctors and the staff. There was every chance that I would have been shot if they caught us. She would have been sent God only knows where. It was insane." He shook his head. She could see the same look in his face again.

"What happened?"

"They whisked me away in the middle of the night. There was no chance to say goodbye. She must have come to my cell in the morning, and I simply wasn't there. I'm sure that they would have told her nothing about my destination. After all, the deal that Horst made with the Russians was something rather secret. I expect she thinks I'm dead."

He could see the distant light of the trolley winding its way toward him.

"I'm so sorry, Eric. Is there a chance that you might be able to find her, now that the war is over?"

"I don't know. I'll certainly try."

The trolley stopped, and they embraced. He got on and waved to her as it began to clatter away. Slowly she turned and went back to the house.

It was early August when the paper work was completed that allowed Eric and Reinhildt to return to Germany. Horst decided to take a last trip to the schloss, though Diana said that she preferred to remember it the way it was on the only night that she had seen it. She remained in Stockholm with Manfred.

It was a strange pilgrimage, taking a circuitous route. The Paris Nord Express got them as far as Bremen, where Horst managed to rent a car.

They were appalled at the damage that they saw. Most of the cities were utterly demolished, with building bricks and starving children in the streets. There were food lines and general misery. Frankfurt had been heavily bombarded in the last days of the war. When they got there, Reinhildt asked Eric to drive to Grünebergweg.

The entire front half on number seven was in the street, and a crew was clearing away the rubble and piling it in dump trucks. Most of the houses on the block were the same. She asked about Erika Trost, but none of the people in the area seemed to know about her. Reinhildt gave up. It had only been a thought to see and thank the woman who had saved her and Ernst.

They spent the night in a small hotel and then drove on to Tübingen.

The schloss had been half gutted by fire, and Reinhildt wept when she saw it. She had told Horst and Eric about Schmidt and about starting the fire to delay the SS, and they had assured her she had done the right thing. Still, she felt sick when she looked at the ruins of what had been so magnificent.

They went through the door, which, to their surprise, had been repaired from the bomb damage. The front hall was still partially demolished, though there were signs that some repairs had been started. As they moved down the hall, a side door opened, and a woman came from the kitchen. All three of them stopped suddenly. It took them a second to recognize her. Anya.

Her hair was pulled back severely, and her clothes were old and worn. There were deeply etched lines around her mouth and eyes. She could have been a woman in her late forties rather than in her middle thirties.

"What do you want here? This is my place now. Mine and

Heinrich's. So is the company. So, go away. You are not welcome."

Horst took a step forward. "Who the hell do you think you are? You were the darling of the Nazis, if I remember rightly. What happened? Did they miss you in the count of the Nazi scum? Or did they decide to let you out of the cage?"

She took a step forward and spat words at him.

"You fool. I earned what I got. It is *mine* now. Kurt held the company, and when he died, it became mine. I finished the de-Nazification program, and the Allies love me. I am going to help them rebuild the German industries to keep them away from the big bad Russians. Now, get out. I have things to do."

Eric stepped forward. "Anya, we will only be a few minutes. Was my room damaged in the fire?"

"No. None of the back of the house was. It's intact. Why?"

"I just wanted to get a few personal things that had been left up there. Then we will go."

She thought for a moment, then nodded imperceptibly. "Very well. But do it quickly and get out."

They went up the stairs and into Eric's room. He walked to one side of the bed and took a picture from the wall, revealing a rectangular outline in the paper. Eric took a pocket knife and pried open the small hinged door of a tiny wall safe. He reached inside and pulled out a slightly rusty locked box, which he tucked under his arm. "That's all I really wanted. We can go now."

Anya was nowhere to be seen as they left. Horst guided the car down the long poplar-lined drive and into the town.

Eric stopped at the clinic and was happy to find that many of the staff were still there. Frau Slodski was gone, along with the other Jews who had vanished into the camps during the war, but there were some familiar faces, including Grette, who hugged him and cried when she saw him.

They wandered around the clinic for more than an hour and were just leaving when a jeep with three Americans pulled up and screeched to a halt. The man in the right front seat was an officer, and the other two men were military police, Eric could see from their brassards.

The officer approached Eric. "Do you speak English?"

Eric nodded. "Yes."

"I am looking for Dr. Eric von Kleist."

"I am he."

"Dr. von Kleist," he said as he pulled a sheaf of papers from his jacket, "I am Major Walters of the American Military District government. Sir, I have a warrant here for your arrest."

"What for?" Eric was stunned.

"Sir, it's from the Nürnberg Tribunal. You are accused of war crimes."

## 37

Eric was taken by the Americans to Stuttgart and then on to Nürnberg, where a case was being prepared against him. Horst wired Diana, and she flew down to Frankfurt, taking Ernst back to Stockholm with her. A few days later the press got hold of the story. In the midst of what was being called "War Crimes Fever," the media made the most of it. In the British and American papers, Eric was being billed as a high criminal, one who used slave labor during the war in von Kleist plants. Thousands had died, the headlines read. Old newsreels were exhumed that billed Eric as the "Head of the Nazi War Machine." Even a picture of him at the grave of his father became evidence.

The arraignment was a farce. Eric was held for trial and remanded to Spandau prison, where the highest-ranking Nazi war criminals were being held. It was guilt by association when photographers managed to get shots of Eric walking in the exercise yard only a few yards from Hess and Goering.

Horst flew to the United States to confer with his father-in-law, while Reinhildt stayed in Germany to help muster Eric's defense. She searched vainly for Erika Trost, who seemed to have dropped from the face of the earth. She took ads in German newspapers and bought radio time to try to get in touch with the woman, all unsuccessfully.

She might be dead, or emigrated to . . . where? With Walter Trost dead, she was the only person who could confirm Eric's connection with the underground. But with only two weeks to the trial, and no results in the search, Reinhildt knew what she must do.

In the United States, things were even more frustrating. Horst tried to find the OSS officials with whom he had worked during the war; they knew that Eric had given Trost's name to Horst in the first place. But neither Hurley nor Weatherow could be located. Indeed, Horst was told that there was no OSS any more. A wartime expediency, it had been replaced by a new organization called the Central Intelligence Agency, and, Horst was informed, it kept little track of wartime OSS operatives. He didn't believe this, but he recognized that the government's priorities had shifted, due to the vagaries of the international situation. The Soviet Union, a wartime ally, was fast becoming a foe. What Churchill called the Iron Curtain was descending on Eastern Europe, and the last thing the US government wanted to associate itself with was the ransom of a Nazi "war criminal" from the Russians in 1944. Dejected, Horst flew back to Germany.

Eric's indictment was pushed from the front pages as the real stars of the war crimes trials were brought to the dock: Goering, Hess, Doenitz, and Speer were now splashed across the front pages, and Eric's trial was remanded to a small room at the side of the main trial facility at Nürnberg. His lawyer was Louis Rauschenberg, a former law partner of Werner Altenhoff. The man was one of the best trial lawyers in Germany. But, here, he did not have a jury to sway. Rather, he had a tribunal of three officers: one French, one

English, one American. Despite the fact that the four-way translations slowed the process, it was clear from the outset that the trial would be brief.

The prosecution counsel was an American colonel, a lawyer named Willis, who had already gotten several convictions in similar cases. Rauschenberg was not happy; the prosecution's opening was strong, however circumstantial the evidence.

"Gentlemen of the tribunal," Willis said as he paced in front of the bench, "perhaps the most vivid indication that we have of the complicity of Mr. von Kleist in war crimes is contained in a series of films. I submit them for your consideration."

Eric had known that the films were coming, when he had seen the projector at the back of the courtroom. What he didn't know was how damning they really were.

The projector flickered to life, and a German newsreel flashed on the screen.

There were shots of the von Kleist complexes interspersed with shots of Eric meeting with workers and managers. The narration was directly out of Goebbels's Ministry of Propaganda.

"Herr Eric von Kleist, oldest son of the greatest industrial giant in all of Germany, helps his family and the entire German war effort as he tours his family's plants, insuring that the Reich is on a war footing. Herr Doktor von Kleist has been vital in the transition of the industrial complexes into arsenals of the Reich."

There was a shot of Eric with a ragged group of workers in the background. Eric pointed to them and then spoke to Gunther. As there was no sound track except for the voice-over, none of the real dialogue between Eric and Gunther could be heard. The prosecutor ordered the frame frozen.

"You clearly see here that Herr von Kleist is speaking to one of the plant managers, a man named Gunther, who did not survive the war, about the disposition of the slave workers in one of the plants."

"Objection." Rauschenberg was on his feet in an instant. "There is no way that the prosecution can state what was being said there. There is no sound."

The head of the tribunal nodded. "I'll sustain that."

The objection was valid, though Rauschenberg knew that the damage had been done by simply showing Eric in the proximity of the slave workers.

"The prosecution would like to call Georg Wichowski to the stand."

A tall, lean, bald man with a pronounced limp shuffled to the front of the court. With him came a translator who was to translate from Polish into German.

"You were an officer of the rank of captain with the Polish Third Army?"

"Yes."

"You were taken prisoner in the first week of the war?"

The man nodded. "Yes. I commanded a troop of horse cavalry. Our horses were killed by the Stukas, and the same day we were overrun by panzers and infantry."

"Where were you sent from there?"

"Along with some others, I was shipped to a factory that I later found out was a von Kleist plant in a town called Höchst."

Eric listened with a hardening knot of frustration in his stomach.

"Was it there that you saw the accused?"

"Yes. I saw him several times. On one occasion, I saw him speak to one of the guards. It was only minutes after that, when the guard told me I was not working hard enough. He hit me in the side with his rifle butt and knocked me to the ground."

"Could this have been done at Herr von Kleist's order?"

"I thought it was."

Again, Rauschenberg was on his feet, objecting that the statement was speculation as much as the one about what had been said in the film. The objection was sustained, but again the damage was done.

Wichowski went on to detail the poor food, long hours, and lack of medical care at the plant.

"Where were you at the end of the war?"

"I was a prisoner in Auschwitz."

"Did you see any indication of von Kleist assistance to the war effort while you were there?"

"Oh, yes. Much. They were the firm that sold the Germans the materials for many of the barracks, not to mention the gas chambers and crematoria. They also supplied the Buna camp."

After a few more questions, Wichowski was excused, with Rauschenberg not wishing to cross-examine. The sooner the man got off the stand, the better for Eric.

Several other witnesses followed, each detailing seeing Eric in factories and seeing a plethora of von Kleist goods in the war effort. The rest of the prosecution's case took only an hour, after which Willis rested.

Rauschenberg began the defense by calling Horst as the first witness.

"You claim that you worked with the American OSS during the war?"

"That's correct, and so did Eric."

"In what capacity?"

"I assisted two OSS agents named Hurley and Weatherow in the establishment of prime targets in the von Kleist industries in the Ruhr."

"How did your brother assist you in this?"

"After we managed to get him from Leningrad to Stockholm, he helped me in pinpointing further von Kleist targets for Allied air raids. You see, he was more conversant with the plants themselves. I had not even seen them in more than ten years. He had been on inspection tours of them at the beginning of the war."

Rauschenberg concluded, then yielded Horst to the cross-examination of Willis, who did not waste any time getting to the point.

"Is there any way to substantiate this collaboration with the Allies, Mr. von Kleist?"

"I am under oath. Is that not enough?"

"I don't question oaths, sir. I simply ask if there is any more to this than your unsubstantiated word?"

"The Allies have records of all of this. Those records were with the OSS at the end of the war."

"Where are they now?"

"Well, the OSS has become another agency now—one called the CIA. They were not willing to release records."

"So then, there is no proof?"

"Yes, there is, Colonel. There is. It's just that we have not been able to get our hands on it."

Horst was excused. It was clear that no one in the tribunal would believe the unsubstantiated testimony.

Rauschenberg looked to the back of the room. "The defense calls Frau Reinhildt Altenhoff."

Eric's head snapped back. He was stunned. He had expected that Reinhildt would not testify. He had prevailed on his counsel to avoid calling her. Apparently, she had conferred with Rauschenberg in private. As Reinhildt came to the front of the room, Eric's eyes riveted those of Rauschenberg. The lawyer came to him at the defense table. "There was no choice, Eric... not after Horst failed to get the documentation. She has to. I'm sorry."


"Eric loathed the Nazis and all that they stood for." As Reinhildt spoke she sat with her hands knitted together. Her knuckles were white and tense. Her voice was filled with emotion. She could feel herself in a dream. Who would have thought that things would have come to this? Eric on trial... and losing.

"And you say that he worked with the underground?"

"Yes... before he went to Russia. He had contacted a man named Walter Trost and had been working with him. Unfortunately, Herr Trost is dead... killed as a result of the plot to kill Hitler in 1944. But, his daughter is alive—she helped me and my son get out of Germany."

"Why did you have to flee?"

Reinhildt paused and took a deep breath. She was going to have to lay it all out... all of the things that Eric wanted to remain secret.

She painfully told the story of Karl Mittenberg and the fact that they had planned to be married. She relived the night of his arrest and detailed the attempts that Eric had made to save him.

"And what happened the night that Doctor Mittenberg, your fiancé, was arrested?"

"He was to be shipped to Dachau . . . at least that was what we were told. Eric tried to intercede and get him released. He failed. My fiancé died there."

The cross-examination was relentless. Wasn't this simply a case of vested interest, a case in which Eric had a personal interest . . . a family interest? Mittenberg had been more than an illiterate Polish slave who could be battered. Reinhildt raised her tear-streaked face to the tribunal: the three judges were impassive. She had sacrificed everything—and lost.

She looked away—out over the spectators. Suddenly her eyes went wide, and her hands flew to her mouth. She again started to cry.

At the rear door of the courtroom stood Erika Trost!

"And your father was a leader of the underground?"

"He was."

"Can you prove that, Fraülein Trost?" Rauschenberg asked, hoping that there was something more than her word to go on.

There was. She took from a case letters of commendation from several high-ranking Allied generals. Validation was there.

"My father had contacted Mr. von Kleist, ah, Dr. von Kleist, as early as a year before the war began. He told me that the man could be a reliable member of the underground, and he felt sure that he could be called on at any time. As it happened, the doctor was conscripted and sent to Russia before we could use him. I can assure you, though, he was touring factories to try to improve conditions for those poor wretches. Whatever those films say, it was the doing of Goebbels and not of Eric von Kleist!"

After the summations, the tribunal sat for only an hour. Eric was acquitted.

# 38

It would be more than two decades before the von Kleists again joined together in something more than an occasional social gathering. After his acquittal, Eric did exactly what he had told Horst he would do. He took the gold that he had secreted in Zurich and started to invest it. Acting on tips from Horst, he put a substantial amount in Lassiter stock, which prospered in the postwar American building boom. He reinvested the dividends and then reinvested again. Strangely, another source of income was the von Kleist stocks he still controlled; they grew in value as the conglomerate, like the Phoenix, rose from the ashes, to supply steel rebuilding Germany. Thanks to the Marshall Plan, American funds assisted in reconstructing the Ruhr complexes. Eric never forgot the words of Anya on his last visit to the schloss: the Americans would spend a lot of money to keep West Germany away from the big bad Russians. They did.

With capital in hand and credit starting to flow again from the German banking system, Eric opened a series of clinics across the German landscape. He staffed them with young doctors just out of medical school and arranged with the German medical board for the clinic work to be considered part of the internship requirement. It was a totally novel idea. The new doctors, working under the supervision of a resident, would treat the patients, be paid a modest salary, and get credit at the same time. As the salary for the individual doctor was low, Eric managed to keep expenses down. With the savings, he opened more clinics. In less than five years from the time of the war crimes trial, the operation was thriving.

*Tonisha!*

The thought of her never left him, and he attributed his success to the energy that he poured into his work as he tried, unsuccessfully, to forget her.

In the first years he had written letter after letter, first to the German consulate in Moscow and then in Leningrad. They could not help him. The records of Russian Jews were the property of the Russians, and they did not easily part with them, especially to German diplomats. Eric tried writing to the Russian government directly but had been getting the same cool, noninformative answers for more than two years before a break came. He was invited to Moscow to address a conference of medical school faculty about the success of his clinics. Specifically, they wanted to know how Eric managed to hold the program together. There was a strong hint that they would welcome advice on how his internship system might be integrated into Soviet clinics.

As Eric got off the plane, the bitter wind of a Moscow December bit into him, recalling his last Russian winter. A group was coming to the ramp, and Eric recognized a small, florid-faced man in a Russian cap as Doktor Vladimir Lozenko, director of the Lenin Institute of Medicine.

"Doktor von Kleist?"

"Yes. And you are Doktor Lozenko?"

"Ah. We both have good intelligence networks. Yes. Meet my staff."

There were introductions, and Eric gave up trying to remember all of the names, though he was surprised the see that half of the staff was made of women. They drove him to a hotel, the best Moscow could offer, though it was pitiful by German standards. The electricity and hot water were intermittent, and the food was mediocre. Still, Lozenko wined and dined Eric in the finest Soviet tradition and worked with him on the speech that he was going to give the next day. Lozenko was obviously impressed and gratified by the fact that Eric had come to Moscow at his own expense and was speaking for free. It was late in the evening in Eric's room, and both men had drunk a great deal of vodka before Lozenko got to the point.

"Eric—if I may call you that—a number of my colleagues suspect your motives in coming here. The NKVD is nosing around. They don't know whether to put more surveillance on or not. They are . . . puzzled about why you wanted to come here."

Eric pondered the remark. Perhaps it was the time to mention his personal mission. There was something about Lozenko that seemed trustworthy.

"You must forgive me, Vladimir. There *is* another motive aside from the possible—" He stopped for a second. His tongue was thick, and he knew it. "For the mutual agreement that we might reach. It · more of a personal reason."

"Well, what is it? We will do the best that we can. We have been known to move even bureaucrats on occasion."

Eric wondered if Vladimir already knew about it. If he did not, why would he have mentioned bureaucrats? He pushed the thought away, assuming that much of Russian life was governed by bureaucrats.

"I'm looking for someone. . . ."

He explained about Tonisha. Vladimir listened silently, nodding occasionally. Then he agreed that he would arrange an interview, after the cc ference presentation, of course, with the appropriate department.

On the following day, the presentation was magnificent, and Eric was given a standing ovation by the staff of the institute. It was two hours before he could pull himself away to join Vladimir. They drove from the institute to a gray building not far from Red Square. The office that they sought was on the third floor. It was bleak, decorated only with pictures of Stalin and Lenin. Two clerks sat at adjoining desks. There was an inner office in the distance with walls lined with bookcases.

Vladimir strode to the first desk and spoke in Russian to the clerk, who, after a minute, got up and scurried through the inner door. In a matter of minutes a tall, thin man with dark features and spectacles came out, spoke to Vladimir for a moment, and then turned to Eric, suddenly speaking fluent German.

"Dr. von Kleist, I am Ivan Kolok. How can the records office help you?"

Eric explained as they moved with Vladimir to Kolok's office, which was more elegantly appointed.

Sure that Eric was in good hands, Vladimir agreed to pick him up in an hour.

Kolok sat behind his desk and listened as Eric explained. When he was finished, Kolok shook his head. "The records of the period, especially those from Leningrad, are fragmentary. There was so much bombing at the time, which you would know since you were there, and—there were different records kept for Jews at the time. I can assure you, though, that many of them have been centralized since then. What we can do is to go through them and look. We have a name and a town of birth. That is something to start with. Beyond that, there is a chance that we can query other offices. Let's look."

They got to work, and for more than an hour they plied the records, with Eric looking at the pictures on the files as he could not read Russian. There were a number of Durovs, and several from the general area where Tonisha had been born. Still, after the hour, it appeared that there was no record of her. Kolok was apologetic. He promised to look further and took Eric's address, assuring him that there would be another exhaustive search.

Eric went back into the hall and down into the street to wait for Lozenk . The wind whipped at him, and it seemed to have more bite than before. He could feel in his heart that he would never find her.

He returned to Frankfurt, dove into his career, and tried to forget. There was no word from the Russians in a year, and in the second year there was a polite and apologetic letter from Kolok, saying that they had exhausted their resources and there was no trace of a Tonisha Durov. Eric found himself living with little more than a ghostly memory, something fleeting, like a wisp of smoke. In that way, he was like his sister, who lived with the ghost of Karl Mittenberg.

By the early sixties, there were more than thirty von Kleist clinics across Germany. Eric, flooded with administrative duties, was forced to incorporate and hire a staff.

Eventually, he developed the funding for a foundation that would focus on disease research. By 1966, he found himself at the head of a medical empire that was one of the largest in Germany. He thought it strange that, in his mid-fifties, he suddenly was the medical equivalent of what his father had been to munitions and weapons. And if he was that, he mused, his younger brother Horst was fast becoming an exact duplicate of Johann in the steel business.

Richard Lassiter died quietly in his sleep in 1951, leaving control of Lassiter Steel to Horst and Diana. Over the following fifteen years, riding through recession and boom, Lassiter grew. Horst had a keen eye for innovation and was one of the first steel company owners to incorporate automation into his plants. After riding a storm of labor problems, he added computers to the steel industry, convinced that it was the wave of the future. By the early sixties, he managed to get his face on the cover of *Time*, which called him the "new Carnegie of Steel." He created trade agreements with Japanese steel competitors, insuring that he would not be undersold. He survived an SEC restriction of trade suit and ended up expanding even more. Horst was fifty when Manfred, he and Diana's only child, graduated from Yale. Ironically, Horst found himself in a similar position to old Johann, years before. He dearly wanted Manfred to come into the company and learn the steel business. Rather, Manfred chose to strike out on his own, blending finance and computers.

Diana contented herself by running their home smoothly, entertaining and impressing important visitors—and maintaining the family ties with Germany. She corresponded regularly with Reinhildt, and over the years the two became close friends. One of the links that bound them together was their mutual antipathy for Anya.

In Germany, Reinhildt dove into the world of finance. She took courses at Goethe University in Frankfurt, earning a degree in business and started an investment counseling firm. Modest at first, it grew into a large operation, though it never could eclipse what her brothers had done—nor did she want it to. Rather, she devoted a good part of her energies to Ernst, who, after passing his entrance exams for the university, announced that he wanted to study medicine. Apparently the constant visits of Uncle Eric over the years had had an impact. Eric and Reinhildt managed to get together for a dinner or a weekend at least once a month. Neither of them ever married: it seemed that the ghosts they both lived with were sufficient company.

And at Schloss von Kleist, Anya raised Heinrich in the image of his father. His bedtime stories were tales of Kurt's heroic sacrifice for the Fatherland. His boyhood and adolescence were rigidly supervised, with Anya carefully meting out her praise and disdain, alternately loving and demanding, to insure that her son would follow in his father's footsteps.

Nor was she alone in this effort. As the dust of war settled and Germany rebuilt, old Nazis came out of hiding. They used assumed names, of course—and code names for their organizations, like ODESSA. It was only natural they should seek out the widow of a hero like Kurt von Kleist, and take an interest in his son—who just happened to be heir to the von Kleist empire. It had served the Reich once; why not again?

Why not? Anya agreed.

## The Negev, 1947

The jeep veered suddenly to the right, looking for cover. There was none. Uri Ben Tabor had not wanted his wife to embark on the mission. He had argued that it was too dangerous, especially in the daytime, to try to get medical supplies to the besieged kibbutz in the Negev. She had overridden his objections, saying that he was needed where he was at an outpost in Galilee that was itself besieged. She had left at dawn with extra fuel and antibiotics, accompanied only by a Haganah soldier to man the jeep's machine gun. But, now, he was dead, killed on the first pass of the strafing Egyptian fighter.

She couldn't see the plane, but she could hear it as it started to dive. She decided to wait until the sound was close and then to veer to the left. She calculated wrong. The fighter was coming from slightly left of center, and as she veered, she caught a burst of fifty-caliber fire in the extra gas cans that she was carrying. The jeep exploded in a blossom of fire. She was killed instantly.

It took more than three days for Israeli patrols to find the body, or what was left of it after the incineration of the jeep. They buried her there, and a day later Uri Ben Tabor, suddenly a widower, stood at a memorial service in his besieged kibbutz. Near him, one of the women of the community held his tiny daughter, Jordanna. He could feel, through the grief, he felt something that he had never felt before. Suddenly he had no further need to be a doctor; it was no longer enough. He looked at his daughter and wearily recalled the horror that had stretched from Dachau to the current war. Her world must be better. . . .

It was less than three days later when he managed to get through to Jerusalem and speak to Isaac Ben Aram.

"You want to what?"

"I said that I want to work strictly with the military. I think that I can give more there."

"Uri. Your wife is dead, and you have a small child. I understand how that might have affected your judgment. But, understand, you are perhaps the best medical officer that we have. Why this—so suddenly?"

"I don't know. But, there has to be something more than the patching up of the wounded. There has to be a defense that will allow us to prevent all of this from happening again. It has to be in the military and in politics. There's no other way."

Isaac sipped hot tea and placed the glass back on his desk. He moved to the window. There were still fires smoldering from an air raid in the distance. A thought struck him. Yes . . . it was perfect. He had been talking to Ben-Gurion about it only that morning. He turned.

"Very well, Karl. We accept your offer. Or, at least I do. All of this will have to be cleared with the Knesset. Are you prepared to accept any assignment that we give you?"

Uri paused and thought. There was no sense in coming this far only to back off. "Certainly."

"Very well. You will be assigned to intelligence. Specifically, your assignment will be Nazis, the ones who are advising the Arabs. There are a great number of them, and you might know some by sight. Also, as a German you speak the language and can understand how they think. Do you accept?"

"Yes."


Over the years, Uri Ben Tabor rose in the ranks to senior Israeli intelligence officer with the rank of brigadier. It was on a warm summer night in 1959 that he was to hear of a ghost from the past.

He waited outside the estate in a small grove of trees. He had come to Damascus as a German merchant. He had shaved his graying head and dyed the fringe black. He had grown a mustache for the mission. Everything had been airtight. During the afternoon, his position outside the estate in the Damascus suburbs had allowed him to see and photograph all of the members of the conference. Of particular interest was a tall German with blond hair and a winning smile. The Arab hosts seemed to fawn over the man. As twilight grew into evening, Uri tuned into the small radio transmitter that had been hidden in the conference room. The conversation was interesting . . . and predictable. It was also frustrating. There were no names mentioned, as if the

Arabs knew they might be overheard. Still, it was clear that the German was making a deal to sell them weapons. He also spoke glowingly of the help that ODESSA could be to the Arabs in any forthcoming holy war. All in all, Uri managed to get some hour of tape to take back to Tel Aviv. He escaped undetected.

After his arrival, he rushed the tape to an audio studio and then got the photos developed. It was late the following afternoon, with his whole staff working relentlessly, when he got a call from Isaac.

"Uri? About this German that you saw?"

"Yes?"

"You have evidence that he has dealt with the Arabs before?"

Uri slammed a fist on the desk. "Isaac, I told you—he is the reason I took the mission. He has been all over the Arab world selling arms. There are a hundred intelligence reports in my files now, all of them inconclusive. None of them can actually identify him."

"We can, now, Uri."

"Well?"

"His name is Heinrich von Kleist."

Anya von Kleist had become the matriarch of the largest steel operation in Europe, and Heinrich had become her emissary. Physically, he was a carbon copy of Kurt, though he was infinitely more clever than his father, developing himself into a master market consultant and salesman for von Kleist. He crisscrossed Europe and the Middle East, garnering markets for his mother. And he had learned his politics at her knee. He was an arch conservative, a violent anti-Semite, and a man who had gone to great pains at a young age to develop intimate ties with the PLO and ODESSA, exploiting the war record of his father. He fast became the darling of the Arab world, especially when he hinted about von Kleist going back into the weapons business.

**Boston, January, 1967**

Horst looked across the desk at Manfred. Unlike many fathers, he did not look for a carbon copy of himself. Rather, Manfred was six-foot-four, a full five inches taller than his father. He had a fair complexion, and his mother's deep blue eyes and red hair. Horst lit his pipe slowly and stared at the hair. It almost reached Manfred's shoulders and somehow looked out of place with the well-tailored blue business suit that his son wore.

"So there's no way that I can induce you?" He puffed the question with a cloud of blue smoke.

Manfred smiled sheepishly. "Perhaps in a year or two. Just recently, I was thinking that I'd like to set up a small computer company. The idea would be time-sharing and services. Hardware is expensive, and many businesses are saddled with more than they can ever use. The big computer outfits keep coming out with new models and building in planned obsolescence so that the users are on a treadmill. What I see is a company that would make a large initial investment in hardware and simply provide services: inventories, payrolls, and the like. From there, we could consult and eventually time-share on our terminals with the master data base we would set up. What do you think?"

Horst gave his son a mock frown. "Much more fun to be in heavy industry."

The two laughed.

"You know, Manfred, a lot of what you are planning here could be applied to Lassiter. I started to incorporate computers into the production operation while you were still in prep school. I admit that I don't know much about how they work, but the data they provide has helped business immensely. What I mean to say is that you could take this idea and bring it home, so to speak."

"Dad, I'd still be the boss's kid. Besides, nowadays, all you do is go from meeting to meeting with an entourage of executives, accountants, and board members. No. Maybe after a year or two, I'll let Lassiter buy me out. But now, I'd like to try on my own. Besides, you're not decrepit—yet."

Horst puffed again on the pipe. "Sometimes I feel close."

"There is another matter I wanted to speak to you about, Dad."

"Hmmm? What?" Horst put the pipe down.

"Well, Mother and I have been talking. I know that this is something that she has thought about for years—at least she said so. And I remember Uncle Eric mentioning it, too. Please don't get upset that I bring this up?"

Horst shook his head and started to laugh. "How can I promise not to get mad about something that I have not heard yet?"

"I guess I didn't put that the right way. Well, anyway, it's about Aunt Anya and the von Kleist conglomerate."

"What about it?" Horst folded his hands across one another and stared at his son. What was he after?

"How is it that you and Uncle Eric and Aunt Reinhildt never made a move at getting back control? I mean, Aunt Reinhildt and Uncle Eric have a great deal of stock in the company now. Why did the three of you hold back rather than going after the old woman?"

"I wish you wouldn't put it that way."

"What?"

"Old woman. She's only a few years older than I."

"Sorry."

"Why, you ask. Well, for one thing, we all developed our own careers and have done rather well. That took a great deal of time. For another, my father rescinded my trust with all of my stock when I stayed in the US rather than going back to Germany. If we had gotten that stock, there might have been an edge, a way to manage a coup. But we never did. A takeover is near impossible. Tell me." He leaned over the table. "Did your mother put you up to this? She has been challenged by Anya for the last twenty years."

"Well...ah...she mentioned it. I must say that. She mentioned it several times in the last year. You are right. She is—intense about it."

"I was told by someone once that I should not ever marry a red-haired woman."

Manfred lifted one of his long locks. "Don't say that, Dad. Where would I be, then?"

Horst looked across the table. Yes, there was something there, something more than his mother. "You obviously have a greater interest in this than would be spurred by Diana, so why not get your tired old father a drink, and we'll speak more about it?"

"Sure." He got to his feet, towering over Horst. "Schnapps?"

"God, no! I stopped drinking that years ago. A glass of chablis."

In a few minutes, Manfred came back with two glasses. He handed one to his father, who had moved to an easy chair in the corner of the room.

"Now, my recently graduated Yale-ee with a degree in computers and business, speak to me. You're challenged by all of this, aren't you?"

"In a way."

Horst shook his head. "The way you just said 'in a way,' was about as sincere as an alcoholic being asked if he wanted to own a distillery and him answering 'in a way.'"

"Well, I have done a little homework—on my own."

Horst looked past him to see Diana go by the door. "You might as well come in, Diana. There's no sense lurking out there."

She came in. She was still the stunning woman he had married. She had kept her lean figure and her sharp good looks and sparkling eyes. He suspected that she touched up the hair to lose a few gray strands, but it didn't matter. His own hair was getting streaked with gray at the temples.

"I was not lurking. I was just passing by."

He smiled. "Sit down and listen to this. You were the one who planted the seed. Perhaps there is a sprout."

"And why would you say that I planted the seed?" she asked as she moved in the direction of the easy chair at the corner of the room.

Horst smiled, knowingly. "There is no secret about the way that you have always felt about Anya."

Diana's smile was forced and tense. Horst noted that she rankled at the mention of the name. "I have nothing against her... after all, there is no reason..." She glanced at Horst and, seeing that he was smiling, she could not keep up the pretense, "...that bitch."

Manfred snapped his head in her direction. "Mother?"

"Yes. I said, 'that bitch.' And don't pretend that you're naive in front of your father." She turned to Horst. "I told him about the way she conspired with Kurt that night years ago. If it were not for Eric, we would still be in Germany... no. We would be dead. Now, she disgraces your family name by fawning over the PLO and the NPD and a dozen other neo-fascist initial groups." She paused and looked at Manfred and then again to Horst. "I'm sorry. I don't want to talk about her unless... well, I just wish to God that we could get the company back from her."

Horst smiled a half smile at her and nodded. He too remembered the snowy night at the schloss and the sacrifice that Eric had made for him. He looked at his son.

"Well, Manfred, what have you unearthed?"

Manfred started to explain, and Horst suddenly realized just how much research his son had really done.

"All of the years that they have rebuilt, the corporation has concentrated on steel. Their one mistake was that they did not diversify. Oh, there is a strong rumor in the international community that they are starting to get into the weapons business in a large way, now. But their corporate diversification should have started a long time ago. Right now, they are a giant with a single product. With the advances that the Japanese have made in the last ten years, not to mention what you have done for the American market, Father, von Kleist could easily be in trouble. That's why Heinrich, the charming cousin I've never met, has to globetrot and charm potential markets."

"How does diversification apply to stock takeovers? Explain." Horst found himself puffing on his pipe like a steam engine as he listened. He, too, was starting to get interested.

"Simple, Dad. Look. They have to have ore to get steel. The competition for ore is much keener now than it was years ago. You know that from the prices that we used to have to pay for ore, before we started to mine our own.

"Well, the corporation never bothered to invest in the ore mines that sold to them. If there was a drought in ore, they could not meet their needs."

"What about backlog? They have to have a large backlog, enough to allow them to recover from a shortage."

Manfred shook his head and folded his arms. "They don't— and that's not strange. They are flooded with orders, and they guarantee delivery in a specific amount of time. They keep backlog very low. That was a mistake that I am sure that Grandfather would never have made. If their ore supply were to be pinched off, levered away from them for a period of say, three months, they would have a problem."

"Exactly what... kind of problem?" Horst asked carefully.

Manfred leaned toward his father. "The essence is a public versus a private corporation. From what you and Mother have told me, Grandfather wanted the company to remain in the hands of the family. And, while he was alive, he kept that desire alive by giving shares to the children. After the war, even with the help of the Truman programs, that was no longer possible. Aunt Anya had to open the corporation and sell stock from her controlling interest to rebuild. As this was in line with the Allied notion of reconstruction, everything went well. The sold or public stock represents a percentage that could mean the swing of control back to you and our side of the family."

"How will it do that?" Horst asked. He could see what Manfred was getting at, but chose to let his son explain all of the plan before commenting.

"I mean, if their raw materials were in short supply, they would lose contracts and therefore cashflow. Quite soon, that would result in the rumor of diminished dividends. Investors would sell the stock. Perhaps there would be enough in sales to . . ."

"To allow the stock to be bought up by . . . ?" Horst made a sweeping gesture around the room with his hand.

"Exactly."

"What do you think, Diana?"

She got up from the couch and smiled at both of them. "I don't know. Remember, this is all just business detail. I just run around planting seeds, remember?" She turned and left the room, chuckling to herself.

"Sometimes I wonder about that woman."

"What do you think, Dad?"

"How do you find and pinch the ore supplies? It would be difficult to find even where they get the balance of the supplies."

Manfred smiled. "Not so. Computers? Remember? There are large number of data areas that can be accessed just from the hardware and the international interlinks that Lassiter has. It could tell you where and the amounts and the purchase price and the back orders of all of the ore that von Kleist purchased in the last three years."

"Sounds like it would take a good deal of time to put that together."

"About a month. I just finished it."

"You what?"

"I told you I kind of got interested."

"His mother's son. Well? Don't stop there. What else?"

"Three companies supply them. There is one in western Canada, another in Minnesota—that's one that also supplies us. The third is an African company that has already dried up. To compensate, they doubled their order to the Canadian firm. That was three months ago. Last month, they doubled again. That would support the notion that they're diversifying into weapons production. But all of the pressure has been on this outfit in Canada. All of the eggs, you see?"

"What do you propose to do?"

"Western Canada Mining is in trouble. They have had poor management for the last five years or so. They made some very poor investments, one of them in that African operation that I mentioned. So, Western will soon be feeling the pinch.

"Dad, I suggest that we make a move to buy them out. Then, we could insure our own supply and create a closed market. Von Kleist would be on the ropes."

Horst finally put the pipe down. It was starting to burn his mouth. "You do all of this research, and you won't work for the company?"

"I'll make a deal with you, Dad. Give me the resources to do this, and if I pull it off, I'll give you von Kleist—and consider working for the company. If I blow it, fire me, and I'll go out on my own."

"I wouldn't be that harsh. But the idea of all of it is exciting. Let me write to Eric and Reinhildt. They've asked us over for a reunion in May. I'll try to explain it the way you have. It might interest them."

"If it interests you the way I think it does, give me a staff of ten and some computer time and some letters of credit, and I'll start on this tomorrow."

Horst paused for a minute, then nodded. "You have a deal." Manfred came across and shook hands with his father.

"You know, Manfred, for the first time in years, I think all of this is going to be fun!"

---

## 39

In the three months that followed, Manfred lived in airports and in front of computer terminals. Using an assumed name, he visited the Canadian firm to look at their operation. He could see that their management was indeed poor, and just from watching their production operation, he could see that they could get more than twice the amount of ore out in less time with updated techniques. After three days of tour and study, he spoke to Jacob Henderson, the president of the company.

As Manfred entered the office he could see at a glance that Jacob Henderson was a traditionalist. The room was walled in mahogany panels, with a deep umber carpet and a huge desk with a lone chair before it. Manfred reasoned that the placement of the chair was meant to be intimidating. He decided to attack immediately.

"Mister Henderson, I see little sense in wasting either your time or mine. I think I should come right to the point."

Henderson smiled tentatively and folded his arms. He was certain that something important had brought the eastern businessman all the way to Calgary. "That's the way we like to do things, too, Mister Walker."

Manfred smiled back. He had decided, with his father's consent, to use assumed names and a series of hastily assembled "front" companies so as to deter Anya and Heinrich from identifying the real source of the plan.

Manfred leaned forward in his chair and fixed the pudgy, silver-haired Henderson's eyes with his own. "Your company is in deep economic trouble, Mister Henderson."

Henderson smiled to cover his surprise and gestured around the room. "Currently, we are in a brief period of consolidation but... I would not say that we were...."

"Deep trouble, Mister Henderson." He glanced at a small card that contained notes. "You are due to pay a five million dollar loan installment to Western Canadian Building and Trust by the end of the month. The odds are that you will not even be able to make the interest payment, let alone the principal. The odds are that you will go into receivership by the end of the quarter." He passed the card across the desk to the suddenly numbed Henderson.

After a few minutes, Henderson looked up from the card. His glance was icy as was his tone. "What do you propose, Mister Walker?"

Opening his briefcase, he passed a sales agreement across the table. The amount that he was prepared to offer was clearly inflated substantially above the true value of the company.

Henderson perused the document and then dropped it on the desk.

"No, Mister Walker."

"No?"

"That's correct. I won't sell."

"You've seen the amount of the offer and you still say no?" It was Manfred's turn to be surprised.

"The offer is generous. I'll give you that. But, I won't do it."

"Is there something in the terms of the agreement that is not correct?" Manfred was playing for time, while he assessed the man's reasoning.

"The agreement seems proper and correct. There are other factors involved."

"Ah . . . might one ask . . . ?"

"One might. This company has been functioning for almost a century and a Henderson has always been at its head. I have to stay in that position. We will try to consolidate and weather the storm. If that means going down with the ship, I'm prepared to do just that. I'm sorry to have caused you a fruitless trip."

"So am I, Mister Henderson. All that you've succeeded in doing has been to make me buy you out the hard way."

After a polite goodbye, Manfred hailed a cab and headed for the airport.

That afternoon, he was grabbing some sleep on an Air Canada flight from Alberta to Ottawa.

Western Canadian Building and Trust was a medium-sized lending institution, specializing in mining ventures. They financed equipment and various indigenous materials in the mining trade. The president, a man named Walters, agreed to see Manfred immediately as Manfred had used his real name this time.

"I'll get to the point, Mr. Walters, as you were so kind as to see me on short notice. You finance a great deal of the Western Mining Company's operation, do you not?"

Walters sat behind his desk, eyeing the son of the most prestigious steel producers in the nation. Manfred could see the man smelling money. He knew that this sort of man was ot likely to be stubborn.

"Yes. I believe that we have a large share of their credit in the market."

"You have eighty-five percent of it, Mr. Walters."

The Canadian smiled. "You have the figures, I assume, Mr. von Kleist."

"I do. I also understand that they are in arrears on a large percentage—say fifty-eight percent or so."

"That's possible."

"Very well. I will be brief. The chances of collecting on more than say, twenty percent of that is meaningless. They will go under."

"How can you say that?"

"Because I just came from there, and their management system is something out of a turn-of-the-century glory hole in California, that's why. I'd give them a year, and you'd recoup perhaps forty cents on the dollar."

"We're in business to take calculated risks."

"Let me offer an alternative to the forty cents on the dollar. Lassiter will buy out their loan and pay five percent additional interest over whatever their loans are rated at. In addition, if the deal can be completed in three days, there will be a ten-thousand-dollar bonus in it for you."

Walters was practically drooling, though he tried to maintain a cool businesslike air. It was the deal of a lifetime. They had millions tied up in Western, and they knew it was a bad risk as well as Manfred. Walters waited a discreet amount of time before he answered.

"I think that we can do business, Mr. von Kleist."

With the deal completed and the liens in his briefcase, Manfred returned to Alberta and confronted the president of Western. The rest took little time. They foreclosed on the company for the balance of the loans, then made them a direct subsidiary of Lassiter—a closed market. All other customers, especially those with shipments waiting, were cut off. Full reimbursement was made, but Von Kleist AG suddenly started to feel itself running out of ore.

One of Horst's operatives moved in on the Minnesota operation. There the tactic was different. Lassiter bought up huge stocks of ore, far more than they usually would. They said that they had to have immediate delivery of prime ore and that if Lassiter would be considered the prime customer, with priority above all others, they would pay ten percent per ton more than the average market price. The officials of the Minnesota company thought that someone at Lassiter had gone insane, but the deal was too good to pass up. It was only three days after the deal was concluded that von Kleist representatives arrived to make a large purchase. The company spokesman told them that they were of a lower priority than a current customer with a huge order. The back order time was going to be six months. That was four months longer than the ore supplies of von Kleist would last.

By April, the European markets were starting to show a steady fall in von Kleist stocks. By mid-month, they were down twenty-eight points, and the rumor in the business world was that the giant was about to fall.

Von Kleist issued more stock. Manfred bought, through several different operatives, so that a takeover bid could not be suspected.


It was the third week in April when the family gathered at a suite in the Hotel Frankfurter Hof, an old and stylish place that reminded Reinhildt, Horst, and Eric of their childhood at the schloss.

The five of them sat in the living room of the suite and sipped coffee and brandy after a fine dinner in the dining room of the hotel. The only interested party who was not there was Ernst, who was studying for his medical entrance exam. Eric could feel for him.

Manfred spread a sea of papers and computer runs on the coffee table.

"Well, shall we start?"

Around the room, all of them nodded. They had no idea how well or poorly the plan had worked.

"You all know, from my father, what the plan has been, and you have all agreed to pool your stocks in von Kleist to see if we could pull this off. Well, the stock dropped as we thought it would, and Lassiter now has a large supply of iron ore— enough to last for a year and a half. We also have a new mining subsidiary that we think will be profitable. With the stocks that we have acquired, it appears that we have managed to amass forty-eight point seven-one-three percent of Von Kleist AG stock. That leaves two percent and a fraction for a simple majority. Is there any other stock that remains outstanding?"

No one spoke.

After a second Eric raised a hand. "Is there any other private holder whom we might have forgotten?"

Manfred looked at the computer sheets. "This is the complete run. If there are other shareholders, Aunt Anya has them in the closet. No. She and Heinrich hold or control directly the rest."

"Well," Eric said, "it was a good try."

Manfred slammed a hand down on the coffee table, rattling a cup and almost toppling it onto the computer printout. "I still think we can do it. All we have to do is hold the stock and keep up the pressure. They will have to make a large capital investment in this new weapons business of theirs. They will need credit. They can't afford to issue any more new stock. They are on the edge now. All we have to do is hold."

"Perhaps we could sell it all, in one huge block, and drop the price on the market. Then we could buy it again the next day at the lower price. If we whip-sawed them enough that way, we might scare off the potential arms buyers, who, by the way, are mostly in the Middle East. If that happened, we'd have a chance," Reinhildt commented. She looked around at the others. No. It was not good.

"I suggest we hold things where they are," Horst said. "We all have a lot of money and stock tied up here. We need to develop a long-range plan."

A thought struck Eric. It slipped from the back of his memory slowly coming into focus. He turned it over and then stopped. No. It was vile, something that would make him no better than his father and his brother had been. He discarded it, as something long dead, to be left in the past.

"Eric?"

"Yes?"

Horst was smiling at him. "Is my older brother slipping away tonight?"

"No . . . just thinking."

"Anything germane to the mess here?"

"Not really." He sighed.

"Well, in that case, I suggest that we adjourn this meeting and have a drink." Horst said.

They agreed. Nothing could relieve the disappointment they felt when Manfred announced the figures, but they agreed to meet the next afternoon after lunch to see if the night's rest had stirred any other ideas.

Few of them had hope that there would be.

## 40

**Inside the Knesset, Jerusalem, the same evening**

"Gentlemen, you don't seem to understand. The air photos are more than clear. You have all just heard the report—the newest shipments of Migs are being deployed as soon as they have been checked out. We have intercepted messages from Cairo that are clearly requests for immediate technical data on the firing mechanisms for SAM missiles. The deployment is tactical and en masse. But that is not the main thing. Bear with me, please. After all, I am a doctor and only a parttime politician."

There was a light murmur of laughter in the cabinet meeting room, as Uri Ben Tabor made the remark. At his side, Jordanna glared at two of the cabinet ministers, and their grins faded. No one could be sure if it was the power of her personality or her striking beauty that stopped them. All the cabinet knew was that they had been in session for ten hours and everyone was tired. It had taken a long time to get to Uri's presentation. He thought that the placement would give him an edge. It had backfired. Instead, they were bleary and bored. Still, he pushed; the threat of war was dire, and they had to know it. And the real threat was something that he was just starting to get used to.

"Please, gentlemen. This is perhaps the most important part of the presentation." He nodded to an aide, who pulled down a projector screen from the ceiling. Another aide snapped off the lights and turned on the projector.

The screen flickered for a second, and then there were a series of German credits. Following that was a clip showing a tank on a test track. The tank was low-slung, with sloping curves on the hull and turret; the gun tube was long, and there was a second, shorter tube next to it. A series of shots showed the tank firing, static, and on the move, with targets exploding at various ranges. In another minute, the film ended, and the lights were flicked back on.

"Colleagues, this is the demon of the piece," Uri said. He ran a hand through his thinning gray hair and looked for a second to Jordanna. She had her mother's dark eyes. There was always love in them—and the support that he needed at times like these. She was more than an administrative assistant and his daughter. He claimed that she was half his brain and eighty percent of his insight.

"It's called the Cobra. It is a main battle tank. Weight is

sixty tons, and she has a range of five hundred miles with a top speed of sixty miles per hour in the desert." He paused to let the thought sink in. She had a longer range than their Centurions by almost two hundred miles. In order to get that range, they had to carry gas cans strapped to the turret; an invitation to become a fiery death trap for the crew.

"But, that is not the most impressive thing. She can raise and lower her suspension, changing her configuration by eighteen inches. This allows for camouflage and misdirection. She carries a hundred-six-millimeter gun that is computer controlled and can fire while she is moving at full speed. Her first round hit ratio is something over ninety-seven percent. In addition, she carries a missile capability that can be used for ground to ground or ground to air, and can penetrate fifteen inches of armor, more than we have on most of our operational tanks."

"Well, Uri, where do we buy them?"

"Mister Minister, we can't. But I can tell you who has. The UAR. They have ordered them and expect delivery in the next six weeks. It is estimated by intelligence that they could be operational in two weeks after that. The crews are being trained on mock-ups now. Of that we are certain."

There was silence in the room. "How many, Uri?" It was the minister. His voice was just above a whisper.

"Six hundred."

"Dear God." It was the army defense chief. "How was it that we did not know about these?"

"It's not your fault, sir. Believe me. We came about this information from a defector. The entire project was secret. It was to go hand in hand with the other war preparations in the UAR. Luckily, the defector also brought us all of the technical readouts on the tank. We have started our technicians developing mock-ups also."

"Is that," asked the minister, "in case we capture one?"

"It—"

"It won't be that way." Again, it was the army defense chief. "We won't get near them. They will tear the Centurions apart. They can stay out of range and blast us, and at full speed. It would be a disaster."

"Excuse me, General," Uri said. "There is a slim possibility that something can be done about the tanks. I emphasize slim. It would have to be something that I would have to do myself. I ask that the cabinet approve a mission that I might undertake to forestall the delivery of these tanks or, at best, prevent it entirely."

There was a buzz in the room. The minister frowned. "Uri, exactly how do you propose doing this?"

"I'd rather not say at this time, sir. But, I assure you that there is a chance of success. I estimate one in perhaps seven or eight. I know that sounds like poor odds, but the odds will be far worse for the country if these Cobras get into the field against us. I need a long-range jet aircraft, and I have to leave tonight."

The minister got to his feet. "Uri, you have never been an alarmist, and I don't think that you are being one now. If there is a chance, then we must take it. If we fail, we'll face that when we must. I'll approve the aircraft and the mission. Where are these tanks being produced?"

"In Germany, sir. They are being built by Von Kleist AG."

It was just past seven in the morning when there was a heavy knock at the door. Eric crawled from bed and pulled on a robe. There was a second knock, this one harder than the first.

He opened the door and was faced with a huge man at least six-foot-six and broad in the shoulders and chest. He wore an ill-fitting suit, and there was a suspicious bulge in the left side of his jacket.

Eric took a reflexive step backward.

"Dr. von Kleist?" The accent was odd.

"Yes," Eric answered tentatively. The huge man stepped aside and behind him stood a ghost, a specter from the past, a shadow drawn from the crematoria and the burial pits of Dachau.

"Karl?" He could feel disbelief, but there were tears starting to fill his eyes.

"Yes. I was, Eric. I have another name now. May I come in?"

Eric nodded dumbly and showed him to a seat. The big man also entered the apartment, but took up a position near the closed door. Eric sat down and stared unabashedly. Yes . . . it was Karl. He was much older, but so was Eric. He was deeply tanned, and there were lines in his face that had not been there before. "You are really Karl."

Uri nodded.

Eric got to his feet and went to the bar. He poured a long shot of scotch and downed it.

"Is that therapeutic, Doctor?"

"Yes. It certainly is."

"Good! Get me one, too."

Eric did, and Uri downed it the same way. They spoke for nearly an hour. Karl/Uri explained the almost pathological need that had developed as a result of Dachau . . . the need to start again . . . the desperate need to forget the past.

Then he explained the problem.

Eric nodded as Karl finished. "I see." He, in turn explained the failed attempt to retake the company from Anya.

Karl leaned forward. "Is there nothing—no pressure that might be applied? I don't have any scruples about this. If those Cobras get into the field in a war—and we are sure that one is coming soon—then we are gone. Israel is gone. We will be driven into the sea. The slaughter will even eclipse Dachau."

Eric shook his head. "I don't—" He stopped. It was there again. What had, the evening before, seemed vile and un- thinkable was suddenly there again. It was something that, God help him, he could use . . . he would *have* to use!

"What is it, Eric?"

"There is something. There is. I don't know if it will work. I have no idea. But . . . yes. I will. I'll try to set it up for today. You will stay, of course?"

"Am I welcome?" He got up from the couch.

Eric took a step forward. Suddenly the tears started to fill his eyes again. The two men embraced.

Karl looked suddenly pensive. "There is something else. I have no right to ask, but . . . is there a chance that I might see Reinhildt?"

"I think she might like that. I think that she might have some things to tell you. But we should wait. Wait until I finish this—task. Stay here if you wish."

"No. I have a room two floors below. I'll wait there. Will this task require protection? I have several bodyguards."

"No. It's something I have to do alone."

The contacts and arrangements took most of the morning. At noon Eric boarded a helicopter at the Frankfort airport, headed to Tübingen.

The remodeled and rebuilt schloss was as magnificent as it had been three decades and more before. As the butler ushered Eric into the office, he was chilled by a memory of his father. Anya sat behind the desk. She looked somehow wizened; the years had been cruel to her. Next to her stood Heinrich; tall, imposing, blond. He bore a terrifying likeness to his father.

Anya motioned him to a chair. "Hello, Eric. Please sit down. What was this urgent meeting all about? We have nothing in common."

"I'm sorry, Anya, but the very fact that you consented to see me at all, let alone on such short notice, says that we do have something in common. You agreed to see me because you know about the stock."

Heinrich looked down at his mother, and she looked up at him. After a second her glanced moved to Eric again. "We knew some of it. We were not threatened by it."

"You were, and you are. You are cornered, and you both know it. I have come to make an offer to buy the controlling two percent of the stock from you."

Anya threw her head back and laughed. "How much are you prepared to offer? How many billions can you and your sister and brother muster? My price is a mark more than that."

"I thought that you would say something like that. Understand that the offer is sincere. I am even prepared to offer fifteen percent above the current going rate for von Kleist stock. That is an honest offer. Remember that I said that, please."

"I told you my price, Eric."

"You force me to do something that I hoped to avoid. Heinrich?"

"Yes?" The man's eyes moved to Eric. They probed, trying to penetrate. His hands moved uneasily, and Eric wondered if he should have accepted Karl's offer of a bodyguard.

"As I understand it, your prime customers are the Arab states—at least, as far as the Cobra is concerned."

Heinrich blinked, and Anya leaned forward in the chair. "How do you know about the Cobra?"

"Accept simply that I do know, and listen to me. I believe that six hundred is the order. The delivery date is sometime in the next six weeks. They are rolling off the assembly line in the Ruhr now, I believe. What would the cancellation of that order mean to you? How much loss? Three million a tank? Almost two billion dollars in contracts? And, if a huge amount of stock were dumped on the market at the same time that the tank deal fell through, I think that would end von Kleist—don't you?"

"The order will not be canceled. It will go through. There is no way to stop it, stock or no stock," Anya snarled.

Eric folded his arms. "Stock will have little to do with it. Something more precious will. You are desperate for ore, and we know it. Our estimates are that you have less than two weeks reserve left. You cannot fill the order with that."

Anya was on her feet and staring at Eric with bitter hatred.

"Damn you. You will *not* stop the sale. We will float a loan from our friends in the Middle East and get the ore from other markets, no matter what the price. You never have been much of a businessman, Eric. Did you think that front corporations for Lassiter steel buying up our ore markets—freezing us out—was something that we did not see? You were right in becoming a country doctor. What a fool I was to ever be interested in you, even thirty-five years ago! We will get the tanks completed and delivered—and the filthy Jews will be pushed into the sea!"

Eric turned and paced toward the window as he pondered how he should raise the next point . . . the one that had been hidden for so long. He turned back to the two of them and began.

"Look at Heinrich, Anya. A fine son. Close to ODESSA because of his fine SS officer father. Close to the Arabs because of his hatred for Israel." He stopped and took a deep breath.

"How will they react when they learn that their fine young Aryan hero is half Jewish?"

"Don't be stupid, Eric," Anya snapped.

"Oh, I'm sorry. *I'm* half Jewish. He is a quarter Jewish, though the distinction will make little difference to the PLO and the others. In fact, you, Anya, are the only Aryan in this room."

"What the hell are you talking about?" Heinrich snapped.

"My mother, Lotte von Kleist, was a full-blooded Jewess, Heinrich. That makes me a half and you a quarter. She wrote it in the last pages of her journal before she committed suicide. I've kept the journal all of these years." He opened the case that he carried and handed a folder each to Anya and Heinrich. "As you can see, it has all been documented there. Lotte von Kleist was formerly Lotte Gelsen. But that was not her real name, either. She had been adopted by the Gelsens, as they could have no children. The parents who gave her up were Jews. That also is documented there. It was the reason that she killed herself as the Nazis were coming to power. You can see that the excerpts of the journal pages have been attested to by experts, who verified them as being in the same handwriting as other witnessed documents written by my mother. The case is airtight. All that is left is for me to

arrange delivery to every embassy in the Middle East." He
paused, to let them absorb the shock. Besides, he himself
was trembling.

"Now, none of this has to go past this room. All that has to
happen is the immediate transfer of the controlling stock.
When that is done, I assure you that all copies of this
document will be destroyed."


It was less than half an hour later when Eric emerged and
boarded the helicopter. While he was in the air, he radioed a
message to Horst in the hotel. They had the stock. He would
explain later. He contacted Manfred and instructed him to
get in touch with the von Kleist administration about the
change of management. They were to cancel all orders for the
Cobra tanks and inform the customers that all deposits would
be refunded.


Karl paced his hotel room. Jordanna sat by the phone:
a line to Tel Aviv had been kept open for more than an
hour. If Dr. von Kleist had failed, not a minute must be
lost.

There was a knock at the door. The huge bodyguard
answered, and a boy from the desk handed him a message,
which had been relayed from a helicopter that was just now
landing in Frankfurt. The message was simple.

> K.:
> Would you like to buy some tanks?
>                                                    E

Karl showed the message to Jordanna, and they embraced.
She ran to the phone, and he headed to the door. He had to
get out of the room—in the hall, anywhere where he could
walk.

He passed a handsome, dark-eyed woman in the corridor—and stopped in his tracks.

"Reinhildt?"

She stopped and turned. "Yes?"

He moved to her. "Reinhildt."

He was a few steps from her when she gasped and turned pale. She shook her head, holding up her hands as if to ward off a blow.

"No . . . no. Who? . . . It's a joke. . . ."

"No, Reinhildt, it's true. It's real. I am real."

She reached out a trembling hand, and he took it. They moved together tentatively, awkwardly. There were no words at first. Then, her eyes, still wide with disbelief, she nodded. "Yes. Come back to life."

"Yes. In a way. Come back to life. I didn't know that until now. My room is here. There's someone you must meet."

"Wait," she said, shaking her head. "I was going to lunch with . . . I mean there's someone that *you* have to meet. His name is Ernst."

"Your husband?"

"No. Were you going to introduce me to your wife?"

"No."

"Well, let me introduce you first." She took his hand, and they walked down the hall.

Eric entered the suite to find Karl and Reinhildt there, with Ernst and a young woman. She was stunning in a dark, wild sort of way. Her beauty struck him. There was something strange and haunting about it, like a distantly remembered dream.

Karl introduced her as his daughter, adding, "She is a perfect image of her mother. She was a fantastic woman."

"Was?" Eric asked.

"Yes. She was killed in an air raid in the 1947 war. But each time I look at Jordanna, I am reminded of my Tonisha."

Eric leaned forward on the couch. "What was her name? Your late wife?"

"Her name was Tonisha. She emigrated from Russia after the war. I met her soon after she arrived."

"Was . . . was she a nurse, this Tonisha?"

"Why, yes. One of the best that I ever worked with. How did you guess?"

Eric looked at Jordanna and then back to Karl. He managed a shrug.

"Well, you're a doctor. . . . It was a good bet."

# EPILOGUE

Eric watched the paper curl into snakelike wisps of ash in the tray. It was over. The weight had been lifted from him . . . the weight he had carried for half his life.

Karl was on his way to Israel to receive delivery of the Cobras. But he would be back—to Reinhildt, to Ernst. And Eric would not be surprised if Jordanna came back with him. Manfred was staying in Germany to help with the transition of the corporation's management—and he and Jordanna had gotten along uncommonly well.

As for himself. . . . Well, the weight was gone. That was enough. He looked out one of the tall windows and saw the blossoming spring colors of the lawns and shrubs.

Perhaps not. Perhaps he, too, could find a new beginning. . . .